Wish
You Were
Eyre

THE MOTHER-DAUGHTER BOOK CLUB

Wish You Were Eyre

Heather Vogel Frederick

Simon & Schuster Books for Young Readers
New York London Toronto Sydney New Delhi

ALSO BY HEATHER VOGEL FREDERICK

The Mother-Daughter Book Club series
The Mother-Daughter Book Club
Much Ado About Anne
Dear Pen Pal
Pies & Prejudice
Home for the Holidays

The Spy Mice trilogy
Spy Mice: The Black Paw
Spy Mice: For Your Paws Only
Spy Mice: Goldwhiskers

Once Upon a Toad

The Voyage of Patience Goodspeed
The Education of Patience Goodspeed

SIMON & SCHUSTER BOOKS FOR YOUNG READERS
An imprint of Simon & Schuster Children's Publishing Division
1230 Avenue of the Americas, New York, New York 10020

SIMON & SCHUSTER BOOKS FOR YOUNG READERS is a trademark of Simon & Schuster, Inc.
For information about special discounts for bulk purchases, please contact Simon & Schuster Special Sales at 1-866-506-1949 or business@simonandschuster.com.
The Simon & Schuster Speakers Bureau can bring authors to your live event. For more information or to book an event, contact the Simon & Schuster Speakers Bureau at 1-866-248-3049 or visit our website at www.simonspeakers.com.
Book design by Krista Vossen
The text for this book is set in Chaparral Pro.
Manufactured in the United States of America, 1213 FFG
2 4 6 8 10 9 7 5 3
Library of Congress Cataloging-in-Publication Data
Frederick, Heather Vogel.
Wish you were Eyre / Heather Vogel Frederick.
p. cm.—(The Mother-Daughter Book Club)
Summary: As the Mother-Daughter Book Club reads *Jane Eyre*, the girls and some of their mothers are involved in some serious competitions, Becca finds romance when the Wyoming pen pals come for a visit, and a wedding brings the British Berkeley brothers and even Stinkerbelle to Concord.
ISBN 978-1-4424-3064-8 (hardback)
ISBN 978-1-4423-4199-9 (eBook)
[1. Interpersonal relations—Fiction. 2. Mothers and daughters—Fiction. 3. Clubs—Fiction. 4. Books and reading—Fiction. 5. Weddings—Fiction. 6. Concord (Mass.)—Fiction. 7. Paris (France)—Fiction. 8. France—Fiction. 9. Brontë, Charlotte, 1816–1855. Jane Eyre—Fiction.] I. Title.
PZ7.F87217Wis 2013
[Fic]—dc23
2012029210

For Alyssa, who started it all,
and Alexandra, who carried it through

Wish
You Were
Eyre

WINTER

"*The eagerness of a listener quickens the tongue of a narrator.*"

—Jane Eyre

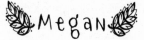

Megan

"... if she were a nice, pretty child, one might compassionate her forlornness; but one really cannot care for such a little toad as that."
—*Jane Eyre*

"Would you like fries with that?"

I frown at the menu. Since when had my grandmother started serving french fries at the tea shop?

I look up to see Becca Chadwick tapping her pen against the notepad she's holding. "Gotcha," she says, grinning at me.

I swat her with the menu. "Dork."

"Hey," she replies, "who's the one with the job, huh? Who's the one earning money right this instant? Speaking of which, you are planning to leave me a big tip, aren't you?"

This is Becca's first day as a full-fledged waitress at Pies & Prejudice, the wildly successful tea shop my grandmother opened here in Concord last year. Things got so busy that Gigi decided to hire some extra help. Becca's been her assistant since the beginning of January. She started out working on Thursday evenings at Gigi's new cooking classes, and today is her first shift waiting tables.

"A big tip?" I pretend to think it over. "I guess it depends if you give me extra whipped cream on my hot chocolate."

"You want a little cinnamon sprinkled on that?" Becca's all business as she writes my order down.

"Of course."

"Got it. Back in a flash." She trots off to a neighboring table to take another order, her apron strings fluttering behind her. Like my grandmother, Becca is wearing the Pies & Prejudice uniform: black dress, frilly white apron, frilly white cap. Gigi had me design them, but I hadn't imagined someone my age actually wearing one. Becca looks kind of like a French maid in a bad sitcom. She's being a really good sport about it, though. She wanted this job so badly. Her father's been unemployed for a while, and working here has been a way to help her family out.

My gaze drifts over to the window, and I note gloomily that it's started to snow again. This has to be some sort of record. Usually this time of year we get New England's famous January thaw, but the month's almost over and so far there's been no sign of it. We've missed more school this winter than any other year I can remember. Not that I'm complaining.

A little while later the bell over the door jangles and Emma Hawthorne and Jess Delaney come in, stomping their snow-covered boots on the mat. They spot me and wave, then cross the room to my table.

"Hey," says Emma, taking a seat. Jess does too.

"Hey back," I reply as Becca reappears with my order.

Heather Vogel Frederick

"I'll take one of those," says Jess, pointing to the hot chocolate that Becca sets down in front of me.

"Ditto," adds Emma. "But hold the cinnamon."

Jess shrugs off her jacket, giving Becca the once-over. "You look good," she tells her. "Just like a real waitress."

"I am a real waitress," Becca snaps.

"I just meant—"

Becca whooshes out a sigh and smiles. "I know. Sorry. I've just got a lot on my mind here. I was hoping for a quiet first day, but we've been swamped. It seems like everybody in Concord's stopped by for something hot to drink."

"Can you blame them?" says Emma, and we all look out the window.

"I sure hope they don't have to cancel tonight's hockey game," says Jess.

"Not to mention my birthday party tomorrow night," I add. I've been planning it for ages—you only turn sixteen once, after all—and I've hardly slept a wink the past few nights, I'm so excited. I think my parents have a surprise up their sleeves, too, because there's been a lot of whispering around the house lately, and they keep giving me these goofy smiles. I'm thinking maybe they got me a car.

"I'm coming if I have to snowshoe up Strawberry Hill to get there," Becca tells me.

As she heads back to the tea shop's tiny kitchen, Emma and Jess and I discuss the odds of the hockey game getting canceled. Emma swears that the snow is tapering off, but Jess is less optimistic. I am

Wish You Were Eyre

too—I've been sitting here for nearly an hour, and it looks to me like the snow is still coming down thick and fast. I don't care as much as the two of them do, though—Emma's brother Darcy and boyfriend Stewart Chadwick both play for the team, plus Jess is dating Darcy. I'm not dating anybody here in Concord, but I know the guys will be really disappointed if they don't get to play.

Becca returns with two more hot chocolates plus a plate of brightly colored round cookies. "On the house," she tells us. "Courtesy of Gigi."

My grandmother blows us a kiss from behind the bakery counter. "*Macarons,*" she calls, pronouncing them the French way. My grandmother loves everything French. "I'm trying out some new recipes in honor of the big birthday."

Somehow my party has turned into a weekend-long celebration. Things kick off tonight after the hockey game, with my friends taking me out to Burger Barn. Then tomorrow night my parents are treating us all to dinner at La Belle Époque, my grandmother's and my favorite fancy French restaurant. Afterward we'll go back to our house for cake and ice cream, and a dance. My father rented sound equipment and hired a DJ, and he's been busy for days turning our family room into an '80s dance club. Becca and Ashley talked me into a retro theme for the evening.

That alone should be enough for anybody, but our next mother-daughter book club meeting is on Sunday afternoon, and that always feels kind of like a party.

I reach for a bright pink cookie and take a bite. It practically melts in my mouth. "Mmm. Raspberry."

Heather Vogel Frederick

"Lemon," says Jess, nibbling on a yellow one. "Dreamy."

"Uh, hazelnut, maybe?" says Emma. She turns around and waves the pale brown cookie in the air. "These are great, Gigi!"

"*Merci beaucoup*," my grandmother replies.

"So what's going on with you guys?" I ask my friends. "I've hardly seen you since the New Year's Eve party, Jess."

Jess goes to Colonial Academy, a swanky private school here in town. She's on a full scholarship, thanks to the fact that she's just about the smartest person I know, and thanks also to Becca's mother, who recommended her for it.

"I know," she replies. "Things have been really busy. Let's see." She starts ticking items off on her fingers. "I got my cast off, but you knew that already. I'm riding again. My MadriGals solo audition is coming up next week and I'm freaking out a little over that. Correction, a lot. Oh, and calculus is really, really hard."

"Poor you." I don't mean for this to sound as sarcastic as it does, but it's hard to work up a lot of sympathy for someone who's taking calculus in tenth grade. Math is Jess's favorite subject. For me, on the other hand, it's sheer torture.

She makes a face at me. "But having Mr. Crandall for a teacher again is great," she continues. "Hey—did you know that Maggie's getting a little brother any day now?"

I'd totally forgotten that the Crandalls were expecting again. "Have they picked a name?"

"Trevor."

"Cute. Maggie and Trevor. I like it." The Crandalls were Jess's houseparents when she started at Colonial back in eighth grade—they're really nice, and all of us have done some babysitting for their daughter Maggie.

Emma turns to me. "Have you heard anything from Simon?"

I nod, smiling. Simon Berkeley is my back-on-again boyfriend, as of New Year's Eve. He broke up with me for a while last fall, telling me he thought we should be free to date other people, which was really awful. Simon is British, and living three thousand miles away from each other is tricky. It's not like we get to just hang out on the weekends and stuff, you know? We have to rely on e-mails and text messages and videoconferencing to stay close. It seems as if we're over our rough patch, though.

"He sent a package for my birthday," I tell her. "I'm dying to open it, but he made me promise I'd wait until tomorrow. Oh, and his father is guest lecturing at some university in the north of England this winter. York, I think. He and his mom and Tristan drive up on the weekends whenever they can to visit him."

"Cool," says Emma, who lived in England our freshman year. That's how Simon and I met—his family swapped houses with the Hawthornes. "We went to York—it's amazing. There's a medieval wall around the whole city, and it has this gorgeous old cathedral."

Emma's cell phone buzzes, and she pulls it out of her pocket and glances at the screen. "Cassidy's still at practice," she tells us. "She's not going to make it here in time to join us."

Heather Vogel Frederick

Cassidy Sloane is our other friend from book club. She eats, breathes, and sleeps ice hockey.

"She says we should have cranberry almond oat scones on her," Emma continues. Gigi's signature scones are Cassidy's favorite treat.

"Tempting, but I've already eaten way too many *macarons*," I reply, pushing the plate away. Cassidy may eat like a horse, but I can't. Designing clothes and sewing—my two favorite things in the world—are not cardio activities.

Before Emma can slip her cell phone back in her pocket, it buzzes again. "Oh good!" she exclaims happily, checking the message. "Zach just stopped by the rink and told Cassidy that the game is definitely on for tonight."

Zach is Zach Norton, the most gorgeous guy at Alcott High School. At least I thought so until I met Simon Berkeley. We all used to be in love with Zach back in elementary school. Okay, and middle school, too. In fact, some of us carried the torch into high school. I give Becca a sidelong look. She's wiping down the table next to us, but I notice her face flush at the mention of his name. She had the biggest crush of all of us, and she's still trying to come to terms with the fact that Cassidy and Zach are dating. Well, sort of dating. It's not like anybody ever sees them holding hands or anything. But they hang out all the time now.

I glance at the clock. The crowd in the tea shop is thinning out as closing time approaches. My father should be here any minute to get Gigi and me. Pies & Prejudice serves breakfast, lunch, and afternoon tea, so he always swings by to drive my grandmother home in time for dinner. Sure enough, a few minutes later the bell above the door jangles and my father appears, right on the heels of Mrs. Chadwick.

"Yoo hoo!" Becca's mother calls, waving at Becca likes she's on the far side of the Grand Canyon. Even though we're the only ones still here except for a lone table of two, Becca turns beet red. Her mother has that kind of effect on people. "That's my daughter," Mrs. Chadwick tells the other customers proudly. "This is her first day waitressing. How'd she do?"

Becca makes a beeline for the back of the shop and dives behind the curtain that serves as a door to the kitchen. I don't blame her. I would too.

As Mrs. Chadwick badgers the trapped customers, my father beckons to me. "See you guys at the game later," I tell Emma and Jess, putting on my jacket and scooping my backpack off the floor. I give my grandmother a kiss on the cheek on the way out.

"Calliope is going to drive me home tonight," she tells me, and I nod.

My father's SUV is parked right outside. As I slide into the front seat, I glance over and notice that he's got that funny smile on his face again. "What?" I ask him suspiciously.

"Nothing," he says, popping one of the *macarons* that Gigi gave him into his mouth. "Oh man, these are good," he mumbles. "How was school?"

"Fine."

"That's it? Fine?"

"It was school."

"Did you have art today?"

I nod.

"And?"

Why is it that parents always want to know every detail about your boring day at school? I heave a sigh and relent. "Art was great. We're working on some woodcuts, and when we're done, Ms. Malone says we might get to do some soapstone carving." I love art class, actually. It's my favorite thing about school.

My father whistles happily to himself as we head down Lowell Road, passing first the Chadwicks' house and then the Hawthornes', and on over the bridge toward Strawberry Hill. Emma was right about the snow; it's tapered off to flurries. Even though I'm pretty sick of this endlessly bleak winter, I still can't help thinking how pretty the snowflakes look drifting across the headlights of our car.

"I guess we're the first ones here," my father says as we pull into the empty garage a few minutes later. He sounds kind of disappointed.

"I think mom had a Riverkeepers meeting this afternoon," I tell him.

"On a Friday? Don't they usually meet on Tuesdays?"

"It got postponed because of the snow."

"Ah."

Leaving our boots on the rack in the garage—my mother hates wet shoes in the house—we go inside and hang our coats in the front hall closet. Then I head down the hall to my room to change. Mirror

Megan—that's what I call my reflection—frowns at me as I pull on my oldest sweats and put my hair up into a sloppy ponytail, but I promise her I'll change before the game tonight. Right now I just want to be comfortable.

Sliding my feet into my favorite pair of slippers (pink bunnies so ratty they've lost most of their fuzz), I notice that one of the ears on the left slipper is flopping forward like it's about to fall off. And that's exactly what it does as I reach down to adjust it. I shrug and toss it in the wastebasket next to my desk. With any luck, I'll get a new pair for my birthday. I've been hinting big-time to Becca, because I know that they're cheap and won't break the bank. With her father out of work, she doesn't need to be buying me expensive presents.

Grabbing my laptop off my desk, I settle cross-legged on my bed, throwing the quilt Summer Williams gave me a few years ago over my shoulders. As I pull it around me, one of the corners flaps over, revealing an embroidered message. I smile when I see it, even though I've long since memorized the words: *To Megan from her pen pal Summer. Friendship is where the best stories begin.*

She's right about that, I think as I check my e-mail to see if there's a new chapter in the Simon Berkeley story.

There is! He sent me an e-card! I click on the link, and it opens to a wintry scene, with snowflakes falling on evergreens and little kids skating on a pond. I smile. Simon has been looking at the Weather Channel again. He likes to do that, so he can see what's happening here in Concord. The snowflakes and skaters onscreen swirl around for a bit while a little tune tinkles in the background, then the snowflakes arrange themselves into the words *Keep warm! Happy almost birthday! XOXO Simon*.

I can't help laughing. It's really cute, and so is he for sending it.

I hop online to check out the weather in Bath, where he and his family live, so I can send him a card back. Not surprisingly, the forecast is for rain. That's what happens in England this time of year. I find a funny card for him with frogs carrying lily pad umbrellas, and add a message: *Keep dry! Miss you! XOXO Megan*.

The garage door rumbles as I press send. My mother must be home. Sure enough, a few moments later the intercom on my wall crackles. Our house is on the large side—Emma calls it sprawling— and my father had this system installed so we don't have to holler at each other. "Megan!" he says. "Your mother's home. Can you come here for a minute?" He sounds excited.

My pulse quickens as I scuff back down the hall to the living room. Maybe this is it. A car of my own would be so cool!

My mom is hanging up her coat in the hall closet. "Where's Mother?" she asks my dad. "I thought you were going to bring her home."

"Calliope Chadwick offered to give her a ride," he replies.

My mother spots me and breaks into the same goofy grin my father was wearing on the drive home. "Hi, sweetie!"

"Hi," I reply cautiously.

She crosses into the living room, where my father is sitting on the sofa reading the newspaper. Or at least he's holding it. Mostly he's smiling at me. What is up with the two of them?

My mother leans down and gives him a kiss, then straightens, frowning. "Has anyone seen my cell phone?" she asks, patting the pockets of her pants. She starts looking behind the sofa cushions. "I know I had it earlier today."

"You probably left it in your coat," my father tells her. "Megan, why don't you go check for her."

"Sure." I scuff over to the hall closet. My mother's winter coat is on a hanger next to my jacket, and I go right to the inside zip pocket where she usually stashes her phone. "Not here!"

"Are you sure?" she calls back. "Did you check all the pockets?"

The keys! I think. *She probably hid the keys to my birthday present in one of the pockets!* I rifle through the rest of them. Nothing. As I slip my hand into the last one, my fingertips touch something soft. Something soft that's *moving.* I snatch my hand back, startled.

The pocket squeaks. Holding it open gingerly, I peer in.

My heart stops.

I gasp in disbelief.

The pocket is full of white fur. White fur that's attached to a *kitten*! Reaching in again gently, I draw out a mewing ball of fluff.

"Omigosh—you little angel!" I whisper, holding it—him? her?—up to my cheek. It's the softest thing I've ever felt. As I kiss its little nose, I spot something out of the corner of my eye, and look over to see the lens of a camcorder peeking around the edge of the closet door. My father is behind it. He's not even trying to hide his broad smile now.

"Surprise!" he and my mother shout.

Heather Vogel Frederick

"Is it really mine?" I exclaim, still stunned. "To keep?"

"It's a she, actually, and yes, she is," my mother replies.

"Happy early birthday, sweetheart," adds my father.

"How . . . when . . . ," I stammer. I've been asking for a pet—or for a sister or brother—for, well, forever. The answer has always been no. My mother's all into zero population growth, plus both of my parents are neat freaks, especially my dad, and they've always said they don't do pets.

"It's all your grandmother's doing," my mother tells me. "She and Shannon Delaney have been twisting our arms ever since the party at Half Moon Farm."

The Hawthornes lost their cat, Melville, last fall, and Jess's family gave them a kitten on New Year's Eve.

My kitten is definitely cuter, though. It yawns and pats at my face with a tiny paw, and I bury my nose in her soft fur again. "This is the best present ever!" I mean it too. A kitten is way better than a car.

"There's more!" says my father. "Come and see."

"More kittens?" I reply, gaping at him.

He grins. "No, silly. More kitten *stuff.*" He herds me down the hall toward my room, then opens the door to the guest room across from it. "Ta-da!"

It looks like Pet Zone made a house call. There's not one but two baskets with pillows in them for snoozing, a pole covered in carpet and what look like branches sticking out of it—some sort of a combination climbing tree/scratching post, I'm guessing—a feeding station, and another basket full of toys.

"And her box will go in your bathroom," my mother says, grabbing something that looks like a big plastic suitcase by the handle and carrying it back across the hall to my bedroom. "I found ecologically friendly cat litter for it."

Of course she did. That's my mother in a nutshell—saving the world, one litter box at a time.

We stand there, my parents both talking at once as they try to film me, pat the kitten, gauge my reaction, and tell me how they managed to keep it a secret all at the same time. They're both so excited that you'd think they were the ones getting a kitten, not me.

"What made you change your mind?" I ask, perching on the edge of my bed and cradling the kitten against my shoulder. I hear the rumbling of a tiny purr as she burrows into my neck, then starts kneading the collar of my sweatshirt.

"I think it was when Shannon sent us the e-mail with her picture, wasn't it, Jerry?" my mother replies, glancing at my father. "She was the last one left in the litter."

He nods. "Shannon said she figured a white kitten couldn't do all that much damage to an all-white house."

I have to smile at this. Trust my parents to pick a cat to match our decor. Our house is really modern, and from the carpets to the furniture almost everything in it is white.

The three of us sit there playing with my new pet until she tires out and curls in a little ball in my lap and goes to sleep. She's so totally adorable I can hardly stand it. I feel like I'm going to burst with happi-

Heather Vogel Frederick

ness. This is shaping up to be the best birthday weekend ever.

My dad is still clutching the camcorder, of course. I think my entire life is preserved somewhere on DVDs.

"What are you going to call her?" asks my mother.

"How about Snowball?" suggests my father.

I shake my head. "Too boring. I'm thinking Coco, after Coco Chanel."

"Cute," says my father.

"Perfect!" says my mother. "Your grandmother will love it."

Coco Chanel is Gigi's favorite fashion designer. I figure it's a fitting tribute, since my grandmother is the one who talked my parents into getting me a pet.

My mother reaches out a forefinger and strokes the kitten's ears. "Do you remember when Cassidy's little sister Chloe was born, and your grandmother tried to get Clementine and Stanley to name her Coco?"

I nod, grinning. "That's what gave me the idea."

A few minutes later my mother stands up reluctantly. "Well, I guess I'd better get dinner started. Why don't you put Coco in her basket, and come keep me company?"

"Do you think she'll be okay by herself?" my father asks anxiously. "Maybe I should install a video monitor so we can keep an eye on her."

My mother winks at me. "She'll be fine," she says. "Leave your door open, Megan. Cats are smart—if she needs us, she'll come find us."

The three of us gather all the pet supplies from the guest room and get Coco settled. As we head back down the hall, my father pulls out his cell phone and taps away at the screen, making notes for himself.

"We'll need another basket in the kitchen," he mutters. "And I think we could probably use one in the living room, too. And another one of those climbing things."

My mother and I smile at each other. Whenever my father decides to do something, he always does it in a big way.

Just as we reach the living room, I hear the scrape of a key in the lock and the front door flies open.

"*Bonsoir!*" trills my grandmother. She trots in, towing a petite dark-haired girl I'm sure I've never seen before, but who still looks vaguely familiar. On the doorstep behind them is a huge pile of luggage.

"Uh, hello," says my mother cautiously.

"This is Sophie," announces Gigi. "She just arrived from France and she's going to live with us!"

My father blinks. Mom looks from my grandmother to the French girl and back again. Then she reaches for Gigi's arm. "Mother, may I speak to you in the kitchen for a moment?"

The two of them disappear, leaving my father and me standing in the middle of the living room with . . . Sophie? Was that her name?

She regards us coldly. I can't tell if she's unhappy to be here specifically, or just unhappy generally. She doesn't say a word, just looks around the room with her eyebrows raised. Her gaze lingers on our white baby grand piano, and I can tell she's impressed. Then she looks at me, and I can see that she's not impressed anymore. My hand creeps up to my hair, which I'm deeply regretting scraping back in a ponytail, and I'm very conscious of the fact that my ancient sweats

Heather Vogel Frederick

are not just ancient, but also now covered in white cat hair.

Sophie, on the other hand, looks like she's just breezed in from a photo shoot. Her curly hair is perfectly tousled, and her outfit is stunning. Simple, understated, but stunning. She's wearing jeans, knee-high black leather boots, a white turtleneck sweater, and a black peacoat, topped with a white cashmere scarf knotted artfully around her neck. Everything about her screams *I am French! I am très chic!*

Which I am most definitely not.

The discussion in the kitchen is getting heated. My mother doesn't like surprises, and she doesn't do houseguests. Add the two things together and it's a surefire recipe for disaster.

"I couldn't just leave her standing there like an orphan!" I hear Gigi wail.

"You could have at least called first!" My mother sounds furious. She's got a point, actually. My grandmother is kind of impulsive sometimes. "This is not your decision to make!"

Sparks are practically flying out from under the kitchen door, and my father gives it a nervous glance. "So, Sophie," he asks. "Do you speak English?"

The French girl shrugs. *"Mais bien sûr,* but of course."

"Right," he says, and vanishes into the kitchen just as I hear Gigi protest, "She was supposed to stay with Peter and Polly Perkins, but after what happened today, they had to drop out of the exchange program!"

A moment later the voices subside. Sophie's lips curl up in a hint of a smile. Not a particularly friendly smile. A minute ticks awkwardly by. She examines her fingernails. Then the kitchen door opens and my mother and father and Gigi appear. "It's settled, then," says my grandmother. "You'll stay with us."

"*Merci,*" says Sophie politely.

"I'm sure you're tired after your long trip," my mother adds, a little stiffly. "Megan will show you to the guest room. It's Sophie, right?"

The French girl nods. "*Oui. Sophie Fairfax.*"

We all stare at her. My heart sinks as I suddenly realize where the resemblance comes from.

"No relation to Annabelle Fairfax, are you?" my mother asks.

Sophie nods. "*Elle est ma cousine.*"

Stinkerbelle has a *cousin*? I gape at Sophie, stunned. No way. Absolutely no way.

There's a small mewing noise behind me, and I look around to see my new kitten hesitating in the living room doorway. I kneel down and stretch out my hand toward her, waggling my fingers. Beside me, Sophie Fairfax does the same.

Coco hesitates for a moment, her tiny tail twitching. Then she scampers straight to the French girl.

I take it all back. This is shaping up to be the worst birthday weekend ever.

❧ Becca ❧

"She was very showy, but she was not genuine . . ."
—Jane Eyre

Flipping on the radio on my bedside table, I dump the bills and coins out of my pockets and onto my bedspread, then flop down on my stomach to sort and count it all. Then I count again to be sure. Twenty-nine dollars in tips! Add that to the regular wages I'm earning, and the total is—well, not bad at all for three hours of work.

Carefully dividing everything into two piles, I deposit it into the pair of big glass jars sitting on my dresser. One is for me—I'm saving for a car, among other things—and the other jar is for my family. My parents are really reluctant to take money from me, but I like being able to help out. It's amazing how quickly it adds up. I started working right after New Year's, just one night a week at first, helping out with Gigi's cooking classes, and I've already contributed nearly a hundred and fifty dollars to our family budget. Now that I'm waitressing and earning tips, too, I'll be able to contribute even more.

My dad is still out of work. He had some promising job interviews this month, but no offers so far. He's trying not to let it show, but I can tell he's getting kind of anxious, especially with college acceptance letters due to start arriving pretty soon. My brother, Stewart, applied to nearly a dozen schools, and tuition is really expensive, even though he's smart and will probably qualify for a bunch of scholarships.

Grabbing one of the yummy little French cookies that Gigi sent home with me—mmm, salted caramel!—I change out of my waitressing uniform and head for the shower. Another nice perk from Pies & Prejudice is the leftovers. My family is happy about that. Tonight we're having the tea shop's chili with homemade croissants, plus more *macarons* for dessert.

Which reminds me, I promised to get dinner started while my mother drove Gigi home. I glance at the clock and hustle down the hall to the shower. I need to get a move on if I don't want to be late for the hockey game tonight. The rink is the place to see and be seen on Friday nights, especially when Alcott High is playing Dracut, our archrivals.

My cell phone is buzzing frantically when I return to my room. I pick it up and see that Megan has sent me a bunch of messages: CALL ME ASAP! WHERE ARE YOU? CALL ME!!!!!

I text her back: WHAT'S UP?

Two seconds later my phone rings. "My life is ruined," she whispers.

"Why are you whispering?" I ask her.

"So she won't hear me."

"She who?"

"Sophie."

"Who's Sophie?" I suppress a wild urge to laugh. This sounds like a bad comedy routine.

Heather Vogel Frederick

"Sophie Fairfax. As in Stinkerbelle Fairfax's *cousin*!"

I gasp. "No way! What's she doing at your house?"

"She's going to live with us for the rest of the school year."

"What! Why?"

"She's part of that exchange program—you know, the one Alcott High does every year. Something happened with the family she was supposed to stay with, and Gigi showed up on our doorstep with her half an hour ago, like she was a stray dog or something."

"Sheesh."

"No kidding," says Megan glumly. "She's unpacking in the guest room across the hall right now."

"That stinks! You never know, though, maybe she's nicer than Annabelle."

Megan snorts. "I don't think so. She's barely said two words to any of us, and the worst part is that my kitten likes her better than she likes me!" Megan's whisper rises to a wail.

I sit down slowly on the edge of my bed, clutching my towel to my chest. "Wait a minute—what kitten?"

"The one my parents got me for my birthday!"

I'm stunned into silence. Megan's parents don't do pets. "Your parents got you a *kitten*?"

"Uh-huh." Megan sniffles. "Gigi finally talked them into it. I named her Coco. Wait until you see her, Becca—she's adorable. Only, now Sophie's here and she's ruined EVERYTHING!"

I can hear the panic in her voice. "Stay calm," I tell her. "We'll figure something out. Maybe there's a different family she can stay with."

"You think?" Megan sniffles again, but there's a tendril of hope in her voice.

"There's got to be. I tell you what—I'm going to call an emergency meeting of the mother-daughter book club. We can duck out of the game for a few minutes at the rink tonight, okay?"

"Okay. Thanks, Becca."

We hang up, and I quickly dry off and get dressed, then head downstairs to the kitchen to heat up the chili. I'm setting the table when my mother walks in. She's on her cell phone.

"Uh-huh," I hear her say. "Unbelievable." She peers into the pot on the stove, then leans over to me and whispers, "Smells good!"

"Chili," I whisper back.

"You're kidding," she says, but not to me this time. "He didn't! Really?" She looks over at the table, then shakes her head and holds up three fingers. *Your brother's already at the rink*, she mouths, and I nod as she wanders off down the hall toward the coat closet, still making shocked noises into her phone.

I take away one of the place settings, then put together a salad and grate some cheese to go on the chili. Working at the tea shop has really upped my skills in the cooking department, that's for sure. I'm just taking the croissants out of the oven where they've been warming as my father comes in through the back door.

"Mmm-mmm," he says, spotting them.

Heather Vogel Frederick

"We're having Gigi's chili, too," I tell him. "Your favorite."

He sets his briefcase down on the floor and hangs his scarf on a peg by the back door.

"Did you have another interview today?" I ask as he shrugs off his coat.

"Yep," he replies. He doesn't say any more, and I figure it's probably better not to ask. He's been trying to keep his spirits up through this whole unemployment thing, but I can tell by his body language that he's feeling a little discouraged tonight.

"Henry, did you hear the news?" my mother calls, trotting back to join us. She's breathless with excitement. My mother loves it when she has a tidbit of gossip to share.

"Nope," he replies, taking a seat. "Enlighten me."

"Mayor Perkins was caught embezzling!"

We stare at her. This really *is* news.

"You can't be serious," says my father. "Peter Perkins?"

My mother nods. "I know! Absolutely unbelievable. Poor Polly."

Polly Perkins and my mother went to Colonial Academy together a zillion years ago. Their daughter used to babysit for my brother and me when we were little. *Good thing she's away at college now,* I think. How embarrassing to have your father caught stealing!

"What happened?" my father asks. "How did they find out?"

"I just got off the phone with Ginny Harper from the town council. Apparently they've been suspicious for a while, but they had to hire a forensic accountant to prove it."

I frown. "What's a forensic accountant? Is that anything like those shows on TV?"

My mother shakes her head. "Not really, honey. Well, kind of, I guess. Only, they solve financial crimes, instead of the other kind."

"What a shame," says my father.

"It's a mess," my mother agrees, sitting down across from him as I dish up the chili. "You wouldn't believe the shock waves it's causing. At the high school, even! Just this evening a French girl who arrived today nearly got stranded when the Perkinses had to pull out of the exchange program. There was a last-minute scramble to find her a spot."

My mother was talking about Sophie Fairfax!

"Sandra Dearborn called to see if we could take her," she continues. "She was practically in tears. She works so hard organizing everything, you know. Anyway, I came this close to agreeing to do it"—she holds up her thumb and forefinger—"but I figured with you out of work, this probably wasn't the best time."

We could have had Stinkerbelle's cousin living with *us*? I shudder, grateful for the very first time that my father is unemployed.

"Yeah, probably wouldn't have been such a good idea," he replies. "Where did she end up?"

"I was in the car driving Gigi home when I got the call," my mother explains. "When she heard what had happened, she made me drive right over to the school and get her. She said Lily and Jerry have plenty of room."

"That's certainly true," says my father, reaching for a croissant.

Heather Vogel Frederick

I reach for one, too.

"It's the perfect solution, actually, since Gigi speaks French," my mother continues. "She put the girl right at ease in what was a terribly awkward situation. It'll be nice for Megan, too—almost like having a sister."

I have to duck my head at this to hide my smile.

"Almost like having a sister!" Megan bursts out at the rink an hour later, when I tell her what my mother said. "Are you kidding me?"

"She didn't put two and two together when she heard Sophie's last name," I reply. "And I didn't tell her." My mother is not a Fairfax fan. Not after Annabelle Fairfax nearly sabotaged the British-American Society's Patriot's Day dinner dance here in Concord a couple of years ago. My mother was in charge of the event, and when Stinkerbelle managed to substitute shaving cream for whipped cream on the dessert pies, my mom was furious. If it hadn't been for Mrs. Sloane-Kinkaid's quick thinking—along with a chocolate fondue fountain—my mother's still convinced the evening would have been ruined.

My cell phone buzzes. It's a text from Ashley. She was supposed to meet us at the rink and go to Burger Barn afterward, but she hasn't been feeling well the last couple of days. NOT GOING TO MAKE IT TONIGHT, she says. FEELING BETTER, BUT MOM SAYS I NEED TO REST CUZ OF PRACTICE TOMORROW AND MEGAN'S PARTY.

Ashley and I are on the cheerleading squad together. I relay the message to Megan, who's spotted Emma and Jess and is waving to them over my shoulder.

"Too bad!" says Megan. "Tell her hi from me."

I'm texting Ashley back as our friends slide into the seats beside us. Cassidy and Zach Norton are right behind them.

I still can't tell if Cassidy and Zach are together or not. He sticks to her like glue around school, and she doesn't seem to mind. But she never talks about going out on dates or anything, and aside from an enthusiastic kiss I witnessed on New Year's Eve, which doesn't totally count because Zach kissed me too, although maybe not quite as enthusiastically, I haven't seen any actual PDA between them. Not that Cassidy has time for a boyfriend, anyway. Her calendar is booked to the max between school and all of her hockey stuff—she plays on an elite team and coaches Chicks with Sticks, a club for younger girls that she started a couple of years ago.

I sneak a peek to see if the two of them are holding hands. Nope. But they're sitting about as close as two people can possibly sit and still be two separate people. I make myself look away. It's really, *really* time to move on.

Megan nudges me. "He's looking at you again," she whispers, her eyes twinkling.

For a split second I think she's talking about Zach, and then I realize she means Third. I scowl at her. "Would you quit it already?" Megan likes to tease me about him. It's true, though—Third, who is sitting rinkside next to my brother Stewart, is staring up in our direction.

Third is actually Cranfield Bartlett III, but nobody calls him that. Back in eighth grade, he and Ashley kind of liked each other, but that

Heather Vogel Frederick

fizzled when we got to high school and she switched to liking a guy on the basketball team. I don't know when it started, but sometime last fall Third started mooning around after me. I've tried to discourage him, but in a nice way because we've been friends since preschool. He doesn't seem to take a hint, though. He's kind of like Kevin Mullins that way.

As if summoned by my thoughts, Kevin suddenly materializes and squeezes in next to Jess. Kevin is so skinny he could squeeze in pretty much anywhere.

"What's the scoop?" Cassidy asks. "How come you two want to call an emergency meeting?"

Megan and I exchange a glance. "Is there someplace we can go and talk privately?" Megan whispers, with a significant nod at her parents, who are seated in the row ahead of us with my parents and the Hawthornes.

"The game's starting any second," says Cassidy. "Don't you want to watch?"

"At halftime, then."

Cassidy looks disgusted. "There is no halftime in hockey, Megan."

"Whatever." Megan is so not a sports fan.

Cassidy sighs. "Yeah, I know a place we can go."

Megan is just finishing showing us pictures of her new kitten when the game starts. We scream our heads off through the first period cheering on the Avengers, but Concord's trailing Dracut by two points by the time the buzzer goes off for the break.

Cassidy stands up and stretches. "Come with me," she tells us. "Not you," she adds to Kevin and Zach. "You two stay here. This is girl stuff."

"Oh," Zach replies, grinning. "Fine. I'll go get us some popcorn and sodas."

Us. That's definitely "us" as in "we're a couple."

Enough, Becca! I remind myself sternly, following Cassidy and my friends down out of the stands.

"Welcome to my office," says Cassidy grandly, pulling out a key and inserting it into the lock of a door on the far side of the lobby.

"You have an office? Wow, I'm impressed!" says Jess.

Cassidy grins. "You won't be when you see it." She flips on the light, revealing what turns out to be a large storage closet. "The rink's owner lets me keep my Chicks with Sticks equipment in here." We all pile in and she closes the door behind us. I'm glad I have my jacket on—it's even colder in here that it is up in the stands.

Cassidy pats a big plastic storage container and Emma and Jess sit down on it. Then she grabs a pair of buckets and turns them upside down for Megan and me. Leaning against the wall, she folds her arms across her chest. "Spill."

Megan does, explaining all about Sophie Fairfax and the foreign exchange student fiasco. I fill in the blanks with what I overheard about Mayor Perkins. Our friends are openmouthed with astonishment by the time we're done.

"She's going to be living at your house until *June*?" says Jess.

Megan nods, and Cassidy gives a low whistle. "Bummer. How unfair is that? And how come we didn't know that Stinkerbelle had a cousin?"

Heather Vogel Frederick

"Why would we?" Emma replies. "It's not exactly headline news."

"Maybe Sophie's different from Annabelle," says Jess.

We all look at her.

"Well, it's true," she adds defensively. "We shouldn't judge ahead of time."

"Haven't you been listening?" says Megan indignantly. "She already stole my kitten! I haven't even had Coco a whole day yet, Jess! And Gigi's acting like she's got a crush or something, just because Sophie speaks French and wears French clothes and is all French and everything. Plus, it turns out she's a vegetarian, so now my mother's acting like she's the one who got a new pet. She even invited her to join our book club!"

Emma groans, and for once I agree. Book club may not be the highlight of my social life the way it is for Emma, but still, it would have been nice if Mrs. Wong had asked us first.

"She'll be at my birthday party tomorrow night, too," Megan continues. "The only reason she didn't come to the game is because she's jet-lagged."

"Coach Sloane to the rescue," says Cassidy, grabbing a clipboard off one of the shelves. She hunts around for a couple of seconds, then pounces on a pen. "First rule of hockey: You have to learn to outthink your opponent. Anticipate their every move. Be one step ahead. The only way to do that is to learn everything you possibly can about them. My team studies film of the other teams so we can learn to spot their favorite plays, their habits, their weak points. I say we do the same thing with Sophie."

"You mean spy on her?" asks Jess, her eyebrows shooting up.

Megan and I exchange a glance. Jess can be kind of a goody-goody sometimes.

"Not exactly," Cassidy replies. "Think of it as collecting information. The more we have, the better our chances of figuring out what she has up her sleeve."

"What if the answer is nothing?" says Jess stubbornly. "I still think you guys are being too suspicious."

Ignoring her, Cassidy points her pen at Megan. "If Gigi and Sophie are chattering away in French, you need to pump your grandmother for information about their conversations. Find out what they're talking about. Get ahold of Simon, too, and see if he knows anything. He's her cousin as well as Stinkerbelle's; he's got to." She turns to Emma. "Maybe you can ask your mother a few casual questions. She's still in touch with Mrs. Berkeley, right?"

Emma nods.

"Meanwhile, I'll find out what Tristan knows. And Becca, do you think you can ask your mother—or if she can ask the lady in charge of the exchange program—why Sophie decided to come here? It just seems like a pretty big coincidence that of all the places she could have gone, she'd pick Concord, Massachusetts." She makes a few notes on her clipboard, then looks up. "So what have we got so far?"

Megan shrugs. "Not much. Her name is Sophie Fairfax. She's our age. She lives in or near Paris—I couldn't quite understand which when she and Gigi were talking earlier at dinner. I'm pretty sure she's

Heather Vogel Frederick

rich because she showed us some pictures of herself with her parents, and her house is practically a castle. Oh, and she's an only child like me. At least I think she is. There weren't any other kids in the pictures."

Cassidy jots this all down. "Right. We'll start with this and go from there. Everybody know what you have to do?"

We all nod, although Jess still doesn't look convinced.

"Then let's get back to the game."

In the end, Alcott High loses to Dracut by one point, which leaks some of the fun out of the rest of the evening. We all drive over to Burger Barn afterward, but the guys especially are pretty subdued, until Cassidy talks everyone into sticking french fries across our upper lips like mustaches while we sing "Happy Birthday" to Megan. That gets us all laughing.

I'm up early the next morning for cheerleading practice. Afterward, Ashley drops me at Pies & Prejudice on her way home.

"Wait until you see what I decided to wear tonight!" she says as I get out of the car. "You're going to crack up!"

The two of us have had a lot of fun figuring out options for our '80s themed outfits. I only hope the guys get into it too, otherwise we're going to look really stupid.

The tea shop is bustling again, which gives me plenty of practice juggling multiple customers. Plenty of exercise, too. Waitressing is a workout! By the end of my shift I'm beginning to feel like I've gotten the hang of it, and I've also earned another thirty dollars in tips. On the walk home I try and figure out how many months it will be before I can afford a decent used car.

"Brr," says my mother as I come through the back door. "Close that quick! It's freezing out there!" She gestures to the chair beside her at the kitchen table. "Come visit with me while I finish this."

I glance over her shoulder to see that she's doing something complicated with graph paper and colored pencils and lists of plant names. My mother is in graduate school, working on her landscape design degree.

I shake my head, yawning. "Sorry, Mom. Between cheerleading practice and my job, I've been running since the crack of dawn. I've got to take a nap or I'm going to fall asleep at the party tonight."

She frowns. "When are you planning to do your homework this weekend? We're hosting the book club meeting tomorrow, you know."

"I know." I promise her that I'll at least tackle my Spanish homework before I head to Megan's, but when I go upstairs and start conjugating verbs, I quickly drift off.

My brother knocks on my door a while later. "Hey!" he says, poking his head into my room. "Mom said to wake you up. I'm leaving for the party in about half an hour, if you want a ride."

I sit up and he grins. "Nice look. New party dress?"

I glance down to see that I fell asleep in my Pies & Prejudice uniform. "Shut up."

He ambles in. Why is it that guys can do nothing but take a two-minute shower and throw on a pair of jeans and a T-shirt—in my brother's case the Stanford one he got when he went out to visit the campus last spring—and still look totally ready for a party? Even one with an '80s theme. At least Stewart bothered to add the white suit jacket he found at Goodwill for a little retro flair.

He pokes at the pile of papers on my bed. "Spanish vocab, huh?"

I nod. "I have a test this week."

He points to the book on my bedside table. "How do you like it so far? *Jane Eyre*, I mean?"

Jane Eyre is our current book club pick. We spent last fall reading the Betsy-Tacy series, thanks to my grandmother who's a rabid fan, and when it came time to choose our next book to read, Mrs. Hawthorne suggested we all write down our top choice and put them in a hat. Then she had Stewart draw one. Jess was really disappointed when he pulled out *Jane Eyre*, because she'd been lobbying for some horse story called *Seabiscuit*. Personally, I think maybe my brother cheated, because he's Emma's boyfriend and he knows that *Jane Eyre* is one of her favorite books.

I shrug. "It's pretty good."

"She's got a lot of spirit, doesn't she? Jane, I mean."

"Yeah." This feels totally weird, talking about a book with my brother. I hope I'm not turning into Emma Hawthorne. That would be a fate worse than death.

Emma is a huge bookworm just like Stewart, and the stuff they read usually spells B-O-R-I-N-G. I have to admit that *Jane Eyre* is not just pretty good, though, it's really good. The story starts out when Jane is a little kid, just ten years old, an orphan living with her horrible aunt and even more horrible cousins. Eventually, she's shipped off to a boarding school called Lowood run by this creepy guy named Mr. Brocklehurst, who barely feeds the girls and makes them cut off their hair and bathe in cold water. I'm just at the part where Jane's finally made a friend. We're supposed to have read up until the point when she leaves Lowood, so I have some catching up to do before our book club meeting tomorrow.

I shoo Stewart out so I can shower and dress. A few minutes later I'm standing in front of my open closet debating my choices. Even though I'm going solo, I still want to look good. For one thing, Zach Norton will be there, and for another, this is my best friend's sweet sixteen we're talking about.

I decide to go with jeans and a satiny blue shirt that I got at the vintage store. Its big puffy sleeves and V-neck scream '80s. Then I pile on the blue eye shadow and blow dry and backcomb my hair until it looks kind of like a bird's nest on top of my head, spraying it securely in place with hair spray. Adding a sprinkling of glitter, I finish off the look with black suede boots and as much sparkly stuff as I can manage to put on without looking like a Christmas tree: rhinestone snowflake earrings and matching necklace, a pile of blue and white bangle bracelets I found at Sweet Repeats, the vintage store in Boston that Megan and I love to shop at, and a long strand of clear crystal beads double-looped around my neck. One final check in the mirror confirms that I've achieved the perfect over-the-top '80s glam look I was going for.

Grabbing Megan's present (I still can't believe she wanted bunny

Heather Vogel Frederick

slippers, but she dropped so many hints I couldn't ignore them), I head downstairs to find Stewart.

We stop by the Hawthornes to pick up Emma, then head for Strawberry Hill Road. The snow has stopped by now, but we still slip around a few times on the drive there. The Wongs live on kind of a steep incline, and even though my mom let Stewart borrow her SUV, it can still be a little scary driving up here when the roads are bad, especially at night.

We're the first to arrive. Megan greets us at the door holding Coco, and Emma and I start squealing the second we spot the kitten, of course. Stewart stands back, giving us some space. Boys don't get the whole concept of cute. Even when it comes in a four-legged package.

He does take a turn holding her, though, and Emma whips out her cell phone and snaps a picture.

"Don't even think about putting that in the school newspaper," Stewart warns her.

"Nah, it's going directly online," she replies, grinning at him.

"Emma!"

"Kidding, you dork! You look so cute with her, though, that I really should."

Stewart hands Coco to me, and I squeal again. I can't help it—she's irresistible. "Megs, she's so adorable!" I tell her, stroking the kitten's snowy white fur.

Megan nods happily. "I know. I still can't believe my parents gave her to me."

"So does she sleep curled up on your bed?" asks Emma. "Melville always slept on my parents' bed, but Lady Jane prefers her basket."

Lady Jane is the kitten that the Delaneys gave to Mrs. Hawthorne at our book club's New Year's Eve party. I guess technically Lady Jane is Coco's sister, although they don't look anything alike. The only white on the Hawthornes' cat is her paws and bib. Otherwise, she's pure gray.

Megan's face clouds.

"Let me guess," says Emma. "Sophie?"

Megan's face clouds. "So far, Coco makes a beeline for Sophie's room most of the time. I'm trying to train her to stay with me."

"Can't you just shut the door or something?" Emma suggests.

"My mother says I have to be extra nice to Sophie," Megan tells her. "I guess her parents' divorce is really upsetting her."

"Ooo, information to add to Cassidy's chart," I reply.

"Yep."

"What chart?" asks Stewart.

"Never mind," I tell him. "It's just girl stuff."

"Speaking of girl stuff, it's good to see that male reinforcements are starting to arrive," says Mr. Wong, poking his head into the entry hall. "Nice to see you, Stewart!" The two of them shake hands. "I could use some last-minute help down in the family room, if you don't mind."

"So where is this mysterious Sophie?" asks Emma, after Mr. Wong and Stewart disappear. She peers over Megan's shoulder toward the living room.

"With Gigi, of course," Megan replies, not even trying to hide the bitterness in her voice.

Heather Vogel Frederick

We follow her across the living room toward the long hallway that leads to the bedrooms at the back of the house. Megan's house is really different from mine. My family lives in an old Colonial-style house. Not as old as Half Moon Farm—that was built in the 1700s, I think—but still old.

Our house is stuffed with antiques; Megan's is ultramodern, with high ceilings and more windows than walls. And everything, from the carpet to the furniture, is white. Or was, before Gigi got hold of a paintbrush and painted one of the living room walls bright red. Mrs. Wong had a cow, but she didn't change it back. It looks pretty good, actually.

I make a brief detour to the dining room, adding my present to the pile on the table. There's crêpe paper and streamers everywhere, and a big banner that spells out SWEET SIXTEEN stretched across the enormous window.

An Eiffel Tower cake rises from the center of the table, in honor of Megan's upcoming trip to France with Gigi. Surrounding it are tiered plates piled high with *macarons*, petit fours, and other assorted goodies, including pink M&M's with the number 16 on them. I'd heard you could special order them that way, but I've never known anybody who did it. It looks like the Wongs pulled out all the stops for the party.

I try not to be jealous, but it's not always easy being friends with Megan. She's totally not some stuck-up rich girl, but her parents have more money than the bank, as my father likes to say, and it's probably true. What's also true is that they're down-to-earth and incredibly generous. Mrs. Wong is on the board of practically every charity in town.

But still, I can't help comparing my life with Megan's sometimes.

My parents probably won't be able to do much for my birthday, unless my father gets a job soon. Maybe it's just as well that I'll be out of town for it this year. I'll be in Minnesota, since my birthday falls during spring break and my grandmother is taking me to Mankato. That's the town where the Betsy-Tacy books are set.

My gaze lingers on the Eiffel Tower cake. One more thing for me to add to the list of things I should try not to get jealous about. When it comes right down to it, Mankato, Minnesota, just isn't in the same spring-break-trip league as Paris, France.

I jog back across the living room and down the hallway past Megan's room and her parents' room and the sewing room and the guest room where Sophie is staying, finally catching up with Megan and Emma as they're starting downstairs.

The lower level of Megan's house has a huge family room, where we'll be having the dance party tonight, a laundry room, Mr. Wong's office, and my favorite part, the guest quarters. That's what Mrs. Wong calls it anyway, or used to, before Megan's grandmother came to live with them. Now everybody just calls it Gigi's place.

It's like a little apartment, with a bedroom, a bathroom, and a tiny sitting room and kitchen. We used to come down here a lot back in middle school to watch movies and hang out with Gigi, but now that she has the tea shop, she's not home as much as she used to be. I miss spending time here.

The door is open, and I hear Sophie before I see her. She has a low,

Heather Vogel Frederick

musical voice, and she's chattering away in a language that must be French. Since I take Spanish, I have no clue what she's saying. I look over at Megan, and she shrugs, too. She switched to French this year, but she isn't very good at it yet. She'll get lots of practice over spring break, lucky girl.

The three of us poke our heads in the door. Gigi and Sophie are sitting at the kitchen counter, sipping tea and looking at a scrapbook of some kind. I recognize it as one of Gigi's photo albums from Fashion Week. Sophie has her back to us, and she's animated and laughing, obviously having a great time.

"*Bonjour*, girls!" chirps Gigi when she sees us. "Come on in. Tea?"

Sophie turns around, and Megan sucks in her breath sharply. At first I don't understand, but then I spot the French girl's earrings. Diamonds the size of peanuts—they've got to be Gigi's. The ones she sometimes lends to Megan for special occasions.

"No thanks," says Megan stiffly, and Emma and I shake our heads, too.

Sophie's smile fades.

Gigi hops down from the stool where she's perched. "*Sophie, je vous présente Emma Hawthorne et Rebecca Chadwick,*" she rattles off in French. Hearing our names, I figure she's probably introducing us.

Sophie slides off her stool as well. She's petite, like Jess, with the same lustrous dark hair as her cousin Annabelle. Hers is curly, though, framing a heart-shaped face and eyes that aren't blue like Annabelle's, but greenish and thickly fringed with lashes. She's very pretty. Especially with the diamond earrings.

"Nice to meet you, Emma," she says politely, shaking her hand. Her English is flawless, with just the right amount of French accent. She turns to me. "You too, Becca."

Uh-oh, I think. She already knows my nickname. This is not a good sign. She's probably been talking with Annabelle. Or am I making too much of it? Gigi could have told her, right?

Megan looks like she's about to cry. I can only imagine how she feels. I mean, the earrings are Gigi's, of course, and she's free to lend them to whomever she wants—she even let me wear them one evening when I was here for a sleepover. But a total stranger? When it's Megan's birthday? It's so not fair.

As if to add insult to injury, Coco starts squirming in Megan's arms and manages to wriggle free. Megan sets her down on the floor, and she runs right over to Sophie.

"*Oh, c'est adorable! Le chaton t'adore vraiment!*" says Gigi as Sophie bends over and scoops up the kitten.

"No it's not," mutters Megan under her breath.

"What did she say?" I whisper.

"That it's cute the way Coco loves her."

The intercom crackles just then. "Megan, your guests are arriving," says Mrs. Wong. "You may want to come back upstairs and greet them."

Megan spins on her heel and stalks out of the room. Emma and I follow her, leaving Gigi looking puzzled.

Heather Vogel Frederick

"This just gets worse every second!" Megan sputters when we're out of earshot. "I was going to ask Gigi if I could borrow those earrings for the party! They'd be perfect with my outfit." She gestures at the dress that we found at Sweet Repeats. It's lavender, with a short, tiered skirt and puffed sleeves like the ones on my blouse.

"Yeah, they really would," says Emma, who's gone for more of a *Flashdance* look, with an off-the-shoulder sweater and enough dark eyeliner to qualify her as a raccoon. "Maybe you should say something to her."

"Sophie?"

"No, dork—Gigi."

Megan shakes her head. "Too late now."

Upstairs, the living room is crowded with our friends from Alcott High. I laugh out loud when I see Ashley's outfit. "I can't believe you picked that one!" I tell her. "I thought you were joking!"

"Ha!" she replies triumphantly, striking a pose. "I told you that you'd crack up." She's dressed in a complete '80s exercise outfit—long-sleeved leotard, tights, leg warmers, little belt at the waist. A sweatband around her forehead peeks out beneath her poufed-up bangs. Mrs. Wong frowns when she sees her.

"Aren't you going to be cold, honey?"

"Don't worry," Ashley tells her, pointing to a sweatshirt draped over the white leather sofa. "I brought that for the car ride, and I'll put it on in if I get chilly."

"Hey Becca," says a voice behind us. I turn around to see Third standing there. He's wearing jeans, like me, along with a polo shirt with an upturned collar.

"Hey," I reply, without enthusiasm.

"Did you hear that Mr. Wong rented a limo to take us to the restaurant for dinner? Cool, huh?"

I nod. Another thing my family definitely won't be doing for my birthday this year.

The three of us talk for a while, and then Ashley nudges me. "Who invited him?" she asks, jerking her chin at Kevin Mullins, who's dangling nervously in the vicinity of Jess and Darcy. He finally got rid of his enormous glasses, but he still looks like an owl because he's not used to his contacts yet and he blinks all the time.

"I did," says Gigi, who has a soft spot for Kevin. "That boy could use some fattening up."

It's true. My dad says that Kevin has to stand up twice to cast a shadow. He used to be practically a midget, but he shot up last summer and now he's the same height as Cassidy Sloane, only about a hundred times skinnier.

Gigi pulls me aside. "Is everything okay with Megan?"

"Uh . . ." I hesitate, feeling trapped.

"She seems a little, I don't know, upset."

I figure I might as well be the one to spill the beans. "It's the earrings," I tell her. "I think she was going to ask to borrow them for the party."

A frown creases Gigi's face. "Oh dear," she says. "I didn't even stop to—it never occurred to me that—oh dear," she says again, and sighs.

Heather Vogel Frederick

"Sophie was feeling badly about what's going on back at home, and because she didn't know about the '80s theme, and I just thought the earrings would spark up that black turtleneck. It gives her an Audrey Hepburn flair, don't you think?"

I look across the room to where Megan's mother is introducing Sophie to the rest of our friends. Gigi is right, of course. Sophie looks dazzling. But then, who wouldn't in diamond earrings like those?

Cassidy Sloane and Zach Norton are the last ones to arrive. They come in just as Mrs. Wong finishes the introductions. Cassidy shakes Sophie's hand, looking like a giantess next to the petite French girl. At six feet tall, though, Cassidy looks like a giantess next to just about everybody.

"Awesome!" breathes Ashley, gaping at her cotton-candy pink prom dress. For once, Cassidy really got into the spirit of things, fashionwise. Her mother must have helped her with her hair, which is just as gravity defying as Ashley's and mine. Cassidy's notoriously bad at doing it herself, and no way is she responsible for getting it to look like that.

She looks kind of ridiculous next to Sophie, though. Gigi was right about the Audrey Hepburn thing—Sophie looks sleek and sophisticated in her jeans and black turtleneck. Even if she didn't get the memo about the '80s theme, it seems to me she could have tried a little harder.

Cassidy and Emma and Jess drift over to where Megan and Ashley and I are standing, leaving the French girl surrounded by a knot of boys.

"Like flies to honey," says Emma ruefully, her gaze lingering on my brother, who's also part of the pack.

"It's the accent," I tell her. "I mean, look at us." I gesture at our flounces and frills and big hair. "Who could resist all this beauty?"

We stare at one another, then burst out laughing. We look ridiculous.

"How did you get your bangs to do that?" Megan asks Jess, whose thick blond fringe has been teased into a sky-high pouf.

"About a gallon of hair spray." She tosses her high side-ponytail back and forth. "My mother helped me. She said she used to wear her hair like this all the time."

"Love the tutu skirt and cropped leggings, but those shoulder pads on your jean jacket look like they need their own zip code," I tell her, prodding at one of them.

"Careful there—I found this in the back of my mom's closet," she replies, laughing again. She turns to Cassidy. "I can't believe you actually wore pink! Voluntarily, I mean."

Cassidy grins. "It's my birthday present to Megan."

"Gee, thanks," says Megan.

A few minutes later Mr. Wong emerges from whatever he was doing down in the family room and claps his hands. "The limo is here!"

"Just one?" asks Emma. "Are we all going to fit?"

We grab our coats and go outside, where we all stop dead in our tracks. At the foot of the driveway is the longest limo I've ever seen in my life. And not just any limo—a Hummer. A *pink* Hummer.

"Sweet ride!" crows Third.

"Jerry, you didn't!" cries Mrs. Wong. "I thought we agreed on the

Heather Vogel Frederick

hybrid." Megan's mother is a die-hard environmentalist.

"Last-minute executive decision," says Mr. Wong, ignoring her disapproval. "This is safer in the snow."

"Whoa, that thing is huge!" says Zach Norton. "I didn't know they came that big."

"Oh yeah, baby," says Cassidy, picking up the hem of her dress and jogging toward it. I hadn't noticed that she's got pink high-top sneakers on. "I am wearing the right color tonight!"

She opens the door and climbs in, and we pile in behind her, leaving the guys outside with Mr. Wong to *ooh* and *aah* over the Hummer's exterior. We're checking out the DVD player and refrigerator filled with soda and snacks when Sophie slips in. She looks around a little uncertainly, then settles into a seat by the nearest window.

"Maybe we should go talk to her," Jess murmurs to me.

I shrug, helping myself to a handful of pink monogrammed M&M's. "Go ahead."

Before Jess can do anything, the door opens again and the boys scramble in. The diamond earrings must have magnetic properties, because most of the guys except Darcy and Zach cluster around Sophie, vying for a seat. Even Third, which is annoying, despite the fact that I don't like him. I mean, I like him, but I don't *like* him.

It's the same thing at the restaurant, where Sophie ends up between Ethan MacDonald and my brother. Emma's on the other side of Stewart, looking a little irritated. More than a little irritated, in fact.

Megan can't hide her annoyance, either, especially when Sophie and Mrs. Wong decide to split a vegetarian entrée.

"I should just wrap her up and put a bow on her and give her to my mother when her birthday comes around," she mutters to me. "Sophie is like the perfect daughter she always wanted."

I squeeze her hand under the table, and she gives me a quick smile. "Thanks, Becca. Glad someone's in my court."

This sweet sixteen party isn't exactly turning out the way I thought it would, and I can only imagine how Megan feels. I don't care if Sophie's got troubles at home; she has no right to sabotage Megan's big day. And no amount of fancy food or presents or even a dance club DJ can make up for the fact that Mrs. Wong and Gigi are falling all over themselves to make Sophie Fairfax happy, and practically ignoring Megan in the process.

La Belle Époque is Concord's fanciest restaurant, and dinner is so amazingly delicious that we manage to enjoy ourselves in spite of Sophie and her perfections. Back at the house the fun continues as we stuff ourselves on Eiffel Tower cake (it's pink inside, a strawberry layer cake—Megan's favorite flavor) and watch Megan open her presents. In addition to the kitten, she gets a fancy new smartphone from her parents, complete with a little telephoto lens that clips on it, "for taking pictures on your trip to Paris," Mr. Wong explains.

"Coco was the main present," her mother tells her, dangling a piece of ribbon above the kitten, who is sitting on her lap. Coco takes the bait and stands up on her hind legs to swat at it.

"You are just so cute I can hardly stand it!" says Emma.

Heather Vogel Frederick

"Why, thank you, Emma," says Mrs. Wong brightly.

Emma blinks. "Um, I wasn't—I didn't mean—"

Mrs. Wong laughs. "I know what you meant," she tells her, handing Coco over. "Here you go."

"Hey! Emma has enough pets—she's mine," Megan protests.

"Open your presents," Emma says, nuzzling the kitten and passing Megan a box with her free hand. "This one's from me and Jess and Cassidy."

The three of them chipped in on this really cool coffee-table book about the history of fashion, which Megan goes nuts over. From the boys she gets the usual assortment of DVDs, movie passes, and gift cards.

"Just two left," says Emma, "a big one and a little one. Which one do you want first?"

"Little one," Megan replies.

Emma hands it to her. "It's from Simon."

"Um, I'm not sure I want to open it here in front of everybody," Megan murmurs.

"Megan and Simon, sitting in a tree!" sings Kevin. His voice cracks and he turns as pink as Megan's birthday cake when everybody looks over at him. "Sorry," he whispers.

Then Sophie laughs, and all the guys laugh, and he looks pleased.

"C'mon, Megs," I coax. "At least take a peek. If it's embarrassing, you don't have to open it all the way."

She peels the wrapping paper off the box slowly, then lifts a corner of the lid. "Oh, how adorable!" she says, lifting it off all the way. There's a necklace inside—a small glittering ice cream cone on a silver chain.

"There's something else in there too," her mother says, peering over her shoulder to see.

"Mom!" Megan protests, whisking the box away. She looks inside again. "You're right," she admits. "Two somethings, actually." She pulls out what looks like a scrap of newspaper and squints at it. "It's in French. I can't read it."

Mrs. Wong frowns. "Aren't they teaching you anything at school?"

"Mom!" Megan says again.

"I'm kidding! Mostly." Megan's mother takes the newspaper clipping from her and hands it to Sophie. "Would you do the honors?"

Sophie shrugs and scans it. "World Ice Dancing Grand Prix to be held at the Palais Omnisports in Paris in April." She looks up. "*C'est tout*—that's all it says."

"Why would Simon send me that?" Megan looks puzzled.

"Duh," says Cassidy. "His brother is an *ice dancer*, remember?"

"You mean—" Megan snatches the clipping back and looks at the dates, then jumps up and shrieks. Startled, Coco gives a tiny hiss and shoots off Emma's lap onto the floor. "That's the same time I'll be in Paris!"

I gasp. "You're going to see Simon!"

"Megan and Si—" Kevin starts to sing again, before Ashley kicks him.

"I thought you said there were two somethings in the box, Megan," her father says.

Heather Vogel Frederick

She reaches in and pulls out an envelope this time. Inside is a tourist brochure. "Um, it's for someplace called 'Glacier Berthillon.'"

"Ahhhh," sighs her grandmother. "The correct pronunciation is *Gla-see-yay Bear-tea-yawn.*" She looks over at Sophie and smiles. "*C'est magnifique, n'est-ce pas,* Sophie?"

Sophie lifts a shoulder, but she can't help smiling back.

"It's an ice cream parlor," Gigi tells us. "But not just any ice cream parlor—the best one in all of Paris, and possibly in all the world. It's on the Île Saint-Louis, not far from Notre Dame Cathedral."

"Better than Kimball Farm?" Emma asks.

Gigi holds up both palms, as if weighing the two options. "That would be a difficult decision," she says finally, and turns to Megan. "Sounds to me like you have a date, *ma chérie.*"

Megan's face flushes, but she looks pleased.

"One more present," I tell her, passing her my box.

"Gee, I wonder what this is?" Megan smiles at me as she slips off the ribbon.

"Haven't a clue," I reply airily.

"Bunny slippers!" She holds them up for everybody to see. "Thanks, Becca—they're just what I wanted." She leans over and gives me a hug.

Sophie's gaze slides over in my direction. She smirks at me, and I can feel my face grow hot. *It's what Megan asked for!* I want to shout at her. *And besides, it's not like you got her anything.*

"My present is waiting for you in Paris," Gigi tells Megan. "You don't mind if you can't unwrap it for a couple of months, do you?"

Megan shakes her head. "I've been waiting for Paris my whole life. I can wait a little longer."

"And now Paris has come to us," says Mrs. Wong, slipping an arm around Sophie's shoulders. "With a wonderful surprise present called Sophie, our borrowed daughter."

Sophie looks down at the floor, but one corner of her mouth quirks up in a half smile. Megan looks like she wants to barf.

"Let's not worry about Sophie any more tonight," Emma tells her a few minutes later, as we all head downstairs to the family-room-turned-dance club. "Let's just have fun, okay?"

For the most part we're successful. Mr. Wong did a phenomenal job with the decorations—there's black fabric draped over all the walls, and pinned to it is a galaxy of silver stars and big silver letters that spell out HAPPY SWEET SIXTEEN, MEGAN! Overhead, the glittering disco ball rotates, sending a shower of sparkles into every corner of the room. The DJ is great, too—he's put together an awesome playlist that has us dancing to everything from Michael Jackson to Cyndi Lauper, the Beastie Boys, and a bunch of other people whose names I don't know but whose music I've heard before.

"So what's the deal with this chick?" asks Cassidy a while later, slouching over to where Megan and Ashley and Emma and I are sitting on a sofa, taking a break. She jerks her thumb across the room to where Sophie is holding court, perched on a stool by the soda fountain that the Wongs imported for the party. Every other guy in the room besides Darcy, who is slow dancing with Jess under the

Heather Vogel Frederick

disco ball, is clustered around, hanging on her every word.

"She's like one of those bug lights that attracts mosquitoes," I grumble.

"Or Velcro," says Megan, and Cassidy grins.

"Mademoiselle Velcro," she says, holding up two fingers to form a V. "Oh yeah."

"It's the cute accent," says Ashley.

"It's her eyelashes—nobody has eyelashes that long," I suggest.

"It's Gigi's earrings," adds Megan with a sigh.

"Whatever it is, it's not fair," says Emma, glumly eyeing Stewart, who's laughing at something Sophie just said.

"It's disgusting," agrees Megan.

"Revolting," adds Cassidy.

"Nauseating," I conclude, turning to Ashley. "This is called the synonym game, by the way."

She smiles. "So that's how it works! I always wondered." Her gaze drifts back to Sophie. "One thing's for sure—she's certainly shaking up Concord, and she hasn't even been here forty-eight hours yet."

"I've about had it with her already," says Emma, standing up. "I'm going to go ask Stewart to dance."

"Better get used to it," I tell her. "She's here until June." I look over at Zach Norton, who appears to be practicing his French. June can't come soon enough for me.

❧ Jess ❧

*"Mrs. Harden, be it observed, was the housekeeper:
a woman after Mr. Brocklehurst's own heart, made up
of equal parts whalebone and iron."*
—*Jane Eyre*

"I'd like to start our meeting this afternoon by welcoming our newest book club member, Sophie Fairfax." Mrs. Hawthorne smiles at the French girl. "We're so happy you can join us."

I glance over at Megan, who doesn't look happy at all. I can't really blame her anymore, now that I've seen Sophie in action. I'm just grateful that Darcy seems immune to her charms. He was polite and everything at the party last night, of course—it's not like he ignored her—but he wasn't falling all over himself to impress her, the way most of the other guys were. Even Kevin Mullins!

And poor Emma. Stewart was right there in the thick of things.

Most of all, though, I feel sorry for Megan. Coco's obvious preference for Sophie is annoying, but more than that, I can only imagine how I'd feel if my family went suddenly gaga over a houseguest the way Megan's family has over Sophie. It reminds me of when we first got Spice, the younger of our two Shetland sheepdogs. Sugar moped around the farm for weeks, certain that she'd been replaced by somebody younger and cuter than she was. Or the way I felt when my mother went to New York to be on a soap opera called *HeartBeats*, and I had to share her with the rest of the world.

"Are you enjoying Concord so far?" my mother asks Sophie. "You certainly arrived on a busy weekend, what with Megan's birthday party and all."

Sophie smiles politely. "Yes, thank you, it is very nice here."

"Can you tell us a little about yourself?" my mother continues. "Do you have brothers and sisters? What do you like to do for fun?"

"No brothers or sisters," Sophie replies, shifting uncomfortably in her chair. "And for fun I like very much photography"—she pronounces it the French way, "fo-to-graph-ee," with the accent on the last syllable—"and also, how you say, cinema?"

"Movies?" Mrs. Hawthorne asks, and Sophie nods. "Wonderful. We all like movies, too, so you'll find plenty of kindred spirits here."

Emma shoots me a look, one that says *I don't think so.*

"*Etes-vous un member d'un club de lecture à Paris?*" asks Cassidy's mother, tucking a strand of her long blond hair behind her ear. I didn't know that Mrs. Sloane-Kinkaid spoke French. Maybe it's because she used to be model a long time ago, before she became a mom. Models probably spend a lot of time in Europe.

Sophie shakes her head and murmurs something rapidly back in French.

"She says they don't have mother-daughter book clubs in France, or at least she's never heard of one," Cassidy's mother tells us, and Gigi nods in agreeement.

"Well, you're in one now, and as I'm sure Megan has told you, we're currently reading *Jane Eyre*," Mrs. Hawthorne continues. "Are you familiar with it?"

Sophie nods. "*Oui.* Yes."

"Wonderful! Feel free to chime in anytime. You'll see how it all works as we go along."

We're sitting in Becca's living room. The Chadwicks' house used to be super formal, but ever since Mrs. Chadwick started her landscape design classes, I noticed she's been changing things up a little. She brought in some big potted plants and rearranged the furniture and added a few bright throw pillows. Just a few small details, but it's made the room a whole lot cozier.

"So, what does everyone think of the book so far? Jess?"

"I like it," I tell Emma's mom. "It's different from the other books we've read, though. It's kind of, I don't know, dark. All that rain and that big gloomy house Jane lives in with her horrible cousins and that awful school and everything."

I can't help it; my eyes slide automatically over to Sophie as the words "horrible cousins" come out of my mouth. She doesn't seem to notice, though. She's too busy patting Yo-Yo, the Chadwicks' Labradoodle.

"It's a good book to read this time of year," says Mrs. Chadwick. "Especially with all this snow. It makes me want to curl up under a blanket with a cup of tea."

My mother laughs. "Every book I read makes me want to curl up under a blanket with a cup of tea," she says. "Speaking of which, pour me a refill, would you, Calliope?"

She passes her cup to Mrs. Chadwick, who reaches for the teapot on the table.

"I know what you mean, Shannon, but *Jane Eyre* gives me that feeling even more than usual," says Cassidy's mother. "Reading it takes me right to those bleak Yorkshire moors."

All the moms nod in agreement. Sophie watches them surreptitiously, her expression unreadable.

"How do you think Jane herself stacks up so far against the main characters in the other books we've read?" asks Mrs. Hawthorne.

"She's different," says Becca. "Spunkier, maybe?"

"Jo March in *Little Women* has plenty of spunk!" protests Mrs. Wong.

"And Elizabeth Bennet is no pushover in *Pride and Prejudice*," adds Emma. She loves Elizabeth Bennet.

"Becca's right, though, Jane is different," says Cassidy. "She's only ten—at least in the part I've read so far—but she doesn't put up with any, uh, you know, crud. I loved the way she stood up to that bratty cousin of hers."

"You mean John Reed?" says Emma.

"Yeah, the fat kid who bullied her and threw a book at her head. Jane was awesome in that scene! If she lived here in Concord I'd recruit her for Chicks with Sticks and have her out on the ice in a hot second."

Cassidy mimes slapping a hockey stick against a puck.

"I can't believe how mean everyone is to her!" says Megan. "Even her aunt—locking her in that creepy red room for punishment."

"The room where her uncle died," adds Gigi with a shudder. "Very bad *feng shui*."

"And as if that kind of mental cruelty isn't bad enough," adds my mother, "she sends her off to that nasty boarding school—"

"—with that awful Mr. Brocklehurst," I finish. Just thinking about him gives me the shivers. Charlotte Brontë's a great writer, and I can totally picture him in my head, all tall and stern with that big nose and prominent teeth.

"A show of hands, please, for everyone who's eager to transfer to Lowood School!" jokes Mrs. Chadwick.

"I'm glad Alcott High isn't like Lowood," says Becca. "I wouldn't have lasted two minutes."

Her mother's smile fades, and she looks at Becca wistfully. She's always saying how so many of her happiest memories are from when she was a student at Colonial Academy, and she's still a little sad that Becca isn't a student there herself. Couldn't be one, really. Becca doesn't have the grades. Even if she did, it's not like she would have wanted to go. Colonial Academy is an all-girls' school, and boys are Becca Chadwick's number one priority in life.

It's not that I don't like boys—I do. Especially Darcy Hawthorne. But I love Colonial, and I feel incredibly lucky to be going there. It still amazes me the way it dropped into my life the way it did, thanks to

Heather Vogel Frederick

Mrs. Chadwick recommending me for the Founder's scholarship. I love all my teachers and classes—even calculus—and I get to go horseback riding for P.E., and sing in MadriGals, and have the fun of living in the dorm during the week. Plus, because it's a local school, I get to keep my regular Concord life with my family and friends on the weekends, too. It's like I have the best of both worlds.

Out of the corner of my eye I see Mrs. Hawthorne prod Emma with her toe and nod significantly in Sophie's direction. Emma sighs and turns to the French girl. "What's your school at home like?" she asks politely.

I'm guessing Emma must have gotten the mom lecture before book club, too. The one that said, "Be nice to Annabelle's cousin; she's a long way from home." I'm pretty sure we all did.

"It's fine," Sophie replies coolly, not bothering to tear her gaze away from Yo-Yo. "School is school."

Emma glances over at her mother and shrugs, as if to say *Hey, I tried*.

Cassidy, who's sitting on the hearth stirring the fire with a poker, suddenly turns around and grins at Becca. "Do you remember when you guys served us cornmeal mush for book club?"

"Whatever, Cassidy. That was ages ago!" Becca sounds a little offended. She's right, though, it was back in eighth grade. We were reading *Daddy-Long-Legs*, and Judy Abbott, the main character, lived in an orphanage, so Mrs. Chadwick got it into her head that serving us the glop they gave the orphans would open our eyes to the plight of the less fortunate. Not exactly fun for a book club meeting, especially when you're expecting maybe cupcakes or something.

"We did go a little overboard, didn't we?" says Mrs. Chadwick with a rueful smile.

"We?" Becca sounds annoyed. "It was all your idea, Mom, remember?"

Her mother raises her hands in surrender. "All right, all right. I accept full responsibility for the loathsome mush. Not one of my better moments. But have I not redeemed myself tonight?" She gestures at the coffee table, which is scattered with the remains of our feast: a high tea direct from Yorkshire featuring seed cake and scones with whipped cream, lemon curd, and jam.

"Oh yeah," says Cassidy, dipping her forefinger into the nearly empty dish of whipped cream. "Definitely. Anyway, I guess reading *Jane Eyre* just reminded me of that night, that's all. Jane's an orphan, too, just like Judy Abbott." She licks her finger pensively. "What's the deal with orphans in books, anyway? There's a ton of them—Anne in *Anne of Green Gables* was an orphan, too."

"Good question, Cassidy," says Mrs. Hawthorne. "Anybody want to respond?"

Emma's hand shoots up.

"Emma!" we all chorus, and she sheepishly takes it down. Old habits die hard, and Emma just can't seem to break this one.

Her mother smiles at her. "Yes?"

"I think there are two reasons for orphans in literature," Emma replies. "One is because everybody feels sorry for them, so using one as a main character makes the reader sympathetic to them right off

Heather Vogel Frederick

the bat. Plus, I read somewhere that a lot of books get the parents out of the way in order for the focus to be on the main character and how they deal with their problems."

"Authors kill off the parents on *purpose*?" Mrs. Wong's voice swoops up indignantly. "Really?"

"Haven't you ever noticed that before, Mom?" says Megan.

Her mother shakes her head. "No! I think it's cold-blooded and horrible, if it's true. What's wrong with having parents in books?"

"Nothing, Lily," says Mrs. Hawthorne, who's probably sorry she brought the whole thing up. "And there are plenty of books out there where the parents are very much alive and kicking. Remember Marmee in *Little Women*? And Mr. and Mrs. Ray in the Betsy-Tacy series?" She digs around in the tote bag by her feet. "Moving right along," she continues, pulling out a folder. "I think it's time for this month's fun facts. And then I have a couple of announcements to make."

She passes us each a handout. Sophie, who has been following this whole exchange quietly, looks at hers without expression.

FUN FACTS ABOUT CHARLOTTE

1) Charlotte Brontë was born April 21, 1816 in Thornton, England.

2) She was the third of six children born to Maria Branwell Brontë, a merchant's daughter from Cornwall, and Patrick

Brontë, an Irishman who rose from humble roots to be educated as a clergyman at Cambridge University. Charlotte had two older sisters, Maria and Elizabeth; two younger sisters, Emily and Anne; and a younger brother, Branwell.

3) Reverend Brontë was appointed to St. Michaels and All Angels Church in the village of Haworth when Charlotte was four, and the family moved into the parsonage. A large, plain stone house, it stood across from the church graveyard and had for its backyard the sweeping Yorkshire moors where the Brontë children loved to roam and play.

4) Charlotte was just five years old when her mother died. Her father made several unsuccessful attempts to remarry (no one seemed interested in taking on a widower with six children under the age of eight). Eventually, the children's aunt Elizabeth, a spinster, moved in with the family to help care for them. She wasn't especially fond of children, but the Brontës also had a warm-hearted housekeeper, Tabitha Aykroyd, whom the family called Tabby, who loved to tell stories and local legends around the kitchen fire.

5) When Charlotte was eight years old, she was sent with Maria and Elizabeth to the Clergy Daughters' School in Cowan Bridge, Lancashire. Its harsh conditions would later become

the model for Lowood School in her novel *Jane Eyre*.

6) Both of Charlotte's older sisters died after contracting tuber-culosis at the school. Charlotte and her sister Emily, who had joined them in Cowan Bridge by this time, were brought home by their father. Charlotte would eventually immortal-ize her beloved older sister Maria as Jane's angelic, doomed friend Helen Burns in *Jane Eyre*.

"What a sad childhood," I exclaim. "I can't believe how many people in her family died. Her mother *and* both her older sisters?"

I see Cassidy and her mother exchange a glance, and could have bitten my tongue. Sometimes I forget that Cassidy's father died. It was a long time ago, but still.

"You'll want to pay close attention to the details of Charlotte's life as we learn about them," says Mrs. Hawthorne. "She's a writer who drew a great deal on her own experience for her novels."

"You mean like Lowood School?" asks Becca, looking at our handout.

"Exactly," says Mrs. Hawthorne.

"I figured she was exaggerating when she described it, but I guess not."

Mrs. Hawthorne shakes her head. "On a happier note," she says, "I've arranged a special treat for next month's meeting. Tristan and

Simon Berkeley will be joining us via videoconference, with more 'fun facts' direct from Yorkshire!"

A current of excitement ripples through the room. I see Megan perk up at the mention of Simon's name, and so does Sophie, who looks interested for the first time all afternoon.

"How did you manage to arrange that, Phoebe?" my mother asks.

"Sarah Berkeley sent me an email the other day, and she mentioned that Simon's taking an elective at school this year in filmmaking," Emma's mother replies. She looks over at Sophie. "Maybe Alcott High has one, too, since you're interested in cinema and photography."

"Great idea! I'll check into it when we register her tomorrow," says Mrs. Wong, making a note.

"At any rate," Mrs. Hawthorne continues, "I knew that Professor Berkeley is lecturing at the University of York this winter and that Sarah and the boys have been visiting him on the weekends. I just connected the dots. It occurred to me that perhaps they'd be open to filming some of the Brontë hot spots—the Haworth parsonage, that sort of thing—since we can't be on location this time around."

"We can show everybody some of our pictures, too," says Emma, whose family visited Yorkshire when they lived in England last year.

"You bet," her mother replies. "And I have some brochures and maps and things I'll bring to next month's meeting as well. Meanwhile, let's plan to read through chapter fourteen. The setting will move from Lowood to a grand country house called Thornfield Hall, where you'll meet a young French girl by the name of Adele Varens—"

Heather Vogel Frederick

"Annoying plot device!" whispers Emma.

"Emma!" says her mother, frowning at her.

"Sorry, Mom, but you've got to admit that's what she is."

Ignoring her, Mrs. Hawthorne turns again to Sophie. "I'm hoping you might be willing to help us with some of the French phrases and passages, when we get to them," she says. "Charlotte Brontë doesn't always translate them for us in her text." Sophie nods, and Mrs. Hawthorne continues, "You'll also be meeting one of the most famous men in English literature: Edward Rochester."

Mrs. Wong sighs happily. "Right up there with Mr. Darcy, right, Phoebe?"

Mrs. Hawthorne gives her a withering look. "No one is right up there with Fitzwilliam Darcy." Emma's mother is nuts about Jane Austen's books, and she's totally in love with Mr. Darcy from *Pride and Prejudice*. Emma calls it a "literary crush."

"I guess it's a matter of taste," says Cassidy's mother. "I've always liked the dark, brooding types myself."

My friends and I look at one another and burst out laughing. Stanley Kinkaid, Cassidy's stepfather, is short and bald and cheerful, and about as far from dark and brooding as you could possibly get.

"I have one more announcement to make," says Mrs. Hawthorne. "My friend Melanie Jacobs called over the weekend, and it looks like the Wyoming girls are finally coming to Concord! They're planning to head our way over spring break."

"But I'll be in Paris!" wails Megan.

"And I'm going to Minnesota with Gram!" says Becca.

"Not to worry," Mrs. Hawthorne replies. "You'll all be here—spring break in Wyoming falls the week before ours."

"So we'll be in school the whole time?" says Emma. "That's no fun!"

"We'll arrange it so that they do their sightseeing during the day while you girls are in classes—you've seen all the places they're going to want to visit anyway—and we'll plan lots of activities for after school and in the evenings," Mrs. Hawthorne explains.

"Maybe your boss will even give you some time off," Gigi tells Becca, who smiles.

I'm really excited to hear this news. The same year we read *Daddy-Long-Legs*, we teamed up with a mother-daughter book club out West, and were each assigned one of the girls as a pen pal. We all ended up going out to Wyoming for a summer vacation, which was amazing because we got to stay at a dude ranch and ride every day. Ever since, our pen pals have been hoping to come see us. And now it's finally happening!

"In honor of their upcoming trip," Mrs. Hawthorne continues, "they've decided that a little solidarity is in order, so they're reading *Jane Eyre*, too. I thought we'd plan a special joint book club meeting while they're in town. Among other things we'll plan for them, of course."

"They must visit Walden Pond," says Mrs. Chadwick, whipping out a clipboard from who knows where and making a note. Becca's mother is addicted to clipboards. "And the historical sites, of course—the Old

North Bridge, Sleepy Hollow Cemetery, Ralph Waldo Emerson's home."

"Bet that's at the top of their list of must-sees," whispers Cassidy at the mention of this last destination, which has to be one of Concord's most boring museums. I stifle a giggle.

"Don't forget Orchard House," adds Emma.

Orchard House is where Louisa May Alcott lived when she wrote *Little Women*, and it's always been one of Emma's favorite places in town. She wants to be a writer someday, and she practically worships Louisa May Alcott.

"Right," says Mrs. Chadwick, making another note.

"I'll get started on packets for them," says Mrs. Wong. "They'll need maps, too."

Megan's mother loves packets and maps almost as much as Mrs. Chadwick loves clipboards.

"I can see that their itinerary is in good hands," says Mrs. Hawthorne. "Any other ideas of things they should do, girls?"

"Will Kimball's be open?" asks Megan.

"Probably not," says my mother. "It's a bit early in the season for ice cream."

"The Red Sox won't be playing, either," says Cassidy, sounding disappointed.

"But they can come to a Chicks with Sticks practice," Emma points out, and Cassidy brightens at this idea.

"How about we schedule a welcome party at the tea shop in their honor?" says Gigi. "A real Pies & Prejudice feast."

"Excellent." Mrs. Chadwick jots this down, too. "And perhaps they'd like a tour of your cheese-making operation at Half Moon Farm, Shannon?"

My mother nods. "Absolutely." Our family raises goats, and a few years ago my parents started selling goat cheese commercially. The business has really taken off since then.

Mrs. Sloane-Kinkaid leans forward in her chair, her eyes alight with excitement. "I've got an idea! How about I talk to Fred Goldberg, my producer, and see if we can work in a *Cooking with Clementine* episode featuring both book clubs?"

"Fun!" says Mrs. Hawthorne. "I'll bet the girls from Gopher Hole would love that."

Sophie looks puzzled. "Gopher Hole? What is Gopher Hole?"

"Where, not what," Mrs. Wong tells her. "It's the name of the town in Wyoming where the girls live."

"But isn't a gopher a . . ." She pauses, searching around for the right word " . . . a rat?"

Megan's mother looks at Mrs. Hawthorne for support.

"Technically, a gopher is a rodent," Mrs. Hawthorne concedes. "But they're much cuter than rats. They're also called prairie dogs."

Sophie's lips curl up in a smirk. "Gopher Hole," she repeats softly. I guess for someone who lives in a chateau, a little town in Wyoming with a name like that must sound really podunk. And I have to admit, we thought it was funny at first too. But it's still not very nice of her to laugh at it.

Heather Vogel Frederick

"*C'est une ville très charmant,*" Gigi tells her. "*Vraiment. C'est le Wild West, avec les cowboys et les chevaux!*"

"Something about cowboys and horses," Megan whispers to the rest of us.

Stewart drifts in just then, eyeing the lone remaining scone on the tea tray.

"Help yourself," his mother tells him, and he does, settling down on the floor by Emma. Sophie, who is sitting across from them, suddenly comes to life. She quickly rearranges her smirk into a big smile, and Stewart smiles back at her.

Cassidy elbows me and flashes a surreptitious *V* sign. "Mademoiselle Velcro," she mutters, and I nod.

Emma is scowling at Stewart, but he's oblivious because he's too busy grinning like a doofus at the French girl. What is it about Sophie? It's like one of those pheromones I learned about in AP biology, that invisible scent thing that insects give off when they're attracting a mate. Sophie's definitely got something major in that department going on.

I decide that this calls for a new Latin name, like the one I gave Becca Chadwick a couple of years ago: *Chadwickius frenemus. Chadwickius* because that's her species, and *frenemus* because she can be a frenemy sometimes. I frown, watching Sophie, who only has eyes— big green eyes, with ridiculously long eyelashes—for Stewart.

Fairfaxium flirtium, maybe? You'd think that Stewart would see right through Sophie, she's so obvious, but he's swallowed the bait hook, line, and sinker. I think Cassidy's already got the best name for her, though. Mademoiselle Velcro fits her to a T.

Our moms have gotten up by now and are busy clearing away the dishes and gathering up books and papers and coats. They linger in the front hall for a few minutes, talking about the scandal involving Mayor Perkins. Then my mother pokes her head back in the living room.

"Jess? Time to go, sweetheart, if you can peel yourself away."

I glance at the clock on the mantel and scramble to my feet. I'm due back on campus in fifteen minutes. I told my roommates I'd meet them for dinner.

Our dorm has a tradition on Sunday nights called Movie Madness. Mr. and Mrs. McKinley, our houseparents, started it years ago. They're both kind of crazy about old movies, so they show one on the big screen TV in the basement rec room every week. We all come in our pajamas and robes. You don't have to go if you have too much homework, but almost everybody does. It's too much fun to miss.

"Bye, guys!" I tell my friends. Grabbing my jacket, I follow my mother out the front door.

She dangles the car keys in front of me as we head to where our car is parked. I take them from her and slide in behind the wheel. My birthday was last month, but I had to wait until I got my cast off to get my license. I'm still not used to driving the new minivan, though. My parents finally replaced the old car, which we'd had for as long as I could remember. I'm glad they didn't replace the farm truck—it's still going strong, even though it's ancient. I like driving it best, because it

Heather Vogel Frederick

smells like barn and I love sitting up high. It's kind of like riding Led or Zep, one of our big Belgian horses. The minivan isn't nearly as fun, but it's practical, what with my not-so-little-anymore brothers and their swim team friends to haul around, plus all of Half Moon Farm's cheese and produce deliveries.

It's just a short drive to school, and a few minutes later I pull into a parking spot by the front gate.

"Break a leg tomorrow, sweetheart," my mother tells me. "Well, not really. One broken leg is enough for a lifetime." She smiles. "You know what I mean, though. And call me afterward, okay?" She knows how hard I've been working on my MadriGals solo audition.

"I will."

We both get out of the car, and she comes around to my side to give me a hug. "Don't forget this," she says, shoving a cookie tin into my hands.

My mother made her special triple chocolate cookies for me and my roommates. I'll have to hide them when I get to the dorm. Fights have been known to break out over these cookies.

"Thanks, Mom," I tell her, slipping the tin into my backpack. I wave as she drives off, feeling a tiny pang as I imagine what's waiting for her back home. My dad always makes waffles for Sunday supper in the wintertime, and then, after any last chores, we have what he calls our tech-free night—no cell phones, TV, video games, or anything with a plug or switch allowed. Instead, we all hang out by the fire in the keeping room, the small family room off our kitchen, where we read, play board games, catch up on homework, and just talk. It's my favorite night of the week.

Sunday nights are fun here at school as well, though, I remind myself, and shouldering my backpack I head through the front gates and across the quad to the dining hall.

I'm happy to see that waffles are on the menu for supper here at Colonial, too. It's like a little reminder of home. Not that I get homesick anymore. It's hard to believe that I ever did, since Half Moon Farm is just a couple of miles down the road. But I was pretty miserable when I first started going here back in eighth grade.

"Hey roomie—how was Megan's party?" Frankie asks as I plunk my tray down beside hers at one of the long tables. Frankie is Francesca Norris. She has dark curly hair and dark eyes, and she's from New York City. Adele Bixby, one of our other roommates, is sitting across from her. Adele is from San Francisco, and she's the exact same height as Frankie. From the back it's hard to tell them apart, except that Adele's hair isn't curly. Plus she has blue eyes. Adele sings in MadriGals with me; Frankie's a dancer.

I launch into a description of our hilarious '80s getups, then pull out my cell phone to show them all the pictures.

"Who's that?" asks Adele, pointing to a picture of Sophie. "She's really pretty."

"Who's pretty?" asks Savannah Sinclair, sliding in beside us and flipping her long, chestnut-brown hair back over her shoulder. "Are y'all talking about me again?"

Heather Vogel Frederick

Frankie grins and tosses a piece of waffle at her. "Whatever."

Savannah laughs. Sometimes I still can't believe we're friends. She's a senator's daughter from Georgia, and the two of us were bitter enemies most of my first year here. Now we're roommates by choice. She's in MadriGals, too.

I explain all about Sophie Fairfax, and her effect on the boys at the party, not to mention Megan's parents, her grandmother, and Coco.

"Megan's kitten likes the French girl better than her? Wow, that's harsh," says Frankie.

I nod. "I can only imagine what it's going to be like tomorrow when she lands at Alcott High. I'm picturing hallways littered with twitterpated males."

"*C'est horrible*," says Savannah with a shudder. She speaks fluent French, thanks to a bunch of au pairs and nannies she had when she was growing up. "It's like the worst birthday ever."

"Yeah, Megan's not too happy. I thought she was overreacting at first, but then I saw Sophie in action."

After dinner, we clear our trays and head back to the dorm. The four of us are sharing a quad this year on the top floor of Elliot, the sophomore dormitory. We busy ourselves with homework, and somehow I manage to wrestle through the remainder of my calculus problems in time for Movie Madness.

"Who's making dessert this week?" asks Adele as the four of us change into our pajamas and robes and troop downstairs. Every week a different part of the dorm is responsible for the treats.

"Uh, B Hall I think," Savannah replies. "I heard someone mention gingerbread."

Sure enough, big platters of warm gingerbread are waiting for us in the rec room. I help myself to a piece before settling next to Frankie on one of the sofas. The McKinleys got wind of the fact that my book club is reading *Jane Eyre*, and they picked an old black-and-white version for us to watch tonight.

"It's not terribly true to the story," our house pop tells us by way of introduction, "but it's one of Mrs. McKinley's favorites, thanks to the brooding presence of a young Orson Welles." He cups his hand by his mouth and whispers conspiratorially, "I think I have some competition!" We all laugh. "And speaking of young," he adds, "be on the lookout for Elizabeth Taylor in a very early, uncredited film role, as Jane's friend Helen."

I pull my cell phone out of my bathrobe pocket and text Emma to see if she's seen this version.

OH YEAH, she texts back. KIND OF STUPID. MY MOM AND I LIKE THE ONE WITH TIMOTHY DALTON BEST.

"And now, ladies, cell phones off, and please enjoy the show."

"I hope I find my Mr. Rochester someday," sighs Adele later, as we're heading back upstairs to our room.

I smile to myself, thinking of Darcy. I already have.

My roommates and I promised each other that we'd turn the lights out early, since three of us have solo auditions tomorrow. I lie there for a while in the dark, letting my thoughts drift. Colonial

Academy is no Lowood, and my life here is pretty great. Unlike Jane Eyre, I have lots of friends. I love my roommates, and I love our attic room with its view out over the athletic fields and the equestrian center to the woods beyond. I love singing in MadriGals, and I can deal with all my classes even though calculus is hard. There's a good chance I'll get straight As again this term, if I can just ace a few more math tests. I tell myself I don't have to worry about that right now. Right now I need to close my eyes and get some sleep, so my voice will be rested for tomorrow.

I wake up to the sound of dripping. I open my eyes and see sun flooding through the window across from my bunk, melting the icicles that line the eaves outside. It looks like New England's famous January thaw has finally arrived. A wee bit late, though, since it's now officially February.

The sunshine puts everyone in a good mood, and the headmistress's announcement at breakfast makes us even happier.

"The Crandalls had their baby last night!" she tells us, and the whole dining hall erupts in cheers. The Crandalls are really popular houseparents. "Trevor James Crandall arrived shortly after midnight, and mother and baby are doing well. As a reminder, girls, don't all rush over to Witherspoon at once to see him. Kate will be posting a sign-up sheet for visiting hours starting later in the week. Meanwhile, give the family a little space for rest and privacy."

When I walk into calculus a little while later, I'm startled to see an unfamiliar face behind the teacher's desk. I'd totally blanked on the fact that we'd be having a sub! But of course we are—Mr. Crandall is hardly going to show up in the classroom a few hours after his new baby's arrival.

"Pupils, take your seats," she tells us as we file into the room.

Pupils? Really? Does anyone still use that word? I slide into my usual spot in the second row and look her over. My first impression is that she's old. Seriously old—she must be pushing ninety at the very least. Her face looks like one of those wrinkled-up dried-apple dolls you see at craft fairs.

"My name is Mrs. Adler," the sub continues, "and I'll be filling in for Mr. Crandall while he's out on paternity leave."

Mrs. Adler looks as if she disapproves of paternity leave, and of babies in general. She doesn't look very happy with us either, and as the hour wears on, she looks even less happy. Calculus is intense, and Mr. Crandall is really great about joking around with us to keep things fun. Well, as fun as calculus can be. This lady never even cracks a smile.

"I understand you have an examination scheduled for Thursday," she says as the bell finally rings. "I'll be holding review sessions every afternoon this week for those who wish to prepare. I encourage you all to attend."

She hands a schedule to each of us as we file out of the room. I glance down at it; unfortunately, I'm not going to be able to make it to any of the review sessions. This afternoon I have my audition, tomorrow is my regular voice lesson, and on Wednesday I snagged a slot on

Heather Vogel Frederick

the sign-up sheet for Emma and me to see the Crandalls' new baby. Looks like I'm going to be on my own for this test.

The rest of my classes zip by, and before I know it it's time for my audition. Adele and Savannah and I meet up in the living room of Elliot and walk over to the Arts Center together. None of us says much on the way. We're all nervous.

We warm up with the rest of the MadriGals in one of the classrooms, and then the auditions start. My name is called first. I can feel my heart pound as I walk into the music room. Mr. Elton, our choral director, smiles at me, and I flash him a quick smile in response. I take my place beside the piano, swallow hard to try and settle the butterflies, then nod at the accompanist.

"Listen, breathe, connect," my voice teacher told me last week. I take her advice and close my eyes, really listening as the pianist plays the last few bars of the lead-in to the piece I chose. "Dreaming" is an old-fashioned song that hasn't been popular for about a hundred years. My grandmother brought the *Betsy-Tacy Songbook* with her when she visited us last Thanksgiving, and I found it in there. I really like it, and it's different, which I'm hoping might give me an edge. People tend to pick the same old Broadway numbers and stuff.

The tempo is *andante*—slow—the melody tender and bittersweet. I cling to that mood as I take a deep breath and launch into the first verse. "Out in the still summer's evening, into my heart comes a feeling . . ." Concentrating on the lyrics as I sing, I try and imagine myself many years from now, thinking back on my life. "Dreaming of days when you loved me best, dreaming of hours that have gone to rest ..." I connect to the song in a way I never have before, and I can feel my eyes swimming with tears when I'm done.

"Thank you, Jess," says Mr. Elton quietly. "Well done."

This is high praise from Mr. Elton, and I leave the music room floating on air.

"How'd it go?" asks Savannah.

I shrug. "It's hard to tell, you know? I gave it my best."

"You totally deserve a spot this year," Adele whispers to me after Savannah's name is called and she heads into the music room.

"Thanks," I whisper back. There's no way of knowing who's going to get picked, though. There are only a handful of solo spots, and the upperclassmen tend to snag most of them. Mr. Elton usually picks a few people for some duets and trios, too, and one of those would be great, as far as I'm concerned. Especially after last year, when I was completely shut out of everything.

"I'll meet you guys out in the hallway afterward, okay?" I tell Adele. "I promised I'd call my mom."

She nods, her eyes glued to her sheet music.

I grab my jacket and leave the room. After I talk to my mother, I call Emma. The two of us made a pact a couple of years ago: BFBB. Best friends before boyfriends. We both try really hard to honor it.

"You're going to get a solo, I just know it," she tells me.

"Thanks, Em," I reply. We arrange to meet at Elliot after school on Wednesday for our visit with the Crandalls, and I hang up.

Heather Vogel Frederick

There's a text waiting for me from Darcy: SECRET LIBRARY RENDEZVOUS THIS WEEK?

I smile. The thing is, Colonial Academy students aren't allowed off campus in the evenings without special permission. During the week we can go into town after classes, but everybody's due back at the dining hall by dinnertime, and the gates are closed after that. There's only one exception, and that's if you request a pass to the Concord Library, which is just across the street.

Darcy never has time to see me in the afternoons, because he's a three-season athlete and always has some practice or another— football in the fall, hockey in the winter, and baseball in the spring. So we've figured out a way to see each other during the week, by meeting at the library. I feel a little guilty about it, but it's not like a real date. We just happen to meet up and sit next to each other while we do our homework together, that's all.

THURSDAY WORKS FOR ME, I tell him, adding that the audition went well. My calculus test will be over by Thursday, too, so I'll be able to relax a little, I figure. As much as I can relax, what with the audition results being posted Friday morning.

YAY YOU! he texts back. SEE YOU THURSDAY—SAME TIME SAME PLACE! XOXO

Tuesday drags by, complete with another dull-as-dishwater math class with the decrepit sub. Mrs. Adler is cranky as well as ancient, and she snaps at me several times when I'm slow in answering a question. I think she's mad that I didn't come to yesterday's study session, even though I told her about the audition.

I don't make it to this afternoon's session, either, thanks to my voice lesson, and I end up staying up really late struggling with our homework assignment. The problems are tough, but I finally manage to plow through them. On Wednesday, Emma comes over after school as planned, and the two of us head to Witherspoon, the eighth-grade dorm, to see the Crandalls.

Trevor couldn't be cuter, and Maggie is proud to be a big sister. "My baby," she keeps telling me as I take a turn holding him, and I nod solemnly in agreement.

"That's right, Maggie. He's your little brother."

"Brudder," she echoes. I can't believe she's three already—and that I've been here at Colonial nearly as many years.

"How's calculus class going, Jess?" asks Mr. Crandall.

I shrug. "Okay."

"I hear that my replacement came out of retirement to help out."

It wouldn't have surprised me to hear that she came out of the crypt, not just retirement. "Yeah. We really miss you."

"Hang in there just a few more weeks and I'll be back," he says. "Meanwhile, feel free to drop by if I can help you with anything."

I nod. "Thanks, I may do that." I hand Trevor back, then hug Maggie good-bye.

As Emma and I are crossing the quad, we run into Mrs. Chadwick, who tells us she's just been in an alumni board meeting.

Heather Vogel Frederick

"Good heavens," she says, spotting a figure in an ankle-length black cape creeping toward the dining hall. "Is that Bernice Adler?"

"Uh-huh," I reply.

"Whoa, scary," says Emma. "Who is she?"

"The calculus sub I was telling you about," I tell her.

"Bernice is *subbing*?" exclaims Becca's mother. "She taught math when I was here!"

Emma and I gape at her.

"Wow, she really is old," I say.

Mrs. Chadwick smiles. "Thanks a bunch, Jess."

"I didn't mean—"

Mrs. Chadwick laughs. "I know you didn't." Her gaze drifts back toward Mrs. Adler. "Bernice was ancient even when I was a student. Or at least we thought she was. Poppy Sinclair and I used to call her the Battleaxe. You know, since her initials are B. A. and since she's kind of—"

"Crabby?"

"Exactly."

"What's with the cape?" asks Emma, watching as Mrs. Adler disappears inside the dining hall.

"She's always worn one," Mrs. Chadwick replies. "It's her fashion statement, I guess."

"Um, and what exactly would that statement be?" says Emma. 'My other car is a broom,' maybe?"

"Emma!" Shocked, I glance over to see if Mrs. Chadwick is offended. She's laughing again, though.

Mrs. Chadwick offers to drive Emma home, and I say good-bye to them at the entrance gates. Afterward I stop by the dining hall for a quick dinner—steering well clear of the faculty table where Mrs. Adler is sawing away at a pork chop—then head back to my dorm to study for tomorrow's test.

It's a long evening. I think about going over to Witherspoon to ask Mr. Crandall for help, but then I decide not to disturb him. I know that new parents don't get much rest or quiet time. Instead, I call Darcy. He's taking calculus as well, and even though we're not studying the same units, he's able to help me with most of my questions. The rest I just have to figure out for myself. In the end, I don't get to bed until after midnight, but I feel as prepared as I'll ever be.

Thanks to my marathon study session, I sleep through my alarm the next morning.

"So nice of you to join us, Miss Delaney," says Mrs. Adler, her creaky voice dripping with sarcasm.

"Sorry," I murmur, sliding into my seat. *Battleaxe.* I smile at the memory of Mrs. Chadwick's nickname for her.

Mrs. Adler looks at me sharply. "Is something amusing, Miss Delaney?"

I wipe the smile off my face. "Uh, no, Mrs. Adler."

She makes a big point of waiting until I'm settled, then shuffles down the aisles, passing out the tests. "Please keep your examinations facedown on your desk until I tell you it's time to start." Returning to her seat, she looks up at the clock. "You may begin."

I can feel Mrs. Adler's eyes on me as I turn my test over. It's unnerving, and I fumble with my pencil. It drops and rolls under my neighbor's chair.

"Sorry," I whisper, bending down to grab it.

Mrs. Adler's eyes narrow. I hold my pencil up, to show her I was just retrieving it, then turn my attention to the exam on my desk.

We're allotted a full hour, but I finish in forty-five minutes. Surprised, I look around to see if anyone else is done, but every head in the room is bent over in concentration. I go back over the questions to see if I've missed anything. After double-checking my answers, I stand up, grab my backpack, and walk to the front of my room.

Mrs. Adler raises her bristly eyebrows as I hand her my test. "That was surprisingly swift, Miss Delaney," she says, her raspy voice as sharp as a paper cut.

Not sure how to respond, I mutter, "Yeah, I guess," and head out of the classroom.

I can barely sit still through the rest of the day's classes. It's a huge relief to have the test out of the way, plus I'm excited about seeing Darcy tonight. Our library rendezvous are one of the highlights of my week.

After dinner I go back to my room to change into a clean shirt.

"Where are you off to?" asks Savannah, watching me brush and rebraid my hair.

"Library," I tell her.

She gives me a look but doesn't say anything, and she doesn't ask which library. I haven't told my roommates about my secret meetings with Darcy, but I think Savannah suspects. Not that it's that big of a deal, and not that she'd say anything, anyway. Even if she is on Colonial's Community Justice Board. Savannah was the only sophomore to get elected this year—all the other members are juniors and seniors. It's considered a big honor. But going to the library is hardly the kind of thing that gets you hauled before the CJB, even if you do happen to run into your boyfriend there.

Downstairs, I write my name on the sign-out sheet, putting *Concord Library* in the *Destination* column, then grab a pass and cross the quad to the front gates.

Darcy's already at our regular table when I arrive. "Well hello, Miss Delaney," he whispers as I sit down across from him.

"Hello, Mr. Hawthorne," I reply primly.

Looking around to make sure nobody's watching, he leans over and gives me a quick kiss. Darcy's not much for PDA, and neither am I. "How'd your calculus test go?"

I lift a shoulder. "Okay. I get the feeling the sub doesn't like me very much, though."

Darcy frowns. "What's not to like?" He tugs softly on my braid.

I smile at him. It's nice to have a loyal friend, and when that friend happens to be your boyfriend, it's even better.

"Too bad you're not at Alcott," he continues. "Maybe you should transfer back. Ms. Kohler is an awesome teacher."

"So's Mr. Crandall," I remind him. "I just have to stick it out a few more weeks until he's back. Besides, there'd be no point in changing schools now. You'll be gone next year."

He nods. "True."

I don't like to think about that, let alone talk about it. It's going to be so weird when he leaves for college. Darcy's been a part of my life for as long as I can remember, first as Emma's big brother, and then as my secret crush, and now as my boyfriend.

We dutifully turn our attention to our homework, but underneath the library table our knees are touching. And every once in a while we look up at the same time and smile at each other.

About fifteen minutes before closing time, Darcy shoves a piece of paper toward me. My heart skips a beat; I've been waiting for this. Leaning back, Darcy stretches, then gets up and strolls off. I grab the note—actually an origami crane—and unfold it. *Meet me upstairs at 515* is written inside.

I stay where I am for another minute or so, then glance around to see if anybody is watching. They aren't, of course. They never are. I get up and head casually into the stacks, smiling as I find tonight's call letters—515 is a shelf filled with calculus textbooks.

There's no sign of Darcy, though. I peek between the math books to see if maybe he's hiding on the other side of the stacks, and nearly jump out of my skin as someone slips their arms around me from behind.

"Hi there," he whispers.

I lean back against him. "Hi."

"Miss you," he says.

"Miss you too."

"Want to go to the movies Saturday night?"

"Sounds good."

The loudspeaker crackles, announcing that the library will be closing in five minutes.

Two people can do quite a bit of kissing in five minutes.

If they actually had five minutes, that is.

About thirty seconds later, someone clears their throat at the other end of the aisle, and we spring apart guiltily. I look over to see Cassidy Sloane grinning at us.

"Hope I didn't interrupt anything," she says, loping over.

I can feel my face turn beet red, but Darcy just shrugs and shakes his head, smiling.

"Nah, didn't think so," she continues. "Hey, have you heard anything about your MadriGals audition yet, Jess?"

"I find out tomorrow."

"You're gonna get picked," she tells me. "I feel it in my bones. We'll have to celebrate this weekend, after the Lady Shawmuts kick some Bay State Blazers' butt."

She does a little touchdown dance move. Cassidy has a big hockey game on Saturday, one that will put her a step closer to a shot at the championship round if her team wins.

"Good luck to you too," I tell her.

"Thanks." She winks at us. "Well, I'll let you two get back to

Heather Vogel Frederick

whatever it is you weren't doing." She saunters off.

Darcy and I exchange a glance and start to laugh. "Way to spoil the mood, huh?" he says, giving me a hug. "How about I walk you back as far as the gate?"

We go back to the table and gather our things just as the loud-speaker announces that the library is now closed.

"I'll see you Saturday night, then," Darcy says when we reach my campus. "Text me tomorrow as soon as the list is posted, okay?"

I promise I will, and we say good night and I head back across the quad to my dorm.

Between the kiss in the library stacks and nervousness about tomorrow, I'm way too keyed up to sleep. I lie in bed tossing and turning. I should be tired, but my audition song keeps playing in my head, and I keep wondering if it was good enough to earn me a solo. In the bunk below me, I can hear Adele twitching around, too, and I wonder if she's thinking the same thing.

"Are you awake?" I whisper finally, leaning over the edge of my mattress.

"Yeah," she whispers back.

"Nervous?"

"Uh-huh."

The light flips on. Across the room, Savannah is sitting up in the lower bunk of her bed. "You guys can't sleep, either?"

We shake our heads. "I can," says Frankie from the bunk above her, stuffing her pillow over her head. "Keep it down."

"I'm hungry," says Adele. "Anybody have any food?"

"Actually, I do," I reply, suddenly remembering the cookie tin my mother gave me. I've been so preoccupied this week, I'd completely forgotten about it. Slipping out of bed, I fish it from its hiding place in my bottom drawer. Then I cross the room and lift an edge of Frankie's pillow, waving the tin back and forth under her nose. "Mmmm!" I whisper. "Triple chocolate cookies."

The pillow goes soaring across the room as she sits up too. "Are you serious? Gimme one of those things."

"Midnight feast!" says Adele happily, padding over to join us. Frankie climbs out of her bunk and the three of us plunk down on Savannah's bed, wrapping ourselves in her comforter.

"So how was the library, Jess?" asks Savannah innocently.

My face flames. "Uh, fine?"

She grins at me. "Yeah, I'll bet it was."

Uh-oh, I think. *She figured it out*.

"What are you talking about?" asks Frankie.

"Do you want to tell them, or shall I?" says Savannah.

I toss a cookie at her. "I've been meeting Darcy at the Concord Library."

Frankie and Adele both squeal at this news.

"Shhhhh, you guys! Keep it down!" I scold them. "You'll wake the McKinleys."

I can't keep the smile off my face, though. Hanging out with my friends like this is the best part of boarding school.

Heather Vogel Frederick

They pump me for details, and then we talk about boys in general and about MadriGals and I tell them about the Battleaxe—they think Mrs. Chadwick's nickname for Mrs. Adler is hilarious—and finally, yawning, we decide it's time for bed.

We're all excited in the morning, and after breakfast and announcements—there's a dance coming up with Essex Academy, a food drive for a local homeless shelter, and a reminder that next week is School Spirit Week and we all need to be thinking of ways we can show it—Savannah and Adele and I race over to the Arts Center. There's a crowd in front of the bulletin board already by the time we get there, and people start congratulating me before I even see the list. I make my way to the front and see that it's true: I earned a solo spot at our competition!

I'm going to Nationals!

I call my parents and text Emma—BFBB—then finally I share the good news with Darcy.

TOLD YOU SO! he texts back. YOU'RE A ROCK STAR!

Two seconds later another text comes through: CORRECTION: YOU'RE MY ROCK STAR! <3

The bell for first period rings, and we all scatter to our classes. I race from the Arts Center to my calculus class, not caring if I'm late again. *I'm going to Nationals!*

Mrs. Adler doesn't say anything to me this time as I take my seat. In fact, she doesn't even look at me at all. Instead, she shuffles down the aisles, silently handing back our tests. When she reaches my desk, she pauses. I look at her expectantly. The test was difficult, but I'm pretty sure I got at least a B, and maybe even squeaked out a B-plus. Not my usual standard for myself, but calculus is *really* hard.

She places the piece of paper on my desk, tapping a finger against the red letter in the top corner.

At first I don't think I'm seeing it correctly. I blink, but the letter doesn't go away.

It's an F.

A big red F.

I *failed*?

I look up at Mrs. Adler, aghast. I've never failed a test before in my life!

She purses her thin, whiskery lips and regards me sourly. "This is what happens to cheaters."

Emma

"'What awful event has taken place?' said she.
'Speak! let us know the worst at once!'"
—*Jane Eyre*

Halfway through world history, my backpack starts to buzz.

Uh-oh, I think. I forgot to turn my cell phone off before class started. Mr. Turner is merciless when it comes to cell phones. If he hears one, he'll confiscate it for twenty-four hours. I grab my jacket off the back of my chair and throw it down over the bag, hoping the thick insulation will smother the sound. It does, almost.

But not completely. A faint but persistent buzzing is still audible. Mr. Turner spins around and starts walking in my direction, still droning on about something called the Maginot Line.

Thinking quickly, I shove my textbook off my desk. It falls to the floor with a thud, and as I bend over to pick it up, I reach into my backpack with my other hand and fumble for the power button on the phone.

As I switch it off, I see my teacher's shoes appear. The toe of one of them starts to tap impatiently. "Perhaps you can enlighten us, Miss Hawthorne?" Mr. Turner says.

"Uh," I reply, straightening up so fast I bang my head on the underside of my desk. I reach up to rub the sore spot and realize too late that I'm still clutching my phone.

With a sigh, Mr. Turner holds out his hand. I give him the cell phone, and he flips it open. I hold my breath. *Please don't let it be from Stewart!* Mr. Turner's other punishment, in addition to confiscating phones, is reading aloud whatever text messages he intercepts. Sometimes this can be hilarious. But not when it happens to you.

"It's from Jess!" he says, his voice going all high and squeaky, like he's an excited teenage girl. Mr. Turner has a secret life in amateur theater here in Concord. I've seen him in a couple of plays with Jess's mom. He's actually pretty good.

I brace myself, hoping that Jess didn't text me anything super personal.

"Call me right away!" Mr. Turner squeals. "Emergency!" He levels a skeptical glance at me, then adds in his usual voice, "I doubt that very much." Snapping the phone shut again, he dangles it just out of reach. "Since this is your first offense, Miss Hawthorne, I'm going to make you a deal. If you can define the Maginot Line for us, I'll let you keep your phone. But just this once, mind you."

I close my eyes, trying very hard to recall what he was telling us just before my cell phone went off. "Um, France built the Maginot Line between its borders with Germany and Italy," I reply haltingly.

"When?" he asks.

"After World War I, maybe? Before World War II, I think."

"Correct. And it is?"

"A fortification system of, uh, concrete bunkers and machine gun posts and, uh, other stuff."

"Close enough," he says, setting the phone on my desk. "Don't let it happen again."

I shake my head vigorously and shove the phone into the pocket of my jeans.

As the rest of the hour ticks by, I keep thinking about Jess's message. I can't imagine her saying something was an emergency for no good reason. By the time class is over, I've worked myself into quite a state, imagining what might be wrong. What if Half Moon Farm burned down? Or what if something happened to her parents, or to one of her brothers? Could she and my brother have broken up?

I practically fly out of the classroom when the bell rings. Making a beeline for the girls' room, I lock myself in one of the stalls for privacy.

WHAT'S UP? I text Jess.

THE BATTLEAXE GAVE ME AN F! she texts back almost immediately. AN F!!!!!!!!! SHE SAYS I CHEATED!

I stare dumbly at the screen on my phone. Jess, cheating? No way. I tap speed dial. "What's going on?"

Jess is practically hysterical.

"I can't understand you," I tell her after a few seconds. "Take a deep breath and start over."

"I could lose my scholarship, Emma!" she finally manages to wail. "I have to go see the headmistress after school today and everything!"

"But it's not true," I tell her. "You didn't cheat—you'd never do that! Can't you just explain?"

"You haven't met Mrs. Adler."

"Mr. Crandall will stick up for you, won't he?"

She gulps back a sob. "I don't know. He wasn't there when I took the test. How's he supposed to help? This is a nightmare!"

"So what happened, exactly?"

"I have no idea—all I can think is that there was this one point right at the beginning of class when I dropped my pencil, and she saw me and gave me this weird look. But that's it, I swear."

"I wish I could come right over," I tell her. "But I can't—I have a newspaper editorial meeting at lunchtime I can't get out of, and a dentist appointment right after school and then my skating lesson."

I've finally started taking lessons again. I didn't for a while after Mrs. Bergson died. She just seemed so irreplaceable. But the rink hired a new instructor, and she's good. Totally different, too—she's in her twenties, for one thing—so it's not like I'm constantly comparing her to, or being reminded of, Mrs. Bergson.

"That's okay," says Jess in a small voice.

"I can come over tonight, though," I assure her.

"If I'm still here," she replies miserably. "What if I get expelled?"

I snort. "Jess, they're not going to expel you. Didn't you tell me that Colonial has some sort of justice system? That thing Savannah got elected to?"

"The Community Justice Board?"

Heather Vogel Frederick

"Yeah, that's it."

She's quiet for a minute. "I guess."

"See? You're going to have a chance to explain, and then everything will be fine."

I hear her suck in her breath sharply, and my heart nearly stops. What now?

"I completely forgot—what about MadriGals?"

"What about it?"

"If I get expelled, or if I'm failing a class, I'm automatically disqualified from extracurricular activities!"

I can hear her starting to get worked up again. "See if you can hold it together until this afternoon," I tell her. "I'll meet you in your dorm around four."

"What about your skating lesson?"

"I can reschedule. Have you told your parents?"

"Uh-huh," she says, sniffling. "They're coming over in a little while for my meeting with the headmistress. Don't say anything to Darcy, though. He's got a hockey game tonight and I don't want him to worry."

I promise her I won't, and we hang up. I stand there for a moment, staring at my phone.

"Poor Jess," says Stewart, when I tell him about it at lunch. We're the first ones to arrive in the small conference room off the cafeteria where we have our newspaper meetings. I don't have time to do more than fill him in on the bare bones before the others come in and our conversation quickly turns to the upcoming issue.

At one point in our discussion I look over to see Stewart gazing through the conference room window with a dazed grin on his face. My stomach drops. It's a look I've seen a little too much of this week. Sure enough, when I check to see what's caught his attention, it's Sophie Fairfax. She's carrying a tray of food, trailing a long line of boys behind her. Including Kevin Mullins, which is pathetic and hilarious at the same time.

I watch them for a minute, shaking my head in disgust. It's like she has footmen or something. They should be holding up her train.

I almost want to laugh, except that it's been like this all week, and it's beyond annoying at this point. Sophie Fairfax has been a huge hit at Alcott High School. Well, with the boys, anyway. The girls are a little wary, and understandably so. It's as if the entire male population has fallen under her spell. All she has to do is bat her eyes and trot out that little French accent, and students and teachers alike pretty much roll over and play dead.

Stewart seems to have been bitten by the bug as well, but what's worse is that it may be mutual. Megan told me she caught Sophie looking at a pile of her old *Flashlite* magazines the other night, checking out pictures of Stewart. He hasn't done much modeling this year, what with all the school stuff he's involved in, but he was in a lot of issues last year. It's nothing he takes seriously—just college fund money, he always says, laughing it off—but it seems like Sophie does.

Why can't Stewart take a cue from my brother? Darcy's really

Heather Vogel Frederick

polite with Sophie, but in a distant kind of way that lets her know he's not interested. Stewart is definitely not distant. He's friendly. Too friendly, in my opinion. I should probably talk to him about it, but I'm afraid he'll think I'm being petty.

Stewart turns around just then and sees me watching him. He smiles, and I smile back automatically. Maybe it's all just my imagination.

I text Jess after lunch, but there's no response, so I figure she must be in her meeting with the headmistress. It's so unfair! This whole thing gives me that same indignant feeling I get every time I read the part in *Jane Eyre* when her horrible aunt calls her deceitful. Or when Mr. Brocklehurst makes Jane stand on a stool in front of the whole school and tells them she's a liar who should be shunned. It makes my blood boil!

To have something like this happen to Jess is bad enough, but to have it happen right after she got the good news about MadriGals is awful. She didn't even have time to enjoy her triumph before the wind was completely taken out of her sails.

And there's nothing I can do, unfortunately. It's not like I can rally the mother-daughter book club behind her, or hold a fundraiser or something. All I can do is give her my moral support and hope for the best.

It makes me feel really helpless.

My afternoon classes drag by. I can't concentrate in Spanish, and chemistry is enough to make me want to tear my hair out. It's probably the hardest class I've ever had. The math and science gene in our family seems to have skipped me entirely in favor of Darcy. But then, Darcy has the whole package. He's super smart, he's good at sports, and he knows how to be a good boyfriend to boot.

Maybe I should have him tutor Stewart in that department.

After school I take the bus home and drop off my backpack, then walk downtown to my dentist appointment. I'm done shortly before four, and since the dentist's office is right across the street from Pies & Prejudice, I decide to stop in on my way to Colonial Academy and get something to bring to Jess. A little chocolate can help cheer anybody up.

"Emma!" says Mrs. Wong as I walk through the front door. She's sitting at a table with Mrs. Chadwick and Megan and Sophie. Stewart is with them too. "Just the person I wanted to see."

I head over to the table cautiously, my raised eyebrows sending a *what's going on?* signal to Stewart. In response, he shrugs his shoulders, striking a classic *who knows?* pose.

Is it my imagination again, or is he looking a little sheepish?

Megan flashes me the *V* sign and I smile at her. Cassidy's "Mademoiselle Velcro" nickname for Sophie has stuck like, well, Velcro.

"Have a cookie," says Gigi, coming over with a plate of them. "And a seat. Lily has an announcement to make."

"Thanks." The cookies are ginger molasses, my favorite next to chocolate chip. I take one, and so does Megan.

"I've decided I'm going to run for mayor!" Mrs. Wong announces.

Heather Vogel Frederick

Megan's gingersnap hangs in the air. Her mouth, which was about to take a bite, forms a surprised O.

"Isn't this wonderful news?" says Gigi, her dark almond eyes sparkling with excitement. "Just think, my daughter, the mayor of Concord!"

Mrs. Wong laughs. "I haven't been elected yet, Mother."

Gigi flaps a hand. "Details, details."

"I must say I'm surprised," says Mrs. Chadwick. "This is quite a step, Lily. When did you decide?"

"It's something I've been thinking about for a while now," Mrs. Wong replies. "Running for office, I mean. Now that Megan's in high school and doesn't need quite so much supervision—"

Megan makes a face at this.

"—I thought perhaps I could take on something meatier beyond just volunteering. When I heard about Mayor Perkins being forced to resign, and the special election to replace him, well, it just seemed like the right time."

Megan looks stunned, and decidedly less than thrilled. I can understand—the last time her mother was in the public eye in a major way, she was wearing handcuffs.

It was when we were still in middle school. Jess's family almost lost Half Moon Farm because of some back taxes. Hoping to help publicize their plight, Mrs. Wong handcuffed herself to a tree and alerted the media. It backfired big-time when Becca slipped her picture into the school newspaper with a caption calling her "Handcuffs Wong."

She and Megan's friendship blew up for a while over that.

Mrs. Wong looks over at me. "I was wondering if you and Stewart would consider running my campaign."

Now it's my turn to look stunned. "Excuse me?"

"I need a campaign manager, and I thought who better for the job than our local high school newspaper's coeditors?" Megan's mother smiles at me. "I keep up with the *Alcott Avenger,* you know, and you two are fine writers. I just thought it would be great experience for you both and something for you to put on your college applications in a couple of years, Emma."

"Uh—"

"I've already spoken to Sophie about it, and she said she'd be willing to help out as our official photographer. She's very talented, you know." She puts her arm around Sophie. "And what a wonderful opportunity for our guest to learn about the American democratic process!"

My heart sinks. The last thing I want to do is support something that throws Stewart and Sophie together.

"Sounds like fun to me," says Stewart. "I'd vote for you any day of the week, Mrs. Wong."

Thank you very much, Stewart, I think. The thing is, though, so would I. Megan's mother can be a little intense about things and, sure, she has her quirks, but she cares deeply about our town, she has a good heart, and she's an incredibly hard worker. Plus, George Underhill, the guy who's already announced he's running for mayor, is the kind of person it would be fun to help someone campaign against. He goes

Heather Vogel Frederick

to our church, and he thinks because he donates a lot of money that gives him the right to boss everyone around. My father calls him "that pompous twit," and he's right.

On the other hand, a project like this could be a real minefield. What if we mess up and Mrs. Wong loses the election because of it? She might never speak to us again.

I look over at Megan, who's scowling. So far, her mother hasn't mentioned a thing about needing her help.

If I get involved and help her mother win, Megan might never speak to me again.

Either way, if I sign on for this job, it's going to mean I'll be spending a heck of a lot more time with Sophie Fairfax. And worse, so will Stewart.

I think this is what you'd call a lose-lose situation.

CASSIDY

*"I have not much pride under such
circumstances: I would always rather be happy
than dignified; and I ran after him . . ."*
—*Jane Eyre*

I feel someone's eyes on me and I look up to see my mother standing in my bedroom doorway, shaking her head in disbelief. "I never thought I'd have to say these words to you, Cassidy, but it's time to put the book away."

"I'm almost done with this chapter," I plead. "Five more minutes?"

She smiles at me. "How can I resist? But don't forget, Coach Larson is picking you up early tomorrow."

I nod, and she blows me a kiss and shuts the door and I dive back into *Jane Eyre*. I can't get enough of it.

I know I've bellyached a lot about the stuff our book club has read over the years, and how most of the books are old-fashioned and everything, but I have to admit I've ended up liking most of them. *Jane Eyre*, though, *Jane Eyre* I absolutely *love*.

Jane is—well, she's awesome. She says what's on her mind, and sometimes gets in trouble for it. I can totally relate. It's great the way she doesn't suck up to Mr. Rochester when they first meet either, but just bursts out and tells him right off that he's ugly. Maybe not ugly, but definitely not handsome.

I flip back through the book to find that part and reread it:

"You examine me, Miss Eyre," said he: "do you think me handsome?"

I should, if I had deliberated, have replied to this question by something conventionally vague and polite; but the answer somehow slipped from my tongue before I was aware—"No, sir."

I love that! Things "slip from my tongue" all the time—and I end up in hot water just like Jane does.

The thing is, when you have a boyfriend—which I sort of do now, I guess—you always have to be thinking about how they're going to react to stuff that you say. I feel like I'm walking on eggshells sometimes. Like, if I mess around in class or at lunch with some of my other guy friends, Zach gets a little jealous, which is so stupid. I told him he's totally spoiled, because he's used to girls being head over heels about him, and I'm just not that way. I'm not going to sit around and flap my eyelashes at him like stupid Sophie Fairfax and act all silly and stuff. I just like to have fun, you know?

I think Jane would totally get that. Maybe not the fun part—she doesn't have much of that in her life, at least not in what I've read so far—but the part about not wanting to act like something you're not.

I especially like how she thinks about guys. She wants love, but she wants it on her own terms. She's not going to turn herself inside out for it, the way I see so many girls doing at school.

I reluctantly turn off the light when I finish the chapter. My mother is right, I've got an early start tomorrow. We're caravanning up to Portland, Maine, for our game, and I'm driving with Coach because Stanley's away on business. He's at some accounting convention in Chicago, "which is going to be just as boring as it sounds," he told us when we dropped him at the airport. "I'd much rather stay home with my girls." He gave me a hug and a high five and told me to call him the minute the tournament was over.

My mother had planned to leave Chloe with a babysitter and drive me instead, but her TV show taping yesterday was a disaster. Our dog Murphy managed to escape from the garage and knock over a table with a bunch of cakes and flower arrangements displayed on it. They're going to have to spend most of Saturday reshooting.

I lie in the dark, trying to put *Jane Eyre* out of my mind and focus instead on the game ahead. The Lady Shawmuts are just a couple of wins away from assuring ourselves a spot at the national championships, and with any luck tomorrow will move us a step closer.

Somehow, though, my thoughts keep drifting back to that brooding house in Yorkshire. *Thornfield*. I even like the name of it. It's sort of, what's the word, ominous? With that word "thorn" in there, you know it's not going to be smooth sailing. I stopped at a really exciting part just now too, where Jane is hearing creepy things this one night—weird laughter and footsteps in the hallway. Plus, she just saved her boss's life when a fire broke out in his bedroom.

The next morning I toss the book into my hockey bag at the last

Heather Vogel Frederick

minute, telling myself that I might have an odd minute or two in the car to read. The odd minute or two turns into the entire drive. Zach is carpooling with us too—he's our team's equipment manager—and he keeps trying to talk to me, but my eyes keep straying back to the page. He finally gives up and talks to Coach Larson and my teammate Allegra Chapman in the front seat instead.

"Cassidy!" Coach scolds me a while later, when we're at the rink and I'm lacing up my skates and reading at the same time. After the fire at Thornfield, Mr. Rochester goes away, leaving Jane to wonder what's up. I need to know what's up too. But Coach is right; now is not the time.

"Sorry," I tell her, snapping the book shut and stuffing it back in my bag.

"Mind—and eyes—on the game," she says, and I nod energetically.

Zach skates over after she leaves and hands me a water bottle. "Man, Sloane, what's gotten into you? Since when did my girlfriend turn into such a bookworm?"

Zach's not much of a reader. But then, neither was I before I joined this book club back in sixth grade. "I dunno," I reply, leaving it at that. I don't want to touch the whole "girlfriend" thing. Not now, right before the game.

We've never really talked about it officially, but I guess Zach is my boyfriend. I'm still a little bit on the fence, to tell the truth. I'm just afraid of becoming one of those girls who turn into a puddle of mush once they start dating, you know?

My sister used to do that. I watched her when I was in middle school and she was in high school. It was like the Courtney I knew would disappear right before my eyes and this other weird alter ego would take over, one that was always checking her makeup and giggling at everything the boy of the month said. (Courtney had a lot of boyfriends.)

Fortunately, she doesn't do that anymore. My sister got engaged at Christmastime. She told me that one of the reasons she said yes when Grant asked her to marry him was because she feels so totally comfortable around him. She can just be her own goofy self, and he loves her anyway.

Not that I'm thinking of getting engaged or anything. Or that I love Zach. I like him—a lot. We've known each other since fifth grade, and most of the time I can be myself around him too. But this whole you're my boyfriend/I'm you're girlfriend thing is kind of a sticky issue for me.

Plus, there's something else influencing how I feel about Zach. It's kind of embarrassing to say, but I'll say it: He's not a great kisser.

Not that I have a huge basis of comparison or anything—I've only ever been kissed by one other guy, and just one time—but that kiss was *memorable*. If that kiss went to the National Championships, it would have brought home the trophy. Kissing Zach is more like, I don't know, kissing Murphy or something. Lots of enthusiasm, but lots of slobber, too.

I glance at Zach, suddenly imagining him with a tail wagging back and forth, and I fight a wild urge to laugh.

"What's so funny?" he asks suspiciously.

Heather Vogel Frederick

"Nothing," I tell him. But I can't help wondering what Jane Eyre would do if she were in my shoes.

The whistle blows and I snap to attention. Shaking off all thoughts of Zach Norton and Jane Eyre and comparative kisses, I grab my stick and head out onto the ice, determined to focus with laserlike intensity on the game ahead.

It's a tough match. Rhode Island's top U-16 team is just as eager as we are to make it to Nationals, and they're not about to let us walk away with the game. It takes us until well into the second period to score a goal—an awesome rebound shot off the goalie's pads that Lucinda Quigley puts away—and then we spend the rest of the game trying to keep the Reds from scoring. Somehow we manage it, chalking up a win that takes us one step closer to earning a spot at Nationals.

Coach is thrilled, of course—we all are. She treats us to pizza on the way home to celebrate. Zach sits next to me and tries to hold my hand under the table, but I pull it away. "Not here," I tell him.

Later, in the car on the way home, he leans over and whispers, "What's the matter?"

"Nothing," I whisper back, with a nod at the rearview mirror. Coach Larson is watching us. I swore up and down when Zach volunteered to be equipment manager that we weren't boyfriend/girlfriend (which was true at the time), because Coach doesn't put up with what she calls "relationship drama-rama," and even though I didn't make some big announcement when things between us kind of changed, I'm pretty sure she suspects.

Zach sighs and turns away.

I wait until Coach starts talking to Allegra, then I elbow Zach. "Don't be that way," I whisper. "It's just that I have a lot on my mind. You know—school, Chicks with Sticks, and now Nationals to worry about."

He nods. "Got it." He doesn't say any more, but his knee drifts over to touch mine, and I don't move away.

See? It's complicated.

The next morning Mom asks if I would babysit Chloe for a couple of hours. "I know you have Chicks with Sticks and book club later, but it would be a huge help, and you can put her down for her nap before you leave. I just need an hour or two to whip things back into shape here before Stanley gets home."

"Sure, Mom," I reply. "No problem." And it's true, it's not a problem. I love spending time with my little sister.

The house is still kind of a wreck from the TV retaping yesterday. Even though there's snow on the ground outside, it looks like spring is in full bloom inside, what with the flowers and potted plants everywhere that Mrs. Chadwick brought over. The kitchen countertops and dining room table are still littered with the remains of the show— some kind of a Mother's Day celebration, from the looks of it.

My mother hands Chloe to me and I take her upstairs. Chloe gets all excited, thinking we're going to my room. She loves going in there. Most of the time it's off limits, because it's hard for her to keep her little hands off things. She broke one of my hockey trophies last week, which wasn't that big a deal, really, since it was one from third grade, but I try and remember to keep my door closed, just like it is now.

I latch the toddler gate at the top of the stairs and Chloe-proof the upstairs hallway by closing all the rest of the doors except the one to her room. Murphy doesn't like being shut out of the fun, and he sits on the next-to-the-top step and watches us, whining. I can't let him join us, though, because he gets too excited when we play, and once or twice he's knocked Chloe over.

"Sorry, Murph, you're just going to have to be the referee today," I tell him, getting down on all fours. "Come on, Chloe, climb aboard the horsey!"

She does, squealing, then grabs my hair with both her hands as I trot around the hall with her on my back. We end up in her room, where I tip her carefully off and then tickle her. I love her delicious little belly laugh.

"Time to work on your hand-eye coordination," I tell her, sitting her down at the far end of the area rug. I sit at the other end and we roll a ball back and forth for a while. I think of it as pretraining for her future debut with Chicks with Sticks. As soon as this kid is steady on her feet, I'm getting skates for her.

By now I'm feeling the need for a snack, and I figure Chloe could use one too, so I take her back downstairs—Murphy is ecstatic—and fix us both some PB&J.

"Everything going okay?" my mother asks at one point, poking her head in the kitchen door to check on us. Unfortunately, she chooses the exact moment when Chloe decides to smear the rest of her sandwich in her hair.

"Gross!" I shriek.

My mother laughs. "Welcome to my world. See ya!" She waggles her fingers at us and disappears again.

I heave a sigh and pluck Chloe out of her high chair. "Okay, Miss Messpot, let's get you cleaned up." Carrying her into the downstairs bathroom, I wash off her face and hands and deal as best I can with her sticky hair.

Sprucing her up gives me an idea. "Photo shoot time," I announce, and back upstairs we go, where I put a clean outfit on her—flowered overalls and a striped turtleneck, for contrast—and rummage through the pile on my desk for my camera. It's been gathering dust since our holiday trip to California. I took some great pictures of my friend Hannah surfing, and some fun ones of the rest of the family, but for what I have in mind I need some shots of Chloe all by herself. I'm thinking that a book of family pictures would make a great Mother's Day present.

"Ready?" I ask.

"Dee! Dee! Dee!" Chloe echoes happily, and I scoop her up and walk with her down to the door at the end of the hall, the one that leads to the turret. My sister is almost never allowed up here, and her eyes widen with excitement as I open the door.

The turret is my favorite spot in our old house. It has comfortable window seats beneath the circle of windows, and a killer view. It's a great place to read, or just sit and dream, and the light up here

Heather Vogel Frederick

is phenomenal, particularly for shooting in black and white, which is what I'm using today. I put Chloe on one of the benches and start taking pictures: Chloe sitting there looking thrilled; Chloe standing up and looking down at the snowy yard; Chloe examining the leaded diamond-shaped panes in the windows.

"Okay if I take the van?" I call to my mother, grabbing the keys off the counter a little while later after I put my sister down for her nap.

"Sure, sweetie!" she calls back. "Have fun with your 'chicks'!"

I get to the rink half an hour early, which gives me plenty of time to pull the equipment I need out of the storage closet. After I set everything up, I change out of my down jacket into my warm-ups, and reaching into my fleece pullover pocket, I pull out Mrs. Bergson's silver whistle and loop its lanyard over my head. It's one of my favorite possessions, and easily one of the nicest gifts I've ever received. Mrs. Bergson left it to me in her will. She was the one who helped me start Chicks with Sticks, and I like wearing it as a tribute to her when I coach. Plus, it's a reminder that she had a lot of confidence in my abilities.

I love coaching. Probably as much as I love playing hockey, and sometimes more. It sounds sappy, but it's incredibly rewarding working with kids. Hockey is rewarding, too, but this is different—I love to see my little skaters improve and watch the way they grow more sure of themselves week by week.

Lacing up my skates, I head out onto the ice to warm up and suddenly find myself busting out some ice dancing moves. This isn't easy to do in hockey skates, and I don't try anything fancy, just a few jumps and spins. It feels good to stretch some muscles that haven't been used in a while.

Where did that come from? I wonder. And then I realize it's because I've had a certain someone on my mind this weekend.

A certain someone named Tristan Berkeley.

I swoop around the rink, recalling what if felt like to dance with him. And recalling that one, memorable kiss . . .

"Cassidy!"

I whirl around. It's Katie Angelino. My littlest "chick" isn't the littlest anymore. She's eight now, and on a peewee team. Anybody who'd seen her last year when she first started wouldn't recognize the scrappy, fearless player that she is today.

"Hey, Katie, what's up?" I skate over and pull up to a stop next to her.

"My cousin Ivy wants to know if she can join the club." She points to the chubby, dark-haired girl who's clinging to her hand. She can't be more than six or seven. The timid expression on her face reminds me of how Katie looked the first few times she showed up at the rink.

"Sure you can, sweetheart," I tell her, squatting down so my height doesn't intimidate her. "Your cousin was your age when she started, Ivy, and she's one of my stars now."

Katie beams at this, and her cousin gives her a worshipful look.

We locate Ivy's mother and get things rolling, and pretty soon the rest of my players start to arrive. I'm glad I thought to ask Emma to help me out, as the group has really grown. Emma's not into hockey, but Mrs. Bergson was her figure skating teacher, so she was coached by

Heather Vogel Frederick

the best. She's completely capable of helping the younger girls get comfortable on the ice and learn to do stuff like skate backward and stop, plus all the basic drills. More important, she definitely understands hockey, what with all those years spent watching her brother's games. She didn't know if she'd have time at first, since she's coeditor of the newspaper and all, but she finally said yes. I'm looking forward to having her out here on the ice with me.

My cell phone buzzes and I pull it out of my pocket. It's Emma, texting me to let me know she's not going to be able to make it today.

JESS IS IN MAJOR MELTDOWN MODE.

WHAT'S UP? I text back.

CALL ME LATER WHEN YOU HAVE TIME.

I call her right then instead. "What's going on? Is everything okay?"

"Jess has been accused of cheating," she tells me.

"Whaaaaaaat? Seriously?"

"Yes, seriously. She could lose her scholarship."

"Whoa. Anything I can do to help?"

"Unfortunately not," Emma replies. "The headmistress referred the matter to the Community Justice Board—"

"That thing Savannah got elected to?"

"—yeah, but they aren't meeting again until after their February break."

Suddenly Jess is on the phone. She must have snatched it from Emma. "It's agony!" she wails. "I have to wait nearly two whole weeks!"

Alcott only gets one break between our winter holidays and

summer vacation, but private schools get spring break plus an extra week in February. For those essential ski vacations and trips to the Caribbean, I guess.

"Couldn't you hire a lawyer, or something?" I suggest.

"Not yet," Jess replies. "It has to go through the academy's justice system first."

"Dang, girl, I'm really sorry." Suddenly, my dumb obsession with Zach's merits as a kisser feels pretty insignificant. "Hey, I have to go—practice is about to start, but I'll call you later, okay?"

The afternoon's session on the ice goes pretty well, considering I have so much on my mind. Zach shows up toward the end, a habit he's fallen into lately, which most of the time I don't mind, but tonight feels a little claustrophobic for some reason. Probably since I already spent all day yesterday with him.

I'm a little irritable afterward when he asks if I want to hang out at the snack bar for a while, and then I have to apologize because it's obvious I've hurt his feelings.

"It's just that I have a ton of homework I didn't finish," I explain. Which is sort of true. To be exact, I have a little homework and then I have to finish *Jane Eyre*. Which is homework for book club, technically.

He gives me a quick kiss in the parking lot—too quick to be slobbery—and tells me he'll see me at school tomorrow. And then we get in our separate cars and head home.

After dinner I log onto the computer in the family room and find an e-mail waiting from Megan. It's addressed to Becca and Emma and

Jess and me, letting us know that she's found out a little more about Sophie Fairfax:

I overheard my mother and Gigi talking, and I guess she ended up in the exchange program because of her parents' divorce. Mrs. Berkeley was the one who suggested it. Sophie's grandfather was worried that all the arguing would be stressful for her, and Mrs. Berkeley told him that Concord was a safe haven.

I make a mental note to add this new info to the list we've been keeping. *Got it,* I e-mail back. *Good work, Megs.*

I'm about to log off and go upstairs, when all of a sudden Tristan Berkeley's icon pops up on IM.

He's online.

I look at the clock. It's midnight in England. Too late to message him? Nah.

Hey, Tristan! I sit there waiting, hoping he'll see my message. A few seconds tick by, and then the screen flashes with a reply: *Hey back!*

I did some ice dancing at the rink today. Just thought you'd want to know.

Really? How'd it go? Ready to compete again?

Ha! Not really, I tell him. *But it was fun anyway.*

There's a pause, and then: *I miss dancing with you.*

Me too, I reply.

Our words hang in cyberspace, shimmering on the screen.

Can I ask you a question? I continue finally.

Sure.

How is your family related to the Fairfaxes again? I forgot.

Funny, he replies. *Megan asked Simon the same thing a little while ago. My mother, Annabelle's father, and Sophie's father are all cousins.*

Which makes the girls your . . . ?

Second cousins, I think.

Got it, I tell him, jotting it all down furiously on my clipboard.

Hey, I should probably go. It's getting late.

I could kick myself for wasting so much time talking about stupid Sophie Fairfax! *Yeah, me too,* I tell him reluctantly.

See you at the next videoconference! Simon and I are working on a killer video—you lot are going to love it.

Can't wait! See you then!

Bye!

Bye!

I linger a moment, hoping he'll sign off "Fondly, Tristan," but he doesn't. That's what he wrote in the book he gave me for Christmas, and I've practically worn out the page running my finger over the words.

I sit there for a while, staring at the screen. It's been a strange weekend. Strange—and confusing. I'm completely in the dark here and have no idea where things stand. Zach and Tristan, tied, maybe? Cassidy, clueless?

I shut the computer down and head upstairs to bed. Time to see if *Jane Eyre* can help me figure out the score.

SPRING

"Merry days were these at Thornfield Hall; and busy days, too . . ."

—Jane Eyre

 Emma

*"When I saw my charmer thus come in accompanied by
a cavalier, I seemed to hear a hiss, and the green snake of
jealousy, rising on undulating coils from the moonlit
balcony, glided within my waistcoat, and ate its way
in two minutes to my heart's core."*
—Jane Eyre

Dear Emma,

Spring can't come soon enough for me, how about you?

The calendar says that the season should be changing

soon—two weeks from now I'll be on a plane to

Boston for spring break, yay!—but apparently no one

told Gopher Hole, because we're still up to our ears in

snow, snow, and more snow.

I put Bailey's letter down for a moment and gaze out my bedroom
window at our yard. It may not be covered with snow like Wyoming,
but it's still a long way from looking anything like spring. Late February through April means mud season in New England, and right now
Concord looks as grim as the grounds of Lowood School.

Which pretty much sums up the way I'm feeling these days.

I glance at my watch. Quarter after three. I need to get going soon; I'm due at a campaign brainstorming session. We're gearing up for Mrs. Wong's first debate in a few weeks. I pick up Bailey's letter again.

You wouldn't believe how excited we all are about the trip! The only one of us who's been back East before is Madison, and that was to Disneyworld, which doesn't really count. Everything I know about New England is either what I've seen in movies or what I've read in nineteenth-century novels, which probably isn't very helpful, is it? You guys aren't, like, super formal or anything, are you?

I laugh out loud at this. "Us, formal?" I ask Pip, who's curled up next to me on my bed. Pip is our golden retriever, and it's totally against house rules for him to be up here, but he's so adorably thrilled when I give in and let him that it's hard to resist.

Pip's eyes stay closed, but his tail thumps softly against my leg, which is his way of participating in the conversation.

I scan the rest of the letter quickly: Bailey's working part-time after school now at Shelf Life, her mom's bookstore, and she's learning how to knit, thanks to Summer Williams. Summer has expanded her craft horizons to include knitting, apparently. Bailey says that at their last book club meeting, Summer did an elaborate presentation about nineteenth-century needlework that included having everyone pick up a pair of needles and give it a whirl. Zoe Winchester thought the whole thing was stupid of course, but no big surprise there. Zoe is sort of the *Chadwickius frenemus* of Gopher Hole.

Bailey's mention of Zoe reminds me that her mother did a stint as mayor there. I'd totally forgotten about that, and I make a mental note to pick Mrs. Winchester's brain for campaigning tips when she's in town.

Bailey ends by dropping a bombshell.

Guess what? I finally have a boyfriend! Well, maybe not quite officially or anything. We've been on exactly two dates—once to a movie, and once for burgers after a basketball game. You'll never guess who: Owen Parker!

My eyebrows shoot up. Owen is one of Cassidy's pen pal Winky Parker's very cute older brothers. Zoe must be fit to be tied—she's had a crush on him forever.

Zoe is fit to be tied, of course, Bailey continues, and I smile. Great minds think alike. *She practically shoots lightning bolts out her eyeballs every time she sees the two of us talking at school. I think I get just as much satisfaction out of that as I do going out with Owen!*

I laugh, picturing the look on Zoe's face. I prop the photo Bailey sent me against the lamp on my bedside table. It was taken at their last book club meeting, and all five of them are holding knitting needles, pretending to look prim. Zoe is failing miserably; she just looks like she

Heather Vogel Frederick

drank a glass of vinegar. I stare at the picture, thinking about how much everyone has changed since we were in Wyoming two summers ago. I'd still recognize them anywhere, though—Bailey's freckled, friendly face; Winky Parker's mischievous twinkle and one-hundred-watt grin; and of course Zoe herself, who still wears too much lip gloss. Summer Williams and Madison Daniels have changed the most, mainly due to their hair styles. Summer used to have waist-length blond hair, but she wrote to Megan recently and told her that she cut it off and donated it to one of those charities that helps disadvantaged kids. That's such a Summer thing to do—she's one of the nicest people I know. Her new hairstyle is cute, though. Madison has traded in her cornrows for a mane of corkscrew curls that look funky and edgy and awesome. Just right for someone in a band. I wish my hair would do that, but my curls are the more boring variety.

I slide off my bed and cross the room to tuck Bailey's letter into the "To Be Answered" slot in my rolltop desk, right next to the letters from Rupert Loomis and Lucy Woodhouse, my English friends. Well, Lucy's a friend. Rupert's more of a . . . how to describe Rupert? He's like the Kevin Mullins of England, I guess.

The notebook in the adjoining slot catches my eye and I pull it out and flip through its pages. I haven't written anything in my journal in days, and I'm itching to get back to it. Now is not the time, however. I don't want to be late for my meeting.

Life has gotten really busy all of a sudden, what with school and being coeditor of Alcott High's newspaper and now Mrs. Wong's campaign. Plus, Cassidy twisted my arm into being her assistant coach for Chicks with Sticks. I thought she was kidding when she first mentioned it, because I am so not a hockey player, but it's turned out to be phenomenally fun.

It's also turned out to be a really good way to take my mind off Stewart and Sophie.

Stewart and Sophie.

Of all the boys at Alcott High whom Sophie Fairfax could have set her sights on, why did she have to pick Stewart? And why does he have to act so flattered?

Scowling, I stuff my arms into the sleeves of my jacket. Cassidy has started referring to him as Stew-rat, which I don't think is quite fair because it's not like there's anything really going on between him and Sophie. At least I don't think so. He's just—twitterpated is the word, maybe. Or enamored. Charmed. Captivated. Entranced. Take your pick.

Great, I think sourly. I'm playing the synonym game with myself. How pathetic is that?

The thing I most hate is how self-conscious I feel whenever I'm around Sophie, which is due to happen again in about fifteen minutes. It's like being back in sixth grade.

It's just that she's so, so—*perfect*. Her hair is curly like mine, but unlike my shoulder-length tangle or Madison Daniels's wild style, Sophie's forms a cute little halo framing her face. Plus, even if she's just wearing jeans she always looks chic, and her makeup is flawless. She's like this petite little package of perfection. The French accent is just icing on the cake.

I, on the other hand, am far from perfection. I'm just, well, Emma. Definitely not petite, hair almost always messy whether it's long or short, clothes fairly hopeless, and makeup barely even on the radar screen. Next to Sophie, I feel like a real plain Jane.

Which makes me wonder if that expression was coined after *Jane Eyre* came out. I'll have to ask my mother.

"Come on, Pip," I tell him. "No point stewing about Sophie, right? Or should that be 'Stew-ratting'?"

Pip ignores my lame pun, of course, and follows me downstairs to my father's office. "Hey Dad," I say as we troop in. Lady Jane Grey, our new cat, is curled up on his desk beside his laptop.

My father is frowning at the screen and doesn't look up for a few seconds. His expression brightens when he sees me. "Emma! When did you get home? I didn't hear you come in."

My father is a writer, and when he's "in the zone," as he calls it when work is going well, he's kind of oblivious to everything else around him.

"About an hour ago, and now I'm going out again," I tell him. "I have a campaign meeting, and then I'm heading to the rink to help Cassidy. You and Darcy are on your own for dinner tonight. I promised Mom I'd walk her home after Chicks with Sticks—she's working late at the library."

He nods absently, already engrossed again in whatever's on his laptop screen. "Uh-huh," he murmurs. "Got it."

Pip squeezes past me and settles onto the rug by his feet with a grumbly sigh. He and my father took a while to become friends. Dad is definitely a cat person, and Pip makes it clear that he considers him a poor substitute for me, and that he's only tolerating him because I'm not around. I'm secretly glad I'm Pip's favorite, though. He's my dog, after all. I'd been wanting a dog forever, and Pip was my birthday present a couple of years ago from my book club friends.

I shut the front door behind me and pull my hood up. The snow may have vanished, but it's still cold out. Plus, it's damp, too, which makes it feel even colder. It reminds me a lot of the weather in England this time of year.

I walk briskly down Lowell Road, turning right at the corner of Main Street. Pies & Prejudice is just past Vanderhoof Hardware. The sight of the black-and-white striped awning over the front window and Megan's clever sign—a silhouette of a woman in a cap and apron holding out a pie—instantly cheers me up. I think everybody in Concord feels the same way about it, actually. It's been hugely popular ever since it opened.

My smile fades as I enter and see Stewart standing at the glass display case talking to Sophie. He's not the only one, either—she's up to her éclairs in boys. It looks as if half of the male population of Alcott High is crammed in here, buying pastries.

Sophie's been a real boost for business. Because she and Gigi have taken such a shine to each other, she's pretty much a fixture at the

Heather Vogel Frederick

tea shop after school these days. Gigi can't officially hire her because of some red tape with her being French and not having a work visa and all, but there's no law against her hanging out and chatting up the customers. Which suddenly includes a lot of boys. Wherever Sophie and her oh-so-charming accent goes, they go, even if it means to a frou-frou tea shop.

I hesitate for a moment by the door, hoping Stewart will notice me. He doesn't.

Sophie doesn't either. She only has eyes for Stewart. I watch as she gives him a cookie, along with a flirtatious glance. I slap a smile on my face and cross the room to an empty table. I'm not going to give her the satisfaction of knowing she has me rattled. I sit down and grab the menu, then start scanning it as if I haven't already got it memorized.

Becca materializes about two seconds later. "Bonjour!" she says brightly.

I glare at her. I'm not in the mood for waitress banter—especially not in French. "Your nametag is crooked," I snap, pointing to the pocket of her uniform.

"Looks like *somebody* got out of bed on the wrong side this morning," she snaps back.

I heave a sigh. "Sorry. It's just—"

"I know," says Becca, glancing over at the counter. "It's enough to make you gag, isn't it?"

I nod.

"We might as well be invisible," she continues, shaking her head in disgust. "Don't let it bug you, though, Emma. My brother is an idiot—he's oblivious to what's going on, poor boy."

Either that or Cassidy's right and he really is a Stew-rat, I think.

Stewart turns around just then. Spotting me, he breaks into a broad grin and trots over to join us. "Hey, Em!"

"Hey," I say without much enthusiasm. He leans down and kisses me on the cheek and I relax a little, feeling bad for my disloyal thoughts. Maybe Becca's right. Maybe he's just clueless.

"You've gotta taste this," he says, enthusiastically shoving half of a cookie at me. "Sophie made it."

I reluctantly take a bite. It's perfect, of course.

"It's called a 'long dew sha,' or something like that."

"Langue du chat," Gigi calls from where she's standing by the cash register. "It means 'cat's tongue.' They're a French delicacy."

"The cat certainly doesn't have her tongue," Becca mutters, watching Sophie chatter away to her knot of admirers.

"What?" says Stewart.

"Nothing."

He plunks himself down across from me as Becca heads off to take care of another customer. I have a clear view of Sophie over Stewart's shoulder. Her eyes keep sliding over to where we're sitting. *Find your own boyfriend*, I think crossly, pulling the campaign notebook out of my backpack. Before I can open it, though, the bell over the door jangles and Mrs. Wong stomps in, waving a newspaper.

"This is war!" she cries, and the tea shop falls silent. Marching across the room, she flings the paper down onto our table. I suck in my breath sharply. The headline screams "Handcuffs Wong Enters Race For Mayor!"

Beneath it is the picture that Becca took back in seventh grade of Mrs. Wong handcuffed to a tree at the Delaneys'. It was one of Mrs. Wong's more over-the-top moments. Her heart was in the right place—she was protesting an unfair tax that almost cost Jess's family Half Moon Farm—but Megan's mother sometimes lets her passion for just causes get in the way of common sense. At any rate, Becca took the picture and managed to slip it into the middle school paper, under my byline, as a prank. The stunt nearly torpedoed my friendship with Megan.

And now here it is again, dredged up who knows how, fanning the flames of a campaign race that's really starting to heat up. I look over at Becca, but she frowns and shakes her head. She obviously had nothing to do with it this time.

Sophie's entourage comes over to see what all the fuss is about. The boys burst out laughing when they spot the picture.

"I remember that from middle school!" one of them crows. "It was hilarious!"

"It's not funny!" retorts Mrs. Wong, putting her hands on her hips. She's mad, but I can tell she's embarrassed, too, because it looks like there are tears in her eyes. Gigi must sense her mood, because all of a sudden she claps her hands.

"Closing time, everybody!" she announces, and Sophie's flock of admirers reluctantly peel themselves away. "Come back and see us soon." Gigi shoos them out, then locks the door and turns the sign to CLOSED. "Now," she says, crossing the room to join us. "What's going on?"

Mrs. Wong points to the headline. Gigi cocks her head and reads it, frowning. "So?"

"So? That's all you can say, Mother—*so*?"

Gigi gives her shoulder a soothing pat. "What's that expression? If you can't stand the heat, get out of the kitchen. It's just politics, and my daughter is strong enough to stand the heat." She turns to Stewart and me. "Why don't you two go home with Lily and continue the meeting there? Becca and Sophie and I will finish up here and be along in a bit. Dinner for the campaign team is from Leaning Tower of Pizza tonight; my treat."

She picks up the newspaper and hands it to me. I nod and put it into my backpack.

As we start for the door, Sophie corners Stewart and hands him a broom. "If you stay and help, we'll finish faster," she coaxes. "And besides, who's going to drive us home otherwise?"

She's right; Becca doesn't have her license yet, and Gigi doesn't drive.

Stewart sees the look on my face and hesitates, then takes the broom. "She's got a point," he says, a tad defensively. "I'll see you in a while, okay?"

No, it's not okay! I want to shout. But I keep my thoughts to myself

Heather Vogel Frederick

and follow Mrs. Wong out to her car. We're both quiet on the drive up Strawberry Hill. I doubt we're worrying about the same things, though.

We pull into the garage and she shuts off the engine, then looks over at me. "Let me talk to Megan first," she says. "She's not going to be happy about this."

No kidding. Megan flipped out over "Handcuffs Wong" the first time around.

Inside, Coco greets us at the door.

"Hi, cutie!" I coo, picking her up and kissing her fuzzy little face. As Mrs. Wong heads down the hallway to Megan's room, I take off my jacket and hang it up, drop my backpack by the dining room table— official headquarters for the Lily Wong for Mayor campaign—and plop down on one of the sofas in the living room.

I don't have to wait long. Mrs. Wong reappears a couple of minutes later shaking her head. "Be forewarned," she says. "My darling daughter is not a happy camper. Maybe you can help calm her down."

Taking Coco with me, I head for Megan's room. I find her lying on her bed, staring up at the ceiling.

"Why did my mother have to run for mayor?" she moans as I come in.

"You mean Handcuffs Wong?" I reply as cheerfully as I can, figuring that maybe humor is the best way to defuse the situation.

Megan shoots me a look. "Don't, okay?"

"C'mon, Megs, it's not the end of the world."

"Your world, maybe. You don't live in mine. I'm the one whose family is on display for everyone to laugh at. As if I didn't have enough to think about, now that I'm living with Mademoiselle Everybody Likes Me Better Than You Including Your Kitten."

I cross the room and put Coco down on her stomach. "*Voilà le* kitten," I tell her. "While Sophie's away, the mice will play."

"You're not going to run for mayor, too, are you?" she asks Coco, scratching her under the chin.

"Shove over," I tell her, and Megan scoots to the other side of the bed. I perch on the edge, gazing around the room. "Looks like maybe somebody's going to Paris." There are maps and posters and guidebooks piled on just about every surface, and a framed print of the Eiffel Tower that I'm pretty sure wasn't there last time I was here is hanging on the wall above her desk. "Nice," I say, gesturing at it. "New?"

Megan nods. "Gigi. Practically every time I come in here I find something else she's left for me. I think she's more excited about our trip than I am, if that's possible." She rolls over on her side, propping her head in her hand. "The thing is, Emma, this was supposed to be a really happy time for me, you know? All the anticipation, the planning, the dreaming. You remember what it was like when you found out you were moving to England, right?"

"Of course."

"I mean, *Paris*! I've wanted to go there since I was, like, two! And, instead, all I can think about is stupid Sophie Fairfax. And now, on top of that, Handcuffs Wong."

"It totally stinks," I agree.

Heather Vogel Frederick

"Yeah."

We're quiet for a bit.

"Here's the thing, though," I tell her. "Shouldn't all this stuff make you even more excited about going to Paris? Just think, you won't have to give either of them a single thought while you're there! Paris is a Sophie-free, Handcuffs Wong–free zone. You'll be able to just relax and have fun."

"I hadn't thought of it that way."

"Plus, Simon is going to be there!" I grin at her.

"Good point."

The garage door rumbles and Coco's ears prick up. She listens for a second, then hops down off the bed and scampers out the door. Megan gives me a rueful smile. "Looks like you-know-who is home."

I don't say much at dinner. The conversation flows around me as I eat my pizza and consider the new wrinkle in the campaign. Something Mrs. Bergson told me once, that the pen is mightier than the sword, comes to mind.

"So," says Mrs. Wong, looking at Stewart and me. "What do my campaign managers suggest? Time to fight fire with fire?"

"Yes," says Stewart, at the same time that I say "no."

"I vote with Stewart," says Sophie quickly.

Obvious, much? I'd be tempted to laugh if she wasn't so annoying. Or so fixated on my boyfriend.

"I think we need to hear what Emma has to say before we take a vote," says Gigi.

"Agreed," says Mr. Wong.

"It just seems to me that fighting fire with fire is exactly what their camp is expecting," I tell them. "It's almost like they're baiting us. But if we do, this whole campaign will end up as some big mudslinging contest. I'd like to see us do something to set us apart from run-of-the-mill politics, and give voters something positive to latch on to."

"Like what?" says Stewart.

"Well, for starters, we need to remember that we have a secret weapon."

"We do?" Mrs. Wong looks surprised to hear this.

"Sure we do—your sense of humor."

Mrs. Wong blinks at me.

"Remember back in middle school, when you emceed our fashion show?" She nods slowly. "You were funny, Mrs. Wong—really funny. I think that instead of fighting fire with fire, we should fight it with laughter. What if we just turn around and make 'Handcuffs Wong' the centerpiece of your campaign?"

"Are you *kidding* me?" Megan looks aghast at the idea.

"No, Megs—think about it. What slogan could possibly be catchier than 'Handcuffs Wong for Mayor?' Who's not going to want that bumper sticker, especially when they find out about the kind of never-give-up attitude that earned your mother the nickname in the first place?" I turn to Mrs. Wong. "Your commitment and passion is just what this town needs, and I think the opposition just handed you the job on a platter."

Heather Vogel Frederick

Stewart stares at me, openmouthed with admiration. "Emma, you're brilliant."

I can feel myself blush. "Thank you." I flick a glance at Sophie. *Take that, Mademoiselle Velcro!* "Mrs. Bergson used to tell me that the pen is mightier than the sword," I continue, "so let's use the pen. You're going to write a letter to the editor in response, Mrs. Wong, a humorous one poking fun at yourself, while at the same time painting yourself as the candidate voters can count on to stick with something and see it through to the end. Someone who puts her handcuffs where her mouth is, so to speak, and stays true to her principles and values—the same principles and values this town needs."

Mrs. Wong is frowning thoughtfully. Stewart's pen flies across the page as he jots down the ideas I'm spouting off the top of my head.

"I see what you're driving at, Emma," Mr. Wong says. "I like it."

"Me too," says Gigi.

Mrs. Wong still doesn't look convinced. "I'm not sure if I can pull off a humorous letter."

"That's what Stewart and I are here for," I tell her. *Stewart and I.* It has such a nice ring to it. I flick another glance at Sophie, hoping she's listening up. She seems more enthralled with picking lint off her sweater than with paying attention to me, but I note with satisfaction a slight flush on her perfectly sculpted cheekbones. Stewart's praise must have annoyed her, I note with satisfaction.

We all sit around the table for a while brainstorming, and pretty soon we have lists of what we're going to need in terms of bumper stickers, buttons, placards, and posters. Stewart and I flesh out some talking points for the upcoming debate, and we discuss the mailing we want to get out before it takes place. By the time we're done, everyone's fired up about the whole Handcuffs Wong idea.

"Maybe Sophie could take pictures of you handcuffed to things around town, Lily," suggests Gigi. "The Old North Bridge, *oui*? To symbolize your devotion to Concord's heritage."

"Great idea," I tell her, feeling generous.

"Stewart can help me," Sophie replies, instantly souring the milk of my human kindness. "He knows where everything is."

"Sure," Stewart replies, looking pleased. "I'd be happy to."

"Oh, this could be fun!" says Mrs. Wong. "Let's plan on setting at least one shoot at the water treatment plant—it's in need of an upgrade, and I'd like to make that one of the key platforms in my campaign." She looks over at Megan, who hasn't said a word this whole time. "Are you okay with this? The whole Handcuffs Wong thing, I mean?"

Megan shrugs.

"I know how kids at school can be—you're probably going to get teased if I go with this strategy," her mother continues. "I don't want this election to be torture for you, honey, so if you want me to try something different, just say the word."

Megan shakes her head, her dark hair rippling like a waterfall. "No, Mom—what Emma says makes sense. Go for it. I'll be okay."

"All right, then," says Mrs. Wong. "Full speed ahead with Handcuffs Wong for Mayor." She grins. "I can't believe I just said that."

Heather Vogel Frederick

I glance at my watch and jump up, grabbing my backpack. "Gotta go," I announce. "I'm due at the rink in fifteen minutes to help Cassidy."

Stewart gets up too, since he's driving me.

"I've heard so much about Chicks with Sticks," says Sophie, pronouncing it "Cheeks with Steeks." It sounds adorable, of course. "May I come watch?"

I stare at her. Unbelievable! Of all the nerve! She knows very well I can't just tell her not to tag along—that would make me look like a big jerk.

"Fine," I reply shortly.

Not that she's asking my permission. Her eyes are glued to Stewart, as usual.

As we're leaving, Megan holds up two fingers in the V-is-for-Velcro salute. I flash one back at her.

"Hang in there," she whispers as she gives me a hug good-bye.

"I will if you will," I reply.

At least Stewart doesn't let Sophie sit in the front. She keeps up a steady stream of chatter from the backseat, though, and I pretend to be engrossed in my campaign notebook, watching the two of them out of the corner of my eye. From what I can tell, Becca is right; Stewart is oblivious to Sophie's tactics. On the other hand, it doesn't really make a difference. It still hurts.

"Stew-rat on the prowl again?" Cassidy asks a little while later as I skate out onto the ice. She jerks her thumb toward the bench where Stewart and Sophie have taken a seat.

"Don't call him that," I tell her. "He's just not thinking, that's all."

She gives me a shrewd glance. "If it looks like a duck and quacks like a duck . . ."

I give her a little shove and she goes sprawling. She picks herself up, laughing, and hands me a stack of orange cones. "Set these up for me, okay? And then if you could take the three youngest players and just work with them on stopping and starting, keeping steady on their feet and all, that would be great."

If Mrs. Bergson could only see me now, I think to myself a few minutes later as I lead Ivy Angelino and a few of the other newest players out onto the ice. I've come a long way from the complete klutz who started lessons with Mrs. Bergson back in middle school. I may not be the most graceful of skaters, and I'm still not totally comfortable with the hockey skates Cassidy got me as a thank-you for agreeing to help her—they don't have toe picks in the front, for one thing, which means I still spend a lot of time sitting on the ice—but I have what it takes to get the job done, thanks to Mrs. Bergson.

I glance over at the bench a few times during the practice session. Once, Stewart waves. The other times, though, he's too busy talking to Sophie. So much for her line about "I want to watch Chicks with Sticks." It seems all she really wants to watch is Stewart.

One of the best perks for helping Cassidy is extra rink time. The rink closes at nine on most weeknights, but Cassidy's brought in so much new business with her youth program and she logs so many hours here that the owner gave her a key, and he allows her to close

Heather Vogel Frederick

the rink down on Tuesday and Thursday nights. Which means we have the place to ourselves after Chicks with Sticks any time we want. We've had some good times here, just the two of us. Cassidy's taught me a little hockey, as well as some dance moves from when she trained with Tristan Berkeley, and I get in a little extra practice for figure skating. And sometimes we just race each other around the rink at top-speed, laughing our heads off. It's a great way to let off steam.

And I've had a lot to let off lately.

But tonight I don't want to hang around afterward. Tonight I want go home with Stewart. By myself.

Unfortunately, I promised my mother I'd walk her home.

"Can I give you a ride to the library?" Stewart asks when we're outside in the parking lot.

"Thank you; I'll walk," I tell him stiffly. My generosity has evaporated. I stand there, hoping he'll insist. I mentally will him to take my hand and pull me into the car.

He doesn't.

"Um, okay," he says, not sounding too sure. We stand there awkwardly for a moment or two. "Well, I guess I'll see you tomorrow, then."

"Yeah, I guess so."

Sophie shivers, stamping her feet. "I'm cold. Let's go, Stewart. Ciao, Emma."

Stewart waves as they drive away. I give him a halfhearted wave in response, then turn and trudge down the street.

"You're awfully quiet tonight," my mother says as she shuts and locks the main door to the library a few minutes later. We head down the wide stone steps together. "Cat got your tongue?"

I snort. *Langue du chat*. "Yeah."

She frowns at me. "C'mon, Emma, out with it. I can read you like a book, remember?"

I sigh. "You know in *Jane Eyre*, when all the guests come to Thornfield for the house party?"

"Uh-huh."

"Well, I'm getting really sick of one of the guests."

She levels a shrewd glance at me. "A little too much Blanche Ingram, I'm guessing? Or is it annoying plot device Adele Varens?"

"A bit of both," I tell her, grateful that she understands my literary shorthand. It helps having a librarian for a mother.

"What you need," she says, "is a nice cup of tea." She slips her arm through mine and tows me briskly toward Concord's downtown coffee shop, where she orders us a pot of Earl Grey to share. "It's not Pies and Prejudice," she whispers, "but it will do in a pinch."

Even though I still have homework to do, and even though I'm dying to write in my journal—which is the best place in the world to unload when I'm feeling unhappy—right now an even better place to be is right here, drinking tea with my mother.

"Tell me everything," she says, and I do, spilling the beans about the whole Stew-rat/Mademoiselle Velcro mess.

"Sophie is a mighty attractive young lady," my mother says when I'm done.

Heather Vogel Frederick

"Um, you're not making me feel better, Mom."

She laughs. "Don't misunderstand me, sweetheart—it's not that you aren't attractive. In fact, you're infinitely more so, in this totally unbiased librarian's opinion." She sips her tea. "But Sophie's a novelty. She's flavor of the month, and Stewart is just a little giddy with all the attention she's showering on him. My advice is to wait and see. This will likely all blow over, and if it doesn't, well, don't forget, Stewart is your first boyfriend, but he may not be your last. He's going away to college in the fall, after all."

"Now you're *really* not making me feel better!"

She smiles and pats my hand. "The thing is, Emma, you two are so young—too young, really, to be pairing off like this. Life holds so many surprises, and you don't want to close yourself off to them too soon."

"I wish Sophie Fairfax had never come to Concord," I tell her flatly.

"Wishing her away won't fix things," my mother replies. She holds up a finger, the way she often does when she's about to quote something. "'Never grow a wishbone, daughter, where your backbone ought to be.'"

I give her a sidelong glance. "Charlotte Brontë?"

"Clementine Paddleford, early twentieth-century American food writer. Charlotte would have liked her, though. And so would Jane."

"Austen?"

"Eyre. That girl has backbone to spare."

"Yeah, good point." Every time I read *Jane Eyre* I'm amazed at the hardships she has to endure. It would seem over the top if Charlotte Brontë wasn't such a great writer. She makes it all totally believable.

"Have you tried talking to Stewart?"

"Not yet," I mumble.

"Maybe it's time to get your Jane on and do it. That's probably a good place to start."

I sit up a little straighter. As usual, my mother is right. Like Jane Eyre, I do have a backbone. And it's time to use it.

❦ Jess ❦

" . . . a weapon of defence must be prepared—
I whetted my tongue."
—Jane Eyre

The conference table is a mile long.

At least it feels that way.

I'm sitting alone at one end, gazing down its length at the solemn-faced members of the Community Justice Board. Savannah and the other students are seated at the far end, flanked by two faculty mentors—an English teacher and a soccer coach I've seen around campus but don't know personally. Mrs. Duffy, our headmistress, and the Battleaxe are sitting off to the side.

I have no idea what to expect. My heart is thudding at twice its normal rate, and I'm wishing fervently that my parents were here with me, but school rules are clear: only students and staff are allowed at Community Justice Board hearings.

My parents came to the first meeting with Mrs. Duffy a couple of weeks ago, of course. They listened quietly as Mrs. Adler repeated her charge against me, providing details that left my mouth hanging open. All I did was drop my pen on the floor and whisper "sorry" to the person sitting next to me! The way she made it sound, I was habitually late to class, deliberately skipped the review sessions and, as a result, came underprepared and scheming to cheat.

When it was my turn to respond, I did the best I could, but it's intimidating sitting in the headmistress's office with someone like the Battleaxe glaring at you, and I was rattled. As I stammered out my explanation, it sounded lame even to my ears. I kept thinking of the last time I got hauled in here, after all that trouble with Savannah the first time we shared a room back in eighth grade.

The two of us weren't getting along, and a prank war had escalated to the point of disaster. Savannah's father, Senator Sinclair, tried throwing his weight around and demanded she be assigned another roommate; my father got offended and it was all just a big mess.

This time around, of course, it was different—there were no pranks, and no Senator Sinclair. But it was still a big mess.

After Mrs. Adler and I each had our chance to speak that afternoon, Mrs. Duffy looked down at my file—or what I assumed was my file, since it said JESSICA DELANEY on the label—then regarded me with what looked like a glimmer of sympathy in her eyes. At least I'd hoped it was a glimmer of sympathy.

"Jess," she said, "in the two and a half years you've been here at Colonial Academy, you've made a wonderful contribution to our student body. You excel at your studies, you're involved in numerous extracurricular activities, and we all know and admire your wonderful volunteer work with the local animal rehabilitator. Additionally, several of your teachers have come forward to give you glowing character recommendations. In light of all that, I've decided to have this issue remanded to our Community Justice Board."

"What?!" exclaimed Mrs. Adler.

"What's the Community Justice Board?" my mother had asked.

"CJB is Colonial Academy's student-run judicial system," the headmistress explained.

Mrs. Adler was obviously unhappy that her word alone was not enough to convict me. "I hardly see the need to draw this matter out," she'd huffed. "I think it's entirely clear what transpired. Colonial has never coddled cheaters."

"Nor will it," Mrs. Duffy replied mildly. "But this is a grave charge, one with potentially grave consequences, and Jessica deserves a full and fair hearing, and the complete support of our institution's due process."

The Battleaxe pursed her lips. "You never were one for simple math, Betsy," she said waspishly, and Mrs. Duffy's face reddened. I gaped at them both—Mrs. Adler had been the headmistress's math teacher, too? Unbelievable! "Two plus two equals four. It always has, and it always will. This girl is guilty as charged."

"Now see here—" my father started, but my mother laid a warning hand on his knee.

"With all due respect, Mrs. Adler," countered the headmistress calmly, "even in academia one is innocent until proven guilty, is one not?"

The Battleaxe grunted.

"I'll take that as a yes." The headmistress had turned to me then, and this time I was sure her gaze was sympathetic. "I'll contact the Community Justice Board on your behalf, Jessica, and a hearing will be scheduled. Given the timing of this incident, I'm afraid it will have to wait until after our break, and in the meantime I have no other choice but to place you on probation."

"What exactly does that mean?" asked my mother.

"Early curfew, closed campus, supervised study halls, no weekend passes—"

Great, I'd thought glumly. *There go my dates with Darcy.* I wouldn't even be able to meet him at the library anymore.

"How about her involvement in MadriGals?" my father asked. "They're heading to New York in a few weeks for the national competition, as I'm sure you know, and Jess has worked hard to earn herself a solo spot."

The Battleaxe made a dismissive noise, but Mrs. Duffy nodded. "I'm well aware of the competition, Mr. Delaney," she replied. "It's a very exciting time for our school. This will all be settled one way or another before then, but in the meantime, Jessica will need to obey the probation requirements."

And that had been that. Well, almost.

"I'm fully confident that my daughter will be cleared of these charges," my mother had said as we were standing up to leave. "But I'm curious what would happen if she were not."

"You mean if she's found guilty of cheating?" Mrs. Duffy replied.

"Yes."

"I'm afraid she'd lose her scholarship. Mrs. Adler is quite right—Colonial Academy doesn't condone cheating."

"I should think not," Mrs. Adler said smugly.

"She really is an old Battleaxe, isn't she?" grumbled my mother afterward as I walked my parents to their car.

"Yeah."

My father gave me a hug. "Chin up, kiddo. It's only a few weeks."

"We're rooting for you, sweetheart," my mother added.

After they left, I drooped back to my dorm room, where Savannah was lying on her bunk, reading the Cliff Notes to *The Scarlet Letter*. I couldn't blame her—it's a horrible book. Even Emma doesn't like it. I don't know why every tenth grader in this entire country has to get stuck reading it.

Savannah took one look at my face and put the book down. "Didn't go well, I take it?"

"Mrs. Adler tried to get me expelled, but Mrs. Duffy is sending me to the Community Justice Board. Meanwhile, I'm on probation."

"Bummer. I thought for sure you'd be cleared on the spot. The charges are so obviously bogus."

"Not according to the Battleaxe. Who, by the way, was the headmistress's teacher, too, back when she was a student here."

"No way."

"Yes way!"

"Wow. So she really is, like, a hundred, then." Savannah sat up. "Community Justice Board isn't such a bad thing, Jess," she told me. "In fact, it's probably a good thing. You'll get a fair hearing."

"You think?"

Savannah was the only underclassman to get elected to the CJB. It was a big deal when it happened. Some of the juniors and seniors who were running against her were pretty upset. But even they had to admit that Savannah knocked it out of the park during the debates.

"Definitely." She passed me a tissue. "Wipe your nose. We're going for a ride. Not much that fresh air and horses can't cure."

She was right, of course. An hour down at the stables with her, putting Blackjack and Cairo through their paces, had me feeling a whole lot better. Savannah loves horses as much as I do, and she's an awesome equestrienne—she won our school's Silver Spurs Award two years in a row, and will probably win again this year. She's a great riding partner.

As the two of us started back up the path toward the dorms when we were done, she looked over at me.

"Hey, do you remember back in eighth grade when we got into trouble for those pranks, and you helped tutor me afterward even though I wasn't very nice to you?"

I laughed. "Yeah. I thought about that earlier today, actually. Sitting in Mrs. Duffy's office reminded me."

Heather Vogel Frederick

"I've never forgotten that, Jess. I know Mrs. Duffy made you do it and everything, but still."

I shrugged. "No big deal."

Savannah bumped her shoulder against mine. "Yes, it was a big deal—I wouldn't still be here if it wasn't for you. I was on academic probation, remember?"

I nodded, still not sure what she was getting at.

"Anyway, I think it's my turn to return the favor. I'm going to call my father."

"Really?" I shot her a skeptical glance. I didn't see how Senator Sinclair could help, unless she was going to ask him to pay for a new building or something in return for letting me off.

Savannah grinned. "Don't worry, I'm not going to ask him to pull any strings or anything. Not that he could, anyway. But he was a lawyer before he was a senator, you know. He was the one who suggested I run for the CJB."

"Really?"

She nodded. "He said it would be a good way for me to learn how the legal system works. And maybe get a taste of what it might be like to practice law someday."

I looked over at her in surprise. Savannah, a lawyer? I'd always thought of her as doing something with horses, a trainer or a breeder, maybe. "So, what's the verdict? Sorry. Bad pun."

She grinned again. "No kidding. But yeah, maybe. It's been really interesting so far."

Suddenly I pictured Savannah in a power suit, standing in front of a jury. She'd be a formidable opponent, and anybody with any sense would want her on their side. She's smart—not a straight-A student yet, but her grades have improved a ton, plus she has what Emma calls street smarts. And she's quick on her feet and has yards of confidence. Which is probably why she was the only underclassman to be elected to the Community Justice Board in about a decade.

"I could totally see that," I told her. "You'd make a great lawyer. Or Supreme Court judge, even."

She laughed. "Thanks."

That conversation was weeks ago, though, and Savannah's not laughing now. She's at the other end of the table, looking very far away and very serious. She wouldn't tell me what she'd discussed with her father, just that he'd given her a few suggestions and helped her strategize. For a brief second, though, I spot a flicker of a smile on her lips, and it gives me hope.

The gavel comes down with a bang on the table and I flinch.

"This hearing will come to order," says a senior named Susan Biltmore. "Each party will have the opportunity to speak, after which we'll ask questions and reach an agreement as to the outcome."

Mrs. Adler gets to go first again. She says pretty much the same thing she did in the headmistress's office—that I was always late to class, skipped the review sessions, and therefore wasn't ready on the day of the test, which led me to cheat. Which she caught me doing, red-handed.

Heather Vogel Frederick

And then it's my turn. This time I'm feeling a little more prepared. I stand up and take a deep breath. Emma's been lecturing me on backbone for the past few days—she calls it "getting my Jane on," in honor of Jane Eyre—and mine is feeling a lot stronger than it had.

"First of all, I was only late to class once, when I overslept," I state as loudly and clearly as I can. "I apologize for that; it was rude." I try not to look at the Battleaxe, who is glaring at me. Instead, I focus on Savannah, who like her fellow CJB members is taking notes. "As far as the review sessions are concerned," I continue, "I told Mrs. Adler ahead of time that I wouldn't be able to attend, because of prior commitments."

Emma helped me with that wording, too—"prior commitments" has a solid ring to it, she said. Very adult.

"On Monday afternoon I had an audition for a MadriGals solo that I'd spent weeks preparing for"—Savannah looks up from her notes and again I catch that flicker of a smile— "and then on Tuesday I had my regular voice lesson, which I didn't want to cancel, and on Wednesday I went to see the Crandalls' new baby. There was a sign-up sheet, and slots were going fast."

Mrs. Adler sniffs. "Frivolous 'commitments.'"

"You'll have another chance to speak in a moment, Mrs. Adler," Susan Biltmore tells her crisply. "In the meantime, please refrain from any further remarks."

The Battleaxe sniffs again.

"Maybe in retrospect I should have postponed visiting the Crandalls," I admit. "But the fact is, I did prepare for the test. I studied on my own every night, and with my—with a friend. Someone from Alcott High."

The board members confer amongst themselves for a moment.

"Is this friend willing to vouch for that fact?" Susan asks.

I nod. Darcy would be more than happy to help me out. Of course, if he does, my visits to the Concord Library might come to light. But it's better than getting kicked out.

Time to get to the heart of the matter. I take another deep breath. "As for the cheating, it's simple: I didn't."

"Nonsense," cries Mrs. Adler, smacking the table with her hand. "Of course you did! I saw you with my own eyes."

"You saw me bend over to pick up a pencil that I dropped, Mrs. Adler," I reply as calmly as I can. "That's all. I didn't cheat."

Susan Biltmore starts banging the gavel, but Mrs. Adler barges on ahead. "No one finishes a calculus test in half the allotted time without making a single mistake! Of course you cheated."

"I didn't," I repeat, resisting the urge to raise my voice. Emma told me that keeping my cool would boost my credibility. *Backbone*, I remind myself, taking another deep breath. "I didn't cheat."

The Battleaxe starts to sputter again, ignoring the gavel. Finally, the headmistress is forced to step in.

"Bernice, please," she says. "You'll have another opportunity to speak in a minute."

Savannah raises her hand, and Susan turns to her in relief. "The chair recognizes Savannah Sinclair."

Heather Vogel Frederick

Savannah rises to her feet. She's not quite as tall as Cassidy Sloane, but she's tall, and she's dressed today like all the other CJB members, in matching navy blazers over white shirts. From where I'm sitting, she looks every inch Supreme Court material.

"This would seem to be a case of she said/she said," she tells her fellow board members. "It's Jess's word against Mrs. Adler's at this point, with no witnesses, except a possible study partner of Jess's. But no witnesses to the actual alleged cheating incident."

"Go on," says Susan.

"It seems to me that if Jess cheated—and in the spirit of full disclosure here I have to say that she's my roommate and a good friend and that's a very big if, as I find it inconceivable she'd ever do something like that—but *if* she did, the only possible reason she would have done so would be because she hadn't mastered the material, right?"

Her fellow board members look at each other and shrug, then nod slowly. So do the faculty advisors and Mrs. Duffy.

"Well then, isn't there a simple way of proving the validity of this charge?" Savannah continues. "What if we were to give Jess another calculus test right here and now? If she passes it, clearly she understands the material and would have had no reason to cheat. If she doesn't, then we pursue the matter further."

There's another round of nods, and Susan Biltmore looks over at the Battleaxe. "Would that be acceptable to you, Mrs. Adler?"

"How am I to know that the two of you haven't cooked this up between you?" Mrs. Adler replies suspiciously. "She's your roommate, after all, a fact I might add was kept from me until now. Perhaps Jessica knew you were going to suggest this, and has simply studied the test and memorized the answers."

"We'll give her a different one," says Savannah quickly.

It suddenly occurs to me that she's planned this all ahead of time, and a second later, when Mr. Crandall walks in, I'm sure of it. Savannah gestures to him. "In fact, I've asked Mr. Crandall to prepare a new exam."

Mrs. Adler frowns. "If you're going to undermine my authority—"

"We have no intention of doing anything like that," Mr. Crandall says smoothly. "Our intention is simply to determine the truth regarding one of Colonial Academy's star students." He glances briefly in my direction, and I think I detect a wink. My pulse, which has been clocking along at *prestissimo*, slows to *moderato*. "When Savannah came to me with this solution, I instantly saw the genius and practicality of it. Our goal here at Colonial is to see that our students master their subjects, and if Jess completes this exam as accurately as she did the other—on which she scored a hundred percent, by the way—"

"Because she cheated," mutters Mrs. Adler.

Mr. Crandall ignores her. "—then it seems logical that this would give us our answer. If there's no motive, after all, why would there ever have been a crime?"

"Shall we put it to a vote?" asks Savannah, pressing the point. Susan Biltmore nods, and at the other end of the table the board mem-

Heather Vogel Frederick

bers confer for a minute with Mrs. Duffy and the faculty mentors. The result is unanimous: I'm to be given an impromptu exam.

I take my seat. My pulse picks up its tempo again but for entirely different reasons this time. Can I pull it off? So much is riding on the outcome!

Mr. Crandall walks down to my end of the table and hands me the test. His back is to the Community Justice Board and he smiles at me, then mouths the words *good luck*.

Aloud he says, "Take your time, Jess. There's nothing more important than the welfare of one of our students, and we will all sit here quietly"—he glances down the table at Mrs. Adler, whose mouth is pinched into a thin line—"*quietly*," he repeats, "while you complete the problems on the exam to the best of your ability."

He passes me a calculator and a pencil, then takes a seat beside the headmistress. The minutes tick by. The problems are hard, and it doesn't help that everyone is watching me. I can feel the Battleaxe's eagle eyes practically boring holes in my shirt. I will myself to ignore her, along with everyone else in the room. It's just me and the page of problems. My focus finally kicks in, and I start scribbling answers.

Twenty minutes later I'm done.

"You can't be finished," says Mrs. Adler, glaring at the clock as I stand up. "Don't you want to double check your work?"

"I did," I tell her, sliding the piece of paper down the table. Mr. Crandall scoops it up, scanning the first problem as he hands it to Mrs. Adler. He smiles.

The Battleaxe, however, isn't willing to give up that easily. "It will take me some time to grade this," she says, looking as if she just bit into an apple and found half a worm.

Time is the one thing I don't have. I'm supposed to leave for New York first thing tomorrow morning with the rest of the MadriGals.

Mrs. Duffy leans forward in her chair. "Surely we could persuade you to at least take a preliminary look?"

Mrs. Adler grunts, but she glances down at the paper in her hand. A minute ticks by, and then another. "She got the first one right," she finally admits.

Mr. Crandall gives me another sly wink, and I feel a huge weight lifts off my chest. "I think you'll find that the next two are correct as well," he tells her.

The headmistress nods. "Right, then. In light of Miss Sinclair's excellent common-sense solution, I feel confident in recommending that the board cancel Jessica's probation," she says. "Unless the remainder of the test results prove otherwise, I fully expect she will be cleared of all charges."

The board nods their agreement.

"You're free to go," Mrs. Duffy tells me.

Susan Biltmore brings her gavel down on the table again. "This hearing is dismissed."

"Do us proud in New York!" Mrs. Duffy whispers as I pass her on the way out.

"Thank you," I whisper back, barely able to conceal my happiness

Heather Vogel Frederick

and relief. I try not to look over at Mrs. Adler. It would be impolite to gloat.

The minute I'm outside I call my parents with the good news, then text Emma and Darcy as I race for the dorm. Bursting through the front doors, I take the stairs two at a time.

Frankie and Adele are waiting for me in our room. They leap to their feet, looking at me expectantly.

"Yippee!" crows Adele when she sees my face. "You're coming to New York!"

We all start talking at once. I'm still explaining Savannah's brilliant strategy as she comes in.

"Aw shucks," she says, feigning modesty, then laughs. "Actually, it was my dad's idea."

"Thank you, Senator Sinclair!" I exclaim, hugging her.

"You can thank him in New York," Savannah tells me. "He and my mom are flying up to catch the competition this weekend." She kneels on the floor and fishes around under her bunk. "Meanwhile, he sent this for you."

She hands me a box and I open it, laughing when I see that it contains a big packet of chocolate cigars.

"He was sure we'd win, and wanted us to have something to celebrate with," Savannah explains. "I think there's a note in there for you too."

There is. It's written in Senator Sinclair's bold black handwriting on official U.S. Senate stationery:

Dear Jessica,

I have absolutely no doubt as to the outcome of this hearing.

Your reputation is sterling with us! You've done so much for Savannah—your friendship has made a real difference in her life. Congratulations, and see you in New York!

All the best,
Robert Sinclair

"Hurry up and open those chocolates," orders Frankie, dancing around the room in anticipation.

I snag a handful of the cigars for my family and put them in my backpack. "I'd better get going," I tell my friends. "My parents are picking me up in a couple of minutes."

"See you in the morning at the bus," says Savannah. "Bright and early."

"Five a.m. on the dot, Mr. Elton said," adds Adele.

I make a face. "How could I forget? I think I'll come in my pajamas."

"Don't stay out too late tonight smooooooooching," says Frankie, her dark eyes sparkling with merriment.

I can feel my face turn red. "No chance of that, actually," I reply lightly. "Darcy's got an away game tonight and won't be home until long after I'm asleep."

I grab a few things out of my dresser drawer and closet, then say

Heather Vogel Frederick

good-bye again and head downstairs. I find my parents in the lobby, talking to the McKinleys.

"So happy to hear that everything turned out all right," says Mrs. McKinley, putting her arm around my shoulders and giving me a squeeze. "Not that we ever doubted it for a second."

"Thank you," I tell her. "For everything." Savannah told me that the McKinleys were among the faculty and staff members who wrote letters of support.

My brothers are waiting in the van, dressed in their Sunday clothes and looking unusually tidy.

"What's going on?" I ask.

"You are," says my father. "We're going out to dinner to celebrate your victory."

"Yeah! You beat the Battleaxe!" crows Dylan.

"Mom told us your nickname for her," Ryan admits.

"Mo-om!" I protest.

"Sorry," she says, not looking sorry at all. She smiles at me. "How does Harborside sound?"

"You're taking me out for *lobster*?!"

My father grins. "You didn't think we'd go to the trouble of wrestling your brothers into those monkey suits for Burger Barn, did you? This is a major Delaney family victory, and deserves to be celebrated as such."

Lobster is one of my favorite things in the whole world. I eat mine and half of Ryan's—my little brother is surprisingly squeamish when it comes to a meal you basically have to tear apart with your hands—plus a giant heap of steamed clams, two ears of corn, some coleslaw, a biscuit with butter and honey, and chocolate cake for dessert.

"To Jess," my father says, saluting me with a lobster claw. "Our lovely daughter, and a shining example of grace under pressure."

"A shining example of stuffing my face," I reply, leaning back in my chair and groaning. "The only thing under pressure right now is the button on my jeans."

Later, on the way home, my mother reaches over and pats my knee. "Too bad you won't be able to see Darcy this weekend."

"Darcy and Jess, sitting in a tree, k-i-s-s-i-n-g," my brothers sing-song from the back of the van. I ignore them, and my mother and I exchange a smile.

"Yeah, well, maybe there'll be time Sunday night," I tell her.

"We'll keep our fingers crossed, okay? Don't forget we have a get-together planned for your Wyoming friends."

I have an unbelievably busy weekend ahead. Not only am I heading to New York tomorrow, but our pen pals are also arriving on Saturday night, and on Sunday we're having a party to kick off their week in Concord, right around the time I get back from Nationals.

The first thing I do when we get home is change into my barn clothes. "Back in a minute," I tell Ryan, who's setting up a Monopoly board on the kitchen table. I grab a couple of apples from the bowl on the kitchen counter and run across the muddy yard to the barn. After today's ordeal, I need a good dose of home.

Heather Vogel Frederick

"Hey boys," I say to Led and Zep, giving them each an apple. "How are things?"

I pat their velvety noses and visit with them for a bit, then spend some time in the goat pen with Sundance and her daughters Sunbeam and Cedar, the rest of my four-legged family.

"Jess!" calls Dylan a few minutes later. I hear him racing across the barn, and then he leans over the wall of the pen, panting. "Do you want to meet my chicken?"

My brothers are both in 4-H this year. Ryan is raising a goat, like I did with Sundance when I was his age, and Dylan is raising a chicken. Last time I was here it still hadn't hatched yet, and he was as worried as, well, a mother hen.

"Of course I want to meet your chicken," I tell him, standing up and dusting off my knees. "Hey!" I add accusingly. "You grew again behind my back!"

I hadn't noticed in the car or at the restaurant, but Dylan is now taller than I am. Which means Ryan must be too, since they're twins.

My brother grins, looking pleased. "Shrimp!"

"Who's calling who a shrimp?" I holler, chasing him across the barn.

He skips ahead of me to the brooding pen, laughing over his shoulder. Inside, frisking in the sawdust under a heat lamp, is one lone little chick. It scoots away from me when I try and pick it up, but I eventually manage to corner it. Scooping it up, I inspect its fluffy black and gray feathers carefully. "A Barred Rock, huh?"

Dylan nods vigorously.

"Nice. They're my favorite. He looks healthy—or is it a she?"

"I hope it's a she, because I named it Taylor Swift," he replies, grinning again.

"Aren't you worried that she'll be lonely?"

"Nah, I keep the radio on. She likes country music."

"As well she should." All of the chickens at Half Moon Farm are named after Country Western singers. It was my mother's idea originally, and somehow the tradition stuck. I set the chick down again carefully, and Dylan and I head back to the kitchen and our board game, where I beat the pants off the entire family.

"A fitting end to a triumphant day for you, sweetheart," says my mother when she tucks me in later that night. I'm way too old to be tucked into bed, so we don't call it that anymore, but that's what it is, really. She perches on the edge of my mattress and strokes my hair. "I'm really proud of you," she continues. "You handled yourself with such maturity these past few weeks. It's not easy to be accused of something you didn't do."

"Thanks, Mom."

She kisses me good night, and my father pops in a few minutes later and does the same, and then I text Darcy to see how his game went.

BEAT 'EM 3–0, he texts back, and sends a picture of himself and Stewart and the rest of the team, sweaty and grinning. I smile. It's been a good day for everybody.

The next morning my alarm goes off at four a.m. and I stagger out of bed to the shower. I'm not used to farm hours any more, that's for sure. Living at boarding school has turned me into a wimp. My parents are already downstairs and dressed by the time I get to the kitchen.

"I know it's early, but try and eat a little something," my mother says, handing me a banana and a bowl of cereal. "I've packed us some snacks for the trip."

My mother is coming along as a chaperone. She jumped at the chance when she heard Mr. Elton needed a couple of extras.

"We'd better get going," I tell her a few minutes later, anxiously checking the clock on the wall. "Mr. Elton said for us to be there at five o'clock on the dot."

Our group's director has arranged a tour of Juilliard for us this afternoon, so we need to leave Concord early to get there by lunchtime.

"In a minute, honey," she replies, sipping her coffee.

"Why don't you go brush your teeth?" my father suggests.

"Fine," I tell them, dashing upstairs and returning shortly with my suitcase. "Can we go now?"

"Sure," says my father. He turns to my mother. "You get your things, Shannon—I'll do the breakfast dishes." He stands up and stretches, then starts clearing the table. As I tap my foot impatiently, there's a knock at the back door.

"Would you get that, Jess?" my mother asks. "It's probably Josh."

I open the door, expecting to see our farmhand, but to my complete surprise, it's Darcy who's standing on the doorstep.

"Someone order a limo?" he asks, grinning at me.

"We figured you wouldn't mind if Darcy gave you a ride this morning," my father tells me. "I'll bring your mother along shortly." He gives me a hug. "Break a leg, honey. I wish I could be there to hear you too."

My little brothers have a big swim meet tomorrow, and he has to drive them out to Springfield for it. My parents are in what they call divide and conquer mode this weekend.

Darcy picks up my suitcase and I follow him outside. He puts it in the trunk, then opens the passenger door for me.

"Such a gentleman," I tease.

"Only the best for my favorite diva."

The drive from Half Moon Farm to Colonial Academy is a short one, but Darcy manages to make it seem longer by driving super slow. I tell him all about my meeting with the Community Justice Board, and he tells me all about his hockey game.

Eventually, though, even with him driving about five miles per hour, we reach the gates of Colonial Academy.

"Nice ride," he says, peering at the luxury bus idling on the street ahead.

"Yeah, well, I guess Colonial is sending us off in style."

I start to get out, and Darcy grabs my sleeve.

"Wait," he says, leaning over and kissing me. "I hope you have a great trip. I know you're going to do well." He reaches into his jacket pocket and takes out an envelope. "Read this right before your solo, okay?"

"Sure."

Heather Vogel Frederick

"No peeking beforehand."

I promise him I won't, and he passes it to me. The envelope is thick; there's something besides just a note inside. My curiosity is piqued, but I obediently tuck it into my backpack for later.

"I'd better go," I tell him. My parents beat us here, and I can see my mother talking to Mr. Elton, who keeps glancing at his watch.

"Keep me posted?" asks Darcy.

I nod, and he kisses me again, then gives my braid a tug. "For good luck," he tells me. "Not that you need it—you've worked hard for this, Jess."

He carries my suitcase to the bus for me and I climb aboard and slide into the seat beside Savannah. Darcy stands there on the sidewalk waving as we pull away.

"Who's that?" I hear Dinah Robertson, an alto who's sitting behind me, whisper to Adele.

"Her boyfriend," Adele whispers back.

"Lucky Jess."

Uh-huh, I think, smiling to myself. *You've got that right*.

The bus ride is long and boring—just highway and more highway. Savannah and I sleep through most of the first half of it, then play cards and talk with our friends and practice our competition pieces for the rest.

"Sounding good, girls!" my mother calls from the front of the bus.

Shortly before lunchtime we spot the city on the horizon. I don't come to New York very often, and I always forget how huge the skyscrapers are and how small they can make a person feel. I stay glued to the window, gawking as we head up the Henry Hudson Parkway into Manhattan. A few minutes later we cut over onto Broadway, then turn onto 65th Street, pulling up in front of a modern glass-and-concrete building with a sign over the entrance: THE JUILLIARD SCHOOL.

"Wow," I say.

"Look at this location!" echoes Savannah, who's been to New York a lot more often than I have. "Lincoln Center is right around the corner. And the Metropolitan Opera, too!"

We pile out of the bus and follow our choir director inside. Mr. Elton leads us to our first stop, lunch in the dining hall, which is like an upscale cafeteria. Then we meet up with a tour guide from the admissions department who shows us the rest of the campus—the dance and music and drama centers, the library, the concert halls.

"This place is amazing," I whisper to my mother, who's traded in her usual farm mom look for black pants and turtleneck, black leather boots, and a floral-patterned spring raincoat. She looks really pretty. "No kidding," she whispers back.

As we walk around, something inside of me stirs to life. *I can picture myself going here.* The realization comes as a bit of a shock—I've always thought I wanted one of those traditional New England–style college campuses out in the countryside somewhere. New York is a City with a capital *C*. It's about as far away from a farm as you can get. The whole place pulses and thrums with activity, and being here feels like having a bucket of cold water poured over my head.

Heather Vogel Frederick

I love it.

Our last stop is the admissions office, where we're told more about the classes that are offered. I didn't realize that Julliard has a liberal arts program, too. For some reason I always thought you'd just study music or dance or drama at the conservatory and nothing else. They even have something called a Scholastic Distinction honors program that sounds like it's right up my alley. I feel a tingle of excitement as we're all handed brochures. I can't wait to show mine to Emma and Darcy.

We pile back on the bus for the short ride to the youth hostel near NYU where we're staying. Savannah and Adele and I are sharing a room; our fellow MadriGals are in a trio of others nearby. Mr. Elton and our chaperones are down the hall.

The students from the other schools start to arrive as we're getting settled. Nationals is a big deal, and we're competing against finalists from six other regions—the Great Lakes, Northwest, Mid-Atlantic, Midwest, South, and Southwest. The hostel fills up quickly, and the halls are soon buzzing with activity.

"We've drawn last place for tomorrow," Mr. Elton tells us a little while later when we meet him downstairs in the common room. "The drawback is that you'll have to sit through all the other performances before you sing, but the advantage is that you'll be the final group to leave an impression on the judges."

We troop over to one of the practice rooms at NYU to run through our pieces. We'll be singing two: a traditional nocturne called "Radiant

Stars, Above the Mountains Glowing" that Mr. Elton chose to showcase our voices in the pure a capella form. For our second number we're cranking it up a bit with Aretha Franklin's "I Say a Little Prayer," which will allow us to show our range and add a little "flash and sparkle," as Mr. Elton likes to call it. Dinah will even be doing some beat-boxing. This second one is the arrangement with a couple of breakout solos, when I'll be standing on my own in the spotlight. I've already got butterflies thinking about it.

By the time we get back to the hostel, it's time for Savannah and Adele and me to change for dinner. We're heading to some swanky hotel on Central Park where Savannah's parents are staying.

"Too fancy?" I ask, eyeing myself in the mirror a short time later.

Savannah gives my dress—a pale blue Wong original I borrowed from Megan—the once-over. "Nope," she replies. "It's perfect. Besides, nothing's too fancy for New York."

"I look like a cupcake," moans Adele, nudging me aside and tugging unhappily at the neckline of her white dress. "I knew I should have brought the red one!"

"You do not look like a cupcake," I assure her. "I love the ruffles—they're adorable."

"Not exactly the look I was going for," she mutters.

"Adele, you look adorable!" my mother exclaims when we meet her downstairs in the common room. "You're just as pretty as a cupcake."

Savannah and I dissolve into giggles, and Adele shoots us a look.

Dinner is magical. A taxi whisks the four of us across Central Park to the Sinclairs' hotel, where they've booked us a big table in the restaurant off the lobby. It's filled with glittering chandeliers and white linen tablecloths and helpful waiters who fall all over themselves once they find out that Savannah's father is a senator.

We're looking over the menus when one of the other customers sidles up to our table. "Larissa LaRue?" she asks my mother in a low voice. "From *HeartBeats*?"

My mother smiles up at her. "Let's just say maybe in a former life."

"I knew it was you!" the woman crows. "May I have your autograph?"

This pretty much never happens in Concord, mostly because my mother has been off the show for nearly five years, plus she's usually wearing farm clothes when she runs into town to do errands. I can tell she's a little thrilled to be recognized.

Adele is wide-eyed watching this exchange. "I didn't know you were a celebrity, Mrs. Delaney," she says when the woman returns to her table.

My mother laughs. "Hardly a celebrity," she replies. "I used to be on a soap opera, that's all. Senator Sinclair is the real celebrity at our table."

"It's good for him to have a little competition," says Mrs. Sinclair. "We don't want you getting a swelled head, now do we, Robert?"

Savannah's father reaches up and pats his silver hair, pretending to be concerned. "Heaven forbid," he says solemnly. "Especially if it outgrows what's left of my hair."

The waiter takes our order, and then Mrs. Sinclair asks us about Juilliard.

"It was amazing," Savannah tells her. "I just wish they had a law school."

"Chip off the old block!" crows her father. He turns to her mother. "What did I tell you, Poppy? She's hooked!"

Savannah and I launch into a blow-by-blow description of my CJB hearing, and then Adele helps us fill Mr. and Mrs. Sinclair in on our Juilliard tour and the other a cappella groups we've met so far.

"All I can say is, I heard the MadriGals in the practice room this afternoon, and I don't think anyone else stands a chance," my mother says when we're done.

"Doesn't surprise me in the least," says Senator Sinclair, beaming at my friends and me. "Not with the amount of talent at this table."

Later, as we're waiting outside for our taxi to pull up, my mother turns to the Sinclairs. "I can't thank you enough for such a lovely evening."

"The pleasure was all ours, wasn't it, Poppy?" Savannah's father replies, slipping his arm around Mrs. Sinclair's waist.

"Absolutely," says Savannah's mother. She tries to talk Savannah into staying at the hotel with them, but Savannah wants to go back with us, of course. There's a party at the hostel tonight, and she doesn't want to miss it.

My mother kisses us all good night outside her room. "Don't stay up too late, girls," she tells us. "You need your beauty rest, and so do your voices."

Of course we ignore her. It's just too much fun to be in a big city with a bunch of friends, and with new people to meet from so many other places. We change back into our jeans and casual clothes and head downstairs to the common room. It's noisy and crowded, definitely not my usual scene, but Savannah and Adele pull me into the room before I can protest. We each grab a soda and go to look for the other MadriGals.

We find them in a far corner of the room, talking to an all-guys a capella group from Cincinnati. They're really funny, and we clown around and flirt a little—well, Savannah and Adele flirt. I'm not good at it, for one thing, and for another, I'm just not interested. We end up jamming a little with them on a few songs we all know like "Sweet Home Alabama" and "Stand By Me," then segue into Broadway tunes. People around us start to join in, and pretty soon the whole common room is having a spontaneous sing-along.

"Whew," says Savannah, collapsing on the sofa beside me after the last notes of a jazzed-up "Tomorrow" from *Annie* fade away. "That was awesome!"

Adele yawns. "Yup. And the sun is coming out tomorrow sooner than we think. We'd better get to bed. I'm beat, how about you guys?"

I nod sleepily. It's been an incredibly long day, but I've been having so much fun that I forgot that I've been up since four a.m. It's only now starting to kick in.

My cell phone buzzes as the party starts to break up. I glance at the screen and see that Emma's sent me a picture—a close-up of Stewart. He's standing by Walden Pond, and barely visible in the background is Mrs. Wong, who appears to be handcuffed to a sign. CAMPAIGN PHOTO SHOOT UNDERWAY the text that accompanies it reads. OH WAIT. WAS SOPHIE SUPPOSED TO BE TAKING PICTURES OF MRS. WONG? There's a frowny face, and then: HELP!

I nudge Savannah, who's drifted off.

"Huh?" she says sleepily. I show her the picture and the text and she makes a rude noise.

"Mademoiselle Velcro is at it again," I tell her. "Emma needs our help. Got any bright ideas?"

"Dial 1-800-CASSIDY," she replies.

"Brilliant." I forward the photo to Cassidy, who immediately sends back a one-word text: BARF!

WHAT CAN WE DO TO UNSTICK MADEMOISELLE V? I ask her.

LET ME THINK ABOUT IT, Cassidy replies. I MAY NEED SOME-ONE WHO KNOWS FRENCH.

"That would be me," says Savannah after I relay the message. "Thanks to Mademoiselle Estelle. And Mademoiselle Juliette, and Mademoiselle Hélène. My French nannies when I was little."

I used to think stuff like this was obnoxious, but it's just Savannah. She had nannies the way Half Moon Farm has goats.

"Great," I tell her. Between Cassidy's genius for pranks and Savannah's foreign language skills, we can't lose, right?

No time to think about it now, though. Now we need to focus on MadriGals. Adele herds us upstairs to our room. I don't even want to know what time it is. We set our alarm for seven; Mr.

Elton wants us downstairs at eight sharp.

By eight fifteen, my mother is knocking on our door. "Girls!" she calls. "What's going on? Where are you? Breakfast is almost over!"

We overslept! The three of us throw sweatpants and hoodies over our pajamas and race downstairs to the hostel's cafeteria. We have just enough time to slam down a bowl of cereal, then shower and dress, before it's time to head over to the concert hall at NYU.

"Listen and learn, girls," Mr. Elton tells us as we slide into a row of seats marked MADRIGALS/CONCORD ACADEMY. "This weekend is as much an educational experience as it is a competition."

The morning passes quickly. The other groups are fabulous, of course—only the cream of the crop makes it to Nationals each year. I try and ignore the butterflies in my stomach—which seem to have traded in yesterday's soft wings for jumbo jet propellers—and lose myself in the music instead. I tear up at some songs, laugh at others, and leap to my feet and cheer after one or two. My mother is wrong. No way is this competition a slam dunk. Before I know it, Mr. Elton is leaning over and whispering that it's time to head to the practice room for our warm-up.

My mother leads us through some physical exercises she learned as an actress to loosen us up, then we vocalize for a bit with our choral director, and then it's time to go onstage.

The lights are blinding. But then, they always are. My mother says performers never stop feeling nervous in front of an audience; they just learn to channel the anxiety in different ways. I think back to the very first time I was onstage, in *Beauty and the Beast* back in sixth grade. I played the part of Belle, and I thought for a minute I was going to faint, but I focused on the music and pretty soon that was the only thing I was conscious of. I resolve to try and do the same thing now.

As we file onto the risers, I hear Savannah beside me murmuring, "I'm not nervous, I'm excited" over and over to herself. Everybody has their method of coping with stage fright.

Mr. Elton gives us our cue from offstage, and we launch into the first stanza of "Radiant Stars, Above the Mountains Glowing." Its ethereal notes settle over the audience like snowfall, and the auditorium grows still. As we sing, I can practically feel the music rippling out of us, washing our listeners in the pure water of its sound. There are no solos in this one; it's strictly an ensemble piece to show the judges how well our voices blend. We finish to wild applause. I think we nailed it.

"You nailed it," Mr. Elton confirms backstage. "Well done, girls, well done."

This is high praise from Mr. Elton, and we head for the lobby feeling pretty pleased with ourselves. The Sinclairs arranged to have lunch delivered, and we collect our food and take it to one of the tables that have been set up for all of us.

Our competitors are huddled nearby, and although people are still friendly, the mood is a little more subdued, and the boisterous joking around from last night has vanished. Everyone's focused on the competition.

I'm both looking forward to and dreading going back onstage

Heather Vogel Frederick

again. "I Say a Little Prayer" is a bit of a departure for us—we tend to be traditionalists, and Mr. Elton usually picks period pieces and quieter ballads and serious madrigals that we sing in their original languages. This song is bursting with sass and attitude, and it's a real crowd-pleaser when we do it right, the way we did at our Valentine's Day concert at Colonial. We pulled the audience to their feet that night, and had everyone clapping and dancing.

We've also been known to totally lose the beat and miss our cues in rehearsal, in which case the whole thing is a hot mess.

Which one will it be this afternoon? I wonder, setting my sandwich aside. My friends must be feeling the same way, because hardly anyone eats more than a few bites.

"Ten minutes to showtime," Mr. Elton murmurs to us a couple of hours later, after we've sat through another round of performances. We stand up and follow him out of the auditorium.

Showtime—and my solo!

"You're going to be great, honey," my mother tells me in the hallway as we're leaving the practice room a few minutes later after warmups. "Just let the music carry you."

I nod blindly. *You've worked hard,* I tell myself. *You're prepared. No need to be nervous. Remember what Darcy said?*

Darcy! I'd almost forgotten!

"Tell Mr. Elton I'll meet you all backstage," I whisper to my mother, and racing to the nearest ladies' room and the privacy of a stall, I pull the envelope Darcy gave me from my pocket, where I stashed it this morning. Inside, I find a smaller envelope clipped to a big fabric *J*, just like the ones star athletes get to put on their jackets. It's blue and gold, Colonial Academy's school colors. The little envelope clipped to it is addressed "To Jessica Delaney, Varsity Vocalist." Laughing softly to myself, I take out the note inside:

> *Congratulations, you've made the Varsity team! You're going to rock the house! Love, Darcy.*

Love? I clutch the note to my chest, hardly daring to look at it again. I do, though, and sure enough the word is still there. *Love!* My feet barely touch the floor as I float down the hall to where the Madri-Gals are lined up backstage, waiting to go on.

Love, Darcy.

Confidence surges through me. I step out into the bright lights, ready for anything.

Heather Vogel Frederick

CASSIDY

"I have talked, face to face, with what I reverence, with what I delight in . . . I have known you, Mr. Rochester."
—*Jane Eyre*

"Now that," says Coach Larson, "was ice hockey."

She beams at us. We beam back. We're circled around her in the locker room, sweaty and panting, our legs on fire from being pushed past the limit, our throats like sandpaper from all the screaming we just did out there on the ice. We couldn't care less. We just took the state title, earning ourselves a spot at Nationals.

"Hard work, drive, and determination got you here, ladies, and hard work, drive, and determination is what I expect to see at the championships," our coach tells us. "No letting up, okay? Since there are no games this coming week, I've arranged for us to scrimmage with the Alcott High boys' team on Wednesday. You can expect our practice schedule to remain the same between now and Nationals, and I'll be working with each of you to set up individual training regimens for running, weight lifting, and yoga or stretching. Understood?"

We nod vigorously.

She looks around our circle, her eyes bright. "I'm so proud of you all, I could burst," she says. "Now get out of here before I embarrass myself and cry."

Our families are waiting outside, and as we appear they start to chant. "SHAWMUTS! SHAWMUTS!"

Chloe waves her Lady Shawmuts pennant and makes a beeline for me, flinging her arms around my legs. "Dee! Dee!" she squeals. She can't manage "Shawmuts" yet, or even "Cassidy," so she just sticks with her favorite nickname for me whenever the crowd chants for our team.

"Hey, monkey face," I reply, scooping her up with my free arm.

"Don't—" my mother starts to say, then stops herself. It totally bugs her when I call Chloe that, which is why I do it, of course. But today, instead of scolding, she just smiles and hugs me. "Great game, sweetheart." Her voice is kind of raspy. The last period was a nail-biter, as the Lady Shawmuts came from behind and snatched the victory away from the Pilgrims. All the whooping and hollering from our fans practically deafened us.

"Amazing comeback!" adds Stanley. "Proud of you, kid." He gives me a bear hug, then pulls back and does a little touchdown dance. "Can you believe it? Nationals!" I grin. My stepfather looks like a dork, but he doesn't care and neither do I. "I know," I tell him.

"We'd better get going if we're going to make it to our shindig in time," my mother says. Our Wyoming pen pals were due to arrive last night while we were out of town for the state tournament, and the mother-daughter book club is having a big welcome party at Pies &

Heather Vogel Frederick

Prejudice later this afternoon. As I say good-bye to my teammates and gather up my things, I look around for Zach, but there's no sign of him.

"Zach said to tell you he's catching a ride home with Coach Larson," my mother says absently, fishing in her purse. She pulls out her cell phone. "He said it would be easier, since we're going straight to the tea shop."

"Oh." I can hear the disappointment in my voice. Zach gave me a big hug out on the ice, of course—everybody was hugging everybody else—but I was kind of looking forward to dissecting the game with him on the way home. And maybe holding hands in the backseat, too, if truth be told.

Zach's kisses may be a little sloppy, but he's a world-class hand holder. He has really big hands, and they're always warm. They fit mine like a glove.

"I'm e-mailing Courtney to tell her the news," my mother says, tapping out a message on her smartphone. She looks up a moment later and smiles. "She says congratulations, and that she'll call you the minute she's back in the U.S."

My older sister is in Mexico at the moment with her fiancé and his family. This weekend is the beginning of UCLA's spring break, the same as it is for our friends from Gopher Hole. It's kind of stupid that all spring breaks aren't synchronized, in my opinion. It would have been nice to be able to hang out during the day with our Wyoming friends. But instead we'll be in school.

"Too bad Courtney won't be able to make it to Nationals," says my mother, slipping her cell phone back into her purse. "At least the book club will be there to support you."

The National Championships are scheduled the same time as my sister's midterm exams. We knew this might happen if the Lady Shawmuts won State, and it's a bummer, but there's nothing anyone can do about it.

"I'll film the whole thing for Courtney," says Stanley. "Or better yet, I'll ask Jerry Wong to do it. He has that amazing camcorder."

"And maybe Sophie Fairfax would be willing to take some photos, too," says my mother, taking her phone out again to make a note. "I'll ask her at the party this afternoon."

I make a face. Even though I haven't had time to help with the campaign, I still can't help feeling a little left out. Jealous, too. Sophie's photos are really good. The ones that actually have Mrs. Wong in them and not just Stewart Chadwick, that is.

I space out on the drive home, staring at the passing scenery and wishing that Zach had decided to ride with us, and not with Coach Larson. I'm also wishing that Courtney wasn't out of the country right now. I could really use a heart-to-heart. She's the one in the family with all the boyfriend experience—well, recent boyfriend experience. My mother's dates with Stanley don't count, and the last time she dated before that, women wore hoop skirts. Okay, maybe it wasn't that long ago, but still. Courtney's really good at listening and offering advice about my love life.

My love life. If you can call it that. Sheesh. I can't believe I even have

Heather Vogel Frederick

one. Sometimes I wish I didn't—it makes things so complicated. Life used to be a lot simpler. Guys were just friends, and I never used to be interested in romance. And then one day, out of the blue, boom—I was.

I glance at my mother. She's really good at giving me advice about most stuff—school, friends, dealing with my Chicks with Sticks and their parents—but for some reason this whole Tristan and Zach thing just isn't something I feel comfortable discussing with her. Mostly because whenever the subject of guys comes up, her eyes go all misty and she gets that stupid *My baby's growing up!* look on her face, which is enough to make a person want to barf.

There's no way I'm bringing it up to my book club friends—too embarrassing. And Stanley? My stepfather surprises me sometimes. He gives pretty decent advice too, so maybe. . . . As I'm pondering the possibility, he turns around and squishes his cheeks together with the heels of his hands, making his famous rude noise for Chloe, who shrieks with delight and bangs her sippy cup on the arm of her car seat.

Or maybe not, I think.

I could make an appointment with Dr. Weisman, I guess. I try and imagine myself sitting in his office, discussing boy problems.

Nope, that's not going to happen either.

For now I'll just have to tough it out alone until Courtney gets back. I sigh and stare out the window again.

A couple of hours later we pull into Concord. My mother drops Stanley at home, and then she and Chloe and I head over to Pies &

Prejudice. A sign on the door says CLOSED FOR SPECIAL EVENT. Looking through the big front window, I see our friends gathered inside. Winky Parker's face lights up when she spots us. She rushes to the door and flings it open. "Cassidy!" she shouts, launching herself at me.

"Winky!" I shout back. We hug each other, and then both of us start talking at once. Winky's eyes widen as she looks over my shoulder and sees Chloe.

"Omigosh, is that baby Chloe?"

"Not so much of a baby anymore, is she?" my mother replies proudly.

Winky squats down on the sidewalk in front of my little sister. "Hey, Chloe," she says softly, "remember me?"

Chloe sticks her thumb in her mouth and ducks bashfully behind my mother's leg.

"I guess not," says Winky, standing up again.

"Don't worry; the shyness is only temporary," my mother tells her. "You won't be able to pry her away once she's used to you. Now get inside before you freeze to death!"

Winky laughs. "This is practically summer, ma'am. It was five below when we left Laramie yesterday."

As we go inside, my mother grabs my hand and holds it up in the air like a trophy. "Guess who's going to Nationals?"

The room erupts in cheers, and everyone crowds around to congratulate me.

Chloe starts to cry, overwhelmed by all the loud strangers.

Heather Vogel Frederick

"Hey, sweet pea, these are our friends," I tell her, leaning down to pick her up. "You remember Summer and Bailey and Madison and Zoe, don't you? And Winky and all her horsies?" Chloe lifts her head off my shoulder and looks around hopefully, as if maybe a horse is suddenly going to appear in the tea shop. "That's right," I tell her. "We stayed at Winky's dude ranch when you were a baby."

Looking around the room, it seems weird to see all the familiar, and yet not familiar, faces. Everybody looks the same, and at the same time they're different—more grown-up. Summer and Madison especially. Madison's face isn't as round as it was last time I saw her—what did she tell us her father used to call it? The Daniels' moon face? Her cheekbones have emerged and she looks a lot more like her mother now. Well, except for the mane of corkscrew curls.

"Cool hair," I tell her. "Just right for a rocker chick."

She grins. "Thanks."

"Speaking of chicks, wait until yours hear the news about Nationals!" Emma says, swooping in to give me a hug. "They already worship you—now they'll think you're a goddess."

"Doesn't everyone?" I reply with a grin, and she smacks me on the shoulder.

We mill around for a while, talking, as we wait for Jess and her mom and Savannah to arrive. They're still not back from New York yet. Savannah is an honorary book club member this week, since she stayed at Gopher Creek Guest Ranch in Wyoming when we were there and got to know our pen pals, too. She and Jess even got permission from Colonial Academy to sleep at Half Moon Farm all week, so they can spend more time with Madison and her mother. Our Wyoming friends are going to be staying with their respective pen pals, which means Winky and her mother are staying with us.

"Has anybody heard how the MadriGals did?" I ask Emma.

Emma shakes her head. "Jess texted a while ago, and said she'd tell us when they get here. I don't know if that's a good thing or a bad thing."

"Did you ask your brother? She probably told him."

Emma's forehead puckers, and I suddenly wonder if I've said something wrong. Would Emma be hurt if Jess confided in Darcy and not in her? That's another way romance complicates your life—you suddenly have to worry about juggling everybody's feelings.

A few minutes later the bell over the door jangles and Jess and Savannah walk in. They're both holding up two fingers, and I glance over at Sophie because at first I think they're giving us the "V for Velcro" sign. Then I spot Mrs. Delaney right behind them, holding up a silver trophy.

"We took second place!" Jess cries, and the tea shop erupts in another round of cheers.

"Woohoo!" I shout. "Way to go, MadriGals!"

"You should have heard them," Mrs. Delaney boasts. "They were fabulous."

"And Jess knocked her solo out of the park," adds Savannah, which is nice of her, since I know she was disappointed not to get picked for

Heather Vogel Frederick

one. Savannah's come a long way since the days when we used to call her Julia Pendleton, after the snotty queen bee in *Daddy-Long-Legs*.

"Did anyone record the performance?" asks Madison's mother. "I'd love to hear it."

Mrs. Delaney nods. "They'll be releasing a CD of all the songs in a few weeks. I'll make sure you get one."

The other mothers all instantly raise their hands, and Mrs. Delaney laughs. "Okay, okay, you'll all get one, I promise."

"Everyone find a seat," says Gigi. "We have so much to celebrate!"

A bunch of tables have been pushed together to make one long one, and all along its length there are bouquets of flowers and tiered plates piled high with sandwiches and goodies. I plop Chloe in her high chair, then circle the table with everyone else, looking for my place card.

"What, no uniform?" I ask Becca as I squeeze past her.

She grins. "Sorry to disappoint you. I'm off the hook today. Just another customer, for once."

I find my spot and slide in between Winky and Jess.

"Have you come up with any ideas?" Jess whispers. "Helping Emma, I mean."

I glance down the table to where Sophie is sitting between Gigi and Zoe Winchester. "Yep," I reply. "I'm all over it."

Not that I have a plan, but one will bubble up. It always does.

Across from us, Mrs. Hawthorne checks her watch. "We need to keep an eye on the clock here, ladies. It's almost time to call the Berkeleys."

My stomach gives a little lurch at this. In all the excitement, I'd almost forgotten about our video conference. Simon and Tristan have been in Yorkshire all week on their spring break, and Simon's been working on a movie about the Brontës for us. Since our Wyoming friends are in town, we wanted them to see it, and this afternoon is the only time the Berkeleys are available. They're heading back to school this week, which seems lame. Everybody's school vacations really should coordinate.

"Do we have time to eat first?" asks Gigi, emerging from the kitchen with a teapot in each hand. She looks a little worried. "The tea is hot."

"There's always time for tea," says Mrs. Hawthorne.

After our teacups are all filled, Mrs. Wong rises to her feet. "I'd like to propose a toast," she says. "To good books and good friends!"

"To good books and good friends!" we all echo, raising our teacups in the air.

I reach for a sandwich. "I'm starving. Let's eat."

"Cassidy! Where are your manners!" My mother heaves a sigh. "Some things never change, do they?"

"Be glad of it," Winky's mother tells her. "So many other things do. They're growing up so quickly!"

Uh-oh, I think, bracing myself for the misty-eyes-and-proud-motherly-glances routine. Winky catches my eye and makes a face, and I nearly spew tea all over the table trying not to laugh. She's familiar with it too, apparently.

Heather Vogel Frederick

"So what have you all done since you arrived last night?" Mrs. Delaney asks our Wyoming friends.

Everybody starts talking at once.

"I don't know about anybody else, but all I did was sleep," Madison replies.

"Our flight was delayed leaving Laramie—" her mother begins.

"Thanks to the stupid weather—" Winky continues.

"—and we missed our connection in Chicago," Bailey finishes.

"We almost had to spend the night in the airport, but at the last minute we were able to catch a red-eye to Boston," Mrs. Winchester explains.

"Jerry Wong picked us all up this morning," Mrs. Jacobs adds. "He rented a bus."

"Mrs. Hawthorne made breakfast for everybody—" Summer chimes in.

"—actually that was Nick," says Mrs. Hawthorne, who is a great librarian but hopeless in the kitchen. I'm a better cook than she is, which isn't saying much.

"—and it was fabulous, and then we went for a walk," adds Winky.

"Except for some of us, who took naps instead," says Madison, yawning.

Mrs. Delaney laughs. "Got it. I think."

"We'll make sure you get well rested tonight," Mrs. Hawthorne says. "We've got a busy week planned for you all."

My cell phone vibrates in the pocket of my jeans, and I fish it out. It's a text from Zach.

GREAT GAME TODAY! SORRY I DIDN'T GET TO SAY GOOD-BYE. CALL ME LATER?

THANKS, I text back. U BET.

Emma's mother checks her watch again, and my stomach goes into its little tap dance routine. *Only a few more minutes until I see Tristan!* Quick as a slap shot, this thought is followed by a stab of guilt. Technically, I already have a boyfriend, and his name isn't Tristan, it's Zach Norton. So why am I feeling so excited right now?

Mrs. Wong and Mrs. Chadwick stand up. "Lily and I have a couple of announcements before we call the Berkeleys," Mrs. Chadwick says as Mrs. Wong starts distributing manila envelopes to our Wyoming friends. "We've worked up an itinerary for the week. You'll find everything inside your packet."

I flick a scone crumb at Megan, who looks over and smiles sheepishly. We like to tease her about her mother's love affair with packets.

"You'll also find maps, brochures for all of Concord's attractions, a list of important phone numbers and addresses, and some coupons for local businesses," Mrs. Wong continues. "Calliope and I have worked hard to balance educational activities with—"

"Shopping!" says Megan in a stage whisper.

"—yes, among other things," concludes her mother, looking a little annoyed.

"You'll also find a daily schedule," adds Mrs. Chadwick, consulting

Heather Vogel Frederick

her clipboard. I crane my neck to peer over Winky's shoulder as she rummages through her folder and pulls out a piece of paper. I'm curious to see what's planned. In a way, I'm not that sorry that we have school every day except Friday this week—Friday is one of those teacher in-service days—because I have no interest in visiting every historical monument on the Eastern Seaboard. Which is pretty much what Mrs. Wong and Mrs. Chadwick have planned, from the looks of it.

"Monday and Tuesday you'll be here in Concord," says Mrs. Chadwick, "visiting Walden Pond and the Old North Bridge and all the famous homes including—"

"Orchard House!" squeals Bailey, spotting it on the page.

Mrs. Chadwick nods. "You're going there tomorrow morning, because we figured you'd want to see it first thing."

"You figured right," says Bailey's mother. She owns a bookstore and is Mrs. Hawthorne's best friend.

Orchard House is one of our town's most famous tourist attractions. It's where Louisa May Alcott lived when she wrote *Little Women,* and I've been there twice already, once with the book club and once on a school field trip, which is more than enough to last me a lifetime. It's interesting and everything, but it would be more interesting if Louisa had played pro hockey instead of just being a writer. Too bad Cammi Granato didn't grow up in Concord. I'd pay good money to go see her house.

"Tomorrow night we'll have dinner at the Wongs', followed by our official joint book club meeting—"

"Isn't that what we're doing right now?" asks Savannah, looking confused.

Mrs. Hawthorne shakes her head. "This is just a little appetizer to whet your appetite. It's the only time the Berkeleys had available."

"What's this mystery event on Tuesday night, after dinner at Half Moon Farm?" asks Summer, pointing to her schedule.

Mrs. Wong flashes me a glance, then smiles slyly. "You'll just have to wait and see, won't you?"

Emma kicks me under the table. When I first heard that our pen pals were coming, I immediately thought of something I wanted to do with them. They were such good hosts when we visited them in Wyoming, I thought it would be fun to plan something extra special and unique. I ran it by Mrs. Wong and Mrs. Chadwick, who thought it was a great idea. Emma's the only other person who's in on the plan. I haven't even told my mother.

"Wednesday you'll head into Boston and explore the Freedom Trail," continues Mrs. Chadwick, "and that night we'll relax with a movie and games afterward at the Hawthornes. We figured you'd need a break by then, since you'll be pretty pooped from all that walking."

And they'll be pooped from what I have planned for them the night before, I think to myself.

"Thursday is free choice," says Mrs. Wong. "I plan to lead a group back to Boston to tour more historical sites, while others may be interested in staying here in Concord, or in—"

"Shopping!" whispers Megan again.

Heather Vogel Frederick

"Megan Rose!" says her mother, exasperated.

"As you all know," Mrs. Chadwick continues smoothly, "since there's no school for the Concord girls on Friday, that's the day we've chosen to film our *Cooking with Clementine* episode."

Mrs. Parker turns to my mother. "It was so nice of you to arrange that, Clementine! I can't tell you how excited the girls are—heck, how excited we all are. We're really looking forward to seeing what goes on behind the scenes on a TV show."

"You'd be surprised," my mother replies drily.

No kidding, I think. I'm always amazed at the end result. On-screen, my mother looks totally calm and collected, and the kitchen and the food and the house and the garden always look perfect. On filming days, though, it's complete chaos. Furniture is moved and rear-ranged depending on the theme of the episode, decorations are put up and taken down, and the kitchen looks like a hurricane hit it. There are production assistants and cameramen running around and lots of yelling and occasionally even some cussing, especially when Murphy, our dog, gets loose. He about goes hysterical on filming days, trying to patrol and protect everything, so we have to banish him to the garage. He's an escape artist, though.

"Friday night is the debate, of course," Mrs. Chadwick says, and I can't resist, I have to shout "Handcuffs Wong for Mayor!" Everybody laughs except Megan, who gives me a withering look. Apparently, she's still not totally on board with that slogan.

"Which reminds me, Lily, I'd like to schedule a strategy meeting with you and your campaign staff," says Zoe's mother, who used to be mayor of Gopher Hole. "I've got some ideas I'd like to share."

"And then Saturday's our last day together," says Summer mournfully. "This week is going to fly by way too fast."

"But we'll enjoy every minute while you're here," says Gigi, reaching over and giving her a squeeze.

Mrs. Hawthorne glances at her watch again. "Time to call England," she says, and under the table my knee starts bouncing up and down like a jackhammer.

Chill, Sloane, I tell myself sternly. *It's no big deal.*

Mr. Wong set up a laptop and a large flat-screen monitor for us earlier, and Megan goes over and turns it on. Thirty seconds later the Berkeley family is on-screen.

"Hello, Concord!" says Simon.

"Hello, England!" we chorus back.

He and his brother and their parents all wave to us, and we wave back. I think maybe Tristan's waving at me but I can't be sure. I brush at my face, hoping I'm not covered in cookie crumbs or cupcake frosting or something.

"You look fine," whispers Jess.

"Shut up!" I reply, but I'm smiling.

"Hey, Sophie," says Tristan. *"Bonsoir!"*

Sophie, who's been really quiet so far this afternoon, suddenly perks up. *"Bonsoir!"* she replies, looking thrilled to be singled out. I go over their connection in my mind again while they're chatting. What

Heather Vogel Frederick

was it Tristan told me? Second cousins? His mom and her father are related somehow, I'm pretty sure. I watch them surreptitiously, trying to gauge just how cousinly their greeting is.

"How did your game go, Cassidy?" Tristan asks.

I'm so busy thinking about his family tree that his question catches me off guard, and my mother answers before I have a chance to. "They won, which means she's going to Nationals," she tells him.

He gives me a big thumbs up. "Brilliant!"

"Thanks," I reply, feeling suddenly like everybody's staring at me. They're not, but my face goes red anyway. I can't seem to take my eyes off Tristan. With his dark hair and deep blue eyes, he's still the best-looking guy I've ever seen. Not that I'd ever tell him that.

Mrs. Berkeley points at the window behind her. "It's lashing rain outside tonight in true Yorkshire style, as you can see. It's like being inside our own private Brontë novel. We're tucked up snug in Philip's digs here at the university, though, eager to share our latest discoveries with you."

"Digs?" I whisper across the table to Emma.

"Rooms," she whispers back. "Mr. Berkeley's apartment in York."

"We're ready whenever you are," says Mrs. Hawthorne.

"Give me a second here," says Simon, springing up and crossing the room to fiddle with something on the table in front of him. His laptop, probably. Sure enough, a moment later the screen goes dark and the words A DAY IN BRONTË COUNTRY fade in, followed by a shot—obviously taken out the window of a car—of a sign that says HAWORTH, 10 KM AHEAD.

"Oh wow," says Winky, as the camera pans across a stone wall bordering the road to a stunning vista beyond. Sheep and cattle graze in emerald fields, and in the distance the land dips down into a valley, then slopes up again toward an outcropping of gray stone houses clinging to the side of a hill. Overhead, the sky is a patchwork of bright blue amidst dark, ominous clouds. The light is phenomenal.

Dad would love this. The thought pops unexpectedly into my head, and my eyes immediately fill with tears. I look down at my lap for a moment to hide them. My father is the one who gave me my camera and taught me to shoot with it.

"Toto, we're not in Kansas anymore," breathes Summer.

"Nope," I agree.

"We're here today in West Yorkshire, heading to the small town of Haworth," Simon's voice tells us, and blinking back the tears, I look up again as the narration begins. "Nestled between the lush dales and stark moors for which this part of England is famous, Haworth is today as it was then: a rural village set deep in the heart of a wool-producing region. It is also now a tourist destination, thanks to its famous former residents: the Brontë family."

Jess leans over to me. "This is so much better than just plain 'fun facts,'" she whispers, and I nod.

"It's here in Haworth that the three most well-known Brontë sisters—Charlotte, Emily, and Anne—and their brother Branwell,

Heather Vogel Frederick

grew up, and it's here that the girls wrote their famous novels." The scene cuts to a cobblestone street lined with ridiculously picturesque gray stone houses and shops. "We're standing by the Black Bull pub, where brother Branwell spent far too much of his time, and now we're going to walk up High Street, which leads to the parsonage at the top of the hill." Simon's voice gets a little breathless and the camera motion a little choppier. "It's steep, as you can see."

He comes to a stop by a graveyard.

"Note the distinctive gravestones." Tristan is narrating now, and at the sound of his voice I grab my knee to keep it from jiggling. "Flat as tables, they were the perfect place for the village women to spread out their washing to dry, which caused quite a flap in Charlotte's day. Eventually, Mr. Brontë, her father, who was the minister at the church of St. Michael and All Angels"—the camera pans over to a gray stone church—"put a stop to it. We'll give you a tour of the church in a bit, but first let's visit the Brontë home." The camera scans across the graveyard to a square gray house, plain and imposing looking, that's set on a rise beyond. "It was here in this parsonage that the Brontë children grew up. A Georgian structure, it's built of local stone and is today a museum. We'll go inside shortly, but first we want to show you their back garden—or what you Yanks like to call 'backyard.'"

The scene cuts to a broad expanse of grassy moors—near-treeless ground broken up by occasional outcroppings of boulders and lots of stone walls.

"Wow," says Winky again. "It's like the open range back home, but wilder and gloomier, or something."

"This is where the Brontë children spent their childhood, running and playing on the moors." The camera lingers on the rocky landscape, rests beside brooks and waterfalls, then eventually returns to the parsonage. "We've been given special permission to film inside today, thanks to Professor Berkeley"—the camera whisks over to Simon and Tristan's father, who smiles and waves—"who happens to know the curator."

The screen goes black, then fades back in to reveal the interior of a large, stone-floored entryway. An imposing-looking staircase winds to the second story, and an arched window on the landing lets in a chilly light.

Simon is narrating again now. "Some eighty-thousand visitors come through the front door of this parsonage each year, curious to see the house where the Brontës lived and worked. Note the flagstone floors throughout the ground floor."

"Brrr," says my mother.

"There were no carpets or wallpaper until Charlotte became a successful author," Simon continues, "and her father had such a fear of fire that he insisted on no curtains on the windows."

Our first stop is the dining room, where we're shown a portrait of Charlotte over the mantel and then a large table. "And this is where the girls would sit, writing their stories after everyone else had gone to bed."

Heather Vogel Frederick

I glance over at Emma, who is staring at the TV screen, mesmerized. The Brontës' dining room is the only one I've ever seen that has bookcases in it, the way her family's does.

"The kitchen would have been one of the Brontë children's favorite rooms," Simon goes on to tell us as the camera leads us down a passageway.

"Too bad it's not pink," Jess whispers to Emma, whose own kitchen is famously painted that shade. "It would be a lot more cheerful."

Mrs. Hawthorne frowns and puts her finger to her lips.

"It was here, seated by the fire, that their housekeeper Tabby would tell them spooky tales and legends of Yorkshire. Charlotte and her sisters did some writing here, too, as well as cooking and baking."

Next stop is Mr. Brontë's study, where Charlotte's father first read *Jane Eyre*, and then it's time to head upstairs. We see one of the toy soldiers that inspired many of the young Brontës' stories, as well as Charlotte's writing desk. The camera zooms in for a closer look at some of her clothes, which are displayed in a glass case. There's a parasol, a bonnet, shoes, a lace-edged shawl, and a dress.

"Blue-sprigged muslin," murmurs Megan. "And look at how tiny she was!"

"It reminds me a little of the Jane Austen museum in Bath," Emma replies.

"Shhhh!" says Mrs. Hawthorne, frowning again.

Tristan chimes in once or twice, narrating events in what he calls "the family's creative but tragic lives," but for the most part this is Simon's baby. The video lasts about ten minutes, and everyone applauds enthusiastically when it's over. Winky and I whistle loudly.

"Unforgettable," says Mrs. Delaney. "Boys, you've outdone yourselves."

"Take a bow," says Mrs. Wong, and they do.

"I thought the lads did quite well, didn't they?" agrees Mrs. Berkeley. She looks pleased at our response, and so do Tristan and Simon.

"Chips off the old block," says their father. "Got all the best historical bits in."

"I'm going to submit it for credit at school," Simon tells us. Or tells Megan, because he's looking directly at her.

"I'm sure you'll get an A," says Mrs. Hawthorne. "Or 'full marks' as you say over there, right?"

"I miss England!" Emma sighs. "I wish I was there right now!"

"Me too," says her mother.

Me three, I think silently, my eyes sliding over to Tristan. The corners of his lips quirk up in a smile; he's definitely looking back at me now.

"Yorkshire is a far cry from Chawton, isn't it?" says Mrs. Berkeley.

Tristan and I lock eyes. Chawton is the last place where the two of us were together—and where we shared a kiss. *A very memorable kiss*, I think, turning bright red again.

Jess's mother nods. "Totally different vibe. Chawton is beautiful, but this is less manicured and, for me, more soul stirring. All those dark clouds brooding over the wild countryside!"

Heather Vogel Frederick

I know exactly how she feels. It's the kind of place that makes me want to reach for my camera. The kind of place my dad would have loved.

"Mom, that's so poetic," says Jess.

"Why thank you, darling."

"Do you girls have any questions for the Berkeleys?" asks Mrs. Hawthorne.

I risk another peek at Tristan. *If you were here, would you kiss me again?* Is it my imagination, or is his face a little flushed, too? I look away. I really have to stop this—it's getting ridiculous.

Across the table, Emma's hand shoots up.

"EMMA!" we all shout.

She grins and shrugs.

"So how can we help you, ma'am?" asks Simon in his best fake American accent.

"When we visited Haworth last year, we took a walking tour to Top Withens, the house that Emily Brontë turned into *Wuthering Heights* for her novel. Did you get a chance to hike there, too?"

"Alas, we did not," says Mrs. Berkeley. "We didn't quite have time to venture that far on this visit. But we'd like to go back; we all really loved the village and the setting. It's very romantic, isn't it, boys?"

They nod. I notice Simon and Megan staring at each other, and Megan's a little pink, too. It must be catching.

"I suppose we should let you get going," says Mrs. Hawthorne finally. "I'm sure you have to be up bright and early to catch the train home."

"Well, not so bright and early," Mrs. Berkeley replies. "The boys don't go back to school until Tuesday, so we can take our time getting back to Bath." She looks over at Sophie. "Which reminds me, Annabelle sends her love. She misses you, Sophie! She'd been hoping to see you while she's in France for the skating competition, but she's planning to visit with your grandfather at least."

Sophie brightens at this. I, on the other hand, do not. Stinkerbelle is Tristan's ice dancing partner. She spends far too much time glued to him, in my opinion.

"This has been great fun, hasn't it?" says Mrs. Hawthorne. "We'll have to do it again soon."

"Until next time, then!" says Mrs. Berkeley, and we all wave good-bye. I'm tempted to blow Tristan a kiss, but I don't, of course, because that would be incredibly lame and incredibly embarrassing and I'd never live it down.

Besides, Megan may be seeing Simon soon in Paris, but my chances of seeing Tristan again, if ever, are pretty much zero. It's really time to stop thinking about him. I've got more important things to think about, like going to the National Championships. I already have a boyfriend, and Tristan and I are just friends, that's all. Well, okay, friends who shared a kiss. An amazing kiss on an amazing summer evening in an amazing garden in England.

"Huh?" I say, realizing that Winky is looking at me strangely.

"I said, pass me your plate," she repeats.

"Oh, okay." *Man, I need to snap out of this.* Pushing thoughts of

Heather Vogel Frederick

a certain ice dancer out of my head, I stand up to help clear the table.

"Would you take care of Chloe, please?" my mother asks me. "I need to talk to Phoebe for a minute about tomorrow."

I turn to see that my little sister is sound asleep in her high chair with her cheek resting on a half-eaten gingerbread muffin.

"Can I carry her?" Winky begs.

"Sure," I reply, passing her Chloe's limp form.

"Looks like somebody had a good time this afternoon," says Mrs. Parker as she and Winky follow me outside to the car. I transfer their luggage from Mrs. Wong's sedan to the back of our minivan while Winky deposits Chloe in her car seat.

"Wyoming contingent and Concord moms, rendezvous here at the tea shop tomorrow morning at eight thirty sharp!" calls Mrs. Chadwick, as the pen pals start pairing off and heading for their various cars. I flash the "V for Velcro" sign at Jess and Savannah as they get into the Delaney's minivan with Madison and her mother. I need to start thinking up a prank.

Back home, Stanley is waiting to greet Winky and her mother. We all sit in the living room talking for a little while, then Winky asks for a tour of our house.

"Oh, me too, please," says her mother. "I've seen it so often on TV, it's a bit surreal to be here in person."

My mother laughs. "I can't promise it's as clean as it looks on TV, but sure—Cassidy, do you want to do the honors while I put Chloe to bed?"

Winky and her mother ooh and aah as I take them around, which strikes me as funny, because I think where they live is much cooler than our old Victorian. Not that I don't think our house is special—it is. But still, it's just a house, not a dude ranch.

"You still have the rocking horse!" says Winky, when I show them Chloe's room.

"Duh," I reply. "It's her favorite thing ever." The Wyoming book club sent two presents for Chloe's baby shower: a rocking horse with a real leather saddle, and a quilt for her crib that Summer Williams made. I show them the quilt, too, and then lead them up to the third floor.

The turret is Winky's favorite spot, of course. It's always everybody's favorite spot.

"If I had a room like this at our house, I'd never leave," she says, settling on the window seat with a happy sigh and gazing down out at the yard and street below.

"I'll bet you spend a lot of time up here, don't you?" her mother asks, and I nod.

"It's kind of turned into an unofficial book club clubhouse—and jailhouse, too," I reply with a grin. I tell them about the mix-up with the Secret Santa gifts last Christmas, and how we got sent up here on New Year's Eve to untangle the big mess of hurt feelings that caused.

As Mrs. Parker heads back downstairs to unpack and get settled in Courtney's room, which doubles as our guest room when she's away at school, I'm tempted for a moment to tell Winky about Zach and Tristan, and how mixed up I feel. In the end, though, I decide not to.

Heather Vogel Frederick

We hang out in the turret for a little while, talking about other things, and then we head for my room.

"I went ahead and set up the air mattress for you, Winky," my stepfather tells her, poking his head in the door. "Hope you'll be comfortable on it."

"Oh sure, we have one just like it at home."

Stanley leaves and Winky circles the room slowly, looking at all my trophies and team photos and stuff. I still have my Cammi Granato poster on the wall—she's my personal hero—but I gave the one of Henrik Lundqvist, the New York Rangers' goalie, to Courtney as a joke gift when she left for college. I told her she was in here all the time looking at it anyway, so she might as well have it to keep.

"It's funny, our rooms are alike in so many ways," Winky tells me. "I mean, I have all my rodeo trophies and stuff on display, and you have all your hockey stuff."

Winky is a two-time rodeo princess for Albany County, Wyoming, which I used to think was a joke until I found out what was involved in winning that title. She's as much an athlete as I am.

Since we had tea so late, dinner is just soup and salad. While Mrs. Parker lingers in the kitchen talking to my mother and Stanley, Winky and I go back upstairs to my room, where I try and finish up a little homework.

"I can't believe you're reading that," she says as I pull *The Scarlet Letter* out of my backpack. She reaches into her suitcase and holds up an identical copy, and we both laugh.

"Savannah and Jess are reading it at Colonial Academy, too," I tell her.

"What do you think of it?"

"I hate it."

"So do I. How about *Jane Eyre?*"

I give her a thumbs up. "Best book we've read so far in book club."

"Really? I like it a lot, but maybe not that much."

"What are you talking about? Jane is awesome!" I protest. "You've gotta love her independence."

"Oh sure, I like Jane herself well enough. It's just that whole section with St. John Rivers that makes me want to throw the book across the room."

"I haven't gotten there yet," I admit. "I'll let you know if I feel the same way."

We're still debating the book's finer points when my mother and Mrs. Parker come upstairs to say good night.

"I never thought I'd walk into this room and interrupt a literary discussion," says my mother, smiling at us.

Mrs. Parker picks up my copy of *The Scarlet Letter.* "Winky's reading this one, too."

"We were just talking about that!"

"Really?" says my mother. "I had to read it back when I was in high school as well. Can't say that I liked it that much."

"I loathed it," says Mrs. Parker with a shudder.

"So if everybody hates it and they have for ages and ages, why do

Heather Vogel Frederick

they keep torturing high school students with it?" asks Winky.

"Good question," her mother replies. "You can talk about that some more in the morning—please try and get to sleep now. Big day tomorrow."

After they leave, we turn out the light obediently. Two seconds later I sit up and switch it on again. "I just figured out my plan," I announce.

"What plan?" asks Winky.

I explain about Sophie and Stewart, and how Jess and Savannah asked me to come up with a prank that will help un-Velcro the French girl from Emma's boyfriend.

"So what's your bright idea?"

"It's not mine, it's Nathaniel Hawthorne's," I reply, outlining what I have in mind.

Winky squeals with delight when I'm done. "Omigosh, that's *brilliant*, as your English friends would say! Can I help?"

I reach over and turn the light off again. "Definitely," I tell her, and the two of us lie there in the dark brainstorming until we fall asleep.

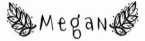 Megan

"I dreamt of Miss Ingram all the night: in a vivid morning dream I saw her closing the gates of Thornfield against me and pointing out another road . . ."
—Jane Eyre

"I can't believe you have your own sewing room!" Summer looks around enviously at the shelves stacked with brightly colored fabric and supplies. "This is so cool!"

I shrug. I guess she's right, but I've had it since sixth grade, so it just feels normal to me.

"I mean, you remember our house in Laramie, how small it is and everything," Summer continues. "My mother used to call herself the old woman who lived in a shoe! It's not so bad now that Andy's off to college along with Ellie and Tessa, but there are still five of us squeezed in under our roof. I can't imagine what it would be like to have a room of my own. I've always had to share with my sisters, you know? Not that I'm complaining or anything. Or envious." Embarrassed, her voice trails off.

Summer talks a lot. I don't mind, though, and the funny thing is, I used to be envious of her! I used to hate being an only child, and I desperately wanted brothers and sisters. She has half a dozen of them. Getting Coco was an improvement, but then I got saddled with Sophie Fairfax, and she's not exactly what I had in mind in terms of a bigger family. Especially since Coco is now her fuzzy little shadow.

"I'm glad your mom is here," I tell Summer, changing the subject. Summer's parents are divorced, and Mrs. Williams single-handedly runs a diner in Laramie called the Cup and Saucer. It's difficult for her to get away from work, and she wasn't sure until the last minute whether she'd be able to come along to Concord or not.

Summer nods, her gaze wandering over to the bulletin board above my sewing table. She points to one of the pictures pinned to it, a black-and-white shot Cassidy took about a year ago. "So tell me about this Simon guy."

My lips quirk up in a smile, as they always do whenever anyone mentions Simon. "Um, what do you want to know?"

"You know, what he's like, that sort of thing."

I consider the question. How to describe Simon? "Well, he's really nice," I say cautiously.

"Duh, of course he's nice," says Summer, "otherwise you wouldn't be dating him. But what's he like?"

I cast around for words and then, in a flash of inspiration, I start grabbing bolts of fabric from the shelves. I toss some midnight-blue corduroy down on the table first. "This is his voice," I tell Summer, taking her hand and running it over the soft ridges and grooves.

"Ooo," she says. "I like his voice."

"Yeah, me too. And this," I continue, reaching for a warm-brown woolen tweed, "is his eyes." Glancing up at her I add, "They're almost the same shade as yours, actually."

Summer smiles.

I fish a skein of buttery mohair yarn from a basket on the floor to represent Simon's curly blond hair, then ponder what to choose next. Aha! The cheerful cotton print I used for my latest Bébé Soleil creation catches my eye. Bébé Soleil is a French company that carries a few of my baby and toddler designs. My grandmother's the one responsible for that—she sneaked an outfit I made for Maggie Crandall into her suitcase a few years ago when she went to Paris for Fashion Week, and all of a sudden I had a job. It's still kind of mind-boggling, but fun—and they pay me, too, so my college fund is fattening nicely.

I reach for the bolt of fabric and hold up a length of it. "This is his smile," I tell my friend, showing off the sunny yellow-and-orange mini-paisley pattern.

"I wish I had a Simon." Summer sighs.

"Do you have a boyfriend?" The two of us didn't get much of a chance to talk after the party yesterday. Sunday night is reserved for *Project Catwalk* around here. It's Gigi's and my favorite reality TV show—we love to see what the fashion designers whip up each week. My parents aren't into it, of course, so it's become a weekly tradition for that to be their date night, while Gigi and I order takeout and hole up in her apartment downstairs. Of course, now that Sophie is here, our cozy twosome has become a threesome. Mademoiselle Velcro sticks to my grandmother the same way she sticks to Stewart Chadwick. I barely ever get time alone with Gigi anymore, or with my mother.

Summer joined us last night while my parents took her mother out to dinner. Her family doesn't have cable, so she's never watched the show. She was completely enthralled, which Sophie seemed to find amusing. She spent nearly as much time watching Summer as she did watching the show. My guess is she's pegged her for a hick. Or a dork. Or both.

Summer's hostess gifts didn't help matters. I was expecting another quilt, but instead it turns out she'd knitted us all matching sweaters. Kitschy sweaters with my mother's campaign slogan on them, along with an image of a pair of handcuffs. Sophie looked bemused when she opened hers.

"*Merci*," she'd said politely, but I could tell from the expression on her face that there was no way she was ever going to wear it. I put mine on immediately, just to spite her.

"I love it, Summer," I said.

"Me too," said my mother, giving her a hug. "What a thoughtful, unique gift."

I look over at Summer now, who still hasn't answered my question. It seems to have rattled her a bit, because her face is beet red. "Boyfriend? Um, no, not really," she says finally. "I've kind of liked Sam Parker forever, though." She gives me a beseeching look. "Don't tell anyone, okay? Especially not Winky. You know how she loves to tease, plus we go to a small high school. It would be really awkward if word got around."

"Hey, don't worry. I understand awkward, believe me."

Speaking of which, my mother comes in just then, trailing Sophie. Coco is frisking at the French girl's heels, as always. My kitten makes a dive for the basket of yarn, and I reach down to head her off at the pass. Summer beats me to it and scoops her up for a cuddle.

"I thought I heard you two in here," my mother says. "It's almost time for your friends to arrive. Maybe you'd like to give Sophie a hand setting up for our meeting?"

"Yes, ma'am," says Summer, springing to her feet.

Cassidy used to say that Summer Williams was so sweet, it made her teeth hurt. That was before we got to know her, of course. Summer *is* sweet, there's no arguing with that, but nice sweet, not icky sweet. And she's polite and thoughtful and really talented, despite the Handcuffs Wong sweaters. She's a little naive, though, too, the way Jess can sometimes be naive, and over the next half hour I watch as she struggles to engage Sophie in conversation.

It's not that Sophie doesn't respond—she does. But she's kind of monosyllabic, the same way she is with me. My mother and Gigi keep telling me to be patient, that she's a long way from home and going through deep waters blah blah blah. Plus, they remind me that English isn't her native language. From what I've observed, however, Sophie communicates just fine whenever there are boys around.

Summer seems blissfully unaware of any tensions between me and Sophie and chatters on, barely pausing for a response. By the time we're done setting up the buffet and bringing extra chairs into the living room,

Heather Vogel Frederick

she's filled Sophie in on all the details about her family, school, her life in Wyoming, the Cup and Saucer, and her passion for quilting and knitting.

"Oh, and my parents got divorced a few years ago," she adds, "which was really awful for a while, but things are better now."

The minute she says this, Sophie drops all pretense of politeness. Without another word she turns and abruptly leaves the room.

Summer stares after her, dumbfounded. "Was it something I said?" she asks in bewilderment.

"It's not you," I assure her. "It's Sophie. Her parents are getting divorced, too, and it's a really touchy subject. I tried to talk to her about it once and she about bit my head off."

The doorbell rings just then, and Summer runs to answer it.

"*Bonsoir*, girls!" calls Mrs. Chadwick, waltzing in with Zoe and Becca and Mrs. Winchester. "What a day we've all had!"

"It's been wonderful," agrees Bailey's mother, who is right behind her with Mrs. Hawthorne and Bailey and Emma.

Mrs. Williams and my grandmother emerge from the kitchen. They've been in there for the last hour and a half, cooking something that smells delicious.

"I thought I heard voices," says Gigi. "Welcome!"

Two minutes later the rest of our friends arrive and the living room echoes with excited voices. Gigi and my mother and I are wearing our "Handcuffs Wong" sweaters, and it doesn't take people long to notice.

"Where did you GET that?" screeches Cassidy, grabbing my sleeve. "I NEED one!"

I explain about the hostess gift, and pretty soon everyone is lined up in front of Summer.

"I'll be knitting from now until the election," she says, laughing as she writes down all the orders. "Better get started now."

I follow her to my bedroom, where she grabs her knitting needles and I grab my sketchbook. I'm in the mood to draw tonight.

Sophie's door is closed. I can hear her talking to someone in French—it's not Gigi, because my grandmother is back in the living room with our friends. I figure she must be talking to her grandfather again, or maybe one of her parents. What Summer said must have set her off.

Summer pauses as we start to pass her door and knocks softly. Without waiting for a reply, she opens it a crack, just enough to see Sophie motioning angrily at us to shut it again. But not before I spot her open laptop. Sophie's not on the phone; she's videoconferencing.

And the face on-screen is Simon's.

All the air whooshes out of my lungs. Summer doesn't seem to notice; she's too busy apologizing to Sophie and closing the door again. I stand rooted to the spot, trying to catch my breath and figure out why on earth Sophie Fairfax is talking to my boyfriend.

There's got to be a logical explanation, right? But what? They're cousins, true. I have boy cousins in Hong Kong. But it's not like we're best friends. I see them once in a while, that's all. We don't talk on the phone and I don't videoconference with them. At least not by myself.

And then I'm struck by an awful idea: Is Sophie the reason Simon broke up with me last fall? If she is, could she be trying to start things up again?

"Megs, are you okay?" asks Becca as I trail back into the living room behind Summer.

"Yup," I tell her shortly. I'm not in the mood to talk right now, not even to my best friend. I take my sketchbook and retreat to the far side of the room, stretching out on the rug under the grand piano, where my suspicions continue to gnaw at me.

"Dinner is served," Gigi announces a couple of minutes later. "Pies and Prejudice's own vegetarian lasagna, accompanied by Victoria Williams's world-famous Easy Cheesy Garlic Biscuits from the Cup and Saucer!"

"Yum!" says Cassidy, diving for the buffet.

"I don't know if they're world famous," says Summer's mother, looking pleased. "But our customers in Laramie seem to like them."

"Aren't you hungry?" my mother asks a few minutes later, bending down to peer under the piano. She holds out a plate.

I shake my head. "Not right now."

She shrugs and takes the plate over to the sofa, where she starts up a conversation with Savannah and Professor Daniels. I notice Savannah glancing over at me once or twice, but I ignore her. Becca, too.

I draw furiously as the conversation flows. Our Gopher Hole friends are buzzing about everything they saw today in Concord and the neighboring towns. I'm just as glad we were in school and didn't have to go sightseeing with them—I've seen the Old North Bridge plenty of times, and Sleepy Hollow Cemetery and Orchard House and the Lexington Battle Green and all that.

"Did you go skinny-dipping in Walden Pond again, Mrs. Chadwick?" Savannah asks when the talk turns to Henry David Thoreau's cabin.

"Savannah!" squawks Mrs. Chadwick, her pale, robin's-egg-blue eyes blinking behind her glasses.

Savannah grins. "Sorry," she says. "My mother suggested I bring it up."

"Your mother is a wicked, wicked woman," says Mrs. Chadwick, but she's smiling now too.

Savannah's mother and Becca's mother were roommates a long time ago at Colonial Academy. When we were in Wyoming, Mrs. Sinclair told us about some of the things the two of them did back when they were students. Like skinny-dipping at Walden Pond.

Normally, I'd be laughing along with everyone else. But tonight the last thing I feel like doing is laughing.

Sophie eventually emerges from her room and takes a seat beside my grandmother. She doesn't even glance in my direction.

"Let's kick off the official part of our meeting with fun facts," says Mrs. Hawthorne as dessert is served—Mrs. Sloane-Kinkaid's killer brownies, which for the first time ever don't even tempt me. My stomach is as tight as a clenched fist. "Most of tonight's facts were covered in Simon's film yesterday, but I thought perhaps you'd all like to add them to your collection, anyway."

Heather Vogel Frederick

I feel my lip tremble at the mention of Simon's name. Usually it brings a smile to my face, but not this time. Not even Coco, who has wandered over to join me for once and is batting happily at the tip of my drawing pencil, can cheer me up.

"Here you go, Megan," says Mrs. Delaney, passing me a sheet of paper.

FUN FACTS ABOUT CHARLOTTE

1) Charlotte and her brothers and sisters early discovered a love of writing. Spurred in part by their father's gift of a dozen toy soldiers to Branwell, they developed a rich fantasy life around the "Young Men," as they called them, inventing a cast of characters and entire worlds for them to inhabit— worlds with such names as Glass Town, Angria, Verdopolis, and Gondal.

2) Charlotte and her sisters and brothers wrote many stories, and from the age of ten she put them into tiny books, bound by hand, and printed in miniscule handwriting meant to mimic real type. These books still exist today and can be seen at the Brontë Museum in Haworth.

3) Charlotte was prolific, writing novels, plays, stories, and poetry. At fourteen, she made a list of her life's work to date;

it included twenty-two volumes, most of them stories written about Glass Town.

4) Charlotte was ambitious, and at age twenty sent some of her poems to Robert Southey, the poet laureate of England, confiding in him her desire "to be forever known." His response was not encouraging. While he admitted that she possessed "the faculty of Verse," he stated flatly, "Literature cannot be the business of a woman's life: & it ought not to be. The more she is engaged in her proper duties, the less leisure will she have for it. . . . "

5) The Brontës loved animals, and they owned several cats and dogs over the years, including Emily's dog Keeper and Anne's dog Flossie, a King Charles spaniel.

6) Patrick Brontë's income was modest, and his daughters would have little, if any, dowry and so were unlikely to find husbands. Realizing he had to prepare them to earn a living, he eventually sent Charlotte to Roe Head School when she was fifteen to learn to be a governess. She had a much better experience this time, making two lifelong friends and rising to become the school's top pupil. (She was also legendary for her storytelling ability, and once scared the wits out of the entire dormitory with a ghost tale.)

Heather Vogel Frederick

7) After teaching for three years at Roe Head, Charlotte found work as a governess. She hated it. "A private governess has no existence," she complained in a letter to her sister Emily in 1839. She stuck it out three months and quit. Eventually, she went to Belgium to learn French so that she could open her own school, a venture that unfortunately proved unsuccessful.

8) Charlotte discovered and read some of her sister Emily's poetry (much to Emily's dismay, for she was very private), and hatched a plan for herself and Emily and Anne to self-publish a small collection of their poetry. They chose the pseudonyms Acton, Currer, and Ellis Bell. Their volume was well-reviewed, but only sold two copies.

9) Encouraged by the reviews, the sisters each set to work on a novel. They formed a sort of family critique group, meeting around the dining room table at night when the rest of the household was asleep. They wrote, read aloud, argued, discussed, and shared their excitement and passion for their work. But who would be the first to publish?

"Nooooo, Mrs. Hawthorne!" Madison protests. "You left us on a cliffhanger!"

"Bwahaha!" replies Mrs. Hawthorne, faking an evil laugh. "You noticed!

Fear not—I'm sending the final fun facts home with your mothers, and the blanks will all be filled in at your next meeting back in Gopher Hole. Meanwhile, does anything here strike you as particularly interesting?"

I listen quietly, still sketching.

"I can't believe that poop of an old poet told Charlotte that writing wasn't for girls!" says Mrs. Delaney. "The nerve!"

"I guess he wouldn't have approved of Chicks with Sticks," says Cassidy.

"It reminds me of something that Jane says at one point—hang on a sec, let me find it." Bailey flips through her copy of the book. "Here it is! Listen to this: 'Women are supposed to be very calm generally; but women feel just as men feel. They need exercise for their faculties, and a field for their efforts, as much as their brothers do . . . and it is narrow-minded in their more privileged fellow-creatures to say that they ought to confine themselves to making puddings and knitting stockings.'"

"What's the matter with knitting stockings?" protests Summer, holding up her knitting needles.

This draws a laugh, and Mrs. Hawthorne continues, "Excellent connection, Bailey. I've often wondered whether Charlotte had Southey's letter in mind when she wrote that."

"Whether or not she did, look who had the last laugh," says Madison's mother. "Today hardly anybody's heard of Southey, but everybody knows Charlotte Brontë and *Jane Eyre*."

"She got her wish to be 'forever known,' didn't she?" says Winky, and everybody nods.

Heather Vogel Frederick

"I noticed something," says Becca. "The Brontës had five daughters, just like the Bennet family in Jane Austen's *Pride and Prejudice*. I mean, before Maria and Elizabeth died they had five. Anyway, they worried about marrying them off just like the Bennets did."

"Another excellent connection," says Mrs. Hawthorne. "And just like the Bennets—and Jane Austen herself—the Brontës worried about money. So many things we take for granted today, like women being able to earn a living in careers of their choice, just weren't options back in Charlotte's day."

"She's like Jane Austen in another way, too," adds Emma. "Jane Austen wrote a lot when she was young, and so did Charlotte and the rest of the Brontë children."

Her mother nods. "Good point. Anybody else?"

I could say something if I wanted to. I could say that I know exactly how Jane Eyre felt when she was betrayed by the person she loved best in the whole world.

But I don't.

"Okay, it's been a long day, and I think we'll wind it up here," says Mrs. Hawthorne.

"Ladies of Gopher Hole, remember we're meeting at the tea shop tomorrow morning at eight thirty again," Mrs. Chadwick announces. "We've got a lot of ground to cover in Boston."

Becca comes over to say good-bye, and I crawl reluctantly out from under the piano.

"Are you feeling okay?"

I shake my head. It's not a lie. Right now all I want to do is go to bed.

"Call me in a bit?" she whispers as she gives me a hug.

I lift a shoulder. "Maybe tomorrow," I tell her. "I'm really tired."

Later, as we're getting into our pajamas, Summer asks, "What were you so busy drawing tonight?"

I shrug. "Nothing much." In fact, I was so worked up I'm not even sure. I wait until she heads through the door to the adjoining bathroom, then reach for my sketchbook to find out.

Simon.

Of course I drew Simon. Who else would I draw? His likeness stares back at me from the page. Around his head, circling like planes trying to land, are question marks.

Lots and lots of question marks.

I climb into bed and pull the quilt that Summer made for me up under my chin. I lie there in the dark, fingering the embroidery that stitches the scraps of velvet and muslin and lace together like puzzle pieces. If I were to take a snapshot of my life right at this moment, it would look exactly like this crazy quilt. Only my patches are Sophie Fairfax, Coco, my grandmother, Handcuffs Wong, and Simon.

The problem is, my puzzle is a mess, and I have absolutely no idea yet how all the pieces fit together.

Heather Vogel Frederick

CASSIDY

"It is vain to say human beings ought to be satisfied with tranquility. They must have action; and they will make it if they cannot find it."
—Jane Eyre

"I think I'm going to sneak Chloe into my suitcase when we head back to Wyoming," says Winky Parker. We're all sitting around the big dining table at Half Moon Farm, and she's cutting up a slice of pizza for my little sister, who's seated next to her in a high chair.

Winky has fallen head over heels in love with Chloe, and it's obvious that the feeling is mutual. My little sister follows her around the way Coco follows Sophie Fairfax. I guess with two older brothers and no sisters, it's kind of a treat for Winky to spend time with a toddler.

My stepfather laughs. "You'll have Murphy to answer to if you try that," he says. "He's very protective."

The dads and brothers have joined us tonight for a Leaning Tower of Pizza feast. We were going to order from Pirate Pete's, but Mr. Chadwick said he'd had enough of their pizza to last a lifetime—he's still working part-time making deliveries for them, until he finds a job. "Besides," he pointed out, "Pete's menu doesn't offer prosciutto and arugula, and it rocks."

He's right; it does. I reach for another piece and my mother gives me a warning look.

"What? I'm hungry!"

"I know, but that makes six pieces so far. There are other people at this table, Cassidy Ann."

I stop mid-bite. "You're counting?"

"Well—"

"Mom! I'm an athlete. I need fuel."

Mrs. Parker pats my mother's arm consolingly. "You should see the way we go through food on the ranch. Hard work makes for big appetites."

"Maybe I'll sneak Cassidy into your suitcase instead of Chloe," my mother says. "Sounds like she'd fit right in." I scowl at her and she adds, "Kidding!" She turns to Winky. "Seriously, though, you can borrow Chloe anytime. In fact, as soon as she's old enough to fly on her own, I'll put her on a plane to come visit you."

"Really?" says Winky. "That would be awesome!"

"AW-SUM! AW-SUM!" shouts Chloe gleefully, banging on her high chair tray with her sippy cup. She's loving all the attention this week.

"Not to change the subject, but what's this mystery event tonight?" asks Madison, changing the subject.

"Yes, do tell us—we're all dying to know," says her mother.

Everybody's been bugging Mrs. Wong and Mrs. Chadwick, trying to find out what's up, but they've been really good about fending off questions. Now, though, I figure it's time to let the cat out of the bag.

Heather Vogel Frederick

"Ladies," I tell them, "start your engines. We're going to the rink."

There's an excited buzz around the table.

"A skating party?" says Summer.

"I'm definitely up for that, y'all," says Savannah. "Sounds fun."

"It'll be more than just fun," I reply. "It's going to be educational, too."

"Uh-oh," says my mother. "Please tell me you're not planning what I think you're planning."

I grin. "Tell them, Emma."

Emma's been really quiet tonight. Probably because Sophie is sitting on the other side of Stewart and has been talking his ear off through most of dinner. *I've got a little something that can help fix that*, I think. *Just wait until Friday morning.*

"We're going to play hockey," Emma says, gamely mustering some enthusiasm.

My mother groans.

"We've been planning it for weeks," I add. "It's gonna be epic."

Mrs. Chadwick looks alarmed. "I haven't skated for years," she protests. "And I've never played hockey."

"It's just like riding a bicycle, Mrs. Chadwick," I assure her, adding slyly, "or skinny dipping. It'll all come back to you."

She tosses an olive at me. "I can see I'm never going to live that one down."

"Not a chance," says Mrs. Hawthorne.

"Can I be on your team, Cassidy?" Dylan begs.

"Sorry, dude," I tell him. "It's ladies' night."

His face falls. "Aw, man!"

"Not to worry," his father says. "I think you and your brother and I should have a boys-only party at the arcade instead."

"Honey!" Mrs. Delaney protests. "It's a school night."

Jess's father lifts an eyebrow. "And that would be why you're going to the rink?"

"Oh fine," she replies, with a rueful smile.

"Gentlemen," asks Mr. Delaney, looking around the table, "would any of you care to join us?" Mr. Hawthorne and Darcy raise their hands, and so do Stewart and Mr. Chadwick and Mr. Wong. "It's unanimous, then. To the arcade!"

"After you do the dishes?" Mrs. Delaney suggests hopefully.

Jess's father makes a long face. "That's right," he replies in his best Eeyore voice. "Go ahead, have your fun, and leave us poor boys behind to slave away." Then he smiles at us. "Of course we'll do the dishes. Off you go, ladies."

"I didn't bring skates," says Summer as we head for the cars.

"No worries," I tell her. "I've got all the equipment you'll need waiting at the rink."

We arrive just as the last skaters are leaving. Mr. Kohler, the rink owner, reminds me to close up tight when we're done. "Have fun!" he calls as he heads out the door.

"Thanks, Mr. K," I call back. "We will!"

I lead my grumbling group over to the supply closet, where I have

Heather Vogel Frederick

a big pile of hockey pads, protective gear, and jerseys waiting. I brought in all my old stuff a few days ago, plus I borrowed a bunch of things from my teammates, too, so that I'd have enough equipment for everyone.

"*Non, merci,*" says Sophie, shaking her head when I hand her a stack of gear.

I grin at her. "That's right, you've got the idea," I reply. "'No mercy.' Everyone's suiting up, everyone's going out on the ice, no exceptions."

She shakes her head again.

"No exceptions," I repeat firmly. "Right, Gigi?"

Megan's grandmother says something in rapid French to Sophie, who sullenly takes the equipment from me.

"I look like a walrus," wails Zoe Winchester, after she's dressed.

"Everybody looks like a walrus when they play hockey," I tell her. "And nobody cares. Who's going to see you?" I make a sweeping gesture. "Check it out—no boys. Not a single one. It's just us girls in here, and we couldn't care less what you look like."

"I still look like a walrus," she mutters.

The person who really looks like a walrus is Mrs. Chadwick, although of course I don't say that. She's a lot slimmer than she used to be, but she's still what my mother calls a "plus-sized gal." Add the hockey pads and the result is, well, pretty walruslike.

Mr. K gave me the key to the skate rentals, too, and once everyone's suited up I take them over to be fitted for skates.

"Same size as me," I say to Megan, surprised, when she asks for hers. "Here, use my skates instead. They're tons better than the rink's."

"Thanks."

I'm not planning on actually playing tonight. That would give whichever side I'm on an unfair advantage. But I don't tell my friends that, as I don't want to start a mutiny. I can tell they're not totally on board with this whole idea yet.

"I don't like hockey," my mother grouses as I help her lace up her skates.

"How would you know? You've never really played before."

"Broom hockey that one time on the Delaneys' pond," she mutters.

"That doesn't count."

"Someone could get hurt."

My mother still worries a lot about that, even though I've played all these years and am still in one piece.

"Mom, no one is going to get hurt, I promise. Seriously, will you look at these pads? Everyone's going to have fun, even you. Just wait and see."

I lace up a pair of rentals and stump around the benches, helping anyone else who needs it. Finally, they're all dressed and ready.

"Look at us!" crows Mrs. Hawthorne. "We need a picture."

"Already got that covered," I tell her, pulling my camera out of my bag. "Grab a stick and line up, okay?"

I snap a group photo, then Savannah takes one with me in it, and then it's time to go out on the ice.

It's pretty comical at first. Bailey's mother takes one step and promptly falls on her behind. Mrs. Williams and Sophie Fairfax both do the same. Others, like Mrs. Wong and Savannah, handle themselves a little more gracefully. We're a really uneven group in terms of ability, though. I watch for a couple of minutes, then pair everybody up, matching weak skaters with stronger skaters.

"Okay, listen up!" I call out, blowing my whistle to get their attention. "What you're going to do is circle the rink slowly a few times with your skating buddy, warming up and getting used to the feel of the ice. Some of you haven't spent much time at the rink"—I look over at my mother, who's clutching Emma's arm—"and some of you are used to figure skates, which have toe picks on the end. Hockey skates don't, as you've probably discovered."

"Yep," says Mrs. Jacobs, rubbing her rear end.

"Off you go, and take your time. This isn't a race."

I take Gigi's arm—I chose her for my partner since she's the one I'm most concerned about. I didn't need to worry, though. She's steady as a rock.

"This is fun!" she cries after we make our first circuit.

"Told you so," I reply smugly.

After we're all warmed up, Emma and I set up for drills. We lead everyone through some basic moves—turning, stopping, that sort of thing—along with some basic stick work.

"You're doing great!" I tell them as they practice maneuvering around the orange cones. "I'll make Chicks with Sticks out of you yet!"

"Chicks with Sticks? More like 'Hicks with Sticks,'" moans Winky a few minutes later, slumping on to the bench. "We stink at this."

"Speak for yourself," says Zoe, zipping by. She's clearly gotten the hang of it.

Winky leaps to her feet and dashes off after her.

"That's the spirit!" I holler, happy to see that her fuse finally got lit. I'd totally get Winky on a team if she lived here in Concord.

Twenty minutes later I decide they're ready to play an actual game.

"Here's how it's going to work," I announce, calling everyone over. They circle around me, huffing and puffing. "For starters, I'm sitting this one out. That will even up the numbers, plus we need a ref. As for who's going to play who—" I gaze at my friends and their mothers, swiftly calculating how best to balance this ragtag bunch.

"How about Concord vs. Wyoming?" suggests Becca.

I shake my head. "I don't think that would be fair—the Concord group has a little more experience, from what I can tell. I'm thinking mothers vs. daughters."

"Oh yeah!" says Emma, and Jess lets out a whoop.

"Team Daughters is going to rule!" cries Madison, her dark eyes sparkling under her helmet.

"Don't count us out yet," says Gigi, shaking her hockey stick in the air. "Go, Team Moms! And Team Grandmas!"

What follows doesn't look like any hockey game I've ever seen, but it's one of the most fun sessions I've ever had on the ice.

For one thing, hockey doesn't usually involve this much laughter. And for another, there seems to be some unspoken agreement that

Heather Vogel Frederick

anytime anybody falls down, the game stops until the person gets up again. Nobody seems to care all that much about scoring goals at first, either—they'd rather chase one another around.

Eventually, though, everyone settles down to business. I've put Mrs. Chadwick in goal, where her walrusness works to her advantage. She's a little tentative on her skates and she's not fast, but she's a take-charge kind of person, and it shows in the determined way that she defends the net.

Down at the other end of the rink, Winky's playing goalie for Team Daughters. She slaps away shot after shot—taken mostly by Mrs. Delaney, who may be petite like Jess but she's a powerhouse. Plus, she skates all the time on the pond at Half Moon Farm, so she's got skills to go with the stamina. Mrs. Parker is surprisingly good, too. She's almost as athletic as Winky is, and before long she's racing up and down the rink like a pro.

Mrs. Jacobs and Mrs. Hawthorne are pretty tentative, and Mrs. Williams and my mother are borderline hopeless. Professor Daniels turns out to have a king-size competitive streak. She gives the daughters a run for their money playing defense and fires off Team Mothers' only goal.

As far as Team Daughters goes, Sophie is fairly useless, which surprises me. I'd thought maybe she'd have some of her cousin Annabelle's skating pizzazz, but she doesn't. Megan, Summer, Madison, and Bailey are pretty much just warm bodies, too, but Zoe Winchester shows some promise. So does Savannah. She and Jess get pretty good at slapping the puck back and forth between them, but it's Emma who makes the team's only goal. This surprises her so much that she falls down, which makes everybody laugh again.

The game lasts almost an hour and ends in a tie.

"A respectable showing, ladies," I tell them.

"I don't know about the rest of you, but I'm ready for a respectable shower," says Mrs. Chadwick, taking off her helmet and running a hand through her sweaty hair.

"We'll be feeling our legs tomorrow, that's for sure," says Mrs. Williams, flopping down on the nearest bench. She puts her arm around Summer. "I can't believe we're supposed to walk all over Boston! You may have to carry me on the Freedom Trail."

Professor Daniels sits down next to them and starts to unlace her skates. "I haven't had this much exercise in years."

"Ditto," agrees Mrs. Hawthorne. "But I haven't had this much fun in years, either."

"You should play hockey more often, Mom," Emma tells her. "There's an adult league that meets here one evening a week."

"Really?" Mrs. Hawthorne perks up at this. "Any Concord moms want to check it out with me? Hockey might be a fun change from yoga."

Emma and I collect all the equipment and put it back in the closet and the skate rental room. The clothing gets stuffed into a giant laundry bag to take home with me, so I can wash everything before returning it to my Lady Shawmut friends. I make one last pass around the

Heather Vogel Frederick

rink to make sure there aren't any stray mittens or trash or anything. The Zamboni crew comes first thing every morning and they like the ice to be free and clear.

The next two days fly by in a flurry of practice sessions and school for me, trips into Boston and shopping for our friends (Winky buys Colonial tricorn hats for her father and her brothers as a joke), and evenings spent with all of us hanging out together. I manage to squeeze in a surprising amount of time with Winky—we stay up late every night before bed talking, and she's used to getting up early on the ranch so she goes running with me before hockey practice, too. I've taken her on some of my favorite routes, including the loop up Monument Street, through Minuteman National Park, and back down Liberty and Lowell to the center of town.

"I love Concord!" she says, throwing her arms out wide as we jog across the Old North Bridge early Friday morning. "It's epic!"

"How do you feel about epic pranks?" I ask with a grin.

"Bring 'em on!"

"Good, because I hear there's one planned for an episode of *Cooking with Clementine* this morning." I pick up the pace, and she matches me stride for stride as we head for home.

I'm eager to finally put my plan into action. I've been texting back and forth with my Concord friends all week, ironing out the details. Winky's the only Wyoming friend who knows, though. We figured we'd have a better chance of keeping the prank a secret that way. Summer's so chatty, she might spill the beans accidentally, and Zoe is, well, Zoe.

After Winky and I shower and dress, we go downstairs to where my mother has set out a light breakfast of muffins along and juice. Our friends are already starting to arrive, along with the camera crew. Everyone is happy and excited, including Megan, which is nice because she's seemed a little down in the dumps all week.

"Tell them your news," Gigi prods her.

"I got an email from *Flashlite* magazine last night!" she says, smiling. "They've asked me to help cover Fashion Week for them while I'm in Paris!"

"Seriously?" says Emma, her voice swooping up an octave. "That's a total dream assignment!"

Megan nods. "I know. Somehow Wolfgang got wind of my trip—"

We all look over at Gigi, who is the picture of innocence.

"—and he's asked me to revive Fashionista Jane and blog about it."

Uh-oh, I think, glancing at Mrs. Wong. There could be trouble ahead. Megan's mother was the one responsible for shutting down the hilariously snarky Fashionista Jane to begin with.

"He said he's going to call you today to discuss it, Mom," Megan hurries to add.

"Is he now?" Mrs. Wong replies coolly.

"It's so exciting!" exclaims Gigi. "My talented granddaughter, reporting on Fashion Week for the world to see! Such an *educational* opportunity."

"Mother, stop trying to influence me," says Mrs. Wong.

"Who, me? I'm just saying."

Heather Vogel Frederick

"Oh Mrs. Wong, you have to let her do it!" begs Emma. "It would be so much fun—almost as if we were all there with her!"

"We'll see," says Mrs. Wong, which is usually mom-speak for "no way." But maybe for once she means it.

It's nice to see Megan looking happy. I think maybe she's a little lonely these days, what with every minute of Becca's time devoted either to cheerleading or waitressing, and her mom and Gigi all enthralled with Sophie. Plus, Simon's so far away.

It occurs to me that this is a definite point in Zach Norton's favor in the boyfriend department. His house is only a few streets away from mine, not halfway around the world.

Becca and her mother and the Winchesters arrive next. Mrs. Chadwick looks like she's about to burst.

"I have wonderful news!" she tells us, before she even takes off her coat. "Henry has a new job!"

Our moms all crowd around to hug and congratulate her, while Becca comes over to join Winky and me and the rest of our friends.

"That's so great!" I tell her. "Where's he going to be working?"

"Some big insurance company in Boston," Becca replies. "He's really thrilled." She looks around. "Where's Sophie?"

I've been wondering the same thing. No Sophie, no prank.

"She'll be here," Megan tells us. "My dad's going to drive her over in a few minutes. Her grandfather called from Paris just as we were leaving."

"Is she wearing her black T-shirt?" We've been counting on this, and it's kind of key to pulling off what we have planned. Fortunately, Sophie wears black a lot. I guess maybe she thinks it makes her look artistic. Or maybe it's just some French thing.

Megan nods.

Winky tugs on my sleeve. "Okay if I show everybody the turret?"

"Sure," I tell her.

As she herds the Wyoming girls upstairs, Megan leans toward the rest of us and lowers her voice. "You guys, I need to tell you something."

"What's up?" I ask.

"I caught Sophie videoconferencing with Simon earlier this week."

Emma gasps.

"I knew there was something wrong, Megs, but that was the last thing I ever would have guessed," says Becca.

We're silent for a moment, contemplating the awfulness of this.

"Well, they are cousins," Jess points out cautiously.

Emma shakes her head. "No way," she says, sounding furious. "No excuses this time, Jess. Stewart's not enough for Sophie? Now she's after Simon, too?"

Any qualms any of us may have had about the prank vanish in the wake of this new information. Sophie totally deserves what's coming.

"Everybody good to go?" I ask, and they all nod.

"Ammunition ready?"

Megan pats her purse. "Right here."

"Be ready for my signal for the hand-off," I tell her. "Winky and I

Heather Vogel Frederick

will take it from there. The rest of you just try and stay between Sophie and Gigi and my mom and anybody else who speaks French, okay?"

They all nod.

I hold up two fingers in the V sign. My friends do the same. My mother sees us and gives me a funny look from the other side of the kitchen, Before she can say anything, Fred Goldberg, the show's producer, walks in.

"Let's get this party started!" he calls, clapping his hand. "Time is money and money's a-wasting!"

Our pen pals come thundering down from upstairs, and soon the house is abuzz with activity. The camera crew gets busy setting up, and we're all funneled through the makeup station while Mr. Goldberg runs around barking out orders almost as loudly as Murphy. I'm used to the chaos, and the Concord book club has been involved in filming a couple of episodes before, so it's not a big deal to us, but I can tell that our Wyoming friends are impressed. Their eyes are round as hockey pucks and their heads are practically swiveling 360 degrees as they watch the crew tape down cables, arrange lights, set up the kitchen and dining room, and start prepping the food.

"Cassidy!" my mother calls at one point, already looking frazzled.

"Yeah?"

"You're on Murphy duty."

I round him up and shoo him into the garage, where he slumps into his crate, resigned to his fate. "Good boy," I tell him. "It will all be over soon, and you can come back inside and terrorize everybody." I give him a pat and a treat and return to the kitchen, shutting the door behind me.

"So what exactly is it that we're filming today?" asks Mrs. Winchester, looking at the fruit on the countertops. "And why are we dressed like this?"

My mother thought it would be fun to keep the episode's subject a surprise. So even though it's late March in New England, which means it's still cold outside, we're all wearing shorts and T-shirts and sundresses, as if it's the middle of summer.

"The one thing we couldn't do with you while you're here in town," my mother replies, "besides taking you swimming in Walden Pond—"

"—or skinny-dipping!" jokes Mrs. Jacobs, and Becca's mother buries her face in her hands in mock dismay.

"Or skinny-dipping," my mother continues without missing a beat, "was a trip to Kimball Farm for ice cream."

Kimball's is closed for the season, which is always cause for deep mourning here in Concord.

"So we figured we'd bring the Kimball's experience to *Cooking with Clementine*, by filming a make-your-own ice cream special," she concludes.

Winky lets out a whoop that's worthy of the rodeo princess she is.

Mrs. Wong frowns. "We're having *ice cream*? At nine in the *morning*? I thought you were planning a simple summer picnic."

"I guess I didn't get that memo, Lily," my mother replies breezily. "And I hate to be the one to break the news, but we're not just making

Heather Vogel Frederick

ice cream, we're making hot fudge sundaes." My mother smiles. "Just think of it as protein and fruit—well, okay, and a little chocolate, too."

Mrs. Wong throws up her hands. "Fine," she says. "No one listens to me anyway."

"Maybe when you're elected mayor you can outlaw sugar," says Mrs. Hawthorne slyly, and we all laugh, even Mrs. Wong.

The back door opens and Sophie comes in. I'm relieved to see that she's wearing a black T-shirt. The makeup crew whisks her away, gives the rest of us a final dusting with powder, and then it's showtime.

As everybody starts lining up around the kitchen island, where we'll be prepping the fruit and nuts and making the sweet cream base for the ice cream, Megan and I hang back and dart into the downstairs bathroom when my mother isn't looking. Megan takes a square of black felt from her purse and passes it to me. I flip it over and quickly slap on a few pieces of the double-stick tape I stashed under the sink earlier.

"Is this really going to work?" she whispers.

"*Oui oui,*" I quip. "Leave it to Winky and me."

We slip back into the kitchen and nonchalantly take our places. Winky has stationed herself on one side of Sophie, just as I told her to. I squeeze in on the other side.

"Ready, everyone?" Fred Goldberg asks. "Ten second warning." The light on the camera starts blinking yellow.

This is our cue! I look over at Winky and nod. She stretches, bumping against Sophie in the process and sending her flying into me. I wince dramatically.

"Ouch!"

"*Excusez-moi,*" Sophie replies.

"It's okay—no big deal." I give her a pat on the back as I say this, neatly transferring the square of black felt to her T-shirt. It's the oldest trick in the book, but still effective if performed properly.

"Three, two, one—roll 'em!" says Mr. Goldberg, and the green light comes on and we're off and running.

I busy myself cutting up strawberries, trying to keep a straight face and not look at any of my Concord friends. The worst thing any of us could do right now is bust out laughing.

On the back of Sophie's T-shirt, in sparkly hot pink letters that Megan glued to the square of felt, are the words PIQUEUSE DE MEC, which Savannah assured us means "boyfriend stealer."

When the show airs, Sophie's shirt will announce to the world what she's done—or tried to do. Thank you, *Scarlet Letter*!

Things get a little tricky when my mother starts moving us around the kitchen to the different work stations, and then to the buffet in the dining room where we assemble our sundaes. Emma and Becca and Megan look like they're performing some intricate dance as they take turns shadowing Sophie, trying to stay between her back and any eyes that might notice something amiss with her T-shirt. She looks at them a little strangely, but our Wyoming friends and the other mothers are so excited to be on TV and so focused on not doing anything wrong that they don't notice a thing. In fact, they probably wouldn't notice if the T-shirt actually caught fire.

Heather Vogel Frederick

Winky catches my eye at one point and I have to cross my arms over my stomach, it hurts so much from trying not to laugh. This is our best prank yet! One for the record books, despite the fact it has a long fuse. It's called delayed gratification—we'll have to keep quiet about it until the show airs in May. But who cares? It's perfect. Subtle, too. People who don't know French won't pay attention; they'll just think it's some random T-shirt slogan. But Sophie will know what it means when she sees the show, and that's the whole point.

The rest of the filming goes off without a hitch, including our exit strategy after the camera stops rolling, when Savannah "accidentally" spills her ice cream on Sophie.

"I'm so sorry!" she cries. *"Excusez-moi!"*

Jess rushes to swat at the front of Sophie's T-shirt with sponges and paper towel, distracting her long enough for me to peel off the sign and stuff it in my pocket.

Final score: The mother-daughter book club goes for the gold! And Sophie Fairfax? Mademoiselle Velcro is going *down*!

Becca

"'I wish he would come! I wish he would come!'"
—*Jane Eyre*

"Mrs. Wong, would you please hold still?" I put my hands on my hips, exasperated. Megan's mother is as jumpy as our dog Yo-Yo during a thunderstorm.

"Sorry," she replies. "But is all this fuss really necessary?"

"Of course it is," says Mrs. Sloane-Kinkaid, who's standing in front of her with a mascara wand poised in the air.

We're at Megan's house, helping her mother get ready for tonight's debate. Filming the *Cooking with Clementine* episode took all morning, and by the time we were done, nobody was hungry for lunch.

"I don't think I want to see another scoop of ice cream as long as I live," Zoe had groaned as we got into the car.

I'd been so focused on our prank that I barely even tasted the ice cream, although just like everybody else, I ate far too much of it. Who can resist homemade vanilla ice cream with homemade hot fudge or salted caramel sauce? Or both, in my case.

After dropping me at home, Zoe and Mrs. Winchester and my mother headed to Half Moon Farm to join the group for a cheese-making demonstration. You'd think girls from rural Wyoming would have had enough barns and four-legged creatures to last a lifetime, but they can't seem to get enough of Half Moon Farm. Not that I don't like spending time there, too, but I had cheerleading practice, and I couldn't skip it. I'm already just barely hanging on to my place in the squad, what with my waitressing job at Pies & Prejudice. Coach O'Donnell has been really great about letting me juggle both, since she knows it's been a help to my family while my dad was unemployed.

And besides, I really didn't want to skip practice. It gave me an excuse to get away from Zoe Winchester for a couple of hours. Zoe is a major pain. What's worse, I know that my friends used to call her Becca West, which is mortifying. Was I ever really like that? Bossy and boy crazy? Plus, she's a lip gloss addict.

Ashley dropped me at the Wongs after practice. She's feeling kind of left out this week, but she's been a good sport about it. I'll see her again tonight; she's volunteered to help set up for the debate over at the high school, which is where most of our group is right now. I stayed behind with Megan and Gigi and Mrs. Sloane-Kinkaid and Zoe's mother, to help Mrs. Wong with hair and makeup and last-minute wardrobe adjustments.

Which isn't proving to be an easy task.

"There's no such thing as too much fuss," Mrs. Winchester tells Megan's mother, who is still frowning at the mascara wand. "Whatever it takes, remember?" Zoe's mother has been coaching Mrs. Wong all week on the ins and outs of campaigning, and she's big on personal appearance.

Mrs. Wong sighs gustily and relents. Cassidy's mother swoops in again as she tilts her face up. "All eyes will be on you tonight, Lily, and you want to look your best," she tells her, standing back to take a critical look. She nods, satisfied, and passes me the wand. "Blush brush," she says crisply, and I slap it into her palm. We're like a surgical team on one of those TV shows.

It's not every day you get to see a former supermodel work her magic with makeup. By the time Mrs. Sloane-Kinkaid is done, I've picked up a few tricks. She's putting on the finishing touches when Gigi comes in carrying a dress bag.

"What's that?" asks Mrs. Wong suspiciously.

"A little surprise from your daughter and me," Gigi replies, unzipping the bag to reveal a bright red skirt and jacket ensemble.

Mrs. Sloane-Kinkaid gasps. "Is that your Chanel suit?"

Gigi smiles. "A flawless copy, thanks to a talented seamstress I know. Lily's too tall to wear mine."

"You mean Megan made that?" Cassidy's mother's eyebrows disappear beneath her perfectly tousled bangs.

Megan nods, smiling shyly. "Gigi bought the fabric, though. She sent for it from Paris."

Mrs. Sloane-Kinkaid whips out her cell phone and starts snapping photos. "This is the perfect kick-off for Fashionista Jane, Paris Edition, Megan," she says. "It gives you total street cred—how many teenage girls can sew a couture knockoff that doesn't look like a knockoff? This could totally pass for the real thing." Tapping away at the keypad she adds, "I'm sending you these pictures right now. You have to promise me you'll use them, okay?"

Megan's eyes slide over to her mother. Mrs. Wong still hasn't said yes yet to reviving the blog. However, she's not listening to Mrs. Sloane-Kinkaid—she's fixated on the red suit.

She reaches out a tentative finger and strokes the jacket sleeve. "It's beautiful, but isn't it a bit frivolous? I was planning on wearing my beige pants and beige sweater set. I want to be taken seriously."

"Beige is boring," says Zoe's mother, who is dressed in an anything-but-boring zebra-striped sweater and black pants. It's a mom look, but a good mom look. "Beige makes you look like a place mat."

I stifle a giggle. She's right, though—Mrs. Wong tends to pick really plain, dull colors most of the time.

"Mom, forget the earth tones," Megan agrees. "Red is your signature color. You always get the most compliments when you wear red."

"I don't know," her mother replies, shaking her head. "This just seems so in your face."

"Which is exactly where your opponent is going to be an hour from now, so you might as well dress the part and go for it too," says Mrs. Winchester, who is starting to sound a little annoyed. "Think of yourself as a boxer going into the ring—you wouldn't droop in wearing some ratty old bathrobe, would you?"

Megan and I exchange a glance, then duck our heads to hide our smiles. Mrs. Winchester has obviously never seen Mrs. Wong's bathrobe. It's incredibly ratty. Mrs. Wong says it's better for the environment to get the most mileage possible out of an article of clothing.

"Of course you wouldn't," Mrs. Winchester continues, oblivious. "You'd enter with your head held high, dressed in your brightest silks. Red is a power color. It lets your opponent know you're confident. In fact," she adds, "I'll bet you anything he'll be wearing a red tie tonight."

This seems to clinch it, because Mrs. Wong takes the suit from Gigi and starts to head out of the kitchen.

"Don't forget these," says Gigi, holding up her diamond stud earrings.

"Absolutely not," says Mrs. Wong.

"They bring good luck," Gigi tells her. "And add sparkle."

"Sparkle? I'll blind the moderator if the spotlight hits me at the wrong angle. You can see those things from outer space, mother."

"Nonsense," says Mrs. Sloane-Kinkaid. "Gigi is right—they're the perfect accessory. Just the right amount of pizzazz."

"Pizzazz, schmizzazz," grumbles Mrs. Wong, but she takes the earrings with her as she leaves the kitchen.

The door swings shut behind her and Cassidy's mother sags against the counter. "Whew," she says. "That was a job and a half."

"My daughter has a stubborn streak," admits Gigi.

"Stubborn can be a useful trait in a politician," says Mrs. Winchester. She glances up at the clock. "We'd better get this show on the road if we don't want to be late."

A few minutes later, we all pile into the Sloane-Kinkaids' minivan and head down Strawberry Hill Road toward Alcott High. Mrs. Wong

Heather Vogel Frederick

is in the front passenger seat, rifling through the three-by-five cards in her hands. I lean over the seat back and pat her on the shoulder.

"Remember Savannah's trick, Mrs. Wong? Just tell yourself 'I'm not nervous, I'm excited.' She says it really helps."

"I'm not nervous, I'm excited," says Mrs. Wong.

"That's it."

"It's not helping."

"Try deep breathing," says Cassidy's mother. "That always worked for me before a photo shoot."

Mrs. Wong is still huffing and puffing as we pull into the high school parking lot a few minutes later. I spot Mr. Wong in front of the entrance to the building. He waves when he sees us.

"There you are," he says, opening the front passenger door. "I was beginning to worry." His eyes widen as Mrs. Wong climbs out of the car. "*Oh là là!* Nice suit."

"See!" wails Mrs. Wong over her shoulder at Mrs. Sloane-Kinkaid. "I told you! Nobody's going to take me seriously in this getup."

"Honey, calm down," says Mr. Wong. "I'm just kidding. You look great."

Megan and Gigi and I hop out, and so does Mrs. Winchester. She and Mr. Wong slip their arms through Mrs. Wong's and propel her through the front door.

"Ah, there you are," says a man in a suit, trotting toward us through the crowded lobby. He has a clipboard in one hand and an earpiece in one ear. "They're ready for you backstage, Lily."

"You're not nervous, you're excited," I whisper.

"I'm not nervous, I'm excited," Mrs. Wong parrots back.

"Deep breaths," adds Mrs. Sloane-Kinkaid.

"You're a boxer, heading into the ring," adds Zoe's mother. "You're going to be fabulous."

"I'm going to throw up!"

"Mom," says Megan. "Do you remember our fashion show back in seventh grade?"

Mrs. Wong nods.

"Do you remember how nervous I was, and how you had to crawl under one of the tables where I was hiding to give me a pep talk?"

Her mother nods again.

"I'll never forget that. You told me you were proud of me, and that I had more talent and gumption in my little finger than most people twice my age." Megan grabs her mother's pinkie. "*So do you, Mom!* You've got a better platform than your opponent does, a better team behind you than he does, and"—she pauses for a moment and grins— "you're way better looking than he is. Dad's right—*oh là là!*"

"Thanks, sweetheart," says Mrs. Wong, her dark eyes shining with emotion. She gives her a trembling smile. "I'm really going to miss you next week when you're in Paris."

Sophie materializes just then with her camera. She circles the two of them, clicking away.

"Would you put that thing down!" snaps Megan. "You're making my mother nervous!"

Heather Vogel Frederick

"*Pardon*, but it's my job, in case you've forgotten," Sophie snaps back.

"Girls!" says Mrs. Wong, her smile fading. "Please."

"Sorry, Mom," mutters Megan, and stalks off.

Shooting Sophie a look, I follow Megan down the hallway to the ladies' room.

"I loathe Sophie Fairfax!" She sniffles, dabbing at her eyes with a tissue. "She ruins everything."

I know Megan means Simon as much as she means things with her mother, but I figure it's best to try and get her to focus on right now.

"C'mon, Megs, don't let it spoil the evening," I tell her.

"Why does my mother always stick up for her?"

I don't have an answer for that.

"One more day to a Sophie-free zone!" I say. "You're going to Paris, Megan. PARIS!"

She lifts a shoulder.

"And you're going to see Simon."

"If he still wants to," she replies in a small voice.

"Of course he still wants to," I tell her. "Give him the benefit of the doubt and call him or e-mail him, will you? Don't be a wimp—get your Jane on and just do it. I'm sure there's a logical explanation, and I'm sure the two of you will straighten this all out. Now blow your nose," I order her, and she obeys.

"You're right," she says. "I don't want to spoil tonight for my mom—I really am proud of her. A little nervous, too."

"No, you're *excited*, remember?"

She gives me a rueful smile.

"That's better," I tell her. "Your mother is going to be great. And she looks fabulous, thanks to your suit."

Megan giggles. "*Oh là là*, right?"

"You said it."

We head back down the hall to the auditorium, passing the huge banners that blare the campaign slogans—UNDERHILL UNDERSTANDS! and RAISE YOUR HAND FOR HANDCUFFS WONG! Gigi said she'd save seats for us, and I spot her in the front row, right next to Mr. Wong and my parents. Megan slips in beside her, and I take a seat between Megan and Emma. Our group of friends takes up the entire two front rows. My brother is sitting on the other side of Emma, and for once, there's no sign of Sophie. Then I spot her roaming the aisles, taking pictures of the crowd.

And it's quite a crowd. The whole embezzlement scandal has been big news in our little town, and Emma told us that some big-name reporters from Boston are here to cover the event. It looks like half of Concord turned out as well. I spot a lot of regulars from Pies & Prejudice, and I'm surprised at how many students from Alcott High are here, too—but then, most of the civics teachers are offering extra credit for attending. Ashley's sitting a few rows back with her new boyfriend. They both wave and I wave back. Third, who's seated with them, waves, too. I toss him a bone and waggle my fingers at him. Megan nudges me and I turn around just as the moderator is coming out on

Heather Vogel Frederick

stage. Mrs. Wong and her opponent are right behind him, and they take their places at the podiums as he steps up to the microphone. Mrs. Winchester was right; George Underhill is wearing a red tie.

"Good evening," the moderator says. "I'm Andrew Johnson, editor of the *Concord Chronicle*, and I'd like to thank you all for coming to tonight's debate. It's an important time for our town, and with the special election just a few weeks away, it all comes down to this—a gloves-off, wide-ranging, no-holds-barred exchange between our two candidates: lifelong Concord resident and longtime selectman George Underhill, and all-around Concord booster and tireless volunteer Lily Wong."

The audience claps enthusiastically, and Mr. Wong waves his HANDCUFFS WONG! pennant. In fact, he does this every time Mrs. Wong's name is mentioned. It's kind of cute, really.

The moderator explains that they flipped a coin backstage to see who would go first tonight, and Mr. Underhill won. "So I'd like to ask you, George, if you could briefly outline your qualifications and why you think voters should choose you when they go to the polls."

Mr. Underhill obviously doesn't understand the definition of "briefly," because he drones on for a full five minutes before finally winding things up. "I think it comes down to whether Concord wants someone with experience, someone with a proven track record, or someone who's—well, let's just say who's willing to do anything as a publicity stunt." He gives the audience a knowing look, and there's a ripple of laughter.

"Publicity stunt?" says Mrs. Wong, leaping right in. "Now wait just a minute, George. If you're speaking of my moment in the spotlight as Handcuffs Wong—which even you have to concede I've made no attempt to avoid after you so conveniently leaked the photo to the press—let's remember that moment for what it was: a sincere, impassioned, whole-hearted attempt to help friends facing an unfair tax bill and the loss of their historic farm. In fact, you must have found me convincing, because you were one of the selectmen who voted to grandfather Half Moon Farm in under the new tax code."

"Score!" Emma says under her breath.

Mr. Underhill reddens. "My point, Lily, is that my record shows I will not do anything to open this town to ridicule."

"What your record shows is that you're not willing to open this town to anything, including progress."

"Oooh," calls someone from the back of the auditorium, prompting a ripple of laughter.

"The floor asks the candidates—and the audience—to recall the rules," says the moderator, frowning. "Politeness and decorum are the order of the evening."

He gives the floor to Mrs. Wong, who goes on to lay out her background as a civic volunteer and outline her campaign platform, which includes fiscal responsibility, upgrading the town's infrastructure, and, of course, preserving the environment.

"Round one: Handcuffs Wong!" whispers Mrs. Winchester when she's done, and heads up and down our two rows bob in agreement. Mr. Wong waves his pennant again.

Heather Vogel Frederick

"And now," continues the moderator, "my first question . . ."

The candidates are off and running. The questions and responses fly fast and furious as the moderator probes their stands on everything from taxes to conservation. Mrs. Wong really gets going when that subject comes up, especially when the moderator asks about the proposed ban on plastic shopping bags that's on the ballot for the next general election. The Riverkeepers are spearheading the initiative, and Mrs. Wong is board chairperson for the Riverkeepers.

"I'm completely opposed to the idea," says Mr. Underhill. "It's an infringement of individual freedom where our local merchants are concerned. It's billed as an environmentally friendly initiative, but what environment are we talking about? If Concord creates an unfriendly environment for commerce, businesses will take themselves elsewhere, and our town will be poorer because of it."

"How about you, Mrs. Wong?" asks the moderator.

"I'm fully in favor of the ban," she replies. "In fact, I think you could say I'm *handcuffed* to the idea."

There's another ripple of laughter at this—it's pretty hard to miss Sophie's pictures of Mrs. Wong handcuffed to a monster made of plastic bags (actually Stewart in full hockey gear, with plastic bags taped to every inch of his body) with a big red circle with a slash symbol on his belly. They're plastered all over her campaign posters and brochures around town.

"That's right," she says cheerfully. "I'm Handcuffs Wong and proud of it." She holds up her hands and crosses them at the wrists, as if she were wearing handcuffs, then raises them overhead first to one side, then the other, in the classic champion's cheer. The audience laughs again.

Mr. Underhill does not.

"On a more serious note, perhaps a better name for me would be the Green Machine," Mrs. Wong continues. "I am a proud member of Riverkeepers, who have placed this important initiative on the upcoming ballot. Studies have shown unequivocally that plastic bags are detrimental to the environment. These bags waste valuable resources in their production, don't biodegrade in any meaningful time frame, contain harmful chemicals that are then ingested by wildlife, and are, needless to say, unsightly when littered, whether deliberately or accidentally." She ticks these off on her fingers. "Concord has a long heritage of environmental activism. It is home, after all, to the original conservationist, Henry David Thoreau. As for my esteemed opponent's argument that passing this ban will drive businesses from Concord, may I remind you all that it was Thoreau who said, 'What is the good of having a nice house without a decent planet to put it on?' If I may paraphrase him, 'What is the good of having a nice business without a decent town to put it in?' Henry David Thoreau's rich legacy here in Concord must be preserved."

To my right, Emma is mouthing the words as Mrs. Wong speaks them. Megan notices, too, and as the audience bursts into thunderous applause, she leans across and pokes Emma. "Emma J. Hawthorne, future White House speechwriter," she whispers, and Emma grins.

Heather Vogel Frederick

The moderator gives each speaker thirty seconds to wind things up.

"Just remember, a vote for Underhill is a vote for experience," says Mr. Underhill, as he concludes his remarks. "Underhill understands!"

But Mrs. Wong has the last word. "If it's the status quo you seek, by all means vote for my opponent. If, on the other hand, you're looking for commitment, for a candidate who won't give up no matter the odds—if that's the candidate you want to hand your vote to, then hand it to me—Handcuffs Wong!"

Our two rows rise to our feet, clapping and cheering. Mr. Wong waves his pennant wildly as the moderator crosses the stage and shakes hands with both candidates. Sophie rushes to the foot of the stage with the rest of the press, snapping pictures.

"I'd say that was a stunning success," says Mrs. Winchester in the lobby afterwards, as our group clusters around the campaign table watching Mrs. Wong being congratulated by a throng of well-wishers.

"It was the earrings," says Gigi breezily. "They always bring good luck. That and the fact that my daughter is smart, hardworking, and never gives up when she knows something is right."

We stick around until the school clears out, handing out brochures and banners and bumper stickers, pennants and buttons, and flyers. Third corners me while I'm taking a turn behind the table, and I'm forced to make small talk with him because Mrs. Winchester and Professor Daniels are there too, and I don't want to look like a jerk.

"Doing anything for spring break?" he asks.

"Yeah," I tell him. "I'm going on a trip with my grandmother."

"Cool. Anyplace fun?"

Not so much, I think to myself. Aloud, I reply, "Minnesota."

His brow furrows. "Why? Isn't it cold there this time of year? We're going to Florida."

Good question, I think glumly. It's getting harder to whip up any enthusiasm for this trip. I haven't even finished packing, and I'm leaving first thing in the morning.

I catch a ride with my parents to the combination debate celebration and farewell party at the Wongs'. Our Wyoming friends are leaving tomorrow morning, too.

"I've had so much fun this week," says Zoe politely to my mother.

That makes one of us, I think. But I nod and smile.

"Me too," says Mrs. Winchester. "Thank you so much for hosting us, Calliope."

"You're welcome," my mother replies. "We're going to miss you."

"And I'm going to miss your campaign tips," says Mrs. Wong, coming over and draping her arm around Mrs. Winchester's shoulders. "I don't think I could have pulled it off tonight without you."

Mrs. Winchester laughs. "Are you kidding me? You're a natural, Lily. I can't wait to send you flowers when you win the election."

Stanley Kinkaid wanders over with a plate heaped with food. "This stuff is great," he says, talking with his mouth full. How come grown-ups can break rules like that and get away with it? "Did Gigi make it?"

Mrs. Wong shakes her head. "No, we had it catered. It's from Mr. Green Dream's."

"That vegetarian place?"

Megan's mother nods. "It was Sophie's idea," she says, slipping her arm around the French girl's waist. "It's fun having a fellow vegetarian in the house."

Megan is standing to the side, watching a little sadly as her kitten twines herself adoringly around Sophie's ankles. Megan spent weeks making that suit as a surprise for tonight's debate, but the only one who seems to get any praise around here is Sophie.

Scooping Coco up, I go over to Megan and link my arm through hers. "Come on, Megs," I whisper. "Let's go to your room for a while."

We do, and I close the door so Coco can't escape. The kitten hops up on Megan's suitcase and bats at the luggage tag.

"Are you excited about tomorrow?" I ask.

Megan nods. "Yeah. How about you?"

I shrug. I've been trying really, really hard not to be jealous, but it's not easy working up enthusiasm for Minnesota when your best friend is going to Paris. You don't need a passport to go to Minnesota.

"I know you're going to have a good time, too," says Megan, accurately reading my thoughts. "Your grandmother is just as much fun as mine."

"That's debatable."

"Come on, Becca—she's great!"

"Yeah, I guess you're right." But a little voice in my head whispers, *If she's so great, why isn't she taking you to Paris instead of Minnesota?*

"Hey, I've got something for you to stick in your suitcase." Megan reaches under her bed and pulls out a flat box wrapped in lavender tissue paper and tied with a silver ribbon. "No opening it until your birthday, though, okay?"

"Okay."

A trip to Minnesota wasn't exactly how I pictured I'd be spending my sweet sixteenth, but when Gram arranged this trip she didn't know that spring break fell the week of my birthday.

"Becca?" My mother's voice echoes down the hallway. She doesn't need an intercom to be heard in every corner of the house.

"Coming, Mom!" I holler back, then turn to Megan. "I guess we're leaving. She wants to make sure I get to bed at a decent hour tonight, and I haven't finished packing yet."

Megan gives me a hug. "I'll see you tomorrow morning, but *bon voyage* anyway!" She smiles at me. "Gotta start using my French sometime, right?"

I smile back. "*Bon voyage* to you, too. Let's try and IM or videoconference this week, okay? And I'll be reading your blog every day."

One good thing that happened tonight is that Mrs. Wong finally gave Megan permission to revive Fashionista Jane. Emma says she must have been filled with post-debate happy hormones or something.

"I'll put stuff in there just for you, I promise," Megan replies.

My mother and father and I head home with the Winchesters, but Stewart stays behind to hang out with Emma. At least that's what he tells us he's going to do, but as we're leaving, the only person I spot him with is Sophie. *Just you wait, Mademoiselle Velcro*, I think, picturing

Heather Vogel Frederick

the PIQUEUSE DE MEC T-shirt as I close the front door behind me. *You are in for one big surprise.*

Early the next morning, we all meet up at Half Moon Farm to say good-bye to our Wyoming friends. I'm catching a ride to Logan Airport with them on the bus that the Wongs hired. The pen pals (well, except Zoe and me) all promise to write to each other, and Summer Williams hands out mittens that she knitted for everyone while she was here. Mr. Wong videotapes the whole thing, and Sophie Fairfax takes a few pictures, too.

"All my bags are packed, I'm ready to go," Madison begins, and Jess and Savannah jump right in as the three of them serenade us with an impromptu a capella version of "Leaving on a Jet Plane."

Things get a little tearful after that as none of us knows exactly when we'll see each other again.

"Next year in Wyoming, maybe?" says Mrs. Jacobs, giving Mrs. Hawthorne another big hug. "We need to give your menfolk a taste of the Wild West, too."

"You're all welcome at the ranch any time," adds Mrs. Parker. She leans over and gives Chloe one last kiss. "Especially you, peanut."

Our Gopher Hole friends climb reluctantly onto the bus, and I follow them, poking my head out the window to wave to my parents.

"Give your grandmother my love," says my mother, blowing me a kiss.

"I will," I promise her.

"Call us when you get there!" says my father.

At the airport, Mrs. Winchester helps me check in and find my gate. It's the first time I've flown alone, and I'm a little nervous. But it's a smooth flight, and three hours later I land in Chicago, where Gram is waiting for me by the baggage claim.

She gives me a big hug. "I'm so excited that you're here!"

"Me too!" I reply, which isn't entirely truthful. No way am I going to spoil this week by being a brat, though. I'm too old for that, and I am not Zoe Winchester. Besides, now that I'm here, I may as well try and have fun, right?

We catch a taxi to Union Station and are soon aboard the Amtrak train that will take us to Minneapolis. Gram was bound and determined to kick off our week together with a Betsy-Tacy style train trip.

"I love traveling by rail," she says, settling into a seat by the picture window with a contented sigh.

I plop down in the seat across from her. I think I'm going to like traveling this way, too. My grandmother sprang for a sleeper compartment for the two of us "just for fun," and in case either of us want to take naps, which we might, since it's an eight-hour trip to the Twin Cities.

The room is small, but efficient, with a pull-down table between us, a closet for our coats, a sink and counter area, and even a tiny bathroom. Plus, two of the seats fold down to turn into a bed, and another berth folds down from above. It's totally cool. I take a bunch of pictures to show Megan and Ashley and the rest of my friends.

"Look!" Gram says happily, pointing to a map. "We'll be passing

Heather Vogel Frederick

through Milwaukee in a couple of hours." As we pull out of the station, she starts to sing: "'There's a place named Milwaukee, Milwaukee, Milwaukee . . .'" She smiles at me. "Remember?"

I nod ruefully. How could I forget? Gram and my mother have been quoting to me from Maud Hart Lovelace's books ever since I was a little kid. Betsy and her friend Tacy make up this stupid poem about Milwaukee when they're, like, five—and then later, when Betsy's in high school, she takes the train there. Which I guess is what we're doing now, even though we're continuing on to Minneapolis and St. Paul.

Gram looks out the window and hums to herself. It's kind of adorable, actually, how giddy she is. I sit back and relax in my seat, then check my watch; it's not quite three.

R U AT THE AIRPORT YET? I text Megan. She and Gigi are booked on an evening flight. They'll arrive in Paris in time for breakfast, even though it will be, like, three in the morning Concord time.

LEAVING SOON, she texts back. STILL PACKING MADLY!

I smile, imagining the chaos in her bedroom. ON TRAIN, I tell her. COOL SLEEPER COMPARTMENT.

R U SPENDING THE NIGHT ON THE WAY?

NO, I reply. ARRIVING 10:30 PM BUT GRAM WANTED TO BE ABLE TO NAP.

HAVE FUN! GOTTA RUN. CIAO 4 NIAO! XOXO

I shove my phone back in my pocket, then pull out my early birthday present from my parents—an e-reader. My mother loaded *Jane*

Eyre onto it for me, and I'm going to try and finish it this vacation. I turn it on and dive back into Charlotte Brontë's world.

There's a mystery afoot at Thornfield—something strange is going on in the attic. Nobody will tell Jane what it is, but she keeps hearing footsteps and weird laughter up there at night, and once, she thinks that someone has crept into her bedroom. Meanwhile, the household is preparing for a party. Somebody named Blanche Ingram is coming to visit, and the housekeeper is sure she and Mr. Rochester are going to get engaged. Adele Varens, the little French girl that Jane has been hired to watch over as governess—the girl Emma calls "annoying plot device"—is all atwitter over the preparations.

Reading about Adele makes me think of Paris again, and I stare out the window wondering if Megan's plane has taken off yet. Is she dreaming of her rendezvous with Simon, her Mr. Rochester?

What about me? I wonder. *Will I ever meet my Mr. Rochester?*

It feels like everybody has a Mr. Rochester but me. Emma has my brother Stewart—well, mostly. The bits of him that aren't Velcroed to Sophie Fairfax. Jess has Darcy, Megan has Simon, and Cassidy has Zach and probably Tristan Berkely, too. The only guy remotely interested in me these days is Third, who's nice and everything, and even, technically, cute I suppose—if you like moose-types with a goofy sense of humor. But still, he's *Third*.

Since when did I become the loser?

The rocking of the train is soothing, and before long my eyes are drooping and Gram is yawning, too. I'm really grateful she got us a

Heather Vogel Frederick

sleeper, because we both end up taking naps in the fold-out beds. By the time we wake up, it's dinnertime.

The dining car is cool—it has real linen tablecloths and waiters and everything. I watch the staff, grateful that Pies & Prejudice isn't on wheels. It looks a little tricky, carrying trays of food and drinks around on a swaying railroad car without dropping anything.

"We won't be getting to the hotel until late tonight, so let's sleep in a bit tomorrow," says Gram after we've ordered. "I want to be sure we're rested up. I thought we'd spend the day sightseeing, maybe visit some landmarks and do a few educational things. That'll make your mother happy."

"Sounds good," I reply, without enthusiasm. Will Megan have to do educational things in Paris?

My grandmother busies herself unfolding her napkin and placing it in her lap, then gives me a sly smile. "But on our way to Mankato, I figured we'd swing by the Mall of America."

I don't have to pretend to be enthusiastic now. This is more like it!

She laughs. "I can tell by the look on your face that you're in favor of that idea. We're going to have so much fun, Becca!"

The next morning we pick up our rental car and drive all over Minneapolis. We visit the Betsy-Tacy sites first, of course, including the Bow Street apartment building where Betsy and Joe (actually the author and her husband Delos) first lived; and the University of Minnesota, which Betsy Ray and her friends all called "the U."

My grandmother was a student here, too, and as she leads me

around campus looking at the buildings, I can't help but think about Charlotte Brontë, who never got to go to college since it wasn't an option for women back then. The second I catch myself thinking about this I tell myself sternly to cut it out. I'm starting to act like Emma Hawthorne.

We tour a university art museum to make my mother happy, grab lunch in the food court at the student union, then hop back in the car to do some more sightseeing. My grandmother wants to show me some of the lakes. It's too cold to go out on any of them today, but we drive by several.

"It would be pretty cool to live in a city with a bunch of lakes right downtown," I tell Gram, looking out at the sparkling water which is still frozen in some spots.

She smiles at me. "I loved it when I was a student here! Your grandfather and I and all our friends used to go canoeing and sailing and swimming in the summer, and skating in the winter."

"Good thing you weren't in Concord last week for the mother-daughter hockey game," I reply. "The mothers would have won for sure."

She laughs.

Next, we drive over the Mississippi River to St. Paul, the other half of the Twin Cities.

"This seems different from Minneapolis," I note, looking around with interest. "It reminds me a lot of Boston. Well, Cambridge, maybe. The buildings, I mean."

Heather Vogel Frederick

"Good eye, Becca! In the nineteenth century, St. Paul was known as 'the last city of the East,' while Minneapolis was 'the first city of the West.'" Gram glances over at me. "Have you ever thought about studying architecture?"

I look at her like she has two heads. *Me? Architecture?* "Uh, no."

"Interesting field," she replies. "You should think about it. The U has a wonderful program."

I haven't thought much about what I might like to do someday. I guess I've always figured I'd decide once I got to college. For a while I thought maybe an acting or singing career would be fun, but the plain truth is that I'm not that good, and I'd hate all the rejection that everybody says comes along with those jobs.

I gaze out the window, thinking about my grandmother's remark. Architecture, huh? I suppose designing houses and buildings could be kind of interesting.

We grab an early dinner at this cool cafeteria-style restaurant called Café Latte, then head back to our hotel. As I look out the car window at the clumps of snow still scattered on the sidewalks and curbs I can't help wondering what the weather is like in Paris. I know I should stop torturing myself, and I really am having a much better time than I expected with Gram, but still, it's hard.

Next morning I'm awakened by a knock on our door.

"I wonder who that could be?" says my grandmother, who's already up and dressed. Winking at me, she trots over to open the door. "Well, look at this—room service! Happy birthday, sweetheart!"

A waiter rolls in a table set with an elaborate breakfast, including a cupcake with a candle in it for me.

"Thanks, Gram!" I say, giving her a kiss.

She lights the candle and I blow it out. There's only one thing I wish for; the same thing I've been wishing for all year: *Mr. Rochester, where are you?*

"I figure we'll shop for your birthday present at the mall today," Gram tells me. "That way you can have the fun of picking it out. I probably should have brought something for you to open this morning, though."

"That's okay—Megan gave me something." I go over to my suitcase and root around for my present. I have a feeling I know what it is, and sure enough, there's a dress inside. "Oh, wow!" I say when I see it.

"Put it on, put it on!" Gram urges me.

It fits me perfectly. The silky gray fabric gathers at one shoulder, falling in ripples as it drapes to the knee-length hem. I look in the mirror, amazed at my reflection. I look so—grown up. Sophisticated. Elegant.

I make a face at myself. I'm turning into Emma Hawthorne again here, spouting synonyms.

"What a labor of love!" exclaims my grandmother. "That's real friendship. And it's a Wong original—you hang on to that dress, Becca. I have no doubt Megan is going to be a famous designer someday."

After breakfast we drive to the Mall of America. My eyes nearly

Heather Vogel Frederick

bug out of my head as we walk inside. This isn't like any other mall I've ever visited before. It's *huge*, like a giant theme park, only indoors, and with about five hundred shops surrounding the central courtyard.

"There's an aquarium we can visit," says Gram, plucking a map from a nearby kiosk. "It has the largest number of sharks in captivity. Oh, and Mrs. Wong would love this—the mall is heated with passive solar energy, and contains thirty thousand live plants and trees. Amazing, huh?"

I nod, looking around in stunned silence. Megan would go nuts over this place.

I'll bet she's going nuts over Paris, my evil inner voice whispers. *She's probably shopping in some trendy little boutique right now.*

"It's hard to know where to begin, isn't it?" says Gram, still frowning at her map. We find a bench so we can sit down and plot a course, then set off. Now that my father has a job again, I feel okay about liberating a little of my waitressing money. I buy presents for my family—a new wallet for my father to celebrate his new job; a gardening book for my mother that she's checked out of the library a zillion times and has been drooling over but hasn't wanted to spring for. I'm tempted to get Stewart a stuffed animal in the shape of a rat, but decide that would be too mean, so I end up picking out a really nice docking station for his iPod that doubles as speakers. I figure he can use it in his dorm next year. He should be getting his college acceptance letters any day now.

Gram talks me into waiting until we get to Mankato to pick out something for my book club friends—she says I should get them

Wish You Were Eyre

263

something Betsy-Tacy–related since we're here, and she's probably right. Still, I can't resist splurging on a really pretty amethyst ring for Megan, and for Ashley, I find a pair of hammered silver hoop earrings.

I manage to talk my grandmother into taking a ride on the roller coaster, which is a mistake because we're both too queasy afterward to eat lunch. We opt for manicures instead, and then we shop for a present for me.

"What do you think about this one?" asks Gram, holding up a necklace with a singe pearl drop. "It would look lovely with your new dress. Or maybe this? It's very *Jane Eyre*, don't you think?"

She passes me a silver locket that opens up to put a picture inside. *Of who?* I think wistfully. There's no Mr. Rochester on my horizon. But it is really pretty, with a fancy *R* engraved on it, and I've always wanted a locket so that's the present I choose.

"We'd better hit the road," says Gram, checking her watch as we're standing at the cash register. "Frannie's expecting us for dinner."

Once we're out of the city, she pulls over and lets me drive. My spirits droop as we plunge further into the countryside. What are we going to DO out here all week? I keep thinking about Megan, who's in Paris right this minute, where there's a whole heck of a lot more to look at than miles of prairie and a road running through it as flat as a stick of gum.

Finally, we see signs for Mankato. As we get off the highway and enter town, Gram shrieks, which startles me so that I nearly drive off the road.

Heather Vogel Frederick

"Pull over, pull over!" she says, and I do, stopping the car in front of a stone building covered with ivy. There's an arched window over the door, and two round windows flanking it. "That's the Carnegie library from *Betsy and Tacy Go Downtown!*" she tells me, her face alight with excitement. "We'll come back tomorrow with Frannie, so she can take a picture of the two of us in front of it for you to show to your book club friends."

My spirits droop even further. Emma should be on this trip; not me. She's the only person I can think of, besides my grandmother—okay, and our moms —who would actually get excited about seeing a library.

I know one thing for sure: Megan's not visiting some stupid library right now. She's probably driving down the Champs-Élysées, while I'm stuck here driving down some podunk street in a podunk town. Life is so unfair!

Get a grip, Chadwick! I tell myself firmly *You're acting like Zoe Winchester.* I slap a smile on my face as my grandmother directs me past a bunch of Betsy-Tacy landmarks—Lincoln Park; the site of the Opera House and the shoe store where Betsy's father worked—and then we drive down a series of tree-shaded streets lined with tidy homes. Some of the houses are really old and big, like Cassidy's, others are smaller and more modest, like the Hawthornes'. None look exactly like ours, but there's still something familiar about this place. I can't tell if it's because it looks so much like what I pictured Deep Valley to be when I read the books, or because it reminds me of home.

"It kind of reminds me a little of Concord," I tell Gram.

"I think so too," she replies. "Well-loved houses in a well-loved town; Concord and Deep Valley have a lot in common."

We pull up in front of a cozy-looking white house, and as we're getting our suitcases out of the trunk, the front door flies open and a silver-haired woman comes charging down the path. She and Gram start squealing and jumping up and down with excitement as they hug each other. It's not exactly the kind of thing you expect to see your grandmother do, but then I guess best friends are best friends, no matter how old they are.

Frannie hugs me too. "I'm so glad to finally meet you, Rebecca!" she says. "We're going to have so much fun this week."

Why does everybody keep telling me that? I think, feeling annoyed. I start to pick up my suitcase and Frannie shoos me away.

"No, no. Leave your bags. I'll get Theo to help with them." She whips her cell phone out of her pocket and punches in a number. "They're here!" she says to whoever's on the other end. "Can you come on over for a minute? We need your muscles."

A few seconds later the front door of the big chocolate-colored house across the street opens and a boy emerges. As he lopes down the front path toward us, my heart does a little somersault. *What's Zach Norton doing here?* Then the boy crosses the street and I see that it's not Zach Norton. He's not quite as tall as Zach, for one thing, and his hair is a darker shade of blonde. His eyes, though, his eyes! They're even bluer than Zach's, and unless I'm completely mistaken, they're looking at me with interest.

Heather Vogel Frederick

Frannie was right about the muscles, too—he has plenty of them.

"Rebecca Chadwick, this is my grandson, Theodore Rochester."

"Call me Theo," he says, extending his hand and smiling broadly.

I almost burst out laughing. *Why on earth would I call you Theo, when I can call you Mr. Rochester?*

"What's so funny?" he asks as we shake hands.

"Nothing," I reply.

Paris? Who needs Paris! Right now Mankato, Minnesota, is the only place on earth I want to be.

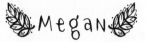

Megan

*"I never saw a more splendid scene:
the ladies were magnificently dressed . . ."*
—*Jane Eyre*

"Mesdames et messieurs, retournez à vos places et attachez vos ceintures, s'il vous plaît. Nous atterrirons à Paris dans quelques minutes. Ladies and gentlemen, please return to your seats and fasten your seat belts, as we will be landing in Paris in a few minutes."

The flight attendant's soft, melodious voice comes over the loudspeaker, interrupting my daydream. I've been awake for a while now, staring out the window as sunrise paints the clouds pink.

I was so excited when we boarded yesterday in Boston that I thought for sure I wouldn't sleep a wink. For one thing, I've never flown first class before. My father takes it all the time when he travels for work, but my mother makes him put the brakes on when we fly anywhere as a family. She says it's a waste of money that could be put to better use (like offsetting our carbon footprint, which she always pays to do whenever we travel anywhere), so we usually just go coach. The only exception was the last time we flew to Hong Kong to see Gigi and my cousins, back when I was in elementary school. My father persuaded my mother that business class would be more humane for such a long flight, and she relented.

For this trip, though, Gigi ignored my mother's protests. "This is a once-in-a-lifetime experience," she told her, "and I intend to pull out all the stops for my favorite granddaughter."

This is a joke, of course. I'm her only granddaughter. Her other grandchildren are both boys.

I have to admit, first class is pretty darn fabulous. A person could really get used to this. Our seats are huge and comfortable, with tons of leg room, and the flight attendants came by constantly during the flight with something yummy or fun—dinner on real china with real linen napkins; ice cream and freshly baked cookies a couple of hours later; free DVD players and headsets; pillows and blankets and even slippers, plus all the soda and juice and hot drinks we wanted.

As if summoned by my thoughts, a flight attendant materializes with a basket of fresh croissants, orange juice for me and coffee for Gigi.

"*Bonjour, Madame Chen. Bonjour, Mademoiselle Wong,*" she says.

"*Bonjour,*" Gigi replies.

"*Merci,*" I add, practicing my French as the flight attendant passes me a croissant. Apparently my accent isn't too hideous because she smiles at me.

A few minutes later she's back again, doling out warm washcloths.

"Doesn't that feel wonderful?" asks Gigi, taking one and dabbing at her face and hands. "It really helps wake you up after such a long flight."

For once in my life I don't feel like I need help waking up. Today's the day I've been wishing for ever since I first got interested in fashion. Even though it's only something like three in the morning Concord time, every cell in my body is on full alert. I feel like a little kid—I want to bounce in my seat and dance in the aisle and sing at the top of my lungs.

Paris! I'm going to Paris!

It's a dream come true.

There are only two possible clouds on my dream's horizon. The first is Simon.

I finally took Becca's advice and mustered the courage to email and tell him I'd seen him talking to Sophie. Becca was right; there was a logical explanation. Sophie had actually been trying to videoconference with Simon's mother. Mrs. Berkeley has been a shoulder for Sophie to cry on during her parents' divorce, and Simon just happened to be using his mother's laptop when she called. I felt like a total idiot for even bringing it up. Now I'm worried that Simon thinks I'm some kind of a snoop as well as jealous.

The other possible cloud is Sophie's grandfather. When he got wind of our trip, he insisted on meeting us at the airport. He's offered to drive us around all week, as a thank you for hosting his granddaughter in Concord. I'm just hoping that he's nothing like Sophie.

Fortunately, he's not.

"Bonjour!" says a white-haired man in a navy blazer as we exit customs a while later. He hurries over to greet us, his face creasing into a broad smile. *"Bienvenue à Paris!"*

Heather Vogel Frederick

"*Bonjour*," says Gigi, extending a manicured hand. I don't know how my grandmother does it. As always, she looks like she just stepped out of the pages of *Vogue* magazine. My face may be clean, but other than that I look like I slept in a laundry hamper. "*Je m'appelle Gigi Chen, et je vous présente ma petite-fille, Megan Wong.*"

"*Enchanté, Madame Chen,*" he replies, taking her hand as he bends over from the waist in a brief bow. "*Edouard de Roches, à votre service.*"

He shakes my hand, too. Sophie's grandfather has the same greenish eyes that she does, but that's where the resemblance ends. He's not particularly tall, but he's not petite like Sophie, either. He's about my father's height, I'd guess, and with his snow-white hair and mustache and the friendliness that he radiates, he reminds me for some reason of Santa Claus. A slimmer, more dapper version of Santa Claus, one who happens to speak French. Although technically I suppose Santa is multilingual.

Sophie's grandfather doesn't blink an eye at the mound of luggage on our trolley. Extending an arm politely to Gigi, he takes its handle from me and sets off at a brisk pace. I trot along behind the two of them, gawking at the French signs everywhere and people chattering away in French, my head spinning as I try to absorb all the new sights and sounds.

I keep thinking about what Fashionista Jane would say. Fashionista Jane Eyre, that is. Although I'm keeping the original blog name, that's how I think of her now. I'm going to do like Becca said and try and get my Jane on, and give the blog a little different spin this time around in honor of our book club. What would Fashionista Jane Eyre say right now? Probably something like "Reader, I'm in Paris!"

"*Voilà*," says Monsieur de Roches as we leave the terminal and pause at the curb in front of an enormous and very elegant car.

"Is that a Rolls Royce?" I whisper to Gigi, spotting the hood ornament.

She nods. "A vintage model," she whispers back.

"*Votre chariot pour la semaine*," says Sophie's grandfather proudly.

I think he just said "your chariot for the week." I sure hope so.

He holds the rear passenger door open politely as we get in, then starts putting our luggage in the trunk.

"Pinch me, I think I'm dreaming," I murmur to my grandmother as I slide in after her. The leather seat is as soft as Coco's fur.

She obliges, her almond eyes sparkling with excitement. "This beats a taxi ride any day."

I figured Sophie's family was rich, what with that picture on her dresser of her house and everything, but a vintage Rolls Royce is a whole different level altogether.

"The Hôtel de Crillon, *oui*?" says Monsieur de Roches as he climbs in behind the wheel. "That is where you are staying, correct?"

"You speak English!" I blurt out, surprised.

His eyes crinkle at me in the rearview mirror. "*Mais bien sûr!*" he says. "But of course. You must pardon my accent, however."

"I'm used to accents," I tell him, pointing to Gigi. My grandmoth-

Heather Vogel Frederick

er's English still carries a hint of Hong Kong.

He laughs. "We will get along just fine then, I see," he says. "Now ladies, if I may suggest *un petit tour*—unless, perhaps, you are tired from your journey and wish to, how you say, make a nap?"

I shake my head vigorously. I don't want to sleep a second more than I have to on this trip. *I'm in Paris!*

"No," says Gigi firmly. "No naps."

"Then allow me to introduce you to my city." Monsieur de Roches drives along whistling cheerfully—I recognize the tune, because Gigi has been humming it practically nonstop for weeks. It's something called "La Vie en Rose," a song from the 1940s that is sort of Paris's theme song.

The Rolls sails along the busy streets as serene as a swan. "You have brought *le soleil* with you, I see," Sophie's grandfather says, glancing up at the cloudless spring sky.

Soleil. I know that word from my work with Bébé Soleil – it means sun. I decide to try out my French in response. *"Oui, c'est une belle journée aujourd'hui."*

"A beautiful day, *oui.* Very good, mademoiselle. I think Paris she will like you very much."

I smother a giggle, and reach into my bag for my sketchbook, jotting down "Paris she will like you very much" and "make a nap." I'm thinking Fashionista Jane might have to have a section on her blog called "Lost in Translation." Or maybe "Roches-isms."

"Where are you going to take us first?" asks Gigi.

"Since it is on our way to the hotel, and since it is such a fine day, we shall start with a view from the top—Montmartre."

"*Ah, bien,*" my grandmother says with a happy sigh.

I grab my guidebook and quickly flip through the pages. Montmartre: Set atop a hill in Paris's Right Bank, this neighborhood has been a magnet for artists, writers, and poets since the end of the nineteenth century. *My kind of place*, I think, and read on about its charming village feel, winding cobblestone streets, and the jewel in its crown—the white-domed Basilica of the Sacré-Coeur, which can be seen from all over the city.

"*Voilà!*" says Sophie's grandfather, pointing out the window at a hill up ahead. The church atop it gleams in the sun like a snowy version of the Emerald City in *The Wizard of Oz.*

It takes us a while to find a parking spot, but we finally do. We head first for the Place du Tertre, the old village square, which is crammed with artists working at their easels. Some of the paintings are pretty good. Then we stroll to the bottom of the steps leading up to Sacré-Coeur, where I gaze open-mouthed at the church's creamy facade. We sit on a nearby bench for a while, chatting and people watching, until it's time for lunch. Monsieur de Roches leads us through a maze of narrow, winding streets to one of his favorite cafés.

There are tables spilling out onto the sidewalk, and since it's such a nice day, we decide to sit at one of them. Gigi puts on her sunglasses as she studies the menu.

I look around, feeling that tingle of excitement again. *I'm in Paris!*

Heather Vogel Frederick

"So what do you ladies have on your agenda this week?" asks Sophie's grandfather, after placing our order in rapid French.

"Well," says Gigi, opening her purse and fishing out a piece of paper with a long list printed on it. She dangles it in the air. "This is what Megan's mother would like us to do."

My heart sinks. This is the first I've heard of any list, and if my mother made it, I can only imagine what's on it. We'll probably have to tour some state-of-the-art wastewater treatment plant, or attend a session of parliament or whatever they call their government over here, or visit a bunch of museums. My mother is big on museums.

"But I have other plans," Gigi continues, and calmly tears the piece of paper in two. She laughs when she sees the look on my face. "Not that we won't visit some museums. No trip to Paris is complete without seeing the Louvre and Rodin's sculpture garden, at the very least." She reaches across the table and squeezes my hand. "But this is our special trip, just for the two of us. And we're going to do whatever we want."

"Ah, spoken like a true *Parisienne!*" says Monsieur de Roches, lifting his glass. "I salute your *joie de vivre.*"

I know what *joie de vivre* means, too. It means spirit, or joy in living. That's my grandmother to a T.

"You're the best!" I tell her, kissing her cheek.

Over lunch, she and Sophie's grandfather launch into a spirited discussion, mostly in French, of all the possible things that we could see and do. They break into English every now and then in an effort to include me, but I'm perfectly happy just watching the world go by.

Before long, my fingers start itching for my sketchbook, so I take it out of my shoulder bag and slip it discreetly onto my lap where I can draw between bites.

The café isn't on a touristy street. I can tell by the kinds of people walking by that they actually live here. Some are pushing strollers, some have tiny dogs on leashes, some are walking arm in arm. Plus, the shops that surround the café are the everyday sort—bakeries, florists, cheese shops, stuff like that. Lots of people go by carrying shopping bags that sprout those long, skinny loaves of bread they call baguettes. Gigi told me that the French really appreciate fresh food and tend to shop every day instead of once a week at the supermarket, the way we usually do at home.

As I sketch, I try and imagine myself living here. What would it be like to have an apartment in Paris, and shop at that *boulangerie* across the street for bread, or at the *poissonnerie* down the block for fish, or buy flowers at the *fleuriste* next door?

It would be heaven.

"What are you smiling about?" asks Gigi, interrupting her conversation with Monsieur de Roches.

I shake my head. "No reason," I reply, still smiling. I can't help myself. *I'm in Paris!*

I'm also getting sleepy. It's midafternoon now, which means it's like nine a.m. back in Concord, so technically my day should just be starting, but the jet lag is starting to catch up with me. Mostly I just catnapped on the plane.

Heather Vogel Frederick

"*Et bien, mesdames,*" says Sophie's grandfather, looking over at my drooping eyelids. "I do think perhaps you are ready to go back to the hotel now and make a nap."

As we wind our way down through the maze of streets from Montmartre into the center of Paris, I catch glimpses of the Eiffel Tower in the distance, and I lean out the window of the Rolls several times to take its picture. I take a picture of our hotel, too, as we pull up in front of it. It looks like a palace.

"The Hôtel de Crillon was a palace built for Louis the fifteenth," says Monsieur de Roches as he shuts off the engine. "It is a masterpiece of eighteenth century architecture, and all of Paris is at your feet."

I know; I've seen the map. We're just a short walk from the Jardin des Tuileries and the Grand Palais and the Carrousel du Louvre and all the other venues where the fashion shows will take place this week, plus we're in the heart of one of the most famous shopping districts in the entire world.

"It's been a delightful day, Monsieur Roches," Gigi tells him as we get out of the car. "We can't thank you enough."

"*Oui, merci beaucoup,*" I echo, trotting out a few more French words I feel confident using.

"*De rien, de rien,*" he replies, which is French for "you're welcome." It literally means "it was nothing." He opens the trunk of the Rolls and a bellhop appears and busies himself with our luggage. "When may I have the pleasure of your company again, ladies? The car is at your service all week."

"Our schedule is quite full tomorrow," says Gigi. "But perhaps Tuesday? Unless you'd care to walk around a bit with us later this evening. I want Megan to see Paris at night—it's so beautiful, all lit up."

Monsieur de Roches gives another one of his brief, dignified bows. "I would be delighted to accompany you both tonight. What time shall I return?"

"Shall we say eight?"

"Eight it is. *À toute à l'heure.*"

"*À toute à l'heure,*" we reply. That means "see you later."

We follow the bellhop into the hotel's palatial lobby. I'm experiencing a combination of jet lag and sensory overload at this point, and can only blink at the elegance—soaring ceilings, marble floors, lots of gilt, crystal chandeliers. The fashionistas are starting to arrive too, judging by the people I see milling around. Either that, or the hotel guests dress in couture all the time.

I follow Gigi upstairs to our room. There are floor-to-ceiling windows with elegant wrought-iron balconies outside, and more chandeliers and gilt. There's a marble fireplace and a tapestry on the wall and more marble in the bathroom. I'm feeling like Jane Eyre must have felt when she first arrived at Thornfield. It's all so unbelievably grand!

"I'm setting the alarm for two hours," says Gigi as I flop facedown on the fluffy comforter and pile of pillows on my bed. "Any longer than that, and we won't sleep tonight. We need to get switched over to Paris time as soon as possible—we have a busy week ahead!"

My nap feels like it's over before it started, and I have to force

Heather Vogel Frederick

myself groggily into the shower after the alarm goes off. I emerge wrapped in a fluffy robe and feeling slightly more awake just as room service is delivering our dinner.

Settling cross-legged on the end of my bed, I help myself to what Gigi calls a *croque monsieur,* a sort of a fancy grilled ham and cheese sandwich.

"Tomorrow we're having breakfast with Wolfgang and Isabelle," she says, consulting our calendar. "Ooo, you're in for a treat. They're taking us to Angelina, one of my favourite spots in Paris!"

"What is it?"

"A *salon de thé,*" she replies. "A tea shop—and it's a restaurant, too, and patisserie. You'll see. It's very special." She looks at the calendar again. "After that, we don't have anything scheduled until your lunch with Bébé Soleil, so I thought maybe we'd walk down the Rue du Faubourg Saint-Honoré and Avenue Montaigne and do a little window shopping. Maybe even real shopping. Give you a bit of an overview."

I nod, taking another bite of my sandwich.

"And of course there's also the Place des Victoires, the Champs-Élysées and the Rue de Rivoli or, if you'd rather, we can scoot over to Les Halles or even Saint-Germain-des-Prés and poke around in some boutiques."

I nod. "Yes."

"Yes, what?" asks my grandmother.

"Yes everything."

She laughs. "That's my girl! I brought you to the right place, didn't I?"

We look over the rest of the week's schedule—it's jammed with fashion shows, of course, but there are also blocks of free time in which Gigi has penciled other destinations such as the Louvre, Versailles, and something called Ladurée.

"Edouard mentioned at lunch that he'd like to take us on a river cruise too at some point, if we have time," Gigi says frowning at the calendar. "But I'm not sure we'll be able to fit it in."

"Edouard?"

"Monsieur de Roches."

"Oh, right. When's our first fashion show?"

"Tomorrow afternoon."

Gigi comes to Fashion Week almost every year, and she says that especially for a first-timer, there's no point trying to go to all of them. There are shows every hour on the hour from ten in the morning until ten at night all week, so nobody can see everything. "Best to pick and choose," she told me when we started planning our trip, even though my inner fashionista was screaming to try and cram them all in.

Back in Concord, my grandmother had me go through the calendar of events and prioritize my choices, limiting them to three or four a day. "Any more than that, and your head might explode," she told me, and Wolfgang agreed. "Gigi is right. See three or four, blog about one or two," was his advice. Once I had my wish list, he went over it and narrowed it down even further, then had *Flashlite* get invitations for Gigi and me.

We've also been invited to a couple of soirées in the evenings, again thanks to *Flashlite*. The biggest one is *Flash* magazine's own farewell

Heather Vogel Frederick

party next Saturday, on our last night in Paris.

My heart skips a beat when I think about Saturday. Simon and I are going to spend the whole day together! His family is arriving Friday night for the weekend, and Tristan said he didn't mind if Simon skipped his ice dancing competition to hang out with me.

I'm allowed to bring a guest to the *Flash* party, and Simon's already said yes. I'm planning to wear a dress I made specially for it. It's a twin of the one I made Becca for her birthday, only mine's not dove gray; it's the same creamy white as Sacré-Coeur.

After dinner Gigi and I get dressed and put on comfortable shoes, then take the elevator down to the lobby to meet Sophie's grandfather. We find him sitting on one of the enormous red sofas reading a newspaper called *Le Monde*. He brightens when he sees us, and offers his arm to my grandmother as the three of us head out. I get that giddy feeling again because Gigi is right: Paris is gorgeous at night.

We walk and walk and walk, across the Place de la Concorde and down to the Seine, the river that flows through the center of the city, dividing it into the Left Bank and the Right Bank. We stroll along the riverbank past the Tuileries gardens and on to the Louvre, where we gawk—well, I gawk, Gigi and Monsieur de Roches have seen it before—at the *Pyramide* in the courtyard of the Louvre, the famous giant glass pyramid thing that's lit up at night. I've seen it in a couple of movies, but the real thing is even more awesome. Some of the fashion shows will be held here, and I can't wait to see it from the inside.

From there we hop on the Metro, a subway kind of like the T in Boston, and head to the Arc de Triomphe, this huge stone arch in the center of a traffic circle that has streets sticking out of it like spokes on a wheel.

"*Mesdames*, may I interest you in *une petite aventure*?" says Monsieur de Roches, whipping three tickets out of his pocket.

Gigi squeals. Right there in public, she actually squeals. I don't know whether to be embarrassed or just go with the moment. I decide to go with the moment.

"We must hurry, though," he says, checking his watch. He herds us inside the base of the arch, where we take the elevator up a ways, then climb a narrow staircase to emerge on the top.

The view is beyond amazing.

"That's the Champs-Élysées," says Gigi, clutching my arm and pointing at the broad boulevard directly beneath us. She's as breathless as I am.

No one needs to tell me what the enormous glowing structure is off to its right. The Eiffel Tower! We can see it in the distance from our hotel room, but from up here, at night, all lit up like this, it's the glowing golden punctuation mark in *I'm in Paris!*

Out of the corner of my eye I see Sophie's grandfather check his watch. He and Gigi exchange a glance and smile at each other, like they have a secret. A moment later he nudges me and whispers, "*Regarde!*"

A spotlight emerges from the top of the tower and sweeps the city in a circle, and then—magic.

Heather Vogel Frederick

"Oh wow!" I gasp, watching in delight as thousands of lights flash randomly up and down the tower's length and across the arch at its base. From a distance, it's like millions of fireflies shimmering against the black velvet of the night sky.

"Some light show, huh?" says Gigi proudly, as if perhaps she designed it. She puts her arm around my shoulders and pulls me close. "Welcome to Paris, sweetheart."

"Did I not tell you?" says Monsieur de Roches with a wink. "Our city, she is sparkling just for you."

I smile. Sophie's grandfather is kind of corny, but I can't help but like him.

By the time we get back to the hotel, Gigi is yawning. She goes right to bed but I'm still kind of awake, buzzing from all the sights and sounds, so I take my laptop in the bathroom and work on a quick blog post.

Reader, I'm in Paris!

Oh là là, Fashionista Jane is here for fashion week. She's staying at a palace (literally) and promises to share with you the very best that Paris has to offer. The best shopping tips, the best behind-the-scenes peeks at all the best shows (she has carte blanche VIP access, thanks to Flashlite magazine), and of course, what Fashionista Jane post would be complete without a little snark? Fashion Faux Pas, Paris edition, coming up! Au revoir until tomorrow!

I upload a few of the best photos I took today, link to *Flashlite*'s website, and post it. When I'm done, I check to see if Simon's online. He's not. I send him an e-mail instead, letting him know that we've arrived safely and that I can't wait to see him next weekend. I send my parents an e-mail as well, and include the picture of the Eiffel Tower all lit up.

Becca has sent me a quick note, letting me know she had a great trip on the train and is being dragged all over Minneapolis by her grandmother and that she loves loves LOVES the dress I made her.

Smiling with satisfaction, I power down my laptop and brush my teeth. When I slip into bed, I nearly slide out the other side. The sheets are smooth as silk. *Fit for a palace*, I think, smiling to myself in the dark.

I'm in Paris!

The next morning I pick out my clothes very carefully. For one thing, it's not every day that a person has a breakfast meeting with the editor-in-chief of *Flash* magazine and her style editor assistant. For another, I don't want to be guilty of some horrible fashion faux pas and end as up the centerpiece of my own blog. Or worse, someone else's blog. I decide on black leggings topped with an oversize white shirt and denim bomber jacket. Add sunglasses and a belt, and it's very urban chic.

"Megan DARLING!" says Wolfgang a little later, as we come through the door of Angelina's. He swoops down on us like some sort of enormous crane, one that bestows air kisses. "And the utterly fabulous GIGI!" Wolfgang is tall and skinny and irresistible, and as

Heather Vogel Frederick

always he's dressed from head to toe in black. Beside him, Isabelle d'Azur, the orange-haired editor-in-chief, looks like a tiny parrot. "I can think of no BETTER way to start Fashion Week than breakfast with our FAVORITE teen blogger, can you, Isabelle?"

"Absolutely not," she says, bestowing more air kisses. "We saw your blog post this morning—it's just perfect!"

"You're already driving *beaucoup* Web traffic to the *Flashlite* site," Wolfgang informs me, sounding pleased.

"Thank you," I reply. "Or maybe I should say *merci*."

"My granddaughter is taking French now at school," Gigi tells them proudly.

We settle into chairs at a table by a large mural. The room is divided by elaborately carved archways, and overhead, the skylit ceiling radiates soft light. The waitress brings us a menu, but Wolfgang waves it away. "There's only ONE thing to order when one breakfasts at La Maison Angelina," he declares. *"Les croissants et les chocolats chauds l'Africains pour tout, s'il vous plaît."*

I shoot my grandmother a questioning look.

"Utterly divine hot chocolate," she whispers. "Trust Wolfgang; he's right."

"Of course I'm right," he says, then pats his tummy, which is nonexistent because Wolfgang is thin as a pencil. "But we only indulge when in Paris, *oui*?"

"Oui," agrees Isabelle.

My grandmother is looking around, and I can tell she's busy taking mental notes on our surroundings. She'll probably end up redecorating Pies & Prejudice when we get home. "Coco Chanel used to come here," she says happily. "Maybe she even sat at this table."

The hot chocolate, when it arrives, is unlike any I've ever seen before. We each have our own pitcher and teacup, for starters, along with individual bowls of whipped cream. I take a picture of everything first—"for my blog," I explain—and I also e-mail it to my mother, just to torture her a little since I know she'll be horrified. This would rank right up there with ice cream sundaes on her list of "Things Not to Have for Breakfast." The cocoa is thick and creamy, somewhere between chocolate syrup and hot fudge sauce, and it smells incredible. I pour myself a cup, then spoon a generous amount of whipped cream on top and take a sip.

"Was I right or was I right?" asks Wolfgang as I let out a groan.

I nod vigorously. "I wish I could dive in, it's so good!"

He looks pleased. "So, we'll see you this afternoon at Chanel, correct?" he asks, and Gigi and I both nod. "And then you are headed to Bix after that?"

"Uh-huh." I'm really looking forward to that one. Not that I'm not looking forward to the Chanel collection—I am, especially since Chanel is Gigi's favorite design house—but Bix is a young, up-and-coming fashion designer and I'm dying to see her work.

After breakfast—if you can call it that, since it was more like dessert—we spend the rest of the morning walking. I'm glad I wore comfortable shoes. Gigi's in high heels, of course, but it's all I can do to

Heather Vogel Frederick

keep up with her as she taps briskly along the sidewalk of the Rue de Rivoli, pausing to peek in the windows of all the fancy designers whose salons dot its length. We walk for what feels like forever.

"This is how Frenchwomen stay so slim," Gigi tells me. "Everyone walks everywhere in Paris."

Has my mother been to this city, I wonder? She would totally approve.

I certainly don't mind walking. It's another gorgeous day, and it's so much easier to get a feel for a city on foot. The energy here in Paris is totally different from Boston or New York. It's hard to describe—less frantic, maybe, but still vibrant and alive.

After a couple of hours of window shopping, Gigi hails us a taxi for our lunch meeting at Bébé Soleil's flagship store.

"Megan Wong! Madame Chen! *C'est un plaisir*," says Madame Simone, the director, greeting us at the door. The shop is just as I imagined it from Gigi's pictures, from the brightly colored garments that burst from the racks and shelves like bouquets to the cheerful orange-and-cream paint scheme to the mural on the back wall of a stylized sun shining on a garden full of flowers that are actually babies.

"In honor of your visit today, we have created a special display," says Madame Simone, leading me to a table placed prominently by the main counter. "Aha! I see that you like it."

Like it? I'm grinning from ear to ear and so is Gigi. The tiny mannequins are dressed in the vivid overalls and pinafore-style dresses, all made from traditional Chinese fabric, that have become my signature line. I take a bunch of pictures to show off to my friends back home. I'll figure out a way to give the shop a plug on Fashionista Jane, too, without revealing my identity. My mother's one stipulation was that the blog remain anonymous.

Madame Simone introduces me to her staff, Kiki and Marie-Claire and Giselle, and we all pose for pictures together, then Gigi and I poke around for a bit. We pick out an outfit each for Chloe, Maggie, and Trevor, the Crandall's new baby, and then it's time for lunch.

"I hope you have brought some new concepts with you," Madame Simone says, as we follow her to a bistro down the street. "Your designs are very popular."

I show her what I've been working on—I'm branching out into more things for boys, for instance, and noodling with a range of little dresses with puffed sleeves and retro smocking for girls. She's very enthusiastic about everything, which is reassuring. Before I know it, it's time for Gigi and me to grab a taxi back to the hotel and get ready for the afternoon fashion shows.

Gigi changes into one of her favorite black Chanel suits, accessorized with pearl rope necklace and pearl earrings. I swap my urban chic look for something a little more polished, exchanging the leggings and layers for a short black skirt, a vintage floral chiffon button-down shirt I found this morning in a tiny shop on Avenue Montaigne, and black heels, since we won't be doing any more walking. I throw on a cropped black leather jacket I found at Sweet Repeats in Boston, make sure I have my camera and sketchbook stowed in my black hobo bag,

Heather Vogel Frederick

then follow Gigi down to the lobby and into yet another taxi. It takes us past the Tuileries gardens—now blooming with huge tents where more shows will be taking place all week—to the Louvre, where Wolfgang is waiting outside the entrance. He whisks us past the velvet ropes and crush of media and curious onlookers, through the security checkpoint, and into the gallery beneath the glass pyramid.

The venue is perfect for Chanel—classy, elegant, and filled with light. Down the center of the gallery, a raised catwalk has been set up. We find our seats in the row right behind Isabelle and Wolfgang and I look around me, trying not to grin too broadly. No point giving myself completely away as the new girl on the block. Beside me, Gigi is settling in with the air of a veteran.

I take out my camera and wait, looking around at the crowd. No fashion faux pas here, that's for sure. From what I can tell, it's a mishmash of fashion elite, journalists, and wealthy patrons, including a sprinkling of movie stars. Or at least I think they're stars, because I sort of recognize them behind their huge sunglasses. I try not to stare.

A few minutes later the music starts. Gigi grabs my hand. "Here we go," she whispers.

I get that giddy feeling again as a *whoosh* of mist blows in from offstage. The music accelerates, its pounding beat matching the racing of my heart. *This is the most exciting thing I've ever done in my life.* Every eye in the gallery is fixed on the large rippling silver curtain at the far end of the catwalk with the designer's trademark interlocked C's projected on it. As the first model emerges from behind it in another cloud of mist, a collective sigh goes up from the audience—her dress is gorgeous, all blue sparkles and bare shoulders. She has an enormous blue plume of a feather in her hair, which is either teased or a wig because it's about two feet high. It's crazy, but somehow it looks perfect.

Close on her heels comes another model, and then another and another in a steady stream of mind-boggling designs. It's quickly apparent that the color of the season is blue, because the women are dressed in every shade of it, from an inky navy to the sheerest, palest sky to bright robin's egg and aquamarine. Also in vogue are luxe fabrics—satins, velvets, silks—to contrast the heavier woolens and tweeds of the fall line.

I snap pictures of outfit after outfit, from überglamorous minis to tailored menswear-inspired ensembles to form-fitting jackets over floor-length, body-hugging dresses. Big, stand-up boatnecks are in. So are ruffles, and a touch of sparkle and shimmer. Even the so-called important pieces—the fall coats and trousers and jackets—have feminine touches like nipped-in waists and belted backs and velvet trim on the pockets and lapels, which I know will thrill my grandmother no end. She's not a big fan of menswear look-alikes.

Some of the styles are over-the-top, like the coat with the enormous balloon sleeves and a dress that's so puffy it almost looks like a bath mat. The skinny little model who's wearing it looks lost. My favorite piece of the show is a sleeveless art deco–style flapper dress with a deep V-neck, a wide, beaded band in a slightly darker shade of blue

Heather Vogel Frederick

under the bust and an identical one low across the hips. Slim vertical pleats give the torso substance, but the hemline wafts away below the knee in a flutter of sheer chiffon. It's exquisite, and the sheer beauty and artistry of it embodies everything I love about fashion. The Asian model who's wearing it looks like an older, much more glamorous version of me, and I can totally picture myself wearing it. Not that I'd have any reason to—it's hardly the type of dress you'd wear to a dance at Alcott High, not even prom. But still, it's dreamy. I snap a picture to pin on the bulletin board in my sewing room at home.

Thirty minutes later the show finishes to a standing ovation. A man with a silver ponytail dressed all in black comes out and takes a bow. It's Karl Lagerfeld! I snap photos of him and of everybody else, too—the models, the designers, the crowd, even the photographers who are taking pictures of the crowd. You never know what will come in handy for my blog, plus I don't ever want to forget a second of my very first Fashion Week show.

I've hardly had time to process what I've just seen before Wolfgang propels Gigi and me upstairs and into another taxi. He barks an address to the driver, then waves us off.

"See you tonight!" he calls as we drive away.

"See you tonight!" we chorus back.

Fifteen minutes later the taxi deposits us at a completely different venue—a graffiti-covered warehouse in an industrial neighborhood. I guess being a younger, edgier designer, Bix decided to choose an up-and-coming place to showcase her designs.

We have to jostle the crowd for seats at this show, which aren't reserved the way they were at Chanel. I lead Gigi to a spot on a riser and we sit down just as the music starts to blare. It's very techno, with strobe lights and a thumping beat. You can feel the energy in the room as the audience's excitement builds. Then the lights stop flashing and the first model appears. She has impossibly long legs that begin beneath a pouf of a pink skirt and end in flirty pink heels. While the bottom half of her ensemble is all feminine, the top is like something out of a robot movie, with an asymmetrical silver metallic jacket and silver hoop earrings the size of dinner plates. She's bald, except for severe black bangs. She looks completely bizarre, but in a totally cool way.

The next model is dressed in tartan shorts and fishnet tights with a matching tartan jacket, and is wearing what looks like a pizza box on her head. She's like a character from some over-the-top Broadway show. I take her picture, along with ones of a gold lamé trench coat over a gypsy skirt and heavy black boots worn by a model with a retro-punk green Mohawk; a menswear-influenced sequined tux; and a knee-length wisp of a lavender kimono worn with a cowboy hat.

It's intoxicatingly different and fun. I can tell my grandmother thinks so too, even though the designs are probably way out of her comfort zone. Her eyes are shining in that Gigi way they do when she's happy, and she's tapping her expensive shoes in time to the synthesized beat.

Because we don't have to rush off to another show afterward, we linger for a while, and I manage to interview Bix briefly for my blog. I

Heather Vogel Frederick

guess the credentials hanging around my neck help, because when I call out her name in the crowd, I see her eyes flicker down to my *Flash* press tag and then back to my face.

"*Oui?*" she says.

"I just want to ask what your main influence is?" I shout, hoping to be heard about the crowd. And hoping she speaks English.

"The street, *chérie*, always the street!" she shouts back. "Is there anything else that's relevant?"

I nod like I understand what she just said, and jot it down dutifully. Gigi takes my arm and we make our way through the crowd to the door, and one more taxi.

Back at the hotel, I collapse in a heap on my bed. "That. Was. *Amazing.*"

"I'm so glad you think so, darling," says Gigi. She's humming that tune again, "La Vie en Rose."

"I can't believe I have four more days of this!" I close my eyes, hardly able to comprehend such bliss.

"What are you going to write about first?" asks Gigi.

I shake my head. "I have no idea." My stomach growls, and I sit up and grin at her. "Can I order a snack? I'm hungry."

"*Mais bien sûr,*" she says. "But of course. And no wonder, after watching all those poor starving girls all afternoon." Crossing to the ornate desk, she passes me the menu. "Order whatever you'd like. Dinner's not for three hours."

We're invited to a party at eight o'clock at a restaurant called Le Soufflé, which sounds promising, but no way will I last until then. And

Gigi is right about the models. They were all about nine feet tall and looked like they could use a trip to Burger Barn. They were beautiful and everything, but some of them were scary-skinny. There were way too many ribs visible. A good stiff breeze would have sent most of them tumbling into the stands.

When I'm a designer someday, I think, *I'm going to make clothes for normal people.* People like me and my friends, not just clothes designed to be worn by the underfed giraffes hired for the fashion runway.

In fact, I decide that's part of what I'll blog about tonight. I order croissants and fruit and yogurt for me and cup of tea for Gigi, then work a bit on my blog post for the day. Afterward we both take naps, and when we wake up, it's time to change again. Gigi selects a beautifully cut red silk cocktail dress she tells me is vintage mid-century Balenciaga, while I'm torn between mimicking the kind of urban vibe I saw this afternoon at Bix or going with classic elegance. I opt for classic elegance. Like Coco Chanel once said, "A girl should be two things: classy and fabulous."

Putting on the black strapless minidress that I made for the cruise last Christmas, I loop a long, narrow turquoise silk scarf around my neck. I leave my hair loose around my shoulders, skip the earrings, and put on my black leather jacket and black knee-high boots for a dash of attitude. One last glance at Mirror Megan—perfect.

Since we're allowed to bring escorts to the soirées, Gigi asked Monsieur de Roches earlier if he wouldn't mind driving us. He's waiting in

Heather Vogel Frederick

the lobby, and his eyes widen when he sees us.

"*Vous serez les plus belles femmes a la fête!*" he tells us. "You will be the most beautiful women at the party."

Gigi laughs and swats him with her sequined clutch.

The restaurant is jammed—and loud. We squeeze our way in and find Wolfgang and Isabelle by a table piled high with mini cheese quiches.

"DARLINGS!" cries Wolfgang, bestowing air kisses all around. Even Sophie's grandfather gets some, which doesn't seem to phase him in the least. "What did you think of the shows?"

"FABULOUS!" I reply, swiping his signature adjective.

He grins. "And Bix? A little different from Chanel, I expect?"

I nod. "I'm going to blog about it tonight. It was over-the-top."

"May I borrow your granddaughter?" he asks Gigi, who nods. "I can see I'm leaving you in good hands," he adds, with a nod toward Monsieur de Roches.

Wolfgang tows me over to meet the fashion critic for *The New York Times* and a bunch of other fashion writers, photographers, designers, assistant designers, models, and various hangers-on and paparazzi. I'm intimidated at first, but eventually I start to relax. *I'm starting to get the hang of this*, I think. All you have to do is look like you belong, and say "fabulous!" a lot.

I glance over at Gigi at one point, grateful that Sophie's grandfather came along tonight to keep her company. I'd hate to have her feel left out. Not that she would—my grandmother is really good at talking to people. But still, it's nice he's here.

It's late when we get back to the hotel, but I stay up a bit longer to check my e-mail. Simon's is brief; all it says is: *Four more days!* I'm laughing about it when an IM message from Becca pops up.

HEY! she says.

HEY BACK! I quickly type.

HAVING FUN IN PARIS?

MAIS BIEN SÛR, I tell her. *OF COURSE. HOW ABOUT U?*

DREAMY, she replies, which isn't the response I'm expecting. Becca's tried really hard these past few months, but I know she was envious of my trip to France.

YEAH?

YEAH. CHECK UR E-MAIL. JUST SENT U A PICTURE.

I do, and there it is, obviously taken on the sly with her cell phone. It's of a guy—a very cute guy who looks a little like Zach Norton.

OOO! I type. *WHO IS HE?*

GRANDSON OF GRAM'S FRIEND FRANNIE. YOU'LL NEVER GUESS HIS NAME.

ZACH?

HA! NOPE—THEODORE ROCHESTER.

It takes me a minute, then I start to laugh. *LOL! MR. ROCHESTER? NO WAY!*

YES WAY! AND I THINK HE LIKES ME. GOTTA GO. WE'RE HAVING DINNER AT HIS HOUSE.

Heather Vogel Frederick

We sign off, and I finish the blog post I started earlier, then head to bed.

Tuesday is even busier, with two shows in the morning and two in the afternoon. Plus, my blog post last night has somehow put me on the Fashion Week radar screen.

"It's Fashionista Jane, *Flash's* new teen blogger," I hear someone behind me whisper as I settle into my seat at the Stella McCartney show. *So much for anonymity*, I think, wondering how word leaked out.

The attention continues all morning. It's a little unnerving. Cameras turn my way; critics ask my opinion; designers take the time to seek me out after both of the shows. It's flattering, but I'm kind of bewildered, too. All I did was write a few brief paragraphs summarizing the Chanel and Bix shows, toss in the *Lost in Translation* quip about "Paris, she will like you," and allow myself a tiny rant about the super-skinny models. ("You could grate cheese on those ribs" was my exact quote.) Oh, and I showcased one Fashion Faux Pas—a picture I snapped at the bistro near Bébé Soleil. *Reader, one should not allow oneself to be charmed by the thought of carrying all of one's belongings around one's waist*, I wrote, under a shot of a tourist wearing one of those fanny-packs that my mother used to be devoted to, before I got on her case. *It is most unbecoming.*

When we ducked back into our hotel to freshen up at lunchtime, though, I saw why people were talking.

"A *thousand* comments? Gigi—check this out!"

My blog post has gone viral.

I do a quick Google search, and all over the Internet people are responding to it—tweeting and writing blog posts and articles and debating and commenting like crazy. Not everyone is happy with me—the size of models is clearly a hot button in the fashion industry and public opinion alike, and I've stirred up a hornet's nest with my criticism of the underfed catwalk models.

I get a text from Wolfgang: FABULOUS! UR LIGHTING UP THE FLASHLITE WEBSITE!

At least he's happy, I think.

Later that afternoon, after Gigi and I stop for tea at Ladurée, a totally awesome patisserie that sells *macarons* in about a zillion flavors, I get a brainstorm. It might not endear me to the fashion industry, but too bad. I decide to throw caution to the winds. Fashionista Jane has a backbone, just like Jane Eyre. She speaks her mind, and so will I. Time to get my Jane on.

NEED A HUNGRY MODEL! I text to Wolfgang. CAN U FIND ME ONE?

He does, and after the next show the three of us duck behind a curtain and set up the shot I have in mind. Handing Wolfgang my camera, I get him to take a picture of me removing the pink ribbon from Ladurée's signature green and gilt box, and feeding a stack of the *macarons* it contains to the celery-stick slender girl in the dazzling couture ensemble.

"She might get in trouble for this," I warn Wolfgang. "Does she know it's for Fashionista Jane?"

The model's eyes light up when hears those two words, and she nods vigorously. Wolfgang says something to her in rapid-fire French, and she shrugs and says something back.

"She's willing to take the risk," he tells me.

I smile at her, and try out a little more of my infant French. "*Comment vous appellez-vous?*"

She smiles back at me. "Albertine."

"Megan Wong," I tell her, sticking out my hand. "Also known as Fashionista Jane. *Merci beaucoup.*"

In my blog post that night, I cover the day's shows in the same kind of admiring and (I hope) Fashionista Jane–worthy detail as I did yesterday, and then I take a deep breath and plunge into another rant, winding it up with something I suspect will make Mrs. Hawthorne proud. I also wonder if maybe I'm more like my mother than I thought I was.

FASHIONISTA JANE'S MODEL FUN FACTS

(OR MAYBE NOT-SO-FUN FACTS)

1. Most runway models today meet the body mass index criteria for anorexia.

*2. Twenty years ago, the average model weighed
8 percent less than the average woman; today's
models weigh 23 percent less.*

*3. Research shows 90 percent of women are
dissatisfied with their body image in some way.*

*Reader, Fashionista Jane cannot help but
wonder if perhaps there is a connection between
this dissatisfaction and what is presented in the
media and on the fashion runways. Shouldn't
both industries take responsibility for promoting
healthy body images? Fashionista Jane herself
has always been told she is beautiful (thank you,
Mom and Dad! Thank you, Gigi!), and to satisfy
the curious she modestly reveals that she is an
entirely normal size and eats entirely normal food.
Including, here in Paris,* macarons *from* Ladurée
and chocolat chaud *from* Angelina. *All things in
moderation,* oui?

I close with the shot that Wolfgang helped me take earlier in the
day of me feeding the model. Underneath it I add a caption: *YOU TOO
CAN END FASHION WORLD HUNGER!*

I read it over, take a deep breath—and post it, hoping I haven't just

Heather Vogel Frederick

bought myself a one-way ticket home from Fashion Week.

The next morning there are nearly double the number of comments waiting.

Emma leaves me one: *Go Megs! The MDBC is behind you 100%!*

So is your mother! says another one, signed Handcuffs. I show it to Gigi.

"And she didn't think a trip to Paris would be educational," she scoffs.

Wolfgang calls to tell me that both *Flashlite* and *Flash* are getting tons of calls and comments, both pro and con.

"We think you're FABULOUSLY brave, darling!" he says. "Keep up the good work!"

Wolfgang thinks any publicity is good publicity, I remind myself, not feeling particularly brave. In fact, this morning I'm feeling downright foolish. It's painful to read the flaming comments from people scoffing at my ignorance—some say I don't understand the industry's "unique demands," while others tell me point-blank to go back to high school, where I belong.

Have I scuttled any chance of a fashion career by opening this can of worms, I wonder?

Gigi's arranged for us to have the afternoon free, so we cram in three shows back-to-back in the morning. Oddly enough, the designers seem to be falling all over themselves trying to court my favor. Maybe Wolfgang is right—any publicity is good publicity? It's hard to tell what's real and what's genuine. Are they fawning over me because my blog is suddenly in the spotlight, not because they agree with me? Just hoping for some free publicity themselves? This is all more complicated than I ever thought it would be.

When we come back to the hotel before lunch, we find our room flooded with swag—boxes and bags from just about every Fashion Week designer and sponsor. There's makeup and magazines, T-shirts and jewelry and silk scarves and even underwear, and larger items, too.

"Oh my goodness," says Gigi, opening one of the bags. She pulls out a gorgeous Bix black leather mini-duffel, a shoulder bag that's the hot item of the week.

"Am I allowed to keep this stuff?" I ask her, incredulous. "Isn't it kind of like bribery or something?"

"We'll talk to Wolfgang," Gigi replies. "I suppose you can always bring it home to give to your friends."

Ashley and Becca would love it, I think, eyeing the loot.

At noon on the dot, we're down in the lobby to meet Monsieur de Roches, who tucks us into the Rolls and drives us out to Versailles. Gigi sits up front with him this time, while I sink into the buttery leather seat in the back with a sigh of relief. It will be good to get away from all the hubbub for a few hours.

Later that night, I blog about our excursion after wrapping up my descriptions of the morning's fashion shows.

Readers, of all the glorious spots in Paris, is there
any so glorious as Versailles? Fashionista Jane likes

Heather Vogel Frederick

to think that perhaps in a former life, she might
have lived at this glittering chateau, complete
with royal courtiers and servants and—oh, never
mind. Alas 'tis but a dream, and she must return
to reality! Reality is no hardship, however, for the
outing included a fabulous lunch (fabulous except
for the escargots, which Fashionista Jane did not
know was a fancy word for snails, and which in her
humble opinion can simply go-go-go), after which
she and her gentle companions toured the fabulous
palace and its fabulous gardens and fountains,
where she was sorely tempted to wash all the cares
of the last few days away.

What? Have you not heard, reader? There is much
hue and cry over Fashionista Jane's plea for hungry
models to be fed. Cheeseburgers for all! Alas
Fashionista Jane was saddened to hear tonight
that a lovely (if too slender) young woman by the
name of Albertine was fired for posing for a certain
photo on a certain blog, and sincerely regrets any
unhappiness she may have caused.

There are another round of comments waiting for me when I get
back to the hotel at lunch the following day, but I ignore them in favor

of the e-mails. My parents have written to tell me how proud they are of me, and Simon's says simply TWO DAYS LEFT!

Becca's e-mail is a little weird, though.

There's something mysterious about my Mr. Rochester. Gram's friend lives right across the street from him, and my bedroom here faces his family's house. Theo's bedroom is on the top floor, and his light is on all night. I mean seriously, all night (I checked). I know it's his room; I borrowed Frannie's binoculars and I can see him moving around in there.

Does that seem creepy to you, or is he just afraid of the dark? What could he be doing over there all night? It's like Thornfield or something.

I laugh at the mental image of Becca peering out the window in the middle of the night with the binoculars, but she's right, it is a little creepy.

Plus, I think maybe he has a girlfriend, she writes.

I'm sure there's some logical explanation for the light, I e-mail back, reminding her of what happened with Simon. *Why don't you just ask him? And while you're at it, ask his grandmother about the girlfriend situation. Get your Jane on!*

On Thursday, we spend the morning at more fashion shows, followed by a special luncheon for journalists. Some people openly snub me, which is awkward and uncomfortable, especially when a couple of models as tall as pro-basketball players corner me to tell me that what I did to Albertine is *très horrible*. Wolfgang has to finally come rescue me from their scolding.

Heather Vogel Frederick

"Don't you worry about Albertine," he consoles me. "Isabelle has already talked to her about coming to work for *Flash*."

"Really?"

He nods. "We like her spirit, and we could use another Paris correspondent, one who knows the ins and outs of the business." He pats my shoulder. "Now put your game face on and let's go back out there. That's all it really is, darling, just a fabulous game!"

I'm not so sure about that, but I do what he tells me, sticking to him like a burr for the rest of the time we're there. I look over to see what Gigi's up to, hoping she's not bored, but she's deep in conversation with Sophie's grandfather and looks perfectly content.

That afternoon I get the shopping itch again. Fortunately my grandmother has carved out time for it in our schedule. I still need to buy souvenirs for everybody back home. We head to a couple of off-the-beaten path neighborhhoods on the Left Bank, hunting for fun boutiques. I end up taking tons of pictures for my blog—everything is so picturesque here! The narrow cobblestone streets, the buildings with ivy growing up the walls, the window boxes, the little parks and sidewalk cafés everywhere—I seriously want to take it all home with me to Concord.

Two stores in particular catch my eye. The first one we stumble upon is Trinket, where I find cute little sterling silver Eiffel Tower earrings for everybody. The other is my favorite. It's called Aubergine, the French word for eggplant, which has nothing to do with the clothes inside but everything to do with the shop's color scheme. The walls and the trim around the doors and windows are painted dark purple. It's gorgeous.

So are the clothes—an eclectic mix of elegant and funky. I spot a pair of shoes in the window that I absolutely have to bring home to Cassidy, especially now that I know we wear the same size, and a really gorgeous silk scarf for my mother. It will look great with the red suit I made for her.

"*Au revoir!*" calls the shopkeeper as we're leaving, and I have a sudden flash to the future: a store of my own right here in Paris. I even know what I'll call it—*La Vie en Megan Rose*, a little play on words for the song that Gigi and Monsieur de Roches keep humming. Wanting to capture the moment, I plunk down on a bench outside and sketch it in my notebook.

"It's perfect," says Gigi, watching over my shoulder as I explain my drawing. "I can see it clearly—you, living here in Paris, me, coming to visit."

"We'll go to Angelina's for hot chocolate—"

"And Ladurée for *macarons*—"

"And be happy as kings at Versailles!" I finish.

The first thought I have when I wake up Friday morning is: *Simon comes to Paris tonight!* I don't have much time to think about him, though, because today is the next-to-last day of Fashion Week, and Gigi and I cram in six shows, which turns out to be too many because my head is swimming by the time the last one finishes. Tonight is the night that Monsieur de Roches has arranged for our dinner cruise on the Seine, but I'm feeling a little under the weather so I send Gigi by herself.

"I'll be fine," I tell her. "Go! Have fun! Enjoy Paris!"

Heather Vogel Frederick

"Well," she says reluctantly, "if you're sure . . ."

I am, and after she leaves I take a long bubble bath, then put on my pajamas and call room service. No escargots for me tonight—I'm craving for comfort food, so I order a cheeseburger and fries. I watch a little TV, or try to, but it's all in French of course, then work on my blog post, which includes some hilarious Fashion Faux Pas that I've been saving up. I do a whole riff on shoes that I call "Putting Your Worst Foot Forward." It includes stuff like pictures of men in sandals with socks ("Fashionista Jane recoils in horror from such terrifying combinations"), American tourists in enormous white sneakers ("one is loathe to make sport of one's countrymen, but reader, Fashionista Jane cannot fathom appearing in public wearing milk cartons"), and a scattering of joggers I spotted in the Tuileries wearing those weird running shoes that look like toe socks ("since when did placing rubber gloves on one's toes become acceptable?"). I also include a picture of a mime inside a red circle with a slash, just for fun.

The phone rings as I'm finishing up. Gigi most likely, checking in on me. I reach for the receiver. "Hello?"

"I'm here!" says a familiar voice. A male voice with an English accent.

It's Simon!

"You're here?" I echo back foolishly.

"Yes I am," he says.

We're both quiet for a minute, and then we both start laughing at the same time.

"I can't wait until tomorrow!" I tell him.

"Me too—what time can you be ready? I have plans for us."

This sounds promising. "As early as you want—where are you staying?"

"We're with friends a little outside the city," he tells me. "It's about a half hour train ride to where you are."

"Maybe after breakfast, then?"

"Perfect. How about I pick you up at nine?"

"I'll be ready."

We say good-bye and I hang up and dance around the room. *I'm seeing Simon tomorrow!* I rummage through my clothes, wondering what I should wear. He said he had plans for us, but he didn't say what they were.

I'm too excited to sleep, so I watch a movie on my laptop. Gigi comes in halfway through, and smiles when she sees me.

"Looks like you're feeling better," she says.

I nod. "Simon called—he and his family are here!"

She laughs. "That will cure everything, won't it?"

I nod again. "Did you have fun?"

"It was glorious. There's nothing like springtime in Paris at night, floating down the river beneath the Pont Neuf and all the other bridges . . ." Her voice trails off and she sighs. "I'm so sorry you missed it."

"Me too. But I just needed a little downtime, you know? And a hot bath."

Heather Vogel Frederick

"I understand completely. A bath sounds good—I think I'll take one myself."

I'm awake at the crack of dawn the next morning and have changed at least half a dozen times before breakfast. I finally settle on jeans, the flowered chiffon shirt I wore to the Chanel fashion show, and some purple suede loafers I bought at Aubergine. I grab a matching purple cardigan just in case. It's supposed to be sunny again, but cooler. I stuff down a room service croissant and hot chocolate—not Angelina's, but not bad—brush my teeth, and am about to head out when I pause by the door.

"What are you doing today, Gigi? I totally forgot to ask."

She smiles at me. "I have appointments at several fashion houses," she says, "and then perhaps a stroll in the Rodin sculpture garden. Monsieur de Roches has offered to be my escort."

"That's nice. Say hi for me, okay?"

"Of course. I'll see you back here tonight."

"Five o'clock at the latest, I promise." The *Flash* farewell party is the biggest party of the week, and we'll need plenty of time to get ready. I wave good-bye and close the door behind me, then jog to the elevator.

I spot Simon before he sees me; I'd know those blond curls anywhere. He's pacing the lobby with his hands behind his back. "Hey, stranger," I say, sneaking up behind him.

He whirls around. "Megan!"

We hug each other. It feels a little awkward, but nice. Really nice. We stand there for a minute, grinning. Then we both burst out laughing, just like last night on the phone, and the ice is broken.

"Come on," says Simon, reaching for my hand. "Let's go see Paris."

When he hears that I haven't made it to any art museums yet, he insists that we make the Musée de l'Orangérie our first stop.

"It's right across the street from your hotel!" he protests. "I can't believe your grandmother hasn't taken you here yet!"

"Sorry," I tell him. "We had other things on our minds."

He shakes his head in mock horror. "Let me guess—clothes, right?"

"Not just clothes—*fashion*."

"There's a difference?"

"A big difference. Fashion is as much art as, as—oh wow."

I fall silent as we step into an enormous oval gallery, flooded with light from a skylight above. Its curved walls are painted with broad murals that I recognize instantly: Claude Monet's *Water Lilies*.

Tears spring to my eyes. So much beauty!

"What were you saying about art?" asks Simon, grinning at me again.

We circle the room, then sit down to just look for a while. "The colors!" I tell him. "I want to swim in those blues and purples. And how did he do that? Up close they're just splotches of paint; stand back and they're beautiful flowers floating in a pond."

"Sometime you'll have to go to his garden at Giverny," Simon tells me. "It's magical."

"All of Paris is magical."

He nods. "I think so too."

The Louvre is next. Simon takes me straight up to the second floor to see *Mona Lisa*, and we hunt down the Venus de Milo sculpture,

Heather Vogel Frederick

too. I've never gotten what Cassidy Sloane calls "mall overload"—I love shopping too much—but I think I finally know what she means by it, because after an hour or so of looking at paintings and sculptures I definitely have a case of museum-overload.

"Seen enough?" asks Simon, and I nod.

Outside, we find a bench in the garden where we sit and talk for a while. He tells me about school, and Yorkshire, and his family, and I tell him about my mother running for mayor.

"When's the election?"

"Ten days from now," I tell him. "I think she has a really good chance of winning."

"I'd vote for her."

"Thanks," I reply. "I'll tell her that."

I show him the latest pictures of Coco my kitten—diplomatically leaving out the part about her devotion to Sophie—and tell him all about my week here in Paris so far, and the flap over Fashionista Jane.

"I love your blog," he says.

"You've been reading it?"

"Of course. I had to make sure you weren't trash talking my brother again, after all."

I give him a sheepish smile. Last year, when the Berkeleys lived in Concord, I posted a couple of Fashion Faux Pas featuring Tristan that caused a rift between us for a while. Thinking about that reminds me of Stinkerbelle, who ratted me out, and thinking about her reminds me of Sophie Fairfax again. I shift uncomfortably. I want to apologize to Simon for doubting him the way I did. But I don't really want Sophie butting in on this perfect day, so I decide to leave it be.

"So what's next?" I ask instead.

"I promised you ice cream, right?" He looks at his watch. "Is it too early in the day for ice cream?"

"On what planet is it ever too early in the day for ice cream?"

"You have a point. Onward!"

We walk hand in hand along the banks of the Seine again, drawing closer to a beautiful stone bridge with multiple arches.

"I suppose you know the Pont Neuf is the most famous bridge in Paris," Simon says as we start across. "It's the oldest in the city, and leads to the Ile de la Cité, the heart of medieval Paris—and Notre Dame."

"The cathedral?"

He nods. "Can't leave Paris without visiting Notre Dame. Which just happens to be in the neighborhood of our ice cream shop."

We walk the length of the island, turning down a side street to find the *glacier*—ice cream parlor—from the brochure Simon sent me. Simon is right; the ice cream is delicious. Especially the strawberry, which it turns out is his favorite flavor, too.

"So what do you think, Berthillon or Kimball Farm?" he asks.

I take another bite, considering the question. "I'd say it's a tie."

"I can live with that."

We spend a long time at Notre Dame. If you look in the dictionary under "cathedral," Notre Dame is what you should see. It's huge, for one thing, like a castle or a landlocked battleship or something. On the

Heather Vogel Frederick

outside, it has these cool things that Simon tells me are called flying buttresses, a support network of stone arches that give the exterior a sort of lacy look. There are statues everywhere, and gargoyles—great gargoyles! I use my new zoom lens to get some close-ups, thinking Fashionista Jane might be able to work them into her final blog post.

If I thought the cathedral's outside was amazing, though, the inside takes my breath away. It's as beautiful as Monet's *Water Lilies*, in a completely different way. The ceilings soar practically to the sky, and the stained glass windows glow like jewels as the sun pours through them.

"It took over two hundred years to build this church," Simon tells me as we wander around. "The architectural style is called Gothic. You can tell by the pointed arches inside and the flying buttresses outside."

"How do you *know* all these things?"

He smiles at me. "My father's a history professor, remember? He's been lecturing Tristan and me about all this stuff since we were little kids."

I take more pictures, and after we've wandered around awhile longer we start to get hungry for lunch. We go outside and find a crêpes vendor, then take our picnic across the other stretch of the Pont Neuf to the Left Bank. There are parks along the river's edge here, too, and we scout out an empty bench and sit down to eat.

"This has been a really fun day," I tell him. "Thank you for showing me around."

"My pleasure," he replies politely.

No kiss? I think, trying not to look too disappointed as he drops me off at the hotel later. I've been hoping for one all day, and I can't help feeling deflated, even though holding hands is really nice. Maybe there will still be time for a little romance tonight. I kind of doubt it, though. We're going to be in a crowded restaurant with a zillion photographers and eyes everywhere.

"We're meeting here in the lobby at seven thirty, right?" he says.

I nod. "Look for Monsieur de Roches. You can't miss him, he's the one who looks like Santa, only thinner. Oh, and wear whatever you want, but I'm going to dress a little fancy."

"I fancy you," he says softly.

Then why don't you kiss me? I want to holler. But I don't. I just smile and wave good-bye and head for the elevator.

There's no sign of Gigi yet, so I hop in the shower and give myself a pep talk. This has been another amazing day, and there's lots to look forward to at the party tonight. It's at some restaurant in the Eiffel Tower, for one thing, and for another, I'm going to get a chance to wear the dress I made for myself. I figure a little free publicity never hurts, and you never know, maybe some designer will see it and find out that I made it and my career will be launched. Well, launched in a way that doesn't include baby clothes or blog rants.

I dry my hair and put on my makeup, then cross to the closet and pull out my dress. As I put it on and look in the mirror, I wonder if maybe I should try and spice up the whole classic elegance thing. The whipped cream color is fine, and it sets off my dark hair and eyes, but it feels like something's missing. Should I go a little edgier and pull a Bix?

Put a blue streak in my hair? Add a cowboy hat?

I don't want to look like a little kid playing dress-up, though; I want to be taken seriously. On the other hand, I don't want to look like I'm playing it safe and end up being boring, either.

What is that quote Gigi read to me earlier this week? "In order to be irreplaceable one must always be different." *Thank you, Coco Chanel.* There's nothing wrong with classic elegance, but there's nothing wrong with putting my own stamp on it either. I march over to the closet and slip off the heels I'd been planning to wear, and instead pull the pair of pink high-tops that I bought as a joke present for Cassidy out of my suitcase.

They're not just regular high-tops, though. They're super-cute wedge heels.

I put them on, and look in the mirror and laugh. So does Mirror Megan, who appears to like being four inches taller because she gives me two thumbs up.

"Who says fashion needs to take itself so seriously?" I ask aloud.

"Who indeed?" asks Gigi.

I whirl around. She must have returned while I was in the shower. She points to the shoes. "Now those," she says, "are pure Megan Rose. *Très* chic, and *très* delightful. But something is missing."

I look at her, worried. Did I miscalculate? Is the look too different? She gives me a mischievous smile and holds out one of her hands. The diamond earrings are resting on her palm.

I gasp. I didn't even know she'd brought them with her to Paris. "Really?"

"Really."

I put them on, then help her with the zipper on her dress. It's a turquoise sheath with a wide, stand-up boat neck that looks a lot like some of the dresses we saw earlier this week but which she tells me she bought thirty years ago on another trip to Paris.

"In fashion, everything old is new again," she tells me. "Things always come back into style."

Downstairs, Simon and Sophie's grandfather are talking in the lobby. They both rise to their feet as we enter, looking at us in open admiration. Monsieur de Roches is wearing a suit; Simon's got a navy blazer on over a white dress shirt and charcoal-gray slacks.

"We four are the belles of the ball," says Gigi, sailing out to the Rolls on Monsieur de Roches' arm. He deposits her up front, leaving Simon to climb in back with me.

"Sweet ride, huh?" I ask him.

"Sweet ride for a sweet girl," he says, taking my hand again.

I could sit here like this forever, I think, wishing it were farther to the Eiffel Tower. But it's not, and a few minutes later we're climbing out of the car again. The restaurant is already crowded, but Wolfgang must have been watching for us because he swoops down the minute we enter.

"Don't you look FABULOUS!" he says, twirling me around. "Love the dress, love the earrings, and the shoes—the shoes are STUNNING. Don't you just ADORE them, everyone?"

There's a smattering of applause, and I can feel my face redden, especially when I spot the smirks from the people who've been snubbing

Heather Vogel Frederick

me all week. For a moment I feel like Jane Eyre when Blanche Ingram makes fun of her at the house party at Thornfield, but then I remember my backbone, and what Coco Chanel said about being different, and I decide right then and there, so be it. If I can't be myself, Megan Rose Wong, in this business, then this business doesn't deserve me.

Lifting my chin, I march into the room. Maybe it's my newfound confidence, or maybe it's Simon, who's looking particularly handsome tonight, but pretty soon we're surrounded by a crush of well-wishers. In fact, it gets annoying after a while. Everybody wants to talk about Fashionista Jane—or suck up to Fashionista Jane, probably hoping I'll blog about them—and I'd rather just be with Simon.

Finally, dinner is served, and we go to find our table. Simon and I are together, of course, along with Gigi and Monsieur de Roches and Wolfgang and a handful of the designers whose shows I wasn't able to visit.

"I wanted to ensure that everyone gets a little face time with Fashionista Jane," says Wolfgang. "Since it wasn't possible for her to be everywhere at once this week."

"Where did you get that divine dress, darling?" asks a tiny man with enormous ears and wire-rimmed glasses. "Such lovely lines."

Omigosh, it's actually happening! Across the table, Gigi smiles at me encouragingly. Taking a deep breath to quell the butterflies, I reply, "Um, I designed it myself."

His eyebrows shoot up, and he passes me his card. "Let's talk soon."

I collect them from everyone else at the table, too. Simon nudges my knee with his under the table.

"May I take Megan for a walk?" he asks Gigi a while later, as dessert is served and the waiter comes around with coffee. "I promise to return her to the hotel safely."

My grandmother hesitates.

"It's Paris—it's springtime—they're young," says Sophie's grandfather softly. "And it's their last evening together."

"I suppose when you put it like that," Gigi replies. She turns to Simon. "Of course you may borrow her. But please have her back by midnight—"

"—or she'll turn into a pumpkin?"

Gigi laughs. "No—at least I hope not. We have a flight to catch early in the morning."

Simon takes my hand and pulls me out of my chair and we slip out of the restaurant and run for the elevator, laughing. The doors open and we step inside, and Simon punches the button for the top.

"I'm not allowing you to go home without seeing the view from the Eiffel Tower," he tells me.

A short ride later we step out of the elevator. All of Paris lies glittering at our feet. We circle the observation deck silently, looking down at the city.

"I don't ever want to forget this," I murmur, leaning on the railing. "Ever." I shiver, more from the sheer gorgeousness of the view than anything, but Simon notices and whips off his jacket, draping it around my bare shoulders. I glance up at him. "Thanks."

"You're welcome," he replies.

Heather Vogel Frederick

Straightening up again, I turn to face him. The shoes I'm wearing put us almost eye to eye. We stand there for a moment, and then finally it happens. He leans over and kisses me.

A collective "aaaahhhhh" goes up from the other tourists on the deck and I step back, embarrassed. But no one's looking at us; they're watching the light show. It's the top of the hour—sparkle time. Simon and I look at each other and grin sheepishly, and then he puts his arm around me and we lean on the railing, watching Paris. The breeze ruffles his blond curls and I lean my head on his shoulder. I have never before in my entire life been this completely and utterly happy. I want to hold onto this moment forever; I don't ever want anything to change.

And then everything changes.

We take the Metro back to my hotel, and Simon gives me a long hug before we go inside. "I'm going to miss you," he says.

"Me too." I have no idea when we'll see each other again.

"Write me, call me, text me, e-mail me?"

"I promise."

He leans down and kisses me one more time. *"Au revoir."*

I love the French. They totally understand romance. Of course they'd have an expression that means "until we see each other again." So much better than just "good-bye."

"Au revoir," I whisper back.

I float across the lobby and into the elevator, smiling all the way up to the room. My grandmother isn't here yet, and I figure she must still be at the *Flash* party. I wander around for awhile, trying to pack as I relive both kisses, but especially the one atop the Eiffel Tower.

A few minutes later the door to our room flies open and Gigi comes waltzing in. Her face is glowing.

"Looks like you had a good time," I tell her.

"I'm engaged!" she cries.

I stare at her blankly. *"What?"*

"Monsieur de Roches just asked me to marry him, and I said yes."

SUMMER

"They had been in London, and many other grand towns; but they always said there was no place like home . . ."

—Jane Eyre

 **Becca**

"There was a mystery at Thornfield . . ."
—Jane Eyre

"What the heck is he doing over there?" I mutter to myself, adjusting the binoculars.

Across the street, a reddish light shines in the third floor window of the chocolate-colored house. I glance at the clock by the guest room bed: it's two thirty a.m.

It's been like this every night since I arrived in Mankato. There's a mystery swirling around Theo Rochester, and I intend to solve it.

But not right now.

Right now, I've got to get some sleep. Setting the binoculars on the windowsill, I cross the room and climb back into bed.

Next morning, I'm up bright and early. The house is quiet; Gram and Frannie are still asleep. I pull on sweats and running shoes, add a hat and gloves since there's still snow on the ground outside, and let myself out the front door. There's no sign of Theo yet, so I jog up and down the street, warming up while I wait.

He runs every morning—I've seen him from my window—and today I plan to "accidentally" bump into him so we can run together.

That will give me a chance to pump him for information.

We've spent a fair amount of time together this week, but always when other people are around. He's been in school, for one thing—spring break here in Minnesota starts next week—so mostly we've been hanging out in the evenings. His parents had Gram and Frannie and me over to dinner once, and then last night he had a basketball game. We all went to cheer him on, which was fun. Plus, it gave me a chance to do a little surveillance. It felt too awkward trying to find out from Frannie if he had a girlfriend, as Megan suggested.

He doesn't.

At least not as far as I can tell.

It's obvious a lot of girls would *like* to be his girlfriend, but that's another thing altogether. I could see the way a few of the cheerleaders down on the court were eyeing him, and how they ran up to congratulate him after Mankato High's win. I know all about how that works. And I spotted a couple other girls heading down from the stands afterward to say hello, too. One even stopped by our table at Mom & Pop's, the ice cream place where we went to celebrate. Gram and Frannie kept calling it Heinz's, after the restaurant in the Betsy-Tacy books, which was kind of embarrassing.

Theo was friendly and polite to everyone, but I don't get the feeling there's anybody special.

Which means the field's wide open for me.

The only problem is, I just have two days left to make my move. And solve the mystery to boot.

I jog back down the street again, my breath puffing out in frosty clouds. I talked to Mom yesterday and she says that spring has definitely sprung in Concord, which makes her ecstatic, of course. She can't wait to get back into the garden again. She said that my father started his new job and loves it so far, and that Yo-Yo misses me, and that Stewart still hasn't heard from any colleges, and is practically camped out by the mailbox.

Up ahead, I see the front door to the Rochesters' house open, and a moment later Theo appears. He takes off down the street at a slow trot. I step up my pace to catch him.

"Hey!"

He looks over his shoulder, sees me, and smiles. "Hey yourself."

"Didn't expect to see you out this early," I tell him, which is stretching the truth, to put it mildly.

"I run every morning," he replies.

"Really? Me too." Which is definitely stretching the truth. I run two, maybe three times a week when I'm at home, but I've slacked off on this vacation.

"Where are you headed?"

"I dunno. Just around the neighborhood, I guess, unless you have a better idea."

"Sure," he says. "Follow me."

He sets his pace to match mine, and we jog along in tandem up and down a few streets before turning onto one that looks familiar.

"Isn't this where the Betsy-Tacy houses are?" I ask him.

Heather Vogel Frederick

He nods. "Yup. Center Street. Nannie Frannie's favorite spot in Mankato."

You gotta love a guy who isn't embarrassed to say the words "Nannie Frannie." But that's really what he and his brother call Gram's best friend.

We jog uphill toward the houses, which are museums now. I know this because I have spent time in both of them this week. A lot of time. The one on the left is Betsy's house—actually Maud Hart Lovelace's when she was a little girl. Across the street is Betsy's best friend Tacy's house—actually Maud's childhood friend Bick Kenney. They're pretty interesting, especially if you've read the books, because they look exactly the way Maud describes them in her stories, and there are all kinds of knickknacks and furniture and stuff on display, real things that Maud pulled from her life to use in her books.

Theo smirks at me as we near the top of the street, where a stone bench sits in a secluded spot at the top of a flight of steps. It's a memorial to the spot where the two girls used to meet when they were little.

"Bet you had your picture taken sitting on that bench, didn't you?" he says.

I laugh. "How did you know?"

He grins at me. "Because Nannie Frannie has about twenty-seven pictures of me sitting on it too. She made me and my brother pose there every Easter for years. She doesn't have any granddaughters, so she has to make do with us."

We turn left past Betsy's house and start up an incline. "Ready for the 'Big Hill'?" he asks. "Don't worry, it's not that big."

The Big Hill is what Betsy and Tacy—or Maud and Bick—used to call the hill behind their houses. I nod at him and we puff our way up to the end of the cul-de-sac at the top, then turn around and head back down toward town. We're almost home again before I muster the courage to ask my question.

"Um, Theo," I begin.

"Uh-huh?"

"I was wondering—I mean I couldn't help noticing—" I hesitate. *Forget it. I can't do it.*

"What?"

"Nothing. Never mind." I know I'm chickening out, but how do you ask a guy about a light in his room that you've spotted from across the street without sounding like some kind of stalker?

Which I sort of am.

Instead, I sort of ask him out.

"What I mean is, I saw that *Space Cowgirls 3* is playing at the movie theater here in town—have you seen it?"

"Nope."

"I thought maybe I'd go tonight," I tell him casually. "Interested? Unless you have basketball practice, of course," I hasten to add.

"Sounds fun," he replies as we slow to a stop between his house and his grandmother's.

I promise to call him after school and let him know what time the show starts, and he disappears inside to get ready for school.

Heather Vogel Frederick

That was easy, I think, leaning over and placing my hands on my knees as I try and catch my breath. *Why didn't I get my Jane on sooner?*

But then it gets a whole lot more complicated.

I walk up the path to the house, eager to hop online and tell Megan and Ashley about this new development. Unfortunately, I forgot to bring my cell phone charger so I'm stuck using Frannie's computer to stay in touch. She and Gram are awake by now, sitting in the kitchen in their bathrobes drinking coffee.

"Nice workout, sweetheart?" Gram calls as I come in.

"Yeah," I call back. I take my running shoes off and pad down the short hall to join them. "Is it okay if I go to the movies tonight?"

"Sure," says my grandmother. "What are you going to go see?"

"*Space Cowgirls 3*," I tell her. "I think Theo's going to go with me."

"I love *Space Cowgirls*!" says Frannie. "I have such a crush on that Jackson Ford."

"Me too," says Gram. "Hey, would you mind if we tag along?"

How am I supposed to say no?

In the end, we all wind up going—me, Theo, Gram and Frannie, Theo's parents and even his brother, Sam. So much for my "date." Theo sits next to me in the theater and we share a bucket of popcorn though, so it almost passes for one. And I notice with satisfaction that heads turn as we come into the theater. Several of the girls I saw sniffing around at the basketball game and the ice cream parlor are not looking too happy about the fact that we're together.

You snooze, you lose, ladies, I think smugly.

"Are you going to run again tomorrow morning?" Theo asks as his parents drop us off in front of his grandmother's house.

"You bet," I tell him, even though I wasn't. Tomorrow is my last day of spring break, and I'd been thinking of sleeping in.

"See you at six, then?"

I nod.

Frannie makes hot chocolate for Gram and me, and the three of us sit around talking for a while, and then I head upstairs to bed. Turning the lights out, I get the binoculars again and sneak over to the window. Sure enough, there's that same eerie reddish light. What the heck can it be?

My last day in Mankato dawns bright and clear. I meet up with Theo for another run, and this time I manage to maneuver him into asking me out, sort of.

"So what's this I hear about some hockey championship that starts today?" I say as we jog toward the cemetery. I dangle this out there, hoping Theo takes the bait. Last night Frannie told me that the whole state practically shuts down to watch, since the games are televised. And she said that the Rochesters are all huge hockey fans. I'm hoping to wrangle an invitation.

I do.

"It's a really big deal," says Theo, lighting up. "It's the state tournament, and eight high schools are competing. Are you a hockey fan?"

I nod enthusiastically. "My brother plays for Alcott High."

Heather Vogel Frederick

"Want to come over and watch with us?"

I pretend to think it over. "Why not?" I reply. "The only thing on our agenda today as far as I know is packing."

It's been a surprisingly busy week. I didn't think that there would be much to do in this little town, but the last few days have been filled with visiting museums, libraries, parks, lakes and all the other landmarks associated with the Betsy-Tacy books. I've felt a little too much like Emma Hawthorne at times, but I can tell it's made Gram really happy to be able to show me everything, and that makes me happy, too.

She and Frannie and I have also done other stuff, of course, like eating at a few restaurants and shopping. The best part for me, actually—well, besides trying to crack the mystery of Mr. Rochester—has been just talking to Frannie. She and Gram grew up down the road from here in a town called St. Peter, and she has tons of pictures of the two of them when they were my age. It seems like there was a story to go with every picture.

"Come on over whenever you're ready," Theo tells me as we circle back to the street where he lives. "The games will be on all day."

Gram and Frannie are having breakfast again when I come in. "Theo invited me over to watch TV today if that's okay—I guess some hockey tournament is on."

"Some hockey tournament?" squawks Frannie, pretending to be outraged. "You're only talking about the most important championship of the year. High school games are a big deal in our state."

I grin. "Important. Got it."

"Of course it's okay," says Gram, shooing me out of the kitchen. "Go have fun. Just make sure you're packed, because we'll be leaving for the airport around two."

I glance at the clock on the wall. That gives me less than eight hours to solve this mystery. Not a lot of time.

I go upstairs and hop in the shower, then check Frannie's computer to see if there's anything from Megan. I e-mailed her after the movie last night, but she hasn't answered yet and she's not online, so there's no chance of an IM. I try and calculate the time difference between Mankato and Paris. She's probably on her way to the airport right now, since she's flying home today, too. I'm dying to talk to her and could kick myself for forgetting my phone charger. Oh well, I'll see her at Logan in a few more hours. Our flights get in about the same time, and Mr. Wong offered to drive me home.

I get dressed, choosing my outfit carefully. It's gotta be jeans for watching hockey, of course, but I glam things up a bit with a super-soft pink sweater that's one of my favorites. Grabbing my jacket, I head back downstairs for a quick bowl of cereal, then jog across the street.

"Becca!" says Mrs. Rochester, answering the door. "Come on in. Theo said you'd be joining us today. Have you had breakfast?"

I assure her that I have.

"Theo's upstairs in his room," she tells me, and I start for the stairs. "Um, better wait for him to come down, okay? He's kind of funny about . . . about entertaining guests up there."

The mystery deepens!

Heather Vogel Frederick

"Oh, okay." I follow the sound of the TV to the family room instead, where Theo's younger brother, Sam, is already sprawled on the sofa. He leaps to his feet when he sees me.

"Uh, hi, Becca," he says.

Sam is five years younger than Theo, who's a junior. He's at that awkward age when some boys get all shy around girls. I remember how my brother and Third and Ethan used to be. Well, how Third still is.

"Hey, Sam. So, has the tournament started?"

He shakes his head. "They're just warming up."

I perch on the edge of a chair, wondering if maybe I should go ahead and go upstairs anyway. But I wouldn't want to embarrass Theo if he's in the shower or something, so I stay put. A few minutes later he appears. "Hi, Becca."

"Hi."

His parents drift in too, and we all settle in to watch some hockey. I'm only half paying attention to the game; the other half of my mind is working on a strategy for sneaking up to Theo's room.

"I love your house," I tell the Rochesters, next time there's a break in the action. "I have a friend back in Concord who lives in a Victorian. It has a turret and everything."

"I've always loved old houses," Mrs. Rochester replies. "I'd had my eye on this one for years, and when it went on the market a few years ago, we jumped."

"Of course, being across the street from my mother-in-law was an added plus," says Theo's father.

We watch a little more hockey, and at the end of the second period I ask, "Um, do you think maybe I could have a tour?"

"Of course," Mrs. Rochester replies. She turns to Theo. "Why don't you take her around, sweetheart? Be sure and show her the coal chute in the basement. I always think that's interesting."

Theo doesn't look too excited at the prospect, but he dutifully stands up and leads me through the dining room, where I ooh and aah over the built-in cupboards and cabinets, and then to the kitchen that, like the Sloane-Kinkaids', has a stained glass window.

"Eww," I say, as we descend into the basement, which is dark and cramped. The ceiling is so low I almost bump my head on it, and Theo has to crouch. "It's kind of creepy down here, isn't it?"

"Lots of spiders, too," he replies, giving me a sidelong glance. "You probably don't like spiders, do you?"

I lift a shoulder. "They're not my favorite thing, I guess, but they're okay. You know—*Charlotte's Web* and all that."

Dang, I really am turning into Emma Hawthorne!

"What's your favorite animal?" Theo asks. He's looking at me strangely, and it occurs to me that this conversation has taken a weird turn.

"Um, our dog Yo-Yo, I guess. Why?"

"I mean besides dogs and cats," he replies, ignoring my question.

I whoosh out my breath. "I dunno, meerkats, maybe—they're cute. And turtles."

"Turtles?" He looks at me with sudden interest.

"Yeah. I had a little pet one once named Herbie. I remember how soft his tiny feet and legs were. Plus, he was just really interesting to watch. Except when he pulled everything in and sat there like a lump . . ." My sentence trails off lamely. What am I doing, talking about a stupid turtle?!

"Let's go back upstairs," Theo says, and I follow him gladly to the kitchen. He shows me the living room, which has this really cool wooden mantel with stuff carved in it, and his father's office, which reminds me a little of Mr. Hawthorne's, all lined with bookshelves. Then we go upstairs.

"Just bedrooms," he says. "No turret."

"Which one is yours?" I ask innocently.

"Um," he says, hesitating. "I—uh, mine is upstairs."

"In the attic?" I try and sound surprised. I'm actually a pretty good actress, when it comes down to it.

He nods and I stand there, looking at him expectantly.

"Turtles, you said?"

"Uh-huh," I reply.

He hesitates, then says, "Well, would you like to see my room?"

Duh. You think maybe? I give him an enthusiastic smile. "Sure!"

"Kids!" His mother's voice floats up from the family room. "Game's back on!"

Theo looks relieved. "Later, okay?" he tells me, and bounds off down the stairs. I follow him, disappointed.

So close!

Mrs. Rochester asks for my help in the kitchen getting lunch ready at the next break, so there's no opportunity to bring up his room then. Gram and Frannie come over and join us for nachos just as the game is finishing. The final score is a disappointment to the Rochesters, apparently, because they let out a collective groan.

Theo stands up. "Ready?" he asks me.

"Where are you two going?" says Frannie.

"I told Becca I'd show her my room."

His mother raises her eyebrows. "Really?"

"Might want to think twice about that, dude," says his father.

"You don't want to scare her off," says Frannie.

"Remember what happened last time," adds Sam, bursting into laughter.

This is r-e-a-l-l-y getting weird, I think. It's like the whole family is in on his secret, whatever it is.

"My granddaughter doesn't scare easily," says Gram calmly.

"Suit yourself," says Mrs. Rochester. She turns to me and smiles. "But don't say we didn't warn you."

My heart is pounding as I follow Theo from the family room. I'm really spooked by now. What is he hiding? What is it that his family doesn't want me to see? How horrible could his secret be, anyway?

My mind rushes from one wild possibility to another—he's a bank robber; he's a mad scientist engaged in shady experiments; he's an alien who hangs his Theo suit on a hook behind his bedroom door.

Heather Vogel Frederick

Theo looks at me nervously as we reach the top of the attic stairs. "Welcome to my world," he says, holding open the door.

At first glance, his room seems completely normal. Bed and dresser, check. Desk, check. Bookcases, check. Cages on top of bookcases filled with—oh.

I get it now.

All of it—the secrecy, the reddish light I see every night, Theo's reluctance to bring me up here.

Mr. Rochester has pet snakes.

I stand there rooted to the spot. There are at least half a dozen glass tanks lining the top of the built-in bookcases by the window. It smells kind of like a jungle in here, and the room is warm from the glow of a couple of heat lamps. I remember having to buy one for Herbie, too.

"Wow," I say politely. "You, uh, have a lot of them, don't you?"

"Yeah," he says sheepishly. "I kind of have a thing for snakes. I want to be a herpetologist someday—that's a scientist who studies them." He walks over to the nearest tank. "Would you like to hold one?"

This is the part where I run screaming from the room. Except I don't. "Sure," says some other Becca, the one who is looking at Theo's gorgeous blue eyes, which are now shining with excitement.

He reaches in and lifts out a red snake with distinctive black and white markings. "This is Arthur. He's a king snake."

"King Arthur?"

He grins. "Yeah. Stupid, I know, but what can I say? I got him when I was ten. He's actually an Arizona mountain king snake, of the genus *Lampropeltis pyromelana*."

Jess would love this, I think.

"Go ahead—you can touch him. He's completely harmless. Just a big baby, really."

Right. A big, scary baby. But a baby with a great sense of design, I have to admit, admiring his markings.

I do as Theo instructs me, and place my hand gently on Arthur. I'm surprised at how warm and smooth his skin is. "He isn't slimy!"

"Nope," Theo replies. "That's a common misconception. Everybody expects snakes to be cold and slimy, but they're not."

Arthur's tongue flickers out and touches me and I flinch. "Don't worry," Theo hastens to tell me. "He's just curious. That's his way of checking you out. Snakes smell with their tongues, you know."

Theo is a fountain of fun facts about the world of herpetology. In short order I learn that Arthur lives on a diet of small rodents, but only eats once a week or so; that snakes are deaf, but can sense sound vibrations; and that they live ten to twenty-five years on average, depending on the species.

"You know, you're the first girl I've been able to talk to about all this stuff," Theo says. "Everybody else thinks it's weird or creepy. This one girl I liked my freshman year freaked out when I brought her up here."

"Was that the one your brother was talking about?"

He grins. "Yeah. It's kind of funny now, but at the time, well—"

"I can imagine." I trace the pattern on Arthur's skin. "I do have to admit it's a little weird," I continue, tempted to confess how I've been watching his window at night. "But you're right; snakes are actually pretty interesting."

"I think so," Theo agrees. "I like all kinds of herps—turtles, frogs, lizards, all sorts of reptiles and amphibians. But snakes are my favorite. There's something about them that's just so . . . mysterious, you know?" He looks at me sharply. "Why are you laughing?"

"No reason," I tell him.

"I've got it all figured out," he continues. "I'm going to get a biology degree at the U, then go to grad school for zoology. I'd like to study snakes in the rain forest. You wouldn't believe how many species there are! Anyway, the Minnesota Zoo has internships, and I've already talked to them about maybe working there this summer, or once I'm in college."

"That's so cool," I tell him, and I mean it. Theo's enthusiasm is catching. "The U, huh?" It occurs to me that maybe I should think about Gram's suggestion, and look into the University of Minnesota's architecture program. Or any of their other programs.

We end up talking until right before it's time for me to leave for the airport. I meet all of Theo's other pet snakes, and he tells me about school and basketball, his other passion. I tell him about my job at Pies & Prejudice, and cheerleading, and my friends at home, and, well, everything. He's really easy to talk to.

"Didn't scare her off, I see," says Mrs. Rochester when we reappear downstairs.

"Nope," Theo replies, grinning. "Becca and Arthur are best friends now, right, Becca?"

I hold a hand up, crossing two fingers. "We're like this," I tell them.

"Good girl," says Theo's father. "There's not too many who pass the attic test."

Sam snorts. "Like, nobody."

"Shut up, Sam," says Theo.

Gram and Frannie have already left to finish packing, so Theo walks me across the street.

"Hey, would you mind if I call you sometime?" he asks. "I like talking to you."

I smile. "I like talking to you too."

"Maybe you can come back and visit someday. Nannie Frannie, I mean. Well, and me."

"I hope so! Or maybe you could come to Concord. We have snakes there, too."

He laughs, and gives me a quick hug. "Bye, Becca."

"Bye."

I barely need a plane to get home, I'm flying so high. Mr. Rochester likes me! And I like him too—snakes and all.

I come down to earth again with a thud when I land in Boston. I spot the Wongs waiting for me by the baggage claim. Sophie Fairfax is with them too, and as I draw closer, I can tell there's some sort of argument going on.

"Mother, I cannot *believe* you would do something so irresponsible!" Mrs. Wong is saying to Gigi. "What were you *thinking*?"

I tap Megan on the shoulder. She whirls around. "Hey!" I say, giving her a big hug. "You'll never guess what . . ." My voice trails off when I see her face. "What's going on?"

"Sophie's grandfather asked Gigi to marry him," she says in a low voice.

I blink at her, stunned. "*What?! Are you serious?"

She nods.

"So is she going to?"

Megan shrugs. "Not if my mother can put a stop to it."

"We know absolutely nothing about this man—his background, his character," Mrs. Wong continues. She looks over at Sophie and presses her lips together. "I'm sorry, Sophie, but it's true, we don't. And besides that—"

"And besides that, it's really none of your business, is it?" says Gigi calmly. "Edouard asked me to marry him, not you."

"Mother!"

Mr. Wong glances around uneasily. The people standing near us are watching with interest. "Let's take the bags to the car, shall we?" he says. "We can continue this discussion at home."

I follow him, still stunned by the news. As Mr. Wong is putting our luggage in the back of the SUV, something suddenly occurs to me. I lean over to Megan and whisper, "If Gigi marries Sophie's grandfather, that means you and Sophie will be related, doesn't it? Like step-granddaughters, or something?"

Megan shudders. *"C'est horrible!"*

Even I don't need a translator to know what that means.

I look over at Sophie. Her face is very pale, and she's staring straight ahead. She must think it's horrible, too, because she doesn't say a word all the way home.

Not a single word.

Heather Vogel Frederick

Emma

*"Gentle reader, may you never feel what I then felt!
May your eyes never shed such stormy, scalding, heart-
wrung tears as poured from mine."*
—Jane Eyre

Concord is abuzz over Gigi's engagement.

Mrs. Wong called the book club moms the moment she got home from the airport, and once Mrs. Chadwick found out, of course, the word spread like wildfire. My mother thinks it's romantic and exciting, but Mrs. Wong is fit to be tied.

"If I'm elected next Tuesday night," she grumbles, "the first law I'm going to pass will be one prohibiting senior citizens from doing crazy things like this. A whirlwind romance! At her age!"

Stewart and I exchange a glance. It's been like this ever since Gigi and Megan returned from Paris. Megan says she can't figure out why her mother's so worked up. It's not that she's thrilled about the whole thing either—especially the suddenly-being-related-to-Sophie-Fairfax part—but she's starting to get used to the idea. She thinks maybe her mom is afraid that Gigi will move to Paris, just when they've started getting along so well. Mrs. Wong and Megan's grandmother got off to a rocky start when Gigi first moved in with them, but now they're practically best friends.

Whatever the reason, it's a touchy subject.

"Um, I think we should talk about this week's action items," I tell her, passing a piece of paper across the dining room table. "Stewart and I drew up a list."

The three of us are sitting around the Wongs' dining room for our final strategy meeting. With the election less than a week away, we've all been working nonstop. Sophie is noticeably absent this afternoon—she's out distributing flyers with a bunch of guys from Alcott High. I think things have been kind of awkward for her here recently, especially since Mrs. Wong is making no attempt to conceal her dismay about the engagement. That can't be easy for Sophie. It's almost enough to make a person feel sorry for her.

Almost.

If she wasn't such a *piqueuse de mec*, of course.

Stewart taps his pen on the table. "Okay, here's what Emma and I think we should do for our final push," he says, now that we've finally got Mrs. Wong's attention. "Our top priority is to line up more phone bank volunteers." He looks over at me. "Did you get a chance to talk to your mom about putting a sign-up sheet on the bulletin board at the library?"

I nod. "Informational flyers and things are fine; sign-up sheets are a no go. The library's supposed to be neutral territory."

"Just like school, I guess," he says, making a note. "Well, maybe we can run a contest for our current volunteers and have them each ask

Heather Vogel Frederick

ten friends. Whoever signs up the most people gets, what, lunch at Pies and Prejudice, maybe?"

Mrs. Wong nods. "I'm sure Mother will be happy to do that." Her face clouds again at the mention of Gigi, and I quickly steer the conversation in a different direction.

"We could also use a few more people to take shifts waving signs at the major intersections over the weekend and on Monday and Tuesday," I tell her. "We've brainstormed some names, but practically everyone we know is heading out of town to watch the hockey championships."

Including our entire mother-daughter book club. Election or no election, no way are we missing out on watching Cassidy and the Lady Shawmuts take a shot at the National Championship.

"Let me give it some thought," Mrs. Wong replies. "I'm sure some of the Riverkeepers would be willing to help us out."

"And finally," Stewart continues, "Mrs. Winchester suggested that we set up a voter registration table at school, and see if we can encourage any last-minute stragglers to do their civic duty. Emma and the rest of the book club are going to staff it during lunch hour through next Tuesday."

"The good thing is, pretty much everybody knows about the election," I add.

The Handcuffs Wong for Mayor campaign has been a big hit, and we've gotten a lot of media attention since the debate. Most of it has been local, but the *Boston Post* and some of the bigger regional radio and TV stations have done stories about us too. Mrs. Wong has even become something of a minor celebrity, thanks to a guest appearance on *Hello Boston!* after a short campaign spot that Sophie filmed went viral.

It wasn't something we were planning to use originally—she and Stewart were just clowning around after one of their campaign photo shoots—but it turned out well, and Sophie ended up submitting it for credit in her filmmaking class at Alcott High. The teacher liked it so much he encouraged her to upload it to the Internet, and somehow it took off. Once the media got ahold of it, we all ended up on *Hello Boston!*

Carson Dawson, the host, interviewed Stewart and me, calling us "precocious teen campaign managers." But he was mostly interested in Sophie, of course—the first time she opened her mouth and that cute little French accent popped out, she had him eating out of her hand.

"What was your inspiration for the video?" he asked her.

"I had heard a great deal about Patriot's Day—she is Concord's big holiday, *oui*?"

"*Oui*," agreed Mr. Dawson, with his folksy chuckle. He's known for that chuckle—and for his sparkly white smile, which came flying out of his mouth a few years ago during a live episode of *Cooking with Clementine*, thanks to a book club prank that backfired. A video of Mr. Dawson's airborne dentures hit the Internet and skyrocketed him to fame, so he knows all about how that works.

Sophie shrugged. "I thought it would be *amusant*—amusing—to use it for *un petit* spoof."

She was laying it on pretty thick, because by now her English is as good as mine, thanks to all the practice she's had over these past few months talking to Stewart and every other guy in Concord. But she had Mr. Dawson practically wriggling in his seat with delight.

"Ah!" he sighed, as if he were French himself. "*Un petit* spoof! How *amusant* of you!"

He ran the campaign spot next, which features Mrs. Wong dressed as a minuteman. She's handcuffing herself to the Old North Bridge while Stewart, who's dressed as a British soldier, marches back and forth across it waving a DOLLARS FOR DEVELOPMENT sign. Sophie intercut this scene with clips of Mr. Underhill at the debate, calling himself "a patriot who will always put Concord first."

"Really?" says the voiceover—she got Kevin Mullins to narrate, of all people. His voice finally changed, and went from squawk to suave. It's still hard to believe that such a skinny body can produce such a deep bass. Who knew our little Kevin had it in him? "Or is he just an opportunist looking to put his own wallet first? George Underhill voted to rezone a parcel of proposed conservation land for development, and the developer turned out to be none other than his brother-in-law. The real patriot in this race is Lily 'Handcuffs' Wong, who's devoted her life to protecting Concord."

The final shot is a speeded-up Keystone Kops–style sequence of Mrs. Wong wrestling the sign away from Stewart and chasing him off the bridge with it. The whole thing is silly, really, but even I have to admit that Sophie edited it cleverly, and it sure caught the public's attention.

Next Tuesday night we'll find out if that kind of attention translates into votes, and if our Handcuffs Wong strategy has paid off.

As Stewart and I pack up our things and head outside to his car, I suddenly realize that this is the first time I've been alone with him in weeks. Between hockey season wrap-up for him, and school and the newspaper and now the campaign on top of it for both of us, there's hardly been any opportunity. And then there's the Mademoiselle Velcro factor. Maybe now is the perfect opportunity I've been waiting for to talk to him about things.

Hello, backbone, it's me, Emma, I think, and taking a deep breath, I plunge in.

"Um, Stewart?" I begin, as we start down Strawberry Hill Road.

"Yeah?"

"I was wondering if we could talk about something?"

"Sure. What's on your mind?"

"It's just that I've been noticing—" My cell phone buzzes, and I sigh and pull it out of my jacket pocket, figuring it's probably campaign business. It's not, though; it's my brother. "Hang on a sec," I tell Stewart. "It's Darcy."

"EMMA!" my brother shouts.

"Ouch!" I hold the phone away from my ear. "Dang, Darcy, what's up?"

"I GOT IN!"

"What? Where? What are you talking about?"

"DARTMOUTH! I'M GOING TO DARTMOUTH!"

Heather Vogel Frederick

I let out a shriek of excitement, and Stewart nearly swerves off the road. "What's going on?" he asks. "Is everything okay?"

"Darcy got into Dartmouth!"

"He got his acceptance letter?" Stewart's mouth drops open. "Omigosh, I have to go right home. Maybe mine have come too."

The car picks up a little speed as I continue to talk to my brother. It turns out he got into every school he applied to except one—no big surprise there, since Darcy is a straight-A student and a star athlete. A bunch of them have offered him really generous financial aid and scholarships, too. "Dartmouth will give me a scholar-athlete award," he says. "It's practically a full ride."

"Did you tell Mom and Dad yet?"

"Yeah," he replies. "Mom says we're going to have to peel her off the ceiling, and she and Dad are dancing around the kitchen. Lady Jane is hiding under the table, and Pip's about going crazy with all the excitement."

I laugh. "So that's what all the barking's about. How about Jess? Have you talked to her yet?"

"I'm heading over to her dorm right now. I thought it would be fun to tell her in person."

"Congratulations," I tell him. "I'm proud of you, bro." This is really a dream come true for my brother—he's wanted to go to Dartmouth since forever.

Stewart pulls into his driveway as I hang up. We've barely come to a stop before he leaps out and sprints up the front path to his house.

So much for finishing our conversation, I think. Resigned, I get out and follow him inside.

"Are they here?" Stewart shouts, sending Yo-Yo into a tizzy. The dog races up and down the hall, barking, as Stewart calls out, "Mom? Dad?"

"In here!" Mrs. Chadwick calls back from the living room. She points to a pile of envelopes on the sofa beside her. "I was just about to text you. The mailman came while I was working in the garden."

I stand in the doorway feeling a little awkward. Maybe Stewart would rather find out the news in private?

But he turns and waves me over enthusiastically. "Come on in, Em," he tells me. "This is so exciting!"

I perch on the arm of the sofa as he sorts through the pile. There are big envelopes and small envelopes, thick ones and thin ones.

"The thin ones are usually no's," he says, frowning at the return addresses.

He pauses when he reaches one in particular, then looks up at his mother and me. "Stanford," he says in a low voice. He opens it. "It's a no."

Mrs. Chadwick reaches over and puts her hand on his knee. "I'm sorry, honey."

"Me too," I add softly. Stanford was Stewart's dream school.

I'm truly disappointed for him, but in my secret heart of hearts I'm a little relieved, too. California is so far away! This means Stewart will be staying on the East Coast, because all the other schools he applied to are closer to home.

He opens the rest of the thin envelopes. "Might as well get the

Heather Vogel Frederick

rejections out of the way first, right?" he says lightly. He gets turned down by two Ivy League schools and a couple more out-of-state schools as well. Then it's time for the thicker envelopes.

"U Mass is a yes," he says. "And so are Bowdoin and Middlebury."

"Vermont would be nice," I tell him.

"Yeah, I really liked that campus."

In the end, he has five rejections and five acceptances, including one from the College of William and Mary in Williamsburg, Virginia.

"Looks like you have a lot to think about," his mother says.

He nods, still looking a bit disappointed.

Mrs. Chadwick fishes her cell phone out of her purse. "This calls for a celebration," she announces. "I'm going to tell your father we'll meet him in Boston for dinner tonight." She turns to me. "We'd love to have you join us, Emma."

I can tell she's trying to cheer Stewart up. "I wish I could, but I think my parents want to take Darcy out. He got his acceptance letters today, too."

"Really? What's the verdict?"

"Dartmouth, probably."

A shadow briefly crosses Mrs. Chadwick's face. She knows that's my brother's dream school, and I can tell she feels bad that Stewart didn't get into his first choice. But she musters a smile. "Tell him congratulations from us, okay?"

I give Stewart a hug and tell him I'm thrilled that he has so many schools to choose from, and that I'll go ahead and walk home.

The following day I try and find an opportunity to talk to him at school, but we're never alone for more than about thirty seconds. After school is no better, as he has to leave our newspaper editorial meeting early to go to a dentist's appointment, and I promised my mother I'd clean the house up and get ready for tonight's book club meeting. Plus, I said I'd make the treats, too.

Jane Eyre has proved difficult in that department—Charlotte Brontë was no foodie, and no way were my mother and I going to fix burnt porridge à la Lowood (been there, done that with Mrs. Chadwick's cornmeal mush). The other choices were slim. In the end, I decided just to go with good old chocolate chip cookies, which I feel pretty sure that both Jane Eyre and Charlotte Brontë would have enjoyed, if they'd ever had a chance to try one. And we're serving tea, too, of course, which is mentioned a lot in the book.

"So I don't understand why you don't just call him," Jess says, swiping a forefinger through the cookie dough. The two of us are in our kitchen, which feels a bit nostalgic—we used to do this all the time back in middle school, but both of us are so busy these days, we rarely get a chance to hang out here anymore. "That's what I would do if I needed to talk to Darcy about something."

That's because my perfect brother is also the perfect boyfriend, I think bitterly. He's already had the big talk with Jess about staying together next year when he goes to college. Stewart, on the other hand, hasn't said a word.

To be fair, he's barely had time to, but it still makes me a little ner-

Heather Vogel Frederick

vous. Cassidy says her sister told her that most high school couples break up when college rolls around, which is depressing. If that really does happen, I want to make the most of my time together with Stewart now. I want a full-time boyfriend, not a part-time one who's dividing his time between me and Sophie Fairfax.

"I started to call him a couple of times," I tell Jess, "and I even wrote him a letter, too, but I didn't mail it. I dunno, this just feels like a conversation that needs to happen face-to-face, you know? I don't want there to be any room for misunderstanding." I don't add that I'm also afraid of sounding petty and possessive.

She nods slowly, helping herself to more cookie dough. "Yeah, I guess I can see that. What about talking to Sophie, then?"

I snort. "Right."

"I'm serious! Why not? She doesn't bite."

"That's debatable." There's no way I'm going to confront Mademoiselle Velcro. I'll just have to be patient a while longer and wait for the right moment for a heart-to-heart with Stewart.

We're just taking the cookies out of the oven as our friends start arriving, including Megan and her mother and grandmother. Sophie is with them, as usual. I give Megan a sympathetic glance. I guess my life could be worse—I could have to live with Sophie Fairfax as well as share my boyfriend with her.

"Looks like the party's already started in here," says my mother, who arrives home from the library just then. She pokes her head into the kitchen where the group has gathered. Cassidy's already digging into the freshly baked treats. "Can I entice you all to join me in the living room?"

My friends follow her down the hall while I put the kettle on and arrange the cookies on a plate, and just as everyone's getting settled the doorbell rings.

"Emma, can you get that?" my mother calls.

"Sure." I take the plate of cookies with me—and just about drop it when I open the front door and see Courtney Sloane standing there. Behind her are Stanley Kinkaid and Chloe. They're all grinning.

Courtney holds her finger to her lips. "Let me sneak in behind you, okay?" she whispers, her eyes dancing with excitement.

"Omigosh, Cassidy is going to faint!" I whisper in reply, then turn and head to the living room.

"Who was that?" my mother asks as I pause in the doorway.

"Um, nobody important," I reply. Across the room, Cassidy's mother is trying to hide a smile. She winks at me. "Just—"

"ME!" cries Courtney, jumping out from behind me.

"WHAT?!" shrieks Cassidy, bounding to her feet. She crosses the room in two long strides and grabs her sister in a bear hug. "No way! What are you doing here? I thought you had midterms?"

"You don't think I'd miss watching my baby sister win the National Hockey Championships this weekend, do you?" Courtney tells her.

There's a lot of laughing after that, plus a few tears from Mrs. Sloane-Kinkaid.

"Happy to have your girls all together again?" asks Stanley, passing her a tissue, and she nods, blowing her nose.

Heather Vogel Frederick

"So that's where you disappeared to after dinner," Cassidy says to him accusingly. "You went to the airport! And here I thought you were just bailing out and leaving me with the dishes."

"Forgive me now?" he replies, grinning.

"Come on in and have a seat," my mother tells him. "We've got cookies hot out of the oven and tea on the way, and we're just wrapping up *Jane Eyre*."

"My favorite book," Stanley says, somehow managing to keep a straight face. From what Cassidy tells me, he's not much of a reader.

"I didn't know you were a Brontë fan," says my mother, looking impressed.

Cassidy's stepfather gives her a sheepish smile. "Clemmie made me watch the DVD with her," he confesses. "It was actually pretty good, though."

When I return with the tea, Courtney is being introduced to Sophie and showing off her ring to my friends. She turns to Gigi as I set the tray down on the coffee table. "What's this I hear about another engagement?"

Her mother makes frantic shushing motions. We've all been tiptoeing around the subject tonight, since Mrs. Wong is still so worked up about it.

"It's fine, Clementine," says Gigi. "There's no reason we can't talk about it. Lily just isn't used to the idea yet, that's all. And yes, I'm engaged—to Sophie's grandfather."

Across the room, Sophie is examining the pattern in the carpet. I can't tell what she thinks about the whole thing—she's been as closed mouthed about it as Megan's mother has been vocal.

"That's so exciting!" squeals Courtney. "Do you have a ring, too?"

Gigi shakes her head. "It was very spontaneous," she says. "It happened last weekend, on our final night in Paris. Edouard is coming to visit in a few weeks, and he's planning to bring the ring with him then."

"I'll believe it when I see it," mutters Mrs. Wong.

My mother says Megan's mother is worried that Monsieur de Roches is after Gigi's money. That doesn't make any sense, though, because Sophie's family is rich, too, right? I mean, she lives in a mansion! I've seen the picture on her dresser.

"So," says my mother, changing the subject. "Let's finish off our discussion of *Jane Eyre*, shall we? What did you girls think of the rest of the book?"

"I was pretty mad at Mr. Rochester there for a while," says Cassidy, shaking her head. She's sitting on the floor, leaning contentedly against her older sister's legs. "He completely blindsided Jane. I almost didn't forgive him."

"How about the rest of you girls? What did you think?"

"Same thing," says Megan. "But he was so lonely, I sort of understood."

"What about that whole attic thing?" asks Becca. "Did anybody else see that coming?"

"See what coming?" says Jess.

We all look at her.

Heather Vogel Frederick

"You didn't finish the book?" I exclaim. "But you gave me that gorgeous copy for Christmas—I thought you'd read it ages ago."

"I'm taking calculus this year!" she protests. "And singing in MadriGals and reading stupid *Scarlet Letter*. You wouldn't have finished it either!"

"How far did you get?" asks her mother.

"Blanche Ingram." Her eyes slide over to Sophie, who appears lost in thought.

"Okay, so no spoilers for Jess," says my mother. "Can we talk in a general way about the choice Jane is faced with?"

"I have one word to describe Jane Eyre," I announce. "Backbone."

My mother smiles at me.

"Jane has grit, I'll give her that," Mrs. Sloane-Kinkaid agrees. "It's not easy to stand up to temptation the way she does."

"It certainly isn't," says Mrs. Wong, scowling at Gigi.

Megan rolls her eyes. Her mother can be like a dog with a bone over stuff. They don't call her Handcuffs Wong for nothing.

"Grit, backbone—those are great descriptions," says my mother. "I'd also call it moral courage. Jane is faced with something that goes against her moral code, and she doesn't give in. She's true to herself, and to her highest sense of right. We can all learn a lesson from that." She looks over at Jess and bites her lip. "I guess we'd better not talk about the ending tonight," she continues. "We'll save that for another time."

"How about fun facts?" says Becca hopefully. "You kind of left us hanging there last time, Mrs. H, remember?"

"I did indeed," says my mother, pulling a folder out of her bag. "Want to help me pass them out, Chloe?"

She gives the sheets of paper to Mr. Kinkaid, and he and Chloe circle the room, handing one to each of us.

FUN FACTS ABOUT CHARLOTTE

1) Beginning in the summer of 1846, the Brontë sisters sent off their novels—Charlotte's *The Professor*, Emily's *Wuthering Heights*, and Anne's *Agnes Grey*—to publisher after publisher, receiving nothing but rejection letters.

2) Meanwhile, Reverend Brontë's eyesight was failing, and he went to Manchester for an operation. Charlotte accompanied him. To keep herself busy while he recuperated, she began work on a new novel called *Jane Eyre*.

3) Both of her sisters eventually received offers to publish their novels, but *The Professor* was turned down again. Bitterly disappointed, Charlotte sent it to one last publisher, William Smith Williams, who also rejected it, but noted its "great literary power," a compliment that encouraged Charlotte to finish *Jane Eyre*. She sent it to Williams in August 1847, and he found the story so compelling that he canceled his plans to go out riding with a friend and skipped dinner in order to finish it in one sitting.

Heather Vogel Frederick

4) Charlotte received an offer within two weeks, and *Jane Eyre* was rushed into print, appearing in bookshops that October, a mere six weeks after its acceptance and, in a quirk of fate, before both of her sisters' novels were published. An instant bestseller, it also received critical acclaim and was called "an extraordinary book" and "decidedly the best novel of the season." The novelist Thackeray praised it; Queen Victoria read it and loved it; everyone speculated as to its authorship. Who was this Currer Bell?

5) The Brontë sisters would eventually reveal their identities, but meanwhile tragedy struck the family yet again. A year later, in the autumn of 1848, Branwell, whose life had spiraled downward into debt and dissolution, died of tuberculosis. Emily, whose *Wuthering Heights* was savaged by reviewers, caught a cold at Branwell's funeral and never recovered, passing away a few months later. Anne swiftly followed, dying of consumption three months after that. Her last words were: "Take courage, Charlotte. Take courage."

6) Faced with this triple bereavement, Charlotte sought refuge in her work. She pressed on with her writing while living quietly at home with her father in Haworth and eventually published two more novels, *Shirley* and *Villette*, earning herself a place among England's literary elite.

7) Charlotte described herself as small and plain—not unlike *Jane Eyre*—but people found her attractive, and she turned down several marriage proposals in her lifetime. One suitor, her father's curate Arthur Bell Nichols, persisted, and after some hesitation (and against Patrick Brontë's wishes) Charlotte finally accepted him. She found to her surprise that marriage agreed with her. "My heart is knit to him," she wrote a friend in 1855. "He is so tender, so good, helpful, patient." Her happiness was short-lived, alas. Less than a year after her wedding, Charlotte died in the early stages of pregnancy, three weeks before her 39th birthday.

8) "As good as she was gifted," is how Charlotte's husband described her, and Charlotte Brontë was indeed gifted. Her novels, with their brilliant, brooding heroes and fiery, independent heroines—not to mention their keen insights into the social conditions of the day—continue to live on, capturing the hearts and minds of readers around the world.

Cassidy flings herself facedown on the rug. "I can't stand it," she moans dramatically. "These are *terrible* facts! First Jean Webster; then Jane Austen; and now Charlotte. Why does every writer we read have to *die*?"

"Take courage," quips my mother. "I don't like it any better than you do, Cassidy, but to some extent, that was just the way things were

Heather Vogel Frederick

in the nineteenth century. We live in a much different world today. For instance, the average life expectancy in the town of Haworth during Charlotte's lifetime was a mere twenty-five years—largely due to poor sanitation."

"They could have used a wastewater treatment plant," adds Mrs. Wong, who never passes up an opportunity to be Mrs. Wong.

We all look at her.

"What?" she says defensively. "I'm just saying."

Cassidy sits up again. "It's still not fair," she grumbles.

"Of course it's not fair," agrees her mother. "Especially when you start thinking about the novels that all those talented women might have gone on to write."

"There's always the After Library to look forward to," I tell them, and my mother nods, laughing.

"What's that?" Cassidy asks.

"My mother's friend Jessica made it up," I explain. "She says if there really is a heaven, it's got to have a big library in it filled with new books by all of her favorite dead authors."

Cassidy snorts, but a smile lingers on her lips. "The After Library. I like it."

Mrs. Sloane-Kinkaid checks her watch. "We'd better get going," she says. "Courtney's been traveling, and must be beat—"

"I'm fine, mom, really," Courtney protests.

"—and Cassidy, you have a busy few days ahead, and I want you rested up before we leave."

"We can't wait to cheer you on," says Jess as we all get up to say good-bye.

"See you this weekend!" I call as they head outside to their car.

Cassidy's tournament starts tomorrow, but we're not caravanning out until Saturday morning. Unless there's some huge upset, the Lady Shawmuts are pretty much a shoe-in to make it at least as far as the quarter finals, and we'll be there in plenty of time for those, since the championship is practically in our backyard. It's being held this year out in western Massachusetts. Everybody's going, except for Mr. Wong, who's staying behind to hold down the fort at Campaign Central, as he calls it, and Mr. Delaney. Several of Half Moon Farm's mama goats are due this weekend, and Jess's dad doesn't want to leave their farmhand to deal with multiple births all by himself.

Since we'll be at the tournament anyway, Stewart and I offered to cover it for the school newspaper. Sophie is going along to take pictures, of course, but I'm hoping Stewart and I will finally be able to squeeze out a few minutes alone at some point to talk.

It doesn't happen on Saturday, as it turns out. There's just too much going on. I've been to some pretty exciting hockey games in my life, what with Darcy having played since I was still in a stroller, but nothing compares to a USA Hockey National Championship. I imagine this is what the Olympics are like, only on a smaller scale, of course. There are teams in town from all over the United States—California, Michigan, New York, New Jersey, you name it. They're all wearing matching warm-up suits in their team colors, and the stands and the

Heather Vogel Frederick

streets and parking lots of Marlborough are ablaze with team colors, too. With so many different age levels competing, from U-12 through the U-16 teams like the Lady Shawmuts to the U-19s, the Sports Center and the hotels and the entire town are jammed with players and visitors.

By the time we arrive, a lot of the preliminary games are already out of the way, and the playing field has been winnowed down to the top eight for the quarter finals.

"We should have brought campaign stuff to hand out," I whisper to Stewart at one point, gazing at the arena. "It looks like half of Concord is here."

We cheer the Lady Shawmuts to an easy victory over a team from Ohio, and they advance to the semifinals.

"Oh yeah!" I crow. "That was easy."

"They won't all be like that," says my brother, who's sitting beside me. He leans across and taps Stewart on the shoulder. "Check it out," he says, pointing down to a cluster of men and women with clipboards standing on the arena floor. "College scouts."

They're out in force, and so is the news media. I spot Carson Dawson rinkside, talking to Sophie. His smile is blinding, even from here.

After the quarter finals we take a break for lunch at a nearby sandwich shop. Cassidy shows up with her team, and they take seats at the table next to us, a mass of red and white.

"I guess you can tell who we're rooting for," says Jess's mother, waggling the end of her red-and-white scarf.

We laugh, because we're all wearing the Lady Shawmuts' colors, too.

"Don't look now," says Courtney, lowering her voice, "but here comes the team from Orange County."

Of course we all look over, and they stare back coolly. The Suns have a bit of a history with the Lady Shawmuts, apparently. Something to do with a disputed call in a game earlier this season. If they both win their semifinal match, they'll be facing off against each other for the championship.

"It's weird to think that Cassidy would be playing for them if we'd stayed in California, isn't it, Mom?" says Courtney.

Mrs. Sloane-Kinkaid nods. "It certainly is. You never know what's around the next bend in the winding hall of fate."

I recognize that expression from one of the Betsy-Tacy books we read last year. It gets me thinking about what lies ahead down that hall for me. Will Stewart still be my boyfriend after he goes to college? Or is a break-up inevitable?

We troop back to the arena after lunch for back-to-back nail-biters. The Suns are up first, against a team from Michigan. It's a close game, with both teams grudgingly giving up a point as they move into the final period. The Suns close it down in the end, though, with a spectacular goal in sudden-death overtime.

"Nice!" shouts my brother, jumping to his feet and pumping his fist in the air.

Jess and I both grab his shirt and tug him back into his seat.

"What?" he says. "It was a great shot!"

Heather Vogel Frederick

"Yeah, but we're Lady Shawmuts fans, not Suns, you dork," I tell him.

Our team is up next against the Chicago Shamrocks. It's another intense match, both on the ice and off, as everybody in the arena knows that a win means a shot at the championship.

"Come on, come on, come on," I hear Mrs. Sloane-Kinkaid mutter in the row ahead of me. She hides her face in her hands as the Chicago girls score, pulling ahead. "I can't watch!" she moans. "Somebody tell me when it's over!"

Beside her, Chloe is sitting on Stanley's lap. She reaches over and pats her mother's hair. "Dee dee dee!" she says—Chloe-speak for "Cassidy" and "Lady Shawmuts." Mrs. Sloane-Kinkaid gives her a kiss. "That's right, Chloe. Cassidy is out there, and we want her to win!"

The ref's whistle blows and the girls skate in for a water break. I see Cassidy and Zach exchange a few words. Something seems a little different between them these days. They're more, I don't know, distant or something. I'm not even sure they're still together. Then again, we've all been so busy lately, what with the election and everything, I'm probably just imagining it.

The team huddles up with Coach Larson for a few seconds. I can't hear what she's saying to them, but it must be good because when the whistle blows again, they blaze through the remainder of the period, scoring two goals in rapid succession.

The Chicago team never quite bounces back after that, and the Lady Shawmuts maintain their lead to win the game.

Back at the hotel, we hang out in the lobby for a while, where

Sophie uploads her photos to her laptop while Stewart and my brother and Mr. Kinkaid and the Delaney twins relive the game point by point. As I work on my write-up for the *Alcott Avenger*, I listen to them with one ear and to Mrs. Wong with the other. She's pacing back and forth, checking in with Mr. Wong on the campaign stuff.

And something else, from the sound of it.

"Did you talk with him?" I hear her say at one point in a low voice. "And?" There a pause, and then, "I knew it! I just knew it! Mother obviously has no idea."

Gigi has no idea about what? My pen hangs in midair as I strain to hear.

But Mrs. Wong has moved away.

"Something's up," I tell Jess when we're upstairs in our hotel room later. She's flopped on her stomach, finishing *Jane Eyre*. I guess we shamed her into it.

"Mmm," she says absently.

"Jess! Listen to me!"

She drags her eyes away from the page. "Okay already! What? I'm listening."

I tell her what I overheard.

"Weird," she says when I'm done. "You're right—it does sound like something's up. Any idea what it could be?"

I shrug. "All I know is it sounds like it has something to do with Gigi's engagement."

We speculate for a while, then turn out the lights and go to sleep.

Heather Vogel Frederick

The next morning Jess sleeps in for once. I get dressed and tiptoe out of the room, then head downstairs to breakfast. Stewart and I are the first to arrive at the buffet.

"Hey, stranger!" he says. "Want to sit with me?"

I look around the empty room, pretending to consider my options. "Well, since you asked so nicely . . ."

He laughs. "Thank goodness there's no competition for me to worry about," he says in mock relief as we sit down at one of the tables.

Finally, the lead-in I've been looking for. "How about me?" I ask. "Do I need to be worried?"

"About what?" he asks, whistling cheerfully as he pours milk on his cereal.

"Competition."

He looks at me blankly.

"You know—Sophie."

"Sophie *Fairfax*?"

"Of course Sophie Fairfax!" I reply, exasperated.

"What the heck are you talking about?"

I can't believe he's being so dense. All the pent-up hurt and anger I've been feeling these past few months boils over. "Stewart! She's been stuck to you like gum on the bottom of your shoe ever since she got here! And from what I can tell, it's not like you've discouraged her or anything."

He gapes at me. "Emma—"

I hurtle on. "You and I have hardly had any time to ourselves in weeks! I can't even remember the last time we went on a date, or—"

"Uh, hello, we've had a campaign to run, remember?"

"—of course I remember! But still, you have to admit, it's like we've become a threesome instead of a twosome."

"What are you talking about? So I've been nice to Sophie, so what? She's over here in a strange country, without her family, her parents are splitting up and she's trying to figure out how to fit into a new school. I was just being friendly."

I look at him. "So that's what it's called."

"Look," he says, reddening, though I can't tell whether it's from anger or embarrassment. This is not going well. "You're blowing this way out of proportion, Emma. Sophie and I are just friends—period."

"Yeah, along with half of Alcott High! The male half, I might add."

"Of course she gravitates toward us guys—we're the only ones who've been nice to her!"

"That's not true!"

"Really? Name one time you've reached out to her, or included her without being forced to, or even tried talking to her!"

I open my mouth to protest and he cuts me off. "And book club doesn't count!" he adds. "Your mothers invited her to join, not you."

I shut my mouth again. Of course we've tried to include her, haven't we? Now that I think about it . . . no, wait! Of course we have. Like that very first time at book club. She was the one who didn't want to talk to me.

"You have no idea what she's been going through, do you?" Stewart continues. "You're so busy judging her, you haven't even tried to get to know her. She could really use a friend or two, Emma—girlfriends."

"What *she's* going through?" I exclaim, stung. "How about what *I'm* going through? My boyfriend's been swiped right out from under my nose, and as far as I can tell he's thrilled to pieces."

Stewart shakes his head in disgust. "That is so unfair."

"It's true!"

He doesn't answer me. We're both silent for a minute, and then he sighs. "Look, this might not be the right time to bring this up, but I've been wanting to talk to you about prom."

My stomach lurches. *Uh-oh*, I think, pretty sure I'm not going to like whatever it is he has to say.

"I was wondering what you'd think about me taking both of you. You and Sophie together, I mean. You and I have talked before about how dances are kind of dumb, and I thought it might be nice for her to go with the two people she's spent the most time with here in Concord. What with all the work we've done together on the campaign, I mean."

My eyes fill with tears. "This is a joke, right?" When he doesn't answer, and I realize that it's not, I throw down my napkin. "Forget it," I tell him. "Take Sophie. That's what you really want, anyway." And I stalk out of the room.

The rest of the tournament is sheer misery.

I sit in the stands, watching silently as the Lady Shawmuts battle the Suns for the championship. Stewart—make that *Stew-rat*—and

I haven't spoken since breakfast. I can tell he wants to talk—he keeps looking up at me from where he's standing by the edge of the rink. But Sophie's there too, of course, so what more is there to say? He's made his choice.

But Sophie's there with him too, of course, so what more is there to say? He's made his choice.

The final seconds of the game unfold as if in slow motion. I see Cassidy and Allegra Chapman skating toward the Suns' goalie. Allegra passes the puck to Cassidy, who takes the shot.

The buzzer blares and I hear the crowd go wild. I see Cassidy and her teammates throw their gloves in the air, screaming their heads off in excitement as the final score is announced.

The buzzer blares and I hear the crowd go wild. I see Cassidy and Allegra Chapman throw their gloves in the air, screaming their heads off as the final score is announced.

"SHAW-MUTS! SHAW-MUTS! SHAW-MUTS!" The chant sounds to me like it's coming from a distance. I watch as Cassidy and the rest of the Lady Shawmuts skate around the rink, their smiles as wide as the banner they're holding, all of them over the moon with happiness.

I know I should be happy for them too, but I'm numb. I feel like I'm underwater, or someplace far away. Not here. Anywhere but here.

Here is too painful.

Heather Vogel Frederick

❧ Jess ❧

"Everybody knows you are the most selfish, heartless creature in existence . . ."
—*Jane Eyre*

"Let's hear it for the new mayor of Concord—Lily Wong!"

Darcy and I toss handfuls of confetti into the air and cheer along with the rest of the crowd. We've been crammed in shoulder to shoulder with many of Mrs. Wong's supporters here at Pies & Prejudice for over an hour, waiting for the election results. Now we have the official word: Megan's mother won by a landslide.

I crane my neck, looking for Emma. I see her family, and I see Stewart standing with Mr. Wong and Sophie Fairfax, but there's no sign of Emma.

"Speech! Speech! Speech!" chants the crowd, and Darcy goes over to help lift Mrs. Wong onto one of the tables. She raises her hands overhead, wrists interlocked in her now-famous Handcuffs Wong pose, and everyone cheers again.

"First of all, I want to thank each and every one of you here tonight for your phenomenal support," she begins as the noise dies down. "If it's true that it takes a village to raise a child—and many of you have had a hand in raising mine"—she smiles at my mother and the rest of the book club moms who are clustered by the pastry display case—"it's even more true that it takes a village to keep the democratic process alive, especially with all that was involved in an unexpected election like this one." She pauses dramatically, then adds: "And I'm here to tell you tonight that the spirit of democracy is alive and well in Concord, Massachusetts!"

Everyone cheers wildly again at this.

"Most of all," she continues, "I'd like to thank my wonderful family and my remarkable campaign staff, especially Stewart Chadwick and Emma Hawthorne who, despite their youth and inexperience, out-worked, outbrainstormed, and, in the end, managed to outmaneuver our worthy opponents. Handcuffs Wong is forever in your debt."

Where is she? I wonder, still searching for Emma as the crowd applauds enthusiastically.

"And of course, I also need to single out Sophie Fairfax," adds Mrs. Wong, "our family's lovely exchange student and the campaign's talented photographer and filmmaker, whose clever ads and video spot caught the eye and the imagination of our town's citizens."

Sophie waves shyly as the crowd applauds again.

Say something about Megan, say something about Megan, I chant under my breath at Mrs. Wong, who is wearing the red Chanel knockoff Megan made her for the debate again tonight. But she doesn't.

As she goes on to pledge her commitment to fulfilling her campaign promises as Concord's new mayor, I finally spot Emma stand-

Heather Vogel Frederick

ing back near the kitchen, half-hidden by the curtain that serves as its door. "Emma, I'm so proud of you!" I tell her after I manage to work my way through the throng. "Isn't this exciting? Your Handcuffs Wong strategy really paid off."

"Yup."

"Next stop, the White House, right?"

She gives a halfhearted laugh, and I look at her keenly. "Is something wrong?"

She lifts a shoulder.

Something is definitely up. Now that I think about it, I haven't seen much of her since Sunday. The two of us didn't get to talk after Cassidy's final game; my family had to skip the celebration party and buzz right home to help out with the baby boom at the farm. "C'mon Emma—you can't hide from me. I know you too well. What's going on?"

She sighs. "Fine. Stewart and I argued."

"Over what?"

"He wants to take both of us to the prom."

"Both of us who?" I ask, puzzled. I'm going with Darcy—Stewart knows that, doesn't he?

"Sophie and me," Emma replies.

I start to laugh.

Emma's eyes well up with tears. "It's not a joke, Jess. I'm serious."

My laughter fades. I stare at her. "He wants to take you and *Sophie Fairfax*? Are you kidding me?"

"I wish I was," she says bitterly.

"Is he completely nuts? This is *prom* we're talking about! Prom! You know, the once-in-a-lifetime deal with the picture that goes in your scrapbook forever?"

Emma snorts. "It won't be going in mine, that's for sure. Not anymore."

"Don't say that! Can't you try and talk to him again? Does he know that you've had your dress picked out since you lived in England?"

She shakes her head and her gaze drops to the floor.

"Look, you're going to go," I tell her, "even if you have to come with Darcy and me."

Her head snaps up again at this. "I am not going to prom with my *brother*!"

"Yeah, I guess that wouldn't be too fun, would it?" I give her a rueful smile. "Maybe if I talk to Stewart, it could help."

"You won't get anywhere, trust me," she replies. "He's convinced that Sophie is this poor, misunderstood creature and that it's his duty to take her under his wing and make sure she has a good time. It's some knight-in-shining-armor complex or something, I don't know."

"What about making sure his girlfriend has a good time?" I stand on my tiptoes, scanning the room and trying to locate our friends. This calls for an emergency mother-daughter book club meeting if anything does. "Leave it to me," I tell her, and push my way back through the crowd again.

The following afternoon the five of us rendezvous at Cassidy's house. After admiring her new medal and her silver co-captain's championship plate, we retreat to the turret, where Emma and I fill everyone in on the latest development.

"Let me get this straight," says Cassidy when we're done. "Stewart actually said, with a straight face, that he wants to take you *and Sophie Fairfax* to the prom?"

Emma nods glumly.

"Put him in the penalty box," says Cassidy in disgust. "Stupid Stew-rat." She turns to Becca. "He's your brother, Becca. What is he *thinking?*"

"Don't look at me!" she protests. "It's not like he asked my advice."

"So what are we going to do?" asks Megan. "To help Emma, I mean."

"I really, really wish our *Cooking with Clementine* episode was running this week, instead of after prom," says Cassidy. "That would give Mademoiselle Velcro something to think about."

We all nod.

"What if we could find Sophie another date?" asks Becca. "Wouldn't that solve the problem?"

"The dance is a week from Saturday," Megan points out. "All the senior boys must have dates already."

"Not necessarily," says Becca. "There are always a couple of last-minute break-ups and cancellations—"

"And there are probably a few shy guys who haven't asked anyone yet," I add.

"Spoken like a true formerly shy person," says Megan, and I stand up and curtsy.

"Too bad we can't sic Kevin Mullins on her," says Cassidy. "That would be a punishment worthy of the crime."

That gets a smile out of Emma—the first one I've seen her crack in days. She starts to giggle, and pretty soon we're all laughing.

Kevin has transferred his affections from me to Sophie and has spent the better part of the semester trailing around after her. It's completely ridiculous, of course, and hugely entertaining to watch—like a chipmunk pining after a panther or something.

"Let me talk to Darcy," I say, pulling out my cell phone. "Maybe he knows somebody who needs a date."

"Hey, you guys," says Emma as I'm tapping out a text, "while we're all here, I told Jess this already, but I overheard something weird at the hotel we stayed at for the hockey tournament." She describes the phone conversation between Megan's parents. "Any idea what that was all about? It sounded serious."

Megan makes a face. "I have a pretty good idea," she replies. "My mother just won't let this whole engagement thing go. She's totally convinced that Sophie's grandfather is some big gold digger. I think she's hired a private detective to check up on him."

"No way!" Cassidy looks shocked.

"Wow," echoes Becca.

Megan nods. "Yeah, no kidding. I don't want to be around when Gigi finds out, either. She's going to hit the roof."

"From what I overheard, it sounds like he discovered something," says Emma.

Heather Vogel Frederick

"Maybe, I don't know," Megan replies. "I haven't gotten wind of anything, but my mother's been all caught up with the election for the past few days, so for all I know she's dropped it. She's not really going to have time for snooping now that she's mayor."

"Isn't Monsieur de Roches coming to visit soon?" asks Cassidy.

Megan nods again. "Next week."

"Maybe she's planning on confronting him then."

We're quiet for a bit, mulling this over. *How awful for Gigi,* I think. I can't imagine which would be worse—finding out some deep dark secret about your fiancé, *à la Jane Eyre,* or finding out that your own daughter hired a private detective to check up on him. It's a lose-lose situation.

"How's your grandmother doing these days, anyway?" I ask.

"She's in her own happy little Gigi bubble," says Megan. "She dances around the house singing "La Vie en Rose" all the time, and when she isn't doing that, she's on the phone with Monsieur de Roches or meeting with the wedding planner."

"They've set a date already?" asks Cassidy.

"Yup. First weekend in June."

"Wow, that's really fast," I tell her.

"Are they going to get married here or in France?" asks Emma.

"Here. They talked about Paris, but Gigi wanted to make sure all of us could be there, and destination weddings are super expensive."

"Is she going to have bridesmaids and everything?" asks Becca.

Megan nods again. "She wants my mother to be her matron of

honor, but that will depend if she and my mother are still talking by then. Right now things are pretty tense at home. And Sophie and I are supposed to be her bridesmaids." She doesn't sound too thrilled about this.

"Hey, just think—you've always wanted a sister!" jokes Cassidy.

"Ha ha ha," Megan replies grimly. "That is so not funny. By the way," she continues, "Gigi's planning a brunch to introduce Monsieur de Roches to everyone after he arrives. Your families will all be getting an invitation in the mail soon—it's a week from next Sunday."

"The day after prom?" Emma asks.

"Yup."

By the following Monday we've lined up a date for Sophie. Jeremy Elliott, a friend of Darcy's from his baseball team, broke up with his girlfriend over the weekend, and he was thrilled at the prospect of having someone else to ask.

"I think he's as much interested in rubbing his girlfriend's nose in it as anything, according to Darcy," I tell Emma.

"That's Sophie's problem," she replies. "I'm just glad she's off my hands. And more important, Stewart's."

The rest of the week zips by, thanks to a rush of baby animals at the rehabilitation center where I volunteer—warmer weather always brings a spate of new cases—and the flurry of preparations for the prom.

"You're so lucky you get to go," sighs Adele, flopping onto her bunk one night as I finish telling them about the latest in the Emma-Stewart-Sophie saga.

That's one drawback to Colonial—there's no prom. There are a couple of private boys' schools in the area that we have dances with during the year, but it's not the same as a traditional high school prom.

"I hear Kevin Mullins is still available," I tell her. "I could totally set you two up."

Frankie laughs. My roommates are only too familiar with Kevin Mullins. He used to ride his bike over here constantly the first year I was Colonial. "Adele Mullins," she says. "Now that has a nice ring to it."

"Thanks a bunch," grumbles Adele.

"Y'all shouldn't make too much fun of that poor kid," Savannah points out. "It's guys like him who end up running computer companies and Internet start-ups."

"Revenge of the nerds?" says Frankie.

"Exactly."

My roommates have all been really good sports about the whole prom thing, and, in fact, have turned the event into a group project. The three of them tagged along shopping with my mother and me when it came time to find a dress, and they helped pick out the shoes and accessories to go with it. This past week they've spent every evening poring over fashion magazines in search of the perfect hairstyle for me.

On Thursday afternoon Emma rides her bike over to join me at Mr. Mueller's rehabilitation center, and I finally get an update.

"Stewart was kind of annoyed when he found out about Sophie's date," she tells me, holding a baby rabbit while I feed it with an eyedropper. "I never let on that we'd pulled some strings behind the scenes. Anyway, he didn't exactly apologize, but we're talking again."

"So you're definitely going to go to prom with him?"

She nods. "Yeah. It still feels a little awkward, but I really don't want to miss it." She gives me a sidelong glance. "I just wish he would—that he was more like . . ." Her voice trails off.

I pretend like I'm not paying attention, and focus on the tiny rabbit instead. I'm pretty sure she was going to say that she wished Stewart were more like Darcy. It hasn't been easy for Emma this spring. It's not that her brother is a perfect boyfriend. He has his faults, too. He can be absent-minded sometimes, especially when sports are involved. He got so wrapped up in some hockey tournament for instance, he forgot to give me the Valentine's Day card he'd bought for me. I got it three days late, along with a huge apology. Still, so far he's showing Stewart up at every turn, and I know Emma can't help comparing her relationship to mine.

On Saturday afternoon the two of us go to the salon together and get mani-pedis and updos. Well, I get an updo. Emma cut her hair short again over spring break, and there's not a whole lot the stylist can do with it besides fluff it up a bit. Still, it looks really pretty. I was just going to wear my hair in its usual braid or maybe leave it loose around my shoulders, but my roommates wouldn't hear of it.

"Prom wouldn't be prom without an updo," Frankie said firmly. "Don't come back without one." She and Adele and Savannah are meeting me at Half Moon Farm afterward to help me get ready.

"See you in a while," I say to Emma when I drop her off at home after we're finished at the salon.

"See you when I'm gorgeous!" she replies, sounding more like her old cheerful self.

"You're always gorgeous," I tell her, and she blows me a kiss.

Emma and Stewart and Darcy and I are going to the prom tonight as a foursome. We decided to keep it low-key, and didn't bother lining up a limo. With Stewart and Darcy both saving for college, it just didn't make sense to spend money on it.

"Too bad I don't have Briggs anymore," Savannah said when she found out. Briggs was her chauffeur, but after our first year at Colonial she begged her parents to recall him to Atlanta and send her a bike instead. She was tired of looking like a total snob. Plus, Concord is so small and Colonial is smack dab in the middle of town, so it's not like she really needed anybody to drive her around.

My roommates are waiting for me upstairs in my room, and Adele squeals when I walk through the door.

"I love the rosebuds the stylist tucked in!" she says, rushing over to inspect me. "They're the exact same shade of pink as your dress!"

Frankie motions with her hand. "Turn around so we can see the back."

I do, and the three of them sigh. There are more sighs when I put on my dress.

"Didn't I tell you?" says Savannah, adjusting the hem. "It's perfect."

Savannah's the one who spotted it. I wasn't convinced at first—strapless is a little out of my comfort zone, plus the spangles on the tulle overlay seemed a bit much.

"Are you sure I don't look like one of the good fairies in *Sleeping Beauty*?" I ask, turning this way and that to inspect myself in the mirror.

Frankie grabs a riding crop off my desk and holds it out to me, her eyes sparkling mischievously. "Your magic wand, milady."

Savannah plucks it away from her. "You're beautiful," she assures me. "And no, you don't look like one of Sleeping Beauty's fairies."

The doorbell rings downstairs, and a moment later my mother calls, "Jess! Darcy's here!"

"I guess it's time," I tell my friends.

"This is so exciting, I think I'm going to cry," says Frankie, dancing up and down.

"I feel like the mother of the bride," says Adele.

"Thanks, you guys," I say, giving them each a hug. "This wouldn't have been nearly as much fun without you."

"Hang on a sec," says Savannah as I turn to go. "We need pictures!" She whips out her smartphone, and they all take turns getting their picture taken with me, and then we manage a group close-up.

"Jess?" my mother calls again.

"Coming!"

My parents get all teary-eyed as I start down the stairs, which is hugely embarrassing. I still feel a tiny bit silly in my dress, as if I'm wearing a costume for a part in a play—Belle, maybe, the character I played in *Beauty and the Beast* back in middle school. But I also feel more than a tiny bit grown up and thrilled, especially when I see the look on Darcy's face.

"So where's my corsage?" he teases as I go to stand beside him.

I laugh, looking up at him. He towers over me – I'm stuck at five-foot-nothing, as my father puts it, just like my mother. Five foot two and a half, to be exact. Exactly a foot shorter than Darcy Hawthorne.

"Can you believe this is our baby?" my mother says, tucking her arm through my father's. "She's all grown up."

Darcy grins. "My parents said the same thing about ten minutes ago."

"To Emma?" my mother asks.

"No, to me! Although I believe the exact words were 'he's all grown up,' not 'she.'"

We pose for pictures, and of course Dylan and Ryan want to get in on the act. They insist on making faces, so my father shoos them away after a couple of shots.

"How about one with all the roommates?" my mother suggests, and Savannah and Adele and Frankie crowd around me.

"We could always just skip prom and stay here tonight," I tell Darcy, as my friends and I smile for the camera. "They're getting takeout from Leaning Tower of Pizza."

My roommates love hanging out at Half Moon Farm almost as much as I do, and they were thrilled when my parents invited them to stay for dinner and a DVD.

"Not gonna happen," Darcy replies, taking my hand and tugging me toward the front door.

"Have fun, you two!" says my mother. "Drive carefully, and give us a call if you're going to be out past midnight."

"We will, Mrs. Delaney," Darcy promises. The door shuts behind us, and he turns to me, smiling. "Whew! Made it out alive!"

We stop by the Chadwicks' to pick up Stewart next who, like Darcy, is wearing a tux. They both look great. So does Emma. She shows up at the Hawthornes' door wearing the lavender dress she bought in England. She picked it because it matched her old glasses, which she doesn't have anymore, but the pale purple shade is still a really flattering color on her.

"Wow," says Stewart when he sees her. "You look beautiful, Emma."

"He'd better tell you that about a zillion times tonight," I whisper to her a few minutes later. "He owes you big-time."

We go through the whole photo routine again with Emma's parents, minus the pesky little brothers, although Pip does manage to wriggle his way into one picture. And then we're off.

Even though we opted not to get a limo, the guys spring for dinner at the Colonial Inn, and it feels like old times again as we talk and joke around during our meal. Stewart has decided on Middlebury, and he and Darcy trade notes on the college classes they're thinking of taking and the summer jobs they're hoping to find. Best of all, Stewart doesn't mention Sophie Fairfax once.

The bubble bursts about halfway through the dance.

Heather Vogel Frederick

I'm floating in Darcy's arms, looking around and thinking how perfect everything is—prom this year is at the Plaza, one of Boston's fanciest hotels—when all of a sudden there's a commotion on the far side of the room.

"How dare you steal my boyfriend!" I hear someone screech.

"Uh-oh," says Darcy, peering over the crowd of couples on the dance floor. "That's not good."

"What's not good?"

"Jeremy Elliott's old girlfriend just showed up."

"In the middle of prom?"

"Looks like it."

There's some more screeching, and then the crowd parts and Sophie rushes by, looking stricken. Stewart darts after her, leaving Emma standing alone on the dance floor.

Things unravel quickly after that. Both Emma and Sophie are in tears, and Emma insists on leaving immediately. I don't want to bail on my best friend in her moment of crisis, so I tell Darcy we need to leave, too. Nobody says much on the drive home. I glance over the back of the seat a few times to where Stewart is sitting between Emma and Sophie. They're all stony faced.

It's really awkward.

Darcy heads for Strawberry Hill first.

"*Merci,*" Sophie says quietly when we drop her off at the Wongs. "Thank you all for rescuing me. I don't know how I would have gotten home otherwise."

"There's this wonderful invention called a taxi," Emma mutters.

"*Emma!*" says Stewart. He turns to Sophie. "Let me walk you to the door."

I hold my breath on the drive back toward town. The atmosphere wafting from the backseat is glacial.

"You can drop me off here," says Emma, when we get to the Hawthornes'. Stewart starts to get out of the car, too, and she shoots him a look. "Don't even think about it."

After a brief stop at the Chadwicks' to let Stewart out, we continue on to Half Moon Farm. Darcy cuts the lights as we pull into the driveway. He parks over by the barn, then turns to me and lifts an eyebrow. "That went well."

I heave a sigh. "Poor Emma."

"It wasn't really anybody's fault," says Darcy. "Talk about bad timing! Who could have guessed that Jeremy's girlfriend would choose the middle of prom to try and get him back?"

We get out of the car and wander over to the fence by the back pasture. It's a beautiful warm May evening, and the sky overhead is thick with stars. Over by the pond, the crickets are out in full force.

"So that was prom," says Darcy, resting his chin on top of my head.

"That was prom," I reply.

"What a disaster! It would be funny if it wasn't so sad."

"I know."

We both laugh softly, so as not to wake anybody inside the house.

Heather Vogel Frederick

Or inside the nearby coop. All we need to top off the evening is to set off the chicken alarm.

"I think you still owe me a dance or two," says Darcy.

"Good thing there's a ballroom handy," I tell him, leading him to the barn. "It's not the Plaza, but it will do in a pinch."

Inside, the radio is playing softly for my brother's 4-H chicken. "Hey, Taylor," I say, squatting down by the brooding pen and clucking softly. The chick, who is now about half-grown, comes scampering over, hoping for a snack.

"Taylor?" asks Darcy.

"Swift," I tell him.

He grins. "You Delaneys and your goofy chicken names!"

"You got a problem with country, boy?" Straightening up, I reach over the pen and crank up the radio—not loud enough to startle any of the livestock but loud enough to dance to—and find a good boot-stomping station. Darcy smiles as I lift the hem of my dress and do a little two-step.

We both kick up our heels for a couple of numbers, laughing and goofing off, then Darcy pulls me closer as a slow tune comes on. It's Patsy Cline's "Tennessee Waltz," one of my mother's favorites. I sing along softly, faltering a bit when I get to the line, "My friend stole my sweetheart from me."

I should call Emma and see how she's doing, I think, pulling away.

"A little too close to home?" Darcy asks, and I nod. That's one of the things I like best about Darcy—he almost always knows what I'm thinking.

He walks me to the back porch, and we pause by the steps. "Thanks for going to prom with me," he says.

"Thanks for asking me."

"I guess I'll see you tomorrow for brunch at the Wongs'?"

I nod. I'm looking forward to meeting Gigi's fiancé, but not to any more drama with Mrs. Wong or Sophie Fairfax.

"Brace yourself for fireworks," I tell him.

"Tomorrow, or right now?" he teases.

"Both," I reply, tilting my face up for a kiss. It's a nice one, well worth putting in my scrapbook with our prom pictures.

After he leaves, I slip inside and up to my room. I try calling Emma, but there's no answer. She doesn't return my text messages, and when I go online there's no sign of her there, either. I send her an e-mail and leave her a voice mail, but in the end I have no choice but to go to bed.

Next morning, my parents let me sleep in and skip church. I try Emma again; still no answer. I text Darcy in frustration to see if he knows anything; he texts me back to say that she's okay, but not acting like herself. By the time we head to the Wongs', I'm starting to get seriously worried.

"I can't wait to meet this beau of Gigi's," says my mother as we pull into the driveway. "It's so romantic, falling in love later in life like that!"

"It's romantic falling in love early in life, too," says my father, reaching for her hand. My parents were college sweethearts.

I look out the window and smile. I'll vote for romance early in life any time. High school, even.

Gigi and Monsieur de Roches are waiting by the front door to greet everyone. Gigi's arm is tucked through his, and she looks radiant.

"I am delighted to meet the famous Delaneys of Half Moon Farm," says Sophie's grandfather after we're introduced. *Megan's right; he does sort of look like a slim French Santa,* I think. It's the whole twinkle in the eye/white mustache thing.

"*Et nous sommes enchantés de faire votre connaissance aussi,*" says my mother, whipping out her high school French. "We're delighted to meet you too."

Monsieur de Roches bows to my brothers, who think that's hilarious. They rush inside and spend the next few minutes bowing to all our friends—and chasing Coco.

Cassidy and Megan and Becca pounce on me the second they spot me.

"What the heck *happened* last night?" asks Megan, pulling me over to a quiet corner of the living room. "Sophie came home in tears and refused to talk about it. She hasn't been out of her room all morning."

I look around. The Hawthornes aren't here yet, and I'm beginning to wonder if maybe Emma's not coming. Stewart is standing by the big picture window, pointedly ignoring us.

"Didn't your brother tell you?" I ask Becca.

She shakes her head. "Total silence. He almost didn't come today. My mother practically had to force him."

I give them a quick rundown of the disaster at the Plaza.

Cassidy lets out a low whistle. "Wow. What a mess."

"So has your mother said anything to Gigi yet?" I ask Megan. "About the private detective, I mean?"

"Not as far as I can tell. She probably wanted to get a good look at Monsieur de Roches first."

"He seems really nice," says Becca.

I nod. "Yeah, I agree. I mean, I've only said hello and everything, but there's something about him that's—"

"Charming?" asks Megan, and I nod.

She sighs. "I know. The thing is, if it weren't for Mademoiselle Velcro, I'd love to have him for a grandfather, you know?"

The doorbell rings again. It's the Hawthornes.

"You're here!" says Gigi happily, introducing them to Sophie's grandfather. "Now the party can really begin."

From the look on Emma's face, a party is the last thing she wants. Keeping her eyes carefully averted from Stewart, she makes her way over to us.

"How are you doing today?" I ask, giving her a hug.

"Horribly," she replies. "I don't think I slept a wink."

"Sophie should be ashamed of herself, ruining prom for you like that," says Cassidy, glowering.

"To be fair, it's not like she planned it or anything," I tell her. "I

Heather Vogel Frederick

mean, come on, you have to admit—wouldn't you have been morti-
fied, too, if some blind date's obsessed ex-girlfriend showed up and
gave you the heave-ho like that?"

Cassidy grunts. "I suppose."

"Still, Stewart didn't have to rush in like the white knight," says
Emma bitterly. "And she could have found another ride home."

The "she" in question emerges from the hallway just then, looking
as pale and unhappy as Emma. She reddens when she sees us, and goes
straight over to her grandfather. My twin brothers rush up to her and
bow.

"Brunch is served!" announces Gigi. "I made dim sum."

Cassidy brightens. "Oh yeah, baby!" Food always cheers Cassidy up.

"Aren't you going to go sit with your friends?" Sophie's grandfather asks her a few minutes later, gesturing to where the five of us are
clustered around the coffee table with our heaping plates of food.

She shakes her head and takes a seat beside him at the dining
room table. "I'd rather sit here with you."

Megan's grandmother looks over at us, pursing her lips. It's pretty
hard to pull the wool over Gigi's eyes, and a few minutes later she
marches over with a plate of cookies in one hand and Sophie in the
other.

"Here, girls," she says. "Why don't you take these down to Megan's
room."

"Uh—" Megan replies, hesitating.

"Now," says Gigi firmly.

"Okay, okay." Megan takes the plate from her. She looks over at us, shrugs, then starts down the hall. Feeling Gigi's eyes on us, we all stand up and follow.

There's an awkward silence when we get to Megan's room. Nobody quite knows what to say. Coco provides the spark that ignites the bonfire when she squirms out of my arms and runs over to Sophie.

Megan snorts. "Figures."

"What?" says Sophie.

"Nothing."

Sophie reddens. "Don't say nothing when you really mean something. Just go ahead and say it."

Megan is silent.

Sophie looks around at us. "*Je ne comprendes pas*—I don't understand," she says. "Why are you all so mean to me?"

"What's not to understand?" says Emma. "You come over here, uninvited, and steal our boyfriends—"

"—and our kittens!" adds Megan.

"I didn't steal anything from anybody!" Sophie protests.

I don't know if it's lack of sleep, or pent-up emotion, or a combination of both or what, but Emma explodes. "If you didn't steal anything, it's because it's always handed to you on a platter!" she snaps. "You're just a spoiled rich girl who thinks she can have anything she wants. Why don't you just go back to your chateau?"

Sophie gapes at her. "What are you talking about? What chateau?"

"The one in the picture you showed us!"

Heather Vogel Frederick

"You know," says Megan. "That picture on your dresser."

Sophie still looks puzzled. Then her brow clears and she laughs. "Oh, I get it now. The *chateau*! But wait, you think it's my home? I thought you knew! I live above the garage there with my grandfather—he's the chauffeur."

Megan's bedroom goes dead silent.

We must all look surprised, because she laughs again, bitterly this time. "*Je comprends maintenant*," she says. "Now I understand. All this time, this is what you thought of me. That I'm just a wealthy spoiled brat. Do you have any idea how lucky you are? All of you!" She looks around at us, her eyes brimming with tears. "You have parents who love you. Mine are so busy fighting that they barely have time to talk to me. I might as well be an orphan!"

We stare at her, stunned. But she isn't done yet.

"Don't you know I would give anything—*tout le monde!* all the world!—to have families like yours? My father is more interested in his work than his family. We haven't had a real conversation in years! My mother isn't like your mothers, someone who would want to spend time with me in a book club, or spend time with me at all. I have no one but my grandfather. And I thought, perhaps, your grandmother, too, Megan, who has been so kind and made me feel so welcome here."

"I didn't know," whispers Megan.

"Of course you didn't," snaps Sophie. "You didn't bother to take the time to find out anything about me."

"I—I had no idea," stammers Emma. "But you—and Stewart—"

"Ah yes, Stewart. Your boyfriend—*your* boyfriend, not mine—is one of the nicest people I know. He has been a true friend to me. I wish I could say the same for you. He deserves better." She turns to go. "My cousin was right about you—about all of you."

"Stinkerbelle?" says Cassidy.

"You're the ones who stink," mutters Sophie.

"Girls?" We whirl around to see Gigi standing in the doorway. Monsieur de Roches is with her, and behind the two of them are our parents. The noise from our argument must have drawn them down the hall. It's obvious from the uncomfortable expressions on their faces that they've just overheard a good chunk of what's been said.

The only one who looks remotely pleased is Mrs. Wong. "I guess the cat's out of the bag, then," she says. "Did you know this, mother? Did you know that your fiancé is actually a chauffeur? I just found out myself from the private detective—"

"You hired a private detective?" The color drains from Gigi's face.

Mrs. Wong suddenly looks a little less sure of herself. "I had to, don't you see? I had to protect you!" Her voice quivers, and it occurs to me that Megan was right. Her mother is afraid. Afraid that Gigi will be taken advantage of somehow, but probably even more afraid that she'll leave Concord—and her.

"I don't need protecting," Gigi says stiffly. "And yes, of course I knew Edouard is a chauffeur. Why on earth would that matter?"

"Mother, you're so naive! You're a wealthy woman, in case you've forgotten, and—"

Heather Vogel Frederick

"—and 'gentlemen in his station are not accustomed to marry their governesses,' *oui*?" says Sophie in a small voice. "Yes, I read *Jane Eyre*, too." She turns and walks out of the room, pushing blindly past Gigi and her grandfather. We hear her door slam across the hall.

"It seems perhaps I have made a mistake in allowing my granddaughter to come here," says Monsieur de Roches in his quiet, dignified voice. "I will take her back to France—I can see she is not wanted." He gives us a sorrowful look as he, too, leaves the room.

My friends and I stare at each other, aghast.

What have we done?

CASSIDY

*" . . . his presence in a room was more cheering
than the brightest fire."*
—Jane Eyre

Forget about *V* for Velcro. How about *V* for Very Big Mess?

"The wedding can't be off—it can't be!" moans Megan, flopping down onto the window seat of the turret. After the showdown at the Wongs, the brunch party ended pretty quickly. Sophie and her grandfather retreated to a hotel, Gigi locked herself in her room in tears, and my friends and I—who are in the doghouse again big-time—fled here to my house to regroup. Darcy was nice enough to drive us. "We have to *do* something!"

"Like what?" says Emma, who's more upset than I've ever seen her. We all feel badly, but this has hit her especially hard, I guess because of the whole Stewart thing. "I doubt Sophie will ever speak to us again. I can't say that I blame her either. Not after the way we misjudged her."

Beside me, Becca stiffens. "Omigosh!"

"What?" asks Jess.

"*Cooking with Clementine!* Isn't our prank episode supposed to run tomorrow?"

I leap to my feet. I can't believe I forgot about it! "If that episode airs, we can kiss this wedding good-bye for sure."

We look at each other, stricken. This is one time in my life when I don't need Dr. Weisman's advice, or my mother's or my older sister's or anybody else's. I know in my heart what we have to do.

It's not going to be easy, though. We're going to need every ounce of backbone we can muster.

"It's time to get our Jane on," I tell my friends, pausing for a moment, before I deliver the bad news: "We have to go talk to my mother."

We find her downstairs, sitting at the kitchen counter with Mrs. Hawthorne and Mrs. Delaney and Mrs. Chadwick.

"Yes, girls?" she says coolly as we troop in. She's got her Queen Clementine face on, which is not a good sign. It's one thing to face off against my mother; it's another thing entirely to go up against the Queen.

"Where's my mother?" asks Megan, looking around.

"Last we saw her, she was lying facedown in the hallway by your grandmother's room, trying to reason with her through the crack under the door," says Mrs. Delaney. "But I don't suppose you girls would know anything about that."

We shift uncomfortably. My friends look over at me, obviously waiting for me to take the lead. They're right; the prank was my idea. I'm team captain here—I need to take responsibility.

"Um, can we talk?" I say, feeling like I'm stepping in front of a firing squad. At best, I'm probably going to be grounded for life. At worst—

actually, I don't even want to think about "at worst."

"Seems like maybe you girls have been doing a little too much talking lately," says Mrs. Hawthorne crisply.

"We're sorry," Emma whispers. "We never meant—"

My mother interrupts her. "What is it you want to talk about?"

I take a deep breath. "Well, you know that ice cream sundae episode?" I begin. "The one that's scheduled to air tomorrow?"

Her forehead creases. "Uh-huh."

I hesitate, and the realization of what's coming dawns on her face.

"Uh-oh," she says. "What did you do?"

When I finish explaining about *piqueuse de mec*, I brace myself for an explosion. Surprisingly, it doesn't come.

"Right," says my mother, standing up. "I'm going to call Fred Goldberg and see if I can catch him at home. Phoebe, Shannon, Calliope—how about if two of you go back to the Wongs to give Lily some moral support, and one of you makes sure that the girls get over to the hotel immediately to try and talk to Sophie and her grandfather?"

She turns to us. "Don't breathe a word about any of this to them."

As if we would, I think, but wisely hold my tongue. I don't want to push my luck.

"What if we're too late?" says Jess.

"Then we'll have to deal with the consequences," my mother tells her. "For now, you have some bridge-building to do, and I have a phone call to make."

She leaves the room along with Mrs. Delaney and Mrs. Chadwick.

Heather Vogel Frederick

Mrs. Hawthorne turns to us and shakes her head. "I'd ask what you girls were thinking, pulling a stunt like that, but I don't even want to know."

"We got the idea from *The Scarlet Letter*," says Emma miserably, like somehow that's going to make it better. "It made sense at the time."

We follow her mother out to the car. None of us says a word on the drive over to the hotel. I know we did the right thing fessing up, and that we're doing the right thing by going to talk to Sophie, but I feel like I've had my nose rubbed in the whole backbone thing this week. I haven't said anything to my friends, but last night, while Emma and Jess were at prom, I finally mustered the courage to have a talk with Zach Norton.

What I had to say didn't go over too well, and I ended up really, really hurting his feelings.

"You just want to be friends?" he said, gaping at me when I was finished. We were sitting in his car in the parking lot outside the movie theater. I could barely concentrate on the dumb action flick we'd seen, because I was so nervous about the conversation ahead. But it had become unavoidable. "Are you kidding me? What's that supposed to mean?"

"Um, what it says, I guess," I'd mumbled. This was all harder to say than I thought it would be. "I like you a lot, Zach. I really do. I like hanging out with you, and talking with you—you're one of my best friends. But the whole boyfriend/girlfriend thing, it's just not, I mean, I don't feel . . ." My voice trailed off and I heaved a sigh, wishing I could explain it better.

"There's someone else, isn't there?" He drummed the steering wheel with his thumbs angrily. "I knew you'd been acting differently lately, but then you just kept telling me everything was fine."

I was quiet. There wasn't really anyone else—just the hope of it. Someday, maybe.

Unfortunately, he took that as a yes.

"I knew it!" he said. "Who is it? Third?"

That made me laugh out loud. Dating Third would be like dating Kevin Mullins. Well, okay, maybe not Kevin Mullins, but still. "No," I told him, shaking my head. "It's not Third. There really isn't anyone else—honest."

I'd hoped we'd still be able to be friends, but now I don't know. Zach was pretty steamed when we said good night, and I could tell he was hurt, too. So much so that I almost regretted saying anything. Part of me wanted to give him a hug and tell him I was kidding, just to put a smile back on his face. Zach has the best smile.

This stuff is all so awkward! You like somebody, you don't like somebody, they like you, suddenly you like them back, they kiss you, and you don't like them again. Or they kiss you and you do like them but they live three thousand miles away! Sheesh. Does life always have to be this complicated?

I didn't get to talk to Courtney about anything while she was here, either. I had to practice every second I wasn't in a game at the tournament, and before I knew it, the weekend was over and she was back on a plane to L.A.

Mrs. Hawthorne pulls into the hotel parking lot. "I'm going to sit right here and wait," she tells us. "Do your best, girls. A sincere apology can go a long way."

There's a surprise waiting for us when we knock on the hotel room door, though.

"What do you want?" says a familiar voice as the door opens a crack.

We stand there, frozen with shock.

Stinkerbelle is back in town!

"Annabelle?" says Emma, gaping at her.

"What do you want?" she repeats crossly, after none of us responds.

"Uh, we want to talk to Sophie," I finally manage to croak.

"Haven't you caused enough trouble already?"

"What are you doing here?" Emma stammers. "The wedding's not for two more weeks."

"Wedding? From what I hear, there isn't going to be one."

My friends and I exchange a glance. Getting past Annabelle Fairfax is going to be a problem.

And then it hits me—if Stinkerbelle is here, Tristan must be too! And all the Berkeleys. She wouldn't just come on her own. Or would she?

As if reading my thoughts, she steps out into the hall and closes the door behind her. Leaning back against it, she crosses her arms over her chest. "Keep your voices down," she whispers. "Everybody's sleeping."

I look at her in surprise. "You're all here? Crammed into that room?"

"No, you idiot." She gestures at the hallway. "We're spread out all over. I'm sharing with Sophie now."

"When did you get here?" asks Megan, looking pleased for the first time all day. Simon is probably here too, of course.

Stinkerbelle shrugs. "A couple of hours ago. Cousin Sarah and Cousin Philip thought it would be fun to surprise you." She snorts. "Turns out we're the ones who're surprised. We've come all this way for nothing."

We stand there awkwardly for a moment. Nobody quite knows what to say.

"Can we please talk to Sophie?" I ask again.

"And the reason I should let you do this is?" she replies coldly.

"We'd like to apologize," Emma tells her, whipping out her best "I am Dorothy, the small and meek" impression from *The Wizard of Oz*. She means it, though, you can tell. "We treated her terribly, and it was wrong of us, and if she leaves now before we get a chance to tell her that, we'll never forgive ourselves and she'll never know how badly we feel about everything. Plus, it's Gigi's life we're talking about here. And Sophie's grandfather's. Please?"

Mrs. Hawthorne was right—sincerity goes a long way. Annabelle regards her sourly for a long moment, then relents. "Oh, well, if you put it that way, fine, I guess." She opens the door again, and we follow her inside.

Heather Vogel Frederick

The room is dark, and Sophie is lying on the bed by the window with her back to us. I can tell she's awake, though. We tiptoe over and stand there, like relatives gathering by a hospital bed. None of us quite knows what to do.

"Uh, Sophie?" says Emma finally. "Can we talk to you?"

No response.

Emma presses on. "We are all so sorry about what happened. Really, truly, sorry. Can you ever forgive us?"

"Please," adds Megan. "For Gigi's sake, if not for ours. She hasn't stopped crying since you and your grandfather left."

This gets a response and Sophie peers at us over her shoulder. "*Vraiment?* Really?" She sounds worried. If there's one thing you can say about Sophie Fairfax, it's that she truly loves Gigi.

Megan nods. "She's locked herself in her room and won't talk to anyone."

Sophie turns away again. "I don't blame her," she replies icily. "What your mother did is *horrible.*" She pronounces it the French way, "hoar-EE-bull."

We all nod.

"What we did was horrible, too," I tell her, thinking about the *piqueuse de mec* prank and hoping with all my heart that my mother has gotten ahold of Mr. Goldberg and is going to be able to put a stop to it in time. "You're completely right—we misjudged you from the beginning."

"Me worst of all," says Megan.

Emma shakes her head. "No, me."

Thinking again about the prank, I jerk my thumb toward my chest. "Definitely me."

Sophie starts to snicker. "You sound like the three Stooges or the three little pigs or something."

"Are you calling us pigs?" says Jess in mock indignation.

"Would I be wrong if I did?" Sophie replies, sitting up and turning around.

Time to go for the goal, I think, and let out my best *oink* sound.

Emma quickly follows. *Snort.*

Snort snort—Becca ups the ante with two in quick succession. Jess produces a really loud, hilarious one, and Megan's is so tiny it sounds like a sneeze. Stinkerbelle stands there, watching and listening openmouthed in astonishment as the five of us proceed to make complete fools of ourselves. It works, though. In the end, Sophie is laughing so hard, she's practically crying.

"Are we forgiven?" asks Megan hopefully.

Sophie lifts a shoulder. "It's a start."

"We still have to talk to your grandfather," says Emma, and Sophie stops laughing.

"That will not be so easy," she tells us. "His pride has been wounded greatly. He takes his occupation very seriously, you know."

"I know," says Megan. "He's an amazing chauffeur. He drove Gigi and me all over Paris." She sits down on the bed next to Sophie. "Back at the house, you know how you said you wished you had Gigi as your

Heather Vogel Frederick

grandmother? Well, I've never met anybody I'd like to have more for a grandfather than yours. He's wonderful."

Sophie starts to tear up at this. Megan does too, and pretty soon we're all blinking back tears and sniffling, except for Stinkerbelle.

"You lot are bonkers," she says. "Crazy. *Completement fou*. I'm going back to bed."

And she flounces over to her side of the room and dives under the covers.

We try and keep our voices down as we wipe our eyes and blow our noses, but it's hard to stop giggling, especially when one or the other of us lets out another little snort. We sober up pretty quickly once we get to Monsieur de Roches' hotel room, though.

Sophie knocks on the door.

"*Oui?*"

"*C'est moi!*" she replies.

"*Entres*," he tells her, and Sophie turns the door handle. We file into the room after her. I can tell by the look on her grandfather's face that we're the last people on earth he's expecting to see.

"Sophie?" he says, giving her an inquiring glance.

"They came to apologize, *Papie*," she tells him. "They want to talk to you too."

He rises from the chair by the window where he was sitting. There's no hint of his Santa-like twinkle now. His expression is stern. "*Oui, mademoiselles?*"

Megan takes the lead this time. "Monsieur de Roches," she says.

"I know you love Sophie very much, and I know that my friends and I were unkind to her and that hurt you greatly. We were wrong, and we're sorry. I also know that what my mother did and said was, well, *horrible*." She pronounces it the French way, too. "She shouldn't have spied on you like that, no matter how afraid she was of losing Gigi. It was wrong. But I also know how much my grandmother loves you, and how happy she's been ever since she met you. I would be so sad"—she pauses, casting about for the right translation, and Sophie whispers *"complètement desolée"*—"I would be *complètement desolée*," Megan continues, "if something were to hurt her chances at happiness."

"Like some boneheaded things a bunch of girls like us may have said, for instance," I offer.

Monsieur de Roches looks over at Sophie, who translates rapidly. When she's done, I detect a glimmer of a smile for the first time since we came into the room.

"I see," he says. "And what does Gigi have to say about all this?"

"We don't know!" Megan bursts out. "She's locked herself in her room and won't come out! All she's done since you left is cry her eyes out!"

"Vraiment?" He frowns, then looks over at Sophie again and rattles something off in French. She nods, and he turns to us. "Well then, girls, what are we waiting for? *L'amour triomphe de tout!*"

"Love conquers everything," Sophie repeats with a grin as we follow him downstairs to the waiting car.

By early evening Sophie and her grandfather have returned to the

Heather Vogel Frederick

Wongs', the rest of us are all home with our families again, the wedding is back on, and the *Cooking with Clementine* fiasco has been avoided.

My mother had to pull a lot of strings to make it happen. It was too late for a re-edit, so she made the executive decision to scuttle the whole episode.

"It's my show," I overhear her tell Mr. Goldberg. "And my call. Yes, I realize there are financial ramifications, and I'll accept full responsibility for that. You can take it right out of my paycheck." She's quiet for a moment, then continues, "Yes, I understand that the network won't be happy. But I'll be even less happy if it does run, and you know what they say, 'If Mama ain't happy, ain't nobody happy.' Trust me, that's never been more true than in this case." She winks at me, and Stanley blows her a kiss.

In the end, she talks the network into replacing the episode with a rerun instead, and my stepfather makes sure she gets Mr. Goldberg to promise he'll send over the master negative as well, just to make certain our prank never accidentally makes it on to the air.

After Chloe has been put to bed, my mother and Stanley call me into the living room.

"We just want you to know that yes, we're angry with you, and yes, there will be consequences," my mother says, "but we're also very proud of you, sweetheart."

"Facing up to your own faults isn't easy," adds Stanley. "Believe me, I know; I've got plenty of them. But it's part of being a grown-up."

I nod, waiting for the ax to fall. I'm grounded for life, right?

My mother surprises me, though. "In the end, despite the fact that what you and your friends did was incredibly thoughtless and stupid, we feel you've learned your lesson and that you deserve credit for your honesty and your desire to try and make things right."

"Can you just please promise us one thing, Cass," says Stanley.

"What?" I ask him.

"Enough with the pranks already, okay?"

I grin, relieved. "I don't think that will be a problem. I've had enough to last a lifetime." I give them both a hug. "Um, I know this probably isn't the best time to ask, but do you guys mind if I go to the rink? Today's been kind of intense."

My mother looks at my stepfather, who shrugs and tosses me the keys to the minivan. "Go blow off some steam," he tells me, and I do.

Mr. Kohler is just getting ready to close up when I pull into the parking lot.

"You know the drill," he tells me. "Just make sure the lights are out and the doors are locked when you leave."

I flip on a single spotlight, then plop down on a bench by the edge of the rink and reach into my bag. I'm startled to find that I grabbed the wrong one—instead of my hockey skates, I brought my figure skates instead. Feeling stupid, I put them on and lace them up. Apparently I have something—or someone—besides hockey on my mind tonight.

I decide I won't bother with music. Sometimes I prefer to skate in silence. I can think better on the ice than anywhere else in the world. It's my refuge, the one place I can go where the world falls away and I can be alone with my thoughts. And tonight I have just one: *Tristan is back in Concord!*

I circle the rink a few times to warm up, then put myself through my paces. I don't bother with a hockey stick; tonight I just want to skate. I do speed drills and crossovers and even a few dance moves. Pausing to catch my breath twenty minutes later, I lean over and rest my hands on my knees, panting.

A noise in the stands brings my head up sharply.

"Who's there?" I call out, figuring it's probably Zach Norton. He has a key to the rink, too, since he's equipment manager for the Lady Shawmuts. I really hope he doesn't want to dredge up everything we talked about in the car again.

But it's not Zach.

It's Tristan.

He steps into the light and smiles at me. "Hullo," he says.

I stand there, too stunned to reply.

"Your mother said I'd find you here. Mind if I join you?"

I nod.

"Yes you mind, or yes I may?"

I grin at him, still not trusting myself to speak. He sits down and laces up his skates, then steps out onto the ice and heads over toward me. We stand there looking at each other for a moment.

"I'm still taller than you," he says. "Thank goodness."

I have to laugh at that.

"May I have this dance?" he asks, holding out his hand.

We don't need music; we make our own, humming the familiar waltz melody as we slip into the rhythm of the routine we performed together last year in England.

I love England, I think as we swoop and swirl across the ice. Especially a certain English garden, where a certain memorable kiss took place.

"I hear you had a busy afternoon," he says.

Annabelle must have told him. Always trying to stir up trouble, especially when it concerns Tristan and me. Stinkerbelle isn't here now though, is she?

One-two-three, one-two-three, step glide release, step glide step. The moves are still in my bones, imprinted by our long hours of practice.

"You know me, never a dull moment," I reply lightly. "I had to make sure that the groom didn't run off."

He laughs.

One-two-three, one-two-three, step glide release, step glide step. We come to a stop and finish humming the final bars of the melody. As the last note fades away, Tristan doesn't let go of me the way he usually does. Instead, he pulls me closer.

That memorable kiss in the garden?

This one is even better.

Heather Vogel Frederick

Emma

"Speak I must: I had been trodden on severely . . ."
—*Jane Eyre*

"Emma! There's a delivery here for you." My mother's voice floats upstairs. I'm curled up on my bed next to Pip, writing a letter to Bailey Jacobs. There's loads to tell her, what with all the excitement around here lately.

"A delivery, huh?" I say to Pip. "Sounds intriguing." His tail thumps in response and I scratch him behind the ears, then reluctantly set my pen and paper aside. "Guess I'd better go check it out—you never know, maybe Stewart sent me flowers."

After the whole Sophie Fairfax meltdown at the prom and the brunch fiasco, things between me and Stewart have been strained, to say the least. I did manage to swallow my pride long enough to apologize for having jumped to conclusions about him and Sophie, and he was good enough not to rub my nose in a pile of "I told you so." But he didn't offer an apology in return, and there are still a few things I feel like I need to say to him.

Maybe tonight after graduation we'll have another chance to talk. Our families are planning to sit together at the ceremony, since

Stewart and Darcy are both graduating, and then we're going to a party afterward at Chadwicks'.

Mostly I want to talk to Stewart about the future. Beyond telling me that he's getting excited about going to Middlebury—he's thinking of a double major in journalism and environmental studies, of all things, thanks to Mrs. Wong's influence—Stewart and I haven't really touched the subject of Us After High School. I'm not sure how I'm going to bring it up without sounding clingy or possessive; I still haven't figured that out yet.

One more chance to get my Jane on, I think. I seem to be doing a lot of that lately.

But first I'd better check out this mysterious delivery.

It isn't flowers.

"Rupert Loomis?" I exclaim, my jaw dropping when I see who's standing in our front hall. "What are you doing here?"

He gives me a clumsy hug, starts to scratch himself, then stuffs his hand in his pocket instead and jingles his change vigorously. Out of the corner of my eye I can see my father watching in amusement. My father adores observing Rupert.

"And don't forget me," says another voice, and I turn to see Rupert's Great-Aunt Olivia sitting in the living room with my mother. "I'm here, too."

My jaw unhinges again.

Miss Loomis smiles. "I see that we've surprised you. I told Rupert we should have written or called first, but he was most insistent upon

Heather Vogel Frederick

the fact that Americans love casual visits."

What would Rupert know about casual anything? I wonder, looking him over. Boarding school has clearly done him a world of good; he's not nearly as awkward as he used to be. And the hug, clumsy as it was, is a good sign. He was always so formal before, like a butler or something.

In fact, Rupert actually looks almost normal. Well, except for his enormous ears. When we lived in England, my mother used to say that he just hadn't grown into them yet. I'm thinking maybe he'll be ninety before he does.

His hairstyle is better, though—someone must have sat him down and told him that a middle part and thick black bangs went out of style in about 1910. To be fair, Rupert was raised by his great-aunt, who probably thought 1910 was a swell year.

"Rupert!" Drawn by our voices, my brother comes clattering downstairs. "Good to see you, man!"

The two of them shake hands, and we all go into the living room to join my mother and Miss Loomis. There's a wicked gleam in Darcy's eye, and as Rupert turns to say something to his great-aunt, my brother looks over at me and mouths the word *MOO!* My mother gives us the evil witch mother eye of death and shakes her head in warning, but I nearly crack up; that was our private nickname for Rupert back in England. Mostly because of the way Rupert always said his name, like he was a radio announcer or something: "Rooopert Looomis."

"My great-aunt and I have brought you something, Emma," Rupert tells me. His voice is as deep as ever, but that mournful quality it used to have, which earned him another nickname from Darcy—Eeyore—isn't as noticeable. I'm guessing life is a lot more fun for Rupert now that he's at boarding school and not rattling around Loomis Hall with only a senior citizen for company.

The senior citizen in question leans forward and passes me a parcel. All of a sudden the air whooshes out of my lungs. I know what this is! Taking it from her eagerly, I rip off the wrapping paper.

"Oh, Emma!" says my mother. "Your book!"

My book!

I'm a published author!

I gaze at the cover, grinning from ear to ear as my father reads the title aloud.

"*Stinkerbelle, the Bad Fairy,* by Emma Jane Hawthorne, with illustrations by Lucy Woodhouse. Now that," he says, paraphrasing one of his favorite poets, "is a thing of beauty and a joy forever."

It really is. The publisher did a gorgeous job with the layout and design, and my friend Lucy's artwork just glows on the gilt-edged pages.

"It's a sample copy," says Miss Loomis. "I've brought along the contract as well, and if the terms are agreeable to you and your parents, you may sign it, and the book will go into full production."

Rupert's great-aunt used to own a publishing company in England. My story was printed in the literary magazine of the school I attended when we lived over there, and Rupert gave it to her to read. She loved it—mostly because it cleverly skewers Annabelle Fairfax, whom she likes about as much as I do.

Anyway, she sent the story to a former colleague, and although I knew it was a possibility that it might get published, I figured it was a long shot. Since I hadn't heard anything about it for such a long time, I just assumed they didn't want it.

"Thank you so much, Miss Loomis!" I tell her, leaning over and kissing her wrinkled cheek. "This is the best surprise *ever!*"

"You're very welcome, my dear," she replies, looking pleased. "One of my greatest pleasures in life has always been helping put talented authors into print."

She just called me a talented author, I think, feeling giddy. *I can't wait to tell Stewart and Jess!*

"Now that you're here, what are your plans?" asks my mother. "Do you have a place to stay?"

"Oh yes," says Miss Loomis. "We've taken rooms at the Colonial Inn."

"We're going to explore greater Boston and its rich history," Rupert booms, sounding like his old pompous self. My father kicks me under the coffee table.

"I hope you'll let us be your tour guides," my mother tells them. "We'd love to show you Concord, for starters. We can begin later this afternoon, in fact. Darcy is graduating from Alcott High in a few hours. Perhaps you'd care to join us and see what happens at an American high school graduation? We happen to have two extra tickets, as my parents had to cancel their trip at the last minute."

"We'd love to," says Miss Loomis warmly. "As long as you're sure we're not intruding."

"Not at all," says my mother. "I'm going to go call Calliope Chadwick and let her know that you'll be at the graduation party afterward. It's just dinner in their garden, very informal, and I know she'll be delighted to show off her roses. She was so impressed with yours last summer at Loomis Hall. Oh, and I'll call the Wongs, too. You remember them from Chawton?"

Rupert and his great-aunt both nod.

"Lily's mother is getting married this weekend, and I feel certain they'll want to invite you to the wedding. The entire mother-daughter book club will be attending, of course, as well as some old friends of yours—the Berkeleys are visiting Concord, too."

"So is Stinkerbelle," I whisper, and everyone laughs.

My father whisks my book behind his back. "Better keep this out of sight," he warns. "We've just managed to put one fire out, no point starting another." Seeing the puzzled look on our guest's faces, he adds, "It's a long story."

My mother volunteers Darcy to drive Rupert and his great-aunt back to the hotel to freshen up, arranging to pick them up later this afternoon on our way to the high school. After they leave, I grab my book and rush upstairs to call Stewart.

I call Jess first, though.

"BFBB alert!" I tell her.

"What's up?"

"You're talking to a published author!"

She gasps. "What? No way—what happened?"

I fill her in on the details.

"Text me a picture right this instant," she demands, and I do. She sighs. "Oh Emma, I'm so proud of you! It's beautiful! This is just *so cool*. You have to bring it with you to graduation, okay? Promise me? I can't wait to see it in person!"

I promise her that I will, and then I call Stewart.

"Awesome!" he says when I tell him what happened. "Congratulations!"

"Can you come over for a few minutes?"

"I wish I could," he replies, "but I think my mother would kill me. She's having a cow over this stupid dinner party. My dad and Becca and I have been slaving away all day helping her get ready for it."

I laugh. "It's okay; I understand. You'll see it later anyway—I promised Jess I'd bring it to graduation."

"Excellent. I can't wait. See you there!"

I'm too excited to finish my letter to Bailey. Instead, I read my book through half a dozen times, examining every little detail. It really is gorgeous.

I'm a published author!

I finally pry myself away in time to shower and dress for graduation, and to wrap the presents I got for my brother and Stewart. Lady Jane Grey, our still-fairly-new cat, wanders in as I'm tying the ribbon and hops up on my bed to bat at the curly ends.

"Not for kitties," I tell her firmly, picking her up and putting her back down on the floor. She blinks at me reproachfully. "Oh all right then, fine," I say, relenting. "Knock yourself out."

I curl a piece of ribbon just for her and dangle it in the air. She leaps and swats at it, finally managing to snag it from me. I laugh as she scampers out of the room with her new trophy.

I sign the card for my brother, then hesitate as I start to sign Stewart's. Love, Emma? Fondly, Emma? Your friend, Emma?

We really need to talk.

I end up signing it *XOXO Emma*, which could go either way.

I got Stewart and Darcy the same thing: leather notepad portfolios with their initials stamped in gold on the cover. I hope it isn't weird that I got them identical gifts, but I think they'll both really like them, and they seemed like a good choice for taking to college.

Before I know it, it's time to leave for graduation, and we head out to pick up Rupert and his great-aunt. It's a bit of a squeeze with six of us in the car, but the high school isn't far and we manage.

I spot Stewart in the crowd of soon-to-be graduates and wave. He waves back, smiling broadly. He looks handsome in his cap and gown. We take our seats; I end up sitting between Rupert and Jess. I can see heads turning in the audience as friends from school look at us, wondering who the heck he is.

"Moo," whispers Jess, and I giggle.

The Wongs are here, too, right down front, and the end of our row

Heather Vogel Frederick

is filled with Chadwicks. Becca is sitting with her grandparents, and she looks over and waggles her fingers at us as the music starts. The audience quiets down at the opening notes of "Pomp and Circumstance." As the seniors start filing in, I see my father take my mother's hand. Mrs. Chadwick, who is already weeping openly, grabs a tissue out of her purse. I'm surprised to find myself suddenly teary, too; the music is stirring, and it seems to tap into a lot of the emotions that have been welling up in me lately. I'm feeling unsettled about Stewart, and Darcy will be leaving soon, and nothing's ever going to be the same.

Jess looks over at me and smiles. Her eyes are brimming, too; she must be having some of the same feelings.

"Why, there's Lily Wong!" whispers Miss Loomis, as Megan's mother takes the stage. "Doesn't she look lovely in that red suit."

"She just got elected mayor," I explain.

Mrs. Wong gives the commencement address, and she totally nails it, sticking to what my dad calls "The Three B's of Speechifying: Be bold. Be brief. Be seated." Stewart and I made that our marching orders for the campaign.

Darcy is next, because he's the valedictorian. I helped edit his speech, just like I helped with Mrs. Wong's. His closing lines take on a deeper significance here today than they did when he practiced in our kitchen at home, however.

"Looking ahead to the future is never easy," he says, his voice echoing through the auditorium. "None of us has a crystal ball; none of us knows exactly what lies ahead. But we can still go forward with confidence, thanks to all of our hard work over the past four years, and most of all thanks to the love and support of our families and friends."

He looks right at Jess when he says this, and I feel that all-too-familiar little pang of envy again. I glance over to where Stewart is sitting with his classssmates, preparing to walk across the stage and claim his diploma. Will he be walking out of my life next September?

We really need to talk.

And, finally, we do.

"I need to stretch my legs," he tells me a few hours later, after the diplomas have been handed out, the hats tossed in the air, the photographs taken.

We're sitting in his backyard beneath a tent; there are half a dozen other tables scattered around us, each holding a circle of our friends and neighbors and relatives. Across from us, my brother and Jess are deep in conversation with Becca and Rupert.

"Sounds good," I tell him, and we stand up and stroll across the yard, Yo-Yo prancing along at our heels.

"Thanks for the portfolio, by the way," Stewart says. "I love it."

"I thought you would."

"And I think your book is amazing."

Stinkerbelle, the Bad Fairy has been a hit this evening, making the rounds of all the tables. Fortunately, Annabelle Fairfax went into Boston with the Berkeleys and Sophie and her grandfather to pick up Sophie's parents at Logan Airport. They've flown in from France for the wedding this weekend.

Heather Vogel Frederick

"Thanks," I reply. I'm feeling shy all of a sudden, which is stupid. *It's now or never,* I tell myself. "Um, Stewart," I begin, glancing over my shoulder to make sure we're out of earshot of the rest of the party, "there are some things I've been meaning to talk to you about."

"Like what?"

"Like Sophie, for instance."

He frowns. "I thought we got all that straightened out."

"Mostly," I agree. "It's just that, well, you really hurt my feelings these last few months, spending so much time with her."

"Emma, I already explained. We're just friends."

I nod, trying to speak calmly. "I know that, and that's not what I'm talking about. What I mean is, because you spent so much time with her, I stopped feeling special. I felt like I was just another friend, too, not your girlfriend."

Stewart leans down and picks up a ball from the grass. "I guess I can see your point," he says grudgingly.

"The thing is, I don't know where I stand anymore."

"What do you mean? You're my girlfriend."

"Then why don't I feel that way?"

Stewart tosses the ball for Yo-Yo, who rockets off into the shadows to retrieve it. "I don't know, because . . . maybe . . . I've been really busy lately? The election, finals, graduation, thinking about college—"

"Can we talk about college?"

He nods.

I pause for a moment, staring off into the darkness. I can just make out the silhouette of the apple tree. Yo-Yo is crashing around in the bushes somewhere just beyond it. "Here's the thing," I say. "I wish I had a crystal ball and could see into the future."

Stewart is quiet, listening.

"I guess I just want to know what's going to happen to us—whether there will even still be an us, you know?"

"It's not like I haven't thought about that, too," he tells me.

Now we're both quiet.

He reaches over and takes my hand. "Do we have to know?" he asks softly. "We're together now, aren't we?"

I nod.

"And we've got all summer ahead of us—my mother hired me to work for her, so I'm not going anywhere. You'll be here too, right?"

I nod again.

"So let's just relax and enjoy each other's company, and try not to worry so much about the future. Maybe it's okay not to look in the crystal ball."

"Maybe." I think I know what Stewart's saying, and it sounds okay to take things a day at a time. I glance down at Yo-Yo and start to laugh. "Oh you poor thing! You heard Stewart say the word 'ball,' didn't you?"

Yo-Yo cocks his head, clearly expecting me to produce one.

"Where's yours, boy? Did you lose it?"

Stewart pulls me over and puts his arms around me. "I seem to

Heather Vogel Frederick

remember we were standing right about here the first time I kissed you," he says, and I smile.

"Well, if you don't count the forehead kiss at Sleepy Hollow Cemetery."

He groans. "You would have to bring that up. Not one of my better moments."

"You chickened out, didn't you?"

"Big time."

I lean into him and rest my head on his shoulder, breathing in his clean, familiar Stewart smell. I'm feeling a whole lot better, even though we haven't really settled anything.

He clears his throat. "Uh, what you were saying about not feeling like my girlfriend lately—would it help if tried a reboot of that first kiss?"

"I think it would," I tell him.

And it does.

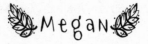

Megan

"Reader, I married him."
—*Jane Eyre*

"I don't think I've ever seen a prettier day in Concord," says my father, sipping his coffee. "Look at that sky! Not a cloud in it."

"Of course it's a pretty day," my mother replies. "I ordered one especially for the wedding." She smiles at Gigi. "I'm the mayor now, remember? I can do that."

I tilt my head back and close my eyes, letting the warmth from the sun wash over my face. My father is right—the sky is gorgeous. *June Blue*, I think, automatically reaching for my sketchbook. I sit up and open my eyes, jotting the words beneath the picture of my grandmother's wedding dress. The bright, robin's-egg shade of its fabric is the exact color of the sky overhead.

My parents and Gigi and I are lingering at the breakfast table out on the deck. I can tell that nobody wants to be the first to move. All of us know this is the last time it will be like this, just the four of us alone together.

After today we'll be six, with Monsieur de Roches—I've got to get used to calling him Edouard—and Sophie rounding out our family circle.

"You know what they say," my mother told me when we talked about it a few days ago. "Be careful what you wish for."

All my life I've wanted a bigger family, and now I have one. Maybe not the one I expected—I bugged my parents to have another baby for years. Sophie's hardly a baby, and neither is her grandfather. I'm totally on board with the whole grandfather idea, of course, and am slowly getting used to the fact that he's part of a package deal. Sophie comes with him, and while she won't exactly be a sister—technically we'll be step-granddaughters, I guess—she'll be spending a lot of time here during her school holidays, in the room right across the hall from mine. I'm going to help her decorate it this summer.

The two of us are getting along a whole lot better now. Especially since a few days after our big apology at the hotel, Sophie admitted that some of the fault was hers, too.

"I can be too much of a flirt sometimes, I know," she told Emma, promising to curb it in the Stewart department. Cassidy suggested she channel her energies toward Zach Norton, who it seems is available again.

And Sophie told me that could see how I got mad at her for spending so much time with my mother and grandmother.

"I guess I was a bit of a, how you say, 'Gigi hog'?" she said, which made me laugh. "But she was so nice to me! And your mother, too."

"It's okay," I told her. "I understand."

And it's true, I do. Especially now that I've actually met her parents. Sophie may have exaggerated about them a bit, because they're not quite the ogres that she made them out to be, but she's right about one thing—as nice as they are, you can tell they're more interested in their own lives than in her. Sophie's father has spent most of his time here shouting into his cell phone, while her mother taps out endless emails on her laptop. I know that they both have busy jobs and everything, but they pretty much leave Sophie on her own most of the time. It's like she's an accessory or something, while my parents always make me feel like I'm the main event.

So does Gigi.

"Nothing's going to change," she keeps telling me, but of course everything is, even though she's still going to be here in Concord running the tea shop. Monsieur de Roches has decided to retire from being a chauffeur so he can help her with it.

"We are thinking of acquiring a delivery truck," he told us. "I am, after all, a very good driver."

My mother stands up and stretches. "Well, I guess we should get cracking," she says. "Big day ahead."

We clear our breakfast dishes and I head down to my sewing room to put the final touches on Gigi's dress. I've spent a good part of the last couple of weeks working on hers, and also on Sophie's. The rest of the time I've spent with Simon.

Heather Vogel Frederick

Simon! It's been heaven having him back in Concord. I'm so glad he and his family decided to come early and surprise us. They've kept busy while we were in school all day, taking Monsieur de Roches and Rupert Loomis and his great-aunt under their wing and showing them the tourist spots. In the evenings, though, all of us have been together, which has been really fun.

Even Stinkerbelle is behaving herself. Well, for the most part. The funniest thing happened—we were at the rink, watching her and Tristan practice for some ice dancing championship they have coming up later this summer, and Third came over to join us and it was love at first sight. I'm not kidding! I've never seen that happen before— although I guess it happened with Gigi and Monsieur de Roches, but older people romance is way different, you know?

Anyway, Third practically started drooling watching Annabelle out there on the ice, and when she came over at the end of the practice session and we introduced everybody, she could barely keep her eyes off of him. She thinks he's hilarious too, which we all think is hilarious because he is such a goofball!

Who would have guessed?

Becca is relieved. She was getting pretty tired of fending him off, plus she's on the phone a lot these days with her Mr. Rochester. She finally told the rest of the book club about what happened over spring break, and everybody cracked up.

"I can't believe you actually found *Mr. Rochester!*" Emma keeps saying. I think she's a tiny bit jealous. Not of Theo, but of the whole idea of meeting someone named after one of your favorite literary characters.

There's a knock at the sewing room door and I look up to see Sophie standing in the doorway.

"I heard you humming in here. May I come in?"

I nod, and she starts to laugh.

"What?" I mumble through the pins in my mouth. I'm kneeling in front of the dressmaker's dummy, trying to get the little band of bows with diamondlike crystals at their center evenly spaced around the hem.

"I'm sorry, but you look so funny! It's like in that scene in *Sleeping Beauty*, you know? Where the mice and the birds all work together to help with the ball gown?"

I sit back on my heels and spit the pins out of my mouth. "Yeah, well bring on the mice," I reply. "I could use some help."

"Let me give you a hand." She crosses the room and sits down beside me, and we work together for a while in companionable silence.

"This dress is so beautiful, Megan," she says.

"Thanks."

She runs her hand across the fabric. "What do you call this fabric?"

"Silk shantung. I love the way it shimmers and drapes, but it's got a crispness and weight to it too, that tailors beautifully." Sensing her interest, I continue, "Gigi wanted something she could wear again, so the basic pattern is modeled on a vintage Chanel that's one of her favorites. I tweaked it, though, here in the bodice"—I stand up and

Heather Vogel Frederick

show her how I added horizontal overlapping bands to the neckline—"and then with the decoration at the hemline, of course. Oh, and there's a bolero jacket that goes with it too, in case she wants to wear it out at night."

She looks at me. "You tweaked Chanel," she deadpans. "Do you hear yourself? How do you know so much about all this, anyway?"

I shrug. "It's just what I do." I've been immersed in fashion for so long, I really don't know the answer to her question. "Maybe it's like you and filmmaking? I'll bet you just kind of instinctively know how to shoot and edit something, right?"

"Yes," she says. "I see." She brushes her fingers across the expanse of blue again. "Why did your grandmother not choose a white dress?"

"Mom tried to talk her into wearing one, but Gigi wasn't having it. For one thing, she said she's too old to wear some big poufy thing, and for another, white is the color of mourning in the Chinese culture—people wear it to funerals."

"Really?" Sophie looks surprised to hear this.

I nod. "Yup. Blue, though—blue is the color of immortality."

We both gaze at the dress.

"This is a good thing for Gigi and Papie," says Sophie softly. "Immortality."

We look at each other and smile.

After we finish up with the wedding dress, I ask Sophie to try on hers. Gigi and Edouard decided to keep the ceremony simple, with just a few attendants each. Sophie's father will be Monsieur de Roches' best man, and Mr. Berkeley and Annabelle Fairfax's father will be grooms-men. On Gigi's side, my mother is her matron of honor, and Sophie and I are the bridesmaids.

The overall look is eclectic, to say the least. Mom and I will be in our *qipao*—traditional midcalf-length Chinese dresses made with brightly-patterned silk brocade. Gigi specifically requested we wear them, as a nod to our heritage.

Mine has a history to it. Gigi's mother had it made for her when she was young, and then it was my mother's, and then Gigi gave it to me for my birthday back when she first came to live with us. It's tur-quoise, with an intricate design of plum blossoms and butterflies— "for long life and beauty," Gigi told me. It still fits me, though I had to let the hem down a little and the seams out at the bust a bit, too.

My mother's *qipao* is one I made for her a few years ago from vintage fabric my grandmother brought with her from Hong Kong. It's bright red, like Gigi's Chanel suit, with gold dragonflies sprinkled across it. Dragonflies symbolize prosperity, harmony, and luck—good things for a mayor, I think.

For Sophie, we settled on a couture knockoff, one based on my favorite dress from Chanel's spring collection. It's soft pink instead of eggplant, and tea length to match the length of our *qipao*, instead of going all the way to the ankles. But the slim flapper style, with tiny pleats across the torso and a flutter of chiffon at the bottom, suit Sophie to a T. She puts it on now and looks at herself in the mirror, smiling.

Heather Vogel Frederick

"A happy customer means a happy designer," I remark. "I'm so glad you like it."

"Like? I love it!" She twirls around, then gives me a hug.

I stand back and look at the dress critically. It really is perfect for her. She looks like a little pink cloud, and the color brings a radiance to her pale skin. "I love it too."

"We are going to look like a little bouquet at the church, *oui*?"

I nod, smiling. That we are for sure. We are blue and red and turquoise and pink, French and Chinese and American. We are a colorful group, this melting pot that is my new family.

I cross the room to where my sketchbook is lying open on the sewing table and write down "bouquet" and "melting pot," to remind myself when I blog about this later. Fashionista Jane has been having a ball covering the wedding preparations.

And she's looking forward to summer, too. After extracting multiple promises that I'd keep the snark dialed back, my mother agreed to let me continue to blog, and she also agreed to let me go to New York for two weeks, at Wolfgang's invitation, to join some other teens from around the country at *Flashlite's* annual Camp Catwalk.

"Megan's awfully young to be doing something like this," she said when he called to tell us about it.

"Mom!" I'd protested. "I've been to Paris, remember?"

"That was different—you were with your grandmother."

"Oh, but you can't say no, it's a FABULOUS opportunity!" Wolfgang told her. "Just imagine, Mrs. Wong, Megan will spend two weeks apprenticing with New York's top fashion designers. And I assure you that all the participants are well-supervised. Think of it as fashion camp, with me as head counselor."

"That's what I'm afraid of," my mother muttered, but she eventually relented.

I'll return home from New York right around the time Gigi and Monsieur de Roches—Edouard—get back from their honeymoon in Greece. If my mother can get away from her new job, my father wants to take the whole family on vacation to France so Edouard can show us his part of the world. He's been a chauffeur at the chateau for so many years that the family who owns it gave him permanent use of a cottage on a corner of their estate as a wedding present. He and Gigi plan to spend part of each year there, probably around fashion weeks in the spring and fall.

There are worse things than having a grandmother with a pied-à-terre in France, that's for sure.

Not to be outdone, my father bought the property next door, and construction has already begun on the little house he's having built there for Gigi and Edouard. Newlyweds need a home of their own, he says.

Gigi didn't want anything too big, and Edouard is used to his small apartment above the chateau's garage, so they're both happy with the modest design. It will be strange not having my grandmother living right here with us, though. Her apartment downstairs will revert to being the guest quarters again.

Heather Vogel Frederick

"You can stay here anytime you like," my mother told Sophie's mother at the rehearsal dinner last night, and I heard her say the same thing to her father a while later.

The sewing room door creaks open a little wider, and Sophie and I look over to see Coco bound in. Truffle is right behind her. His real name is Truffaut, after the French film director, but we all call him Truffle.

The mother-daughter book club threw a bridal shower for Gigi last weekend, and Sophie got a surprise gift—a kitten of her own. A black one this time, which didn't thrill my parents, but my mother's been bending over backward to make Sophie happy ever since the fiasco with the whole private detective thing, so Sophie got to keep him. She's the one who named him. She's really into French cinema, not surprisingly.

"*Bonjour, mes petites!*" says Sophie, squatting down and snapping her fingers. The pair of them run to her, and she picks Coco up and passes her to me, then snuggles Truffle under her chin.

The two cats adore each other, and spend their days chasing each other all over the house. I'm not keeping track of who stays where anymore or with whom. I get plenty of time with both of them, and so does Sophie.

The shower was, as Wolfgang put it, FABULOUS! And it really was. Becca's mother hosted it outside in her rose garden, which is in full bloom this time of year and looks gorgeous. She'd been planning to hold Stewart's graduation party out there anyway, so why not two parties for the price of one, she'd said. There was a big white tent set up in the middle, and flowers twined around all the poles holding it up, and around the backs of the chairs. I've never seen so many flowers in my life. It looked amazing. The entire book club pitched in to help with the food, and a whole lot of friends and neighbors from Concord came. Thanks to Pies & Prejudice, just about everybody knows my grandmother.

They came to see the garden too, though. Mrs. Chadwick graduates from landscape design school in a few weeks, and already has more clients lined up than she can handle. Her yard is all the advertisement she needs.

I remember how worried Becca's father was when she first started ripping things up and replanting. Mr. Chadwick was convinced they'd be the laughingstock of Concord. I guess he imagined that Mrs. Chadwick's design sense would be like her fashion sense—this all happened right after her "it's a whole new me!" phase a few years ago, when she was suddenly big into animal prints and sequined caftans.

But instead of a laughingstock, the yard has made them the envy of the whole town. Mrs. Sloane-Kinkaid did an entire episode about the heirloom rose garden, which was just featured on the cover of some big gardening magazine as well. These days, total strangers are knocking on their door asking to see it. Becca says it's a little creepy, even though she's happy for her mother and everything.

My grandmother got some really cool presents, almost all of them handmade, because she didn't want anyone spending money on her. Emma wrote her a wedding poem, and Becca offered to help with the

Heather Vogel Frederick

flowers. Jess and her mother are making the wedding cake, of course, and I'm doing the dress, which Gigi said was the best present of all.

But it wasn't. The best present came from Cassidy.

"Oh my," said Gigi when she opened the box. Inside was a huge framed photo collage of our book club over the years.

We all clustered around to see.

"Look how young we were!" squealed Emma, pointing to the picture of us dressed up as characters from *Little Women* for a holiday party back in sixth grade. "I can't believe how much we've changed!"

"I don't have braces anymore, for one thing," said Becca ruefully. "Thanks for putting that one in there, Cassidy."

"You're welcome," Cassidy replied, grinning as she draped an arm around her shoulders. "That's what friends are for, Metalmouth."

There was a picture of us in the Delaneys' sleigh, and doing the stupid Maypole maiden dance, and jumping up and down on the beds in a New York City hotel room. We howled at the shots of Mrs. Chadwick looking grumpy on our disastrous camping trip, and of Mrs. Hawthorne pulling a live chicken out of a box at our Betsy-Tacy ornament exchange last Christmas, and of all of us in our horrible middle school uniforms.

Mrs. Sloane-Kinkaid couldn't get over it. "I never knew you took so many pictures, sweetheart!"

Cassidy squeezed everything in there—the fashion show at Half Moon Farm, Stanley and her mom holding baby Chloe right after she was born, all of us on horseback in Wyoming and in costume at the

Jane Austen ball in England and eating ice cream with our families at Kimball Farm right here in Concord.

She'd captured the delighted looks on Emma's face when we gave her Pip for her birthday, and Mrs. Bergson's when she came to her first book club meeting. She got my mother, too, not looking delighted, with green goo all over her face the time we gave one another facials with Madame Miracle's Mint Mud Mask—and another, cheerier one, on election night, surrounded by all of us in our Handcuffs Wong sweaters. There was a picture from our New Year's Eve party at Pies & Prejudice, and one of Becca's first day as a waitress, and down in the corner, where she'd signed it *To Gigi, Love Cassidy*, was a great shot of the National Championships, and all of us crowding around her as she held up her trophy.

"So many wonderful memories," said Gigi softly.

It was definitely the best gift, although my other favorite was the quilt that Summer Williams sent. In the center she embroidered a big heart, and inside it was a quote from *Jane Eyre*, one of the most famous: *Reader, I married him.* Encircling the heart were two more quotes, the first one a line we all loved from one of Charlotte Brontë's letters, when she's talking about her new husband: *My heart is knit to him.*

It turns out Charlotte was actually quoting the Bible when she wrote that, so Summer included the verse from Colossians, too: *That their hearts might be comforted, being knit together in love.*

"Beautiful!" said Gigi, when she finished reading the quotes. "Nearly as beautiful as all of you. So much love here today—what a gift!"

Heather Vogel Frederick

The intercom on my sewing room wall crackles. It's my mother. "Girls!" she says. "It's time to start getting ready. The caterers just arrived and are setting up, and your father wants to be at the church at least an hour ahead of time, Megan."

The wedding is at eleven; then everybody's coming back here afterwards for a brunch reception. We had the rehearsal dinner here last night. It was the easiest place, since things were already set up for the reception. This whole weekend has been one long party.

Everybody came to the dinner, even our friends who aren't actually in the wedding ceremony itself: all of our book club friends and their families, the Berkeleys, Sophie's parents, Stinkerbelle, and Savannah and her parents. Gigi has a soft spot for Senator Sinclair.

Our backyard and deck had been transformed, with white-linen covered tables and twinkle lights and even a dance floor. Madison Daniels sent a wedding present, too—a mix tape that she and her band recorded for us. They're really talented musicians, and they put together a great selection of crowd-pleasing oldies and more high-energy rock numbers. Madison even included "La Vie en Rose," which Gigi and Edouard had fun dancing to while we all watched.

"FABULOUS!" cried Wolfgang, dabbing at his eyes with a black hankie as they spun and twirled under the stars.

We all had fun toasting the engaged couple after that, and there was lots more dancing, along with plenty of laughing and hugging and kissing.

Especially kissing. I witnessed quite a bit of it over the course of the evening, and I got my fair share of kisses myself.

Like I said, it's nice having Simon back in Concord.

I got double French cheek kisses from Sophie's grandfather, too, who made a point of seeking out each of us in the book club and thanking us for not letting him make "the biggest mistake of my life," as he put it.

"For what would I be without my Gigi?" he'd said, tucking her arm through his.

"You managed just fine without me all those years," she teased, but he shook his head.

"*Non, chèrie.* Always my heart was waiting for you." And then there was another kiss, and everyone clapped and whistled.

He winked at me. "*Et voilà!* My patience was rewarded—not only with my angel Gigi, but with another granddaughter to add to my collection."

I'm *definitely* on board with this whole grandfather thing.

As Sophie heads back to her room, I slip Gigi's dress off the dressmaker's form and take it downstairs to her apartment. There's no sign of her, so I drape it on her bed and go back upstairs to take my shower. A little while later, as I'm in my room slipping my *qipao* over my head, someone knocks.

Gigi pokes her head in. "Do you have a minute?"

I nod and she comes in, shutting the door behind her.

"Almost time!" she says, smiling at me.

Heather Vogel Frederick

"Time for what?" I reply, pretending to be mystified. "Oh that's right, somebody's getting married."

"I wonder who that could be?" She does a little pirouette. "Maybe it's me—I have this pretty dress, all I need is an excuse to wear it."

We laugh. I adjust the bodice and smooth out an invisible wrinkle. "You look stunning."

It's true. My grandmother is lovely, from the tip of her perfectly coiffed head to the soles of the ridiculously expensive blue pumps, a present from Wolfgang and Isabelle. It's more than that, though. Gigi's beauty shines from within.

She passes me a small box wrapped in shiny silver paper. I look at it in surprise. "For me?"

She nods. "A little bridesmaid's gift."

I sit down on the end of my bed and open it, sucking in my breath when I see what's inside. *Little gift?* She's given me her diamond earrings! "Gigi, are these really for me?"

She nods again. "I want you to have them now, while I can enjoy seeing you wear them."

I reach out a finger and touch them in wonder. Then I look up, frowning. "But what will you wear today?" We'd planned Gigi's whole outfit around the earrings, even down to the sparkling trim on the hem of her dress.

"These," she says, opening her hand to reveal the most gorgeous earrings I've ever seen. Flashing from her palm like twin suns are two round, flat white pearls, each encircled by a wide band of platinum paved with tiny diamonds. "Edouard gave them to me this morning," she tells me. "They're de Roches family heirlooms, and they'll be Sophie's someday."

We both put our earrings on and stand in front of the mirror side by side, admiring ourselves. Mirror Megan is speechless with delight.

"My beautiful American granddaughter!" says Gigi, giving me a hug.

"My beautiful Chinese grandmother!" I echo, hugging her back.

"I'm so glad to see you and Sophie getting along, finally," she tells me. "This has been a difficult time for her, and it's not going to be an easy transition, spending time in so many places—her mother's house, her father's new apartment in Paris, and now Concord, too."

I nod. "I know."

Gigi has a knack for reading my mind, and she does it again now, framing my face between her soft, birdlike hands. "You are my Megan Rose, and always will be. No one can ever take your place. I want you to know that. But our hearts are both big enough to make room for one more, right?"

I nod again, reassured, and smile at her through my tears.

She reaches for a tissue and wipes them away. "Save those for later!" she scolds me, laughing. "Now let's go and get your grandmother married, shall we?"

The wedding is perfect.

I fasten on small details, holding them as tightly as I hold the

Heather Vogel Frederick

bouquet in my hands: the fragrant roses arched over the doorway to the church; Chloe's delighted laughter as Mrs. Chadwick passes her the tiny basket of rosebuds she's going to carry down the aisle; the shaft of sunlight streaming through the stained glass window on the harpist as she begins to play the first notes of Pachelbel's Canon in D.

Jess picked that one out.

There's an air of hushed expectation in the chapel, and as the music begins, everyone turns to face us. I spot Jess first and give her a little wave. She waves back. She's sitting with her parents and her brothers, and Emma and her family are right behind her. I tuck another detail in my pocket—Darcy Hawthorne, reaching forward and tugging on Jess's long blond braid.

Up in the front of the church, Monsieur de Roches appears through a side door and crosses to take his place beside the minister. Sophie's father and the other groomsmen are with him, all of them looking very dignified.

Sophie starts up the aisle first. Her face is calm, almost solemn, but there's joy in it too. She moves in time to the music, the chiffon hem of the dress I made for her fluttering gracefully just as I envisioned it would.

And then it's my turn. As I step forward, Cassidy flashes me the V for Velcro sign, and from their seats in other rows Becca and Emma and Savannah and Jess do the same. It's obviously a well-rehearsed move, and I almost start to giggle. I manage to compose myself, though, as I continue forward.

Wish You Were Eyre

They each smile and blow me a kiss as I pass by: Becca, who has developed a sudden and inexplicable interest in architecture—and Minnesota. Savannah, who has been talking nonstop to Rupert Loomis ever since they met and he told her he wants to study to be a barrister. That's what they call lawyers in England. And Cassidy, whose red hair is glowing in a shaft of sunlight like a fiery halo—or an Olympic torch. Will she follow in Mrs. Bergson's footsteps someday, I wonder, or does her path lead toward a partnership with a certain dark-haired young Englishman both on the ice and off? Jess's future is equally bright. Knowing her, she'll find a way to blend her love of animals and science with her love of music into a spectacular career. And finally, there's Emma, already a published author. Will she write our story someday?

It's a story worth writing, that's for sure, one brimming with love. I feel it now as I approach the altar, radiating all around me—from Emma's parents, who are holding hands and beaming at me, as are Mr. and Mrs. Delaney, as they try and keep Dylan and Ryan from bouncing up and down in their pew in excitement. I feel it from Isabelle d'Azur and from Wolfgang, who stunned us all by swapping his trademark all-black for all-white in honor of the occasion, and from Becca's parents, and from Cassidy's mother and step-father, whose bald head is glowing pink the way it always does when he's happy. Seated next to them, Courtney and Grant are beaming, too, probably thinking ahead to the day when it's their turn to walk down the aisle. Even Stinkerbelle is

Heather Vogel Frederick

smiling at me. And all the guys have big grins on their faces—Darcy and Stewart and Third, Kevin Mullins and Zach Norton, whose grin slips a little when he looks over at Tristan Berkeley. But then Sophie Fairfax catches his eye, and he can't help returning her smile.

I reach the front row, where my father looks like he might burst with pride. Behind him, Senator Sinclair is already wiping his eyes. Savannah's dad is a total softie.

As I step up onto the platform and take my place next to Sophie, my gaze finally rests on Simon. He smiles at me, and I smile back. Weddings are still in the distant future for me and my friends, and life may take us in unexpected directions down the winding hall of fate, just the way it did for my grandmother, but you never know.

You just never know.

A few moments later my mother steps into her spot beside me. She reaches down and takes my hand, giving it a little squeeze.

I hold on to that detail, too.

As the music swells, little Chloe Sloane-Kinkaid toddles down the aisle ahead of my grandmother, swinging her basket of flowers. Just as she reaches the last row of seats, she trips, sending the basket and its contents flying.

She lets out a howl, but her tears are quickly dried as her mother rushes forward to scoop her up.

"Hush, sweetheart," she consoles her. "No one minds. We're all friends here."

It's so true! *Our hearts are knit together in love*, I think, tucking that truth away to hold close as well.

And as I watch my beautiful grandmother walk down the aisle, her shining eyes fixed with confidence on her Mr. Rochester and their future together, I feel another truth stirring in my heart, one that I've known for always.

There really is no place like home.

Heather Vogel Frederick

"She sighed a sigh of ineffable satisfaction, as if her cup of happiness were now full."
—Jane Eyre

The girls got a negative first impression of Sophie and as a result, weren't very nice to her for a large part of the book. Have you ever judged somebody too harshly based on a first impression? Have you ever been judged wrongly?

One of the recurring themes in the series is that Megan, an only child, has wanted a brother or sister. When Sophie moves in, it's not exactly what Megan had hoped for. Based on Megan's experiences with Sophie, would you want to host a foreign exchange student? From which country? What would you ask them?

Megan takes a long-awaited trip to Paris with Gigi, and she fulfills her dream of going to Paris Fashion Week. If you could take a trip anywhere in the world, where would you want to go?

At the same time Becca travels to Minnesota with her grandmother, and the trip turns out better than Becca had anticipated. Have you had an unexpected experience while on vacation? How did you feel about what happened?

Jess got into trouble for cheating, though she was innocent. Have you ever been accused of cheating? If so, how did you handle it? Do you think Savannah's solution to retake the test was fair? Would you come up with a different defense?

Cassidy was torn between two guys, when she was dating Zach but kept thinking about Tristan. Have you ever liked more than one person at once? How did you handle it?

Both Jess and Cassidy were striving for something they really wanted, Jess in her a cappella competition and Cassidy in her hockey tournament. Have you ever been in a high stakes game or exhibition? How did you handle the pressure? If you won, how did it feel to win? If you didn't win, how did you feel?

Megan decided to blog about the trend toward extreme thinness that has been an issue in the modeling world, but some of the people who worked in fashion didn't think she should have. Did you ever have to make a choice that you felt was right, even though it went against the popular opinion?

Emma and Stewart teamed up to help Mrs. Wong in her campaign for mayor, and everyone helped out on the cooking show hosted by Cassidy's mom. Have you ever helped your parent accomplish one of their goals?

Becca misunderstood Theo's love of herpetology and was a little scared of his snakes, but after she talked to him about it, she thought it was cool. Do you have an unusual hobby? What do people think of it when you tell them? Are you able to change their minds?

Both Emma and Stewart help Mrs. Wong when she campaigns for mayor, and they get an inside view of local politics. Have you ever run for class or club office? What were your strategies? Did anything surprise you about the campaign process?

Jess and Savannah's friendship survived competing for the same soprano solo in the MadriGals. Were you ever in a situation where you competed against a friend? Was your friendship the same afterward?

Cassidy and the girls play a prank on Sophie when they all appear on *Cooking with Clementine,* but they later fess up, even though they know they'll be punished. Have you ever had to own up to something you did wrong? What was the outcome?

Have you ever been to a wedding? Were you watching or did you participate? Did the experience live up to what you thought it would be?

What do you think the future holds for Emma, Jess, Megan, Cassidy, and Becca? What would you hope for them?

The Mother-Daughter Book Club has read a lot of books! Have you ever read *Little Women, Anne of Green Gables, Daddy-Long-Legs, Pride and Prejudice,* the Betsy-Tacy series, or *Jane Eyre*? How many of them have you read? Which ones do you still want to read?

Would you ever want to start your own book club? Who would you invite and what books would you read? If you are in a book club, what books have you read?

What was your favorite book in the Mother-Daughter Book Club series? Who was your favorite character? Have your answers changed as the series went on?

Author's Note

It isn't easy saying good-bye to a world you've come to love.

Even if it's a world of your own creating.

I've spent nearly seven years of my life watching my fictional book club girls grow up, and as sappy as it sounds, I've come to think of them as the daughters I never had (I have two boys!). Even better, writing this series has brought "real" daughters into my life in the form of the many young readers who have come to love my book club girls too, and who are kind enough to send me letters and email telling me so.

But the time has come for me to move on—there are other fictional worlds I want to explore, other books I need to write.

I couldn't do this, however, without one final stop at one final book: *Jane Eyre*. No series about girls reading classic novels would be complete if it didn't pay a visit to Charlotte Brontë's immortal Jane. Spirited, independent, resilient, and thoroughly modern, Jane Eyre was a woman way ahead of her time. Her clarity of thought, strong conscience, and backbone are as much an inspiration to readers today as they were back when the book was first published in 1847. It's no wonder that the book remains so universally beloved. (Of course, having a brooding, romantic love interest like Mr. Rochester doesn't hurt either!) If you've never read *Jane Eyre*, you're in for a treat, and if you have, isn't it time to take it down off the shelf and re-read it again?

As always, there are many friends and colleagues I'd like to thank for their help in the making of this book. First and foremost this time, my husband Steve (my own private Mr. Rochester), whose love and steadfast support are the bedrock of my writing career. Thank you for keeping me in Junior Mints, too, sweetheart!

My wonderful editor and friend Alexandra Cooper is another pillar of support, and I couldn't ask for a better partner-in-crime. The delightful Amy Rosenbaum helps keep us both in line, and Lucy Cummins and the artistic team at Simon & Schuster have outdone themselves in giving this series its unique look. As Wolfgang would say, "FABULOUS, darlings!"

My intrepid agent Barry Goldblatt is in a class by himself, and therefore gets a paragraph to himself. We've come a long way together in the past decade, haven't we, Barry?

The Paris location was greatly enriched by travel tidbits from Isabel Colon, Gabrielle Spiers, Ruth McGregor and above all Pamela Pate, and thanks are also due to Amy Rechner and Andrea Scobie and Rita Allen for DVD recommendations and loans. For Minnesota, I had a number of trusted resources to rely on, including Kathleen Baxter, Ann Wallace, Susan Orchard, Kelly Reuter, and Lona Falenczykowski, while Jonatha Wey has been my boots-on-the-ground in Concord throughout the series. Thank you, dear Jonatha! Jessica Weissman's "After Library" was too irresistible not to include (personally, I can't wait to read Jane Austen's next six novels), and she and the rest of the amazing Betsy-Tacy "Listren" have provided friendship and moral support for several years now. You really *are* the "Ladies Who Know Everything"!

What would a mother-daughter book club installment be without a shout out to Helen Quigley and her hockey rock star daughter

Lucinda? Not only is Lucinda Quigley tops on the ice (her team won the USA Hockey National Championships *two years in a row*), but she's tops off the ice as well in my book, thanks to all the help she's given me over the years. Go, Lucinda!

And finally, remember those two boys I mentioned earlier? I love them dearly and it's high time that I thank them, too. My sons have brought laughter and fun into my life in ways I never could have imagined, and I wouldn't trade them for all the daughters in the world. Ian and Ben, you're the best!

About the Author

Heather Vogel Frederick grew up in New England and spent her middle-school years in Concord, Massachusetts, the town where the Mother-Daughter Book Club series takes place. Today the award-winning author of the Patience Goodspeed books, the *Spy Mice* series, and *Once Upon a Toad* lives in Portland, Oregon, with her husband and sons. You can learn more about the author and her books at heathervogelfrederick.com.